BRICOLAGE
Essays, Journalism and Improvisations

John Howe

Edited by Rosamund Howe

Copyright © 2020 John Howe
All rights reserved.
Printed in the UK by TJ International
First published 2020

ISBN 978-1-5272-6530-1

Bricolage Books
www.bricolagebooks.co.uk
bricolagebooks2020@gmail.com

BRICOLAGE

In memory of John Howe, 1938–2018

CONTENTS

List of illustrations   xi
Acknowledgements   xiii
Preface   xv
Introduction   xix

1. PORTRAITS

Fela Anikulapo Kuti: An Honest Man   3
By Way of Kensal Green   13
Evenings with Our Girl Rene   37

2. CARS

First Wheels   49
Learning Curve: Old News from the Front Line in the Struggle between Motorist and Industry   53
The Knowledge: London Cabbies Learn their Trade the Hard Way   59
Motoring with the Murgatroyds   62
Prototype Boulevard   66
Vehicle of Desire   77

3. AFRICA

Sanitising Nigeria's Capital   91
Letter from Accra: A Bit of Transnational Gossip   95
Anarchy in Vitro: Uganda, July 1980   98
Reporting the War in Chad   128
Polisario Stepping Up Attacks as Morocco Completes Sixth 'Wall'   132
The Crisis of Algerian Nationalism and the Rise of Islamic Integralism   135
Opinion: The Captains and the Kings   154

4. FROM THE MOTO PARK

If You Can't Be Good, Be Careful …	159
Don't You Believe It	161
Keep the Profit, Share the Loss	164
Martyrdom	167
The Devil's Music	170
A Contradiction or Two	173
Technicalities	176

5. LETTER FROM LONDON

31 août 1981	181
29 octobre 1981	185
20 mars 1982	188
21 avril 1982	192
27 juillet 1982	196

6. PSYCHOLOGY

Wilhelm Reich	201
Encounter Group: Right on, Gang, but what about Freud?	209
The Bigger the Car, the Bigger You Are	214
Dope on Dope	216

7. VERSE

Your Mum and Dad	221
Femme Fatale	221
The Marquess of Bath	222
Mothertruckers	223
The Ultimate Late Braker	223
The Marquess of Blandford	224
Currant Bun	224
All the Sixes	225
Six Haiku on Sound	225

8. MISCELLANY

The First North–South War	229
Moving towards Change	234
Holy Water	237
Painting the Lily: Adapting Burroughs for Stage and Screen	253
Going to the Cinema: Trincomalee in the Late 1940s	260
Fragments:	263
Elephant House	263
Blackout	264
Carnival	267
Hoppy	268

ILLUSTRATIONS

Front cover: A fisherman casting his net, River Chari, Chad. John Howe, 1982.

Back cover: Bottle wall built by John (*c.* 1977, Greatham, West Sussex). Lewis Hume, 2020, after a low-res photo by John Howe, 2009.

p. v   John and Ros at Climping. Laura Mulvey, *c.* 1969.

p. xiv   John photographing his daughters and nephew (L–R: Fingo 20, Chad 15, Natalie 10, Frances 5) at Greatham. Laura Mulvey, 1984.

p. xviii   John working on the sitting room at Ladbroke Grove. Francesca Annis, 1974.

p. 1   Fela Kuti at the Shrine, Lagos. John Howe, *c.* 1978.

p. 47   Ros, with John under his Peugeot, at Greatham. Hoppy, 1991.

p. 89   Polisario members cooking over the fire, Western Sahara. John Howe, 1987.

p. 90   John with Koku (Chris's daughter), Tanzania. Chris Elkington, 1980.

p. 157   John (far right) with Larry Sider and (far left) unidentified Polisario member, Western Sahara. Jerry Sider, 1990.

p. 179   A carnival costume, Ladbroke Grove. Hoppy, *c.* 1989.

p. 180   John with Faysal Abdullah at carnival, Ladbroke Grove. Chad Wollen, early 1990s.

p. 199   John in West London. Hoppy, *c.* 1959.

p. 219   'Osteopath' by John Howe, *c.* 2010.

p. 227   John at Greatham. Natalie Hume, 2011.

Images are printed by kind permission of the photographers or their estate (those by Hoppy © 2020 Estate of John 'Hoppy' Hopkins).

ACKNOWLEDGEMENTS

We want to acknowledge the contributions of the portrait subjects – Fela, Priest and Rene – as well as the presence and influence, often implicit, of John's friends and colleagues over the years.

We thank all those who have given their permission to republish texts: Matt Bishop, who commissioned 'The Knowledge' and went to the trouble of finding the relevant issue in his archive to share with us, and the current editor of *Car* magazine Phil McNamara; Daisy Cockburn and Rose Dempsey, owners of Emma Tennant's estate, for 'Motoring with the Murgatroyds'; Susan Watkins and *New Left Review* for 'Fela Anikulapo Kuti', 'Prototype Boulevard', 'Vehicle of Desire' and 'The Crisis of Algerian Nationalism'; Patrick Smith for the 'From the Moto Park' articles; Ilona Halberstadt for 'Painting the Lily' and 'Going to the Cinema'.

We thank the photographers whose work is featured here: Lewis Hume, Francesca Annis, Laura Mulvey, Hoppy (and James Ware for Hoppy's estate), Chris Elkington, Jerry Sider and Chad Wollen.

We are grateful to Patrick Smith for his valuable support and advice throughout the process of building this collection, and to Mark Dallyn for his encouragement.

Julian Rothenstein offered generous guidance and created the styling and front cover; we appreciate his help enormously. Great thanks to Lucas Quigley for patience in working with us on typesetting and layout. Geoff Barlow has been thorough and efficient in seeing the book through production.

Laura Mulvey contributed to all our decisions, from selecting and editing the texts to choosing images. Finally, we could not have completed the book without the love and support of Frances Howe, whose judgement has been essential throughout.

Rosamund Howe and Natalie Hume, June 2020

PREFACE

This book is a compilation of writings by my husband, John Howe, selected from literally hundreds of articles, stories, reviews, verses and random fragments produced over a period of nearly fifty years.

The word *bricolage* in the title, in its evolved usage, means a construction created from a variety of materials at hand. It thus conveys this book's meld of fiction and non-fiction, previously published and unpublished, polished and spontaneous. In its original meaning, *bricolage* is the French for DIY, and signals John's range of skills from plastering to electrical wiring to cabinet making to car maintenance: skills, however, which he could only deploy when inspiration struck at a moment which might take weeks or months to arrive. *Bricolage* also serves as a metonym for the French language, which was important for John in his work as a translator, as a lingua franca in his travels in francophone Africa, and as the language of one of his favourite destinations, Paris.

Selecting the articles for this collection reawakened my memories of John's career as a freelance journalist, a life that is never easy and in which a predictable routine is not a possibility. On the contrary, he always had to be on the lookout for a new and unexpected angle, a new venture, perhaps involving inconvenient, uncomfortable and dangerous travel, in a gamble that might or might not pay off and had to be sold to cynical and parsimonious editors.

As a freelance journalist, many crucial factors are beyond your control. The innovative, interesting publications you are keen to write for have a tendency to founder for lack of advertising revenue, maybe leaving you unpaid. And at the best of times payment is a fraught issue – how can it take an accounts department six weeks to write a cheque? Then the foreign news editor you got on with so well resigns and the new one may turn out to have a pre-existing list of contacts. And the late twentieth century saw the rise of digital television to the detriment of print journalism, with freelancers of course the most vulnerable.

In all these circumstances, a freelance journalist may find it difficult to keep his spirits up, to keep his temper, indeed to keep working, particularly if he is by nature impatient and impetuous and takes a pride in his skills as a writer.

Compiling this book has made me wonder whether I empathised sufficiently with John's experiences in contending with the structural difficulties of his profession. These provoked constant worries, nagging irritations, compared to which the travel felt like an exciting challenge. That said, in his journey to Western Sahara John visited a war zone and witnessed the firing of live ammunition; he visited Kampala when it was in a state of insecurity and lawlessness. Nearer to home, missiles were flying when he covered the 1981 Brixton riots.

For me, these were times of acute anxiety, an escalation of the constant low-level worry I felt during his absences for months at a time. Had I not heard from him because letters take so long to arrive? Or had something bad happened – perhaps he had been arrested? He was once held under arrest very briefly in Tanzania for unwittingly taking a photograph in a military zone. He always said that the only place in Africa where he felt actually frightened was Nairobi, which was not at war and had a government but suffered appalling street violence. But whatever the dangers and worries, he always came home safely.

Even for a dedicated professional, writing to a deadline can feel like a persecution. But particularly towards the end of his life John often wrote not for publication but simply for pleasure. My hope in collecting these diverse pieces for publication is not only to give new life to his previously published articles, but also to disseminate for the first time some of the improvisations he wrote for pleasure.

Rosamund Howe, May 2020

INTRODUCTION

John delighted in language, both written and spoken. On the page, his precision and commitment to the *mot juste* were balanced with playfulness, idiosyncrasy and liberal use of the vernacular. His speech was spontaneous and expressive, the words inseparable from expansive gestures. His morning coffee-making ritual was enlivened by a stream of consciousness – limericks, epithets and spoonerisms, punctuated by choice soundbites from the newspaper or *Private Eye* – uttered, and sometimes sung, in tones that reflected his mood, rapidly changing and always intense. Whether exuberant or irate, he often found expression in torrents of profanity from diverse dialects and languages.

Despite this talent for expression, John had not fulfilled his academic promise at Brasenose College, Oxford, where he read English but left after only two terms. His prior education had been eclectic, because of his father's career in the Admiralty, and he attended a total of eight different schools, including a Sri Lankan prep, a Welsh grammar and, for sixth form, the Jesuit boarding school Beaumont.[1] The conventions and formalities of Oxford must have seemed like yet another tiresome system requiring discipline and adaptation. He was drawn instead to the emerging countercultures coming out of the US, led by the explosive creativity of groundbreakers such as Charlie Parker, Miles Davis, Allen Ginsberg and William Burroughs.

Free of university, John moved to London and began his lifelong relationship with Notting Hill, which was then a cheap and vibrant neighbourhood with a large immigrant population. He identified particularly with the area's Caribbean community, which coalesced around the Fiesta One; the restaurant's owners Larry Forde and Clement Byfield would become some of John's closest friends.[2] John's affinity for West Indian culture, represented by his feelings for the carnival, emerges through his life and writing in numerous ways, from his politics, to social cannabis use, to his loyalty (despite regretting its gentrification) to 'the Gate'. His devotion to the Notting Hill Carnival was deeply personal – both Larry Forde and another of John's close friends, the photographer, film-maker and activist Hoppy,

---

1 Beaumont closed in 1967. John always maintained that the best school he had attended was the Hill School, Trincomalee, despite his misery, as an eight-year-old, at being sent there to board.

2 Clement Byfield (1925–1986) arrived in London from Jamaica soon after the Second World War. He became a distinguished campaigner for the rights of black people in Britain, serving as chairman of the West Indian Standing Conference and general secretary of the Association of Jamaicans. Originally from Trinidad, Larry Forde (1931–2012) remained an active member of the Caribbean community.

contributed to its genesis in the 1960s – and it represented what he loved about the area.[3] The first time John lived in Notting Hill, around 1960, it was in a Westbourne Terrace flat shared with Hoppy, Peter Wollen and Alan Beckett: all three went on to play an important role in John's life.[4] Peter and John would share accommodation once again, as brothers-in-law, when they moved with their families to Ladbroke Grove in 1974. That house, strategically positioned on the carnival route, would be John's home for the next thirty-five years.[5] Each August bank holiday, the local street party was the setting for John's freewheeling birthday celebrations.

During the 1960s John gradually drifted away from a nascent career in market research and began minicab driving, presumably with an emerging plan to write professionally. He began working as a journalist in the early 1970s, writing principally for the specialist Africa press based in London and travelling extensively, including to Nigeria, Ghana, Uganda, Tanzania, Kenya, Mozambique, Chad and Algeria. His first visit to Lagos in 1973 was a memorable experience that probably cemented his interest in the region: 'he was hosted by Fela Anikulapo Kuti, the Afrobeat music star ... They became firm friends and occasional verbal sparring partners on matters political and spiritual.'[6] John admired the ebullience of the city's culture and the resilience of its population, many of them challenged rather than benefited by rapid development. Beyond the specialist press, John covered African stories for general news publications, including the *Guardian* and the *Economist*, particularly in the context of the civil war in Chad during the early 1980s. His most recent trips to Africa, made during the late 1980s and early 1990s, were to Western Sahara, where he took a personal interest in the struggle for Sahrawi independence. Generally impatient with good causes and reluctant to trust politicians, John was

---

3 John Hopkins (1937–2015) was always known as Hoppy. A seminal figure in London counterculture and co-founder of the Notting Hill Free School, a springboard for the Notting Hill Carnival, several of his photographs are reproduced here and John commemorates him in a very short text at the end of the book. Larry later became a mainstay of the Flamboyan carnival collective based in Fernhead Road, where he and his wife Gloria would work unstintingly on costumes for months of every year. John made frequent social visits there, often as part of a long walk with a granddaughter in a pushchair.

4 Before becoming a writer John worked with Alan Beckett (1938–1997) in market research; their friendship, sometimes tempestuous, continued for many decades.

5 Peter Wollen (1938–2019), whom John had first met at Oxford, was an intellectual, writer and filmmaker, whose remarkable achievements are described in a recent *Guardian* obituary: theguardian.com/film/2020/jan/08/peter-wollen-obituary. Peter and John became brothers-in-law as a result of their relationships with sisters Laura and Rosamund Mulvey.

6 Patrick Smith, 'Obituary: John Howe, 1938–2018', *Africa Confidential*, vol. 60, no. 1, 11 January 2019 (www.africa-confidential.com/article/id/12525/John_Howe,_1938-2018). This visit to Lagos had been suggested by John's Nigerian friend JK Brimah, who would also have made the introduction to Fela.

INTRODUCTION

deeply moved by the dignity of a desert culture fighting determinedly for political independence.[7]

Although his professional focus was Africa, John's writing also reflected his broader personal interests. In the 1980s he wrote a regular column on contemporary London and British current affairs for the French daily *Le Matin*. He also contributed more discursive pieces to varied titles from *New Left Review* to *Car* magazine. During the 1990s he gradually moved into French–English translation, both of articles and full-length books. Most of these were non-fiction, with highlights including translations of works by philosopher Régis Debray, anthropologist Marc Augé and film director Jean-Luc Godard.[8] But John received particularly enthusiastic praise for his translation of Jean Vautrin's 2003 historical novel *The Voice of the People* (*Le Cri du peuple*): 'in John Howe, [Vautrin] has found a translator to match his own energy and panache … a version which is resourceful, eye-catching and, when required, ingeniously foul-mouthed … Howe catches all the colours.'[9]

Alongside professional writing, John wrote constantly for himself and for the amusement of friends and family. Often opinionated, with touches of wit and brilliance, these texts include reminiscences, polemics, stories and fragments, as well as verse, which he described as doggerel.

The selection of texts reproduced here represents a tiny portion of John's output, which was considerable in spite of his uneven working habits. John followed his interests, and fractious phases of activity were surrounded by anxious intervals when little was produced. He thrived on crises and worked best with the spur of looming deadlines and an overdrawn bank account. Much work was done very late at night, after hours or days of procrastination. His desk was covered with papers, overflowing ashtrays and old envelopes (including unopened parking fines and bills, accumulated over years) covered with scrawled notes, none of which could be thrown away. John was nevertheless a perfectionist and would compulsively rework his articles, most of which exist in several different versions. Inappropriate editing by careless subs drove him into a rage. We hope this edition – a project we promised him and have planned for many years – would meet with his approval.

---

[7] 'Given his scepticism towards politicians of all stripes, John was not an instinctive campaigner. Yet he threw himself into the fight for a Sahrawi state'. Smith, 'John Howe'.

[8] Debray's *Praised Be Our Lords*, for example, was 'admirably rendered by the translator John Howe'. Jeremy Harding, *LRB*, 9, 7 February 2008.

[9] David Coward, *TLS*, 17 May 2002.

*

The collection features only John's original writing, as opposed to his translations which are available elsewhere. The texts, carefully chosen from a diverse and chaotic repository, are grouped thematically.[10]

The book opens with a section entitled PORTRAITS, comprising three of the most engaging and accessible pieces. 'Fela Anikulapo Kuti' was written as a candid tribute following the musician's 1997 death from AIDS. After opening with a description of his own humiliating triumph as Worst Male Dancer at the Shrine nightclub, John goes on to produce a personal sketch of Fela that also contextualises his professional achievements within a distinct cultural and political milieu.

Elegiac and moving, 'By Way of Kensal Green' describes the very different trajectory of John's old Notting Hill acquaintance Priest. His tragic downward spiral into hard drugs and ill health reflects a wider history of continuing racist persecution, as the country that had beckoned West Indians 'with siren gestures was now making them feel unwelcome'. John was referring to Britain in the 1970s and 1980s, but in the wake of the 2018 Windrush scandal these words feel more relevant than ever.[11] The fundamental message of this piece, anti-racism, was meaningful for John not as an abstract principle but as part of everyday life.

John envisaged these first two portraits as the beginning of a series describing personal friends and Notting Hill characters; the neighbourhood itself features significantly in Priest's story. Other subjects were to include John's brother-in-law Peter Wollen, whose outstanding intellect and creative talent were cut short by early-onset Alzheimer's, and Larry Forde, whose easy-going modesty belied his valuable contribution to Caribbean culture in London. Sadly neither of these texts was ever realised. The only other portrait John completed is also the one text in the book with a woman protagonist: 'Evenings with Our Girl Rene' is a sensitive recollection of its subject, some fifty years on. It affectionately describes the mutual curiosity and subsequent camaraderie that grew up between John's coterie of young bohemian intellectuals and Rene, a prominent local resident.

---

10 We distributed a short collection of favourite pieces at John's funeral. This larger selection is more representative.

11 West Indians of Priest's generation and their children – people who have lived in Britain almost all their lives – have been refused healthcare, detained and even deported.

INTRODUCTION

CARS reflects John's unambiguous enthusiasm for machines, one that began in early childhood. He loved driving and all aspects of motoring, which he considered an art form; as well as being the main subject of this section, cars frequently show up in his writing on other topics as well. Motor racing, specially Formula One, was his only sporting interest. John also maintained and repaired his own cars, including a series of models from the widely despised brand Skoda, which he valued for their economy and functionality, and because they were easy to work on: he spent much time lying under one or another of these, often in side streets off Ladbroke Grove. His self-taught mechanical expertise, accumulated over decades, informs the nostalgic reminiscence that is 'First Wheels', which describes his early days as an inexperienced and irresponsible car owner. 'Learning Curve' continues the theme of car maintenance, describing John's determination to keep a cheap second-hand car on the road during a journey across the United States. It was a feat that required 'mimsing', by which he meant driving slowly, often getting in the way of other traffic – a habit that, under normal circumstances, would send him into a towering rage.

Mimsers were not the only source of frustration John encountered on the road; pushy and aggressive drivers were almost as irritating. As a former minicab driver proud of his own familiarity with London's back streets, he had a healthy suspicion of black cabs, whose owners are notorious for their rudeness in traffic. For 'The Knowledge', John sets his prejudice aside to describe with uncharacteristic sympathy the challenges faced by initiate London taxi drivers.

'Motoring with the Murgatroyds' is John's only published work of fiction and was written under the pseudonym Armel Coussine (the surname borrowed from his maternal Maltese ancestry). The Notting Hill resident and novelist Emma Tennant commissioned it for her avant-garde literary magazine *Bananas*; the spring 1978 issue featured five stories linked only by the name of their protagonist, Murgatroyd.[12] At the time of writing John did not identify with his retrograde principal character, nostalgic for an obsolete form of motoring, but this had changed thirty-five years later when he re-read the story while working on 'Prototype Boulevard'. The latter text explores increasing automation and the prospect of driverless cars that 'will save us money, absolve us of personal responsibility for road crashes and otherwise be seen, when authorised, and not heard, much

---

12 Emma Tennant (1937–2017) was an influential writer and feminist, and close friend of Peter and Laura. The other authors participating in the Murgatroyd issue were John Sladek, Alan Munton, Hilary Bailey and Tom Nairn.

like a well-behaved Victorian child'. Needless to say, this was not a future he relished. 'Prototype Boulevard' was one of two car-related articles produced for *New Left Review*. The other, 'Vehicle of Desire', touches on similar themes of creeping computerisation and planned obsolescence. Opening with a grudgingly appreciative description of Ilya Ehrenburg's 'visionary' 1929 novel that suggests 'Cars … are for suckers', John traces the sociological and literary history of car ownership through the twentieth century, to end on the uneven (and often dubious) benefits of technological innovation and the 'bricolage' required of motorists in poorer regions.

The AFRICA section comprises a fraction of John's prolific writing on this subject between 1973 and the mid-1990s, including some previously unpublished pieces. Describing a rapidly changing environment resulting from an oil boom, 'Sanitising Nigeria's Capital' argues that the 'peculiar ferocity' that so impressed visitors to Lagos was something many of its exhausted residents could do without. Written from the next stop on John's 1977 trip, 'Letter from Accra' is a short, entertaining coda to the preceding text, illustrating the perverse impact of currency fluctuations on petty trade between the two countries.[13]

In 1980 John visited East Africa, and years later he wrote an extended account of his hair-raising stay in the Ugandan capital Kampala where he was reporting on elections following the overthrow of Idi Amin. 'Anarchy in Vitro' is much the longest text included here; it is also one of the most vivid and entertaining, from John's brush with Customs ('I felt like a pet pekinese being given the once-over by a couple of foxhounds'), to the 'furtive slink-and-dash' of moving about the city after curfew, to his fruitless interview with President Obote (about which there was little to be done: 'Your options do not include shouting curses or seizing the interviewee by the throat').

The following two pieces, by contrast, offer a sample of John's reporting. Chad, a huge, underpopulated, landlocked country, had been beset by civil war in different guises since its independence from France in 1960, with long-standing military interventions from Libya. John's 1983 arrival there coincided with a sudden escalation in fighting, centred on the Aouzou Strip, at the Libyan border in the north of the country. The material here comprises

---

[13] John chose to write this piece under a pseudonym, as he had for 'Motoring with the Murgatroyds', but used a slightly different spelling (Armel Grant Cousine).

INTRODUCTION

some of John's short reports from N'Djamena for the *Guardian*.[14] 'Polisario Stepping Up Attacks' resulted from a 1987 visit to the Sahara desert, where John witnessed frontline combat against Morocco by the Polisario Front, fighting for the independence of Western Sahara.[15]

The Sahrawi independence movement foundered in the early 1990s when Algeria, its essential sponsor, was overtaken by troubles of its own: 'The Crisis of Algerian Nationalism and the Rise of Islamic Integralism' traces the country's slide towards religious fundamentalism. For John, who had first visited the country in 1978, this was a sad development; it was also politically disappointing for the international left, which had viewed the country as a beacon of hope when it emerged from its long war of independence against France in 1962.[16]

Short but incisive, 'The Captains and the Kings' is the only text in this section not written from firsthand experience. Alluding to the hypocrisy of colonialism, it compares the 1978 coronation of Bokassa, ruler of the short-lived Central African Empire (otherwise the Central African Republic), with the 'bargain-priced monarchy' of England, and ends with an accusation aimed at both, of 'personalising and trivialising everything'.

John's 'monthly stream of consciousness' for the *West African Hotline* calls for a dedicated section: FROM THE MOTO PARK takes its name from 'the indispensable gathering point for traders, travellers, preachers, all manner of proselytisers and hustlers' to be found in any West African city.[17] Written anonymously, supposedly from the perspective of a local lorry driver, the columns offer unorthodox and entertaining commentary on current events and preoccupations, from safe sex during the AIDS epidemic to religious martyrdom in the context of spreading Islamic proselytism. 'The Devil's Music' starts with a typically satirical observation: 'Foreigners naively convinced that all Africans have an inborn facility for the joyous foot-tapping, hip-swinging, pelvis-rolling, shoulder-twitching dance imposed on the listener by the best African dance music have never watched Catholic intellectuals, Muslim warlords or millionaire politicians

---

14 Despite donations of military equipment from the US and France, Chad's government, led by President Hissène Habré, suffered from lack of assistance.

15 Western Sahara, formerly the territory of Rio de Oro, was decolonised by Spain in 1975 but immediately annexed by neighbouring Morocco and Mauritania (which has since withdrawn).

16 Over subsequent decades, authoritarian policies of industrialisation and agricultural collectivisation, run by a single party, the FLN, failed to deliver economic development to the rapidly growing population.

17 Patrick Smith, personal communication, 29 March 2020. Now editor of *Africa Confidential*, Patrick wrote John's obituary (see above) and gave a powerful tribute at his funeral.

BRICOLAGE

at play.' The examples printed here have been chosen for their range as well as for their individual interest.

LETTER FROM LONDON samples a very different column, the one John produced for *Le Matin* in the 1980s as its London correspondent. In this pre-internet era, his role involved a daily call with the paper's foreign news editor to discuss material, followed by an intense phase of writing before finally dictating the piece over the telephone to the Paris office.[18] As well as bringing energy to the considerable challenge of writing in French, John enjoyed the wide scope of his remit, offering his personal take on topics of the day, including the continuing Troubles in Northern Ireland, London riots, the miners' strike and a royal wedding. One piece printed here focuses on a subject dear to John's heart, the Notting Hill Carnival. Another gives a prescient hint of the 2016 referendum on EU membership: already in 1982, the newly admitted British were behaving like 'bothersome passengers on a bus', testing the patience of their fellow travellers. This sustained coverage of domestic affairs amidst the brutal divides of Thatcher's Britain led John towards an appreciation (or perhaps an acceptance) of realpolitik, and during this period he gradually abandoned what he came to regard as a naïve and ill-informed ultra-leftism.

By contrast, the PSYCHOLOGY section dates from an earlier phase of John's writing career and reflects a keen, if sometimes equivocal, interest in the left and in countercultural thought. Although now largely forgotten, Wilhelm Reich (1897–1957) was a psychoanalyst whose legacy was revived during the 1960s and 1970s; his promotion of sexual liberation and adherence to communism and psychoanalysis made him a hero for younger generations, including the Paris students of May 1968.[19] John describes a visit to Orgonon, Reich's house, research centre and burial place, which remains a monument to the flawed, eccentric work of its owner.[20]

The other three pieces of the section were all written for left-wing weekly *Seven Days*. 'Right on Gang but what about Freud' is a sceptical review of a countercultural conference on the politics of psychotherapy; 'The Bigger the Car the Bigger You Are' adopts Leonid Brezhnev and

---

18 John gives a cameo performance of the job in Peter and Laura's film *Crystal Gazing*, 1981 (his voice heard off screen as he dictates into the telephone).
19 Both the communist and psychoanalytic establishments rejected him as too unorthodox, which only made him more attractive to his countercultural followers.
20 The house, in Maine, is now the Wilhelm Reich Museum.

INTRODUCTION

Edward Heath as case studies for a light-hearted look at the psychology of driving; and the book review 'Dope on Dope' doubles up as a polemic against the specious sanctimony of drug laws.

VERSE represents a segment of John's output that he tended to compose for his own amusement, sometimes shared informally with friends and family. Having long abandoned a youthful ambition to become a poet, his facility for light, robust verse blossomed in middle age and beyond. Many of these compositions benefited enormously from his spoken delivery: the printed version of 'The Marquess of Bath' is a mere relic of John's colourful performances. Since his death we have often wondered how we failed to capture any of these spontaneous recitations on video. The section ends with a shift in mood: the haiku is abstract, contemplative and lyrical.

The book concludes with MISCELLANY. 'The First North–South War' is an unusual take on the Falklands conflict, highlighting the disparity between the British government's attitude to the Falklanders and to the Diego Garcian islanders. Though little publicised, this issue is still pertinent: in May 2019, following a ruling in the International Court of Justice, the UN General Assembly called on the UK to decolonise the Chagos Archipelago of which Diego Garcia is a part, but there has so far been no sign of compliance.[21]

In light of the current migration crisis, the following text also remains relevant: 'Moving towards Change', a book review of the late 1970s, highlights the untenable nature of a world system reliant on gross disparities between rich and poor.

The extended short story 'Holy Water' is an irreverent fantasy about the accidental adventures of a baffled priest (Catholicism had played an important part in John's upbringing), and includes memorable passages about reckless driving and psychedelics. It was written quickly in the wake of 1990s press reports that some factions of the IRA were selling drugs to fund their activities; although never polished for publication, its rough immediacy is part of its charm.[22]

John was enthusiastic about *The Naked Lunch* soon after its 1959 publication, and came to know its author William Burroughs a few years

---

21 un.org/press/en/2019/gaspd696.doc.htm.
22 The Irish Republican Army was then still engaged in open combat with the British Army. The Good Friday Agreement of 1998 brought about a ceasefire, since endangered by Brexit.

later in London.[23] Although disappointed with David Cronenburg's 1991 screen adaptation, he produced a careful review, 'Painting the Lily', at the request of his friend, *PIX* editor Ilona Halberstadt.[24]

By contrast, the other text he wrote for *PIX* is personal and evocative. 'Going to the Cinema' describes a treasured childhood memory from Sri Lanka (then Ceylon), where John had lived between the ages of eight and ten. He never returned to the country, but it occupied a special place in his mind as a vivid interim between the bleakness of wartime Bath and the bleakness of 1950s Fishguard, his father's subsequent posting.[25]

Fragmentary reminiscences, which John recorded in the last decade of his life, form the book's closing series. 'Elephant House' and 'Blackout' are childhood recollections, the latter written in response to a granddaughter's request for help with a school project. 'Carnival' expresses John's rage at the sometimes insensitive – or, at worst, gratuitously violent – policing at the event; it is a reminder, if one were needed, that racist law enforcement has long been the norm rather than the exception in London as well as in the US.[26] The last piece comprises a few impressionistic lines about Hoppy, written soon after his death.

The book opens and closes with tributes to two of John's closest friends. Although often preoccupied by his inner life, John was compulsively sociable and valued his numerous and diverse personal connections; many of those he counted as friends had nothing in common beyond their association with him. The outbursts of irritation and impatience that were familiar to all who knew him well tended to be short-lived and superficial – and were insignificant alongside his generosity of spirit, curiosity and humour which are at the heart of his appeal as a person and as a writer.

Rosamund Howe and Natalie Hume, Spring/Summer 2020

---

23 William S. Burroughs (1914–1997) was celebrated for his experimental writing style as well as for his eccentric personal life.

24 Ilona Halberstadt (b. 1937) was at Oxford with Peter, and later married John's great friend and fellow car enthusiast Glen Kidston (1937–2018); the couple were regular visitors to the house in Ladbroke Grove.

25 Other memories, recounted to his family but sadly never committed to paper, include his close shave with a Sri Lankan pit viper that reared up and struck, narrowly missing his leg, to his mother's great alarm; he also described flying fish and dolphins in Trincomalee harbour and monkeys at Sigiriya.

26 We complete our work on the book amidst ongoing Black Lives Matter protests in the weeks following the unprovoked murder of George Floyd by a policeman in Minneapolis on 25 May 2020.

① PORTRAITS

FELA ANIKULAPO KUTI

An Honest Man

Through an accident – performing a service for a friend of his in London – I was invited to stay in Fela's house the first time I visited Africa. In 1973 the naira was high, Lagos hotels were expensive as well as bad and I was not rich, so I accepted. For six weeks or so, off and on, I was treated as a privileged member of Fela's entourage and spent much time in his company. We were six weeks apart in age, enjoyed one another's conversation and had many noisy arguments.

Despite the inconvenience of my presence, other members of the very large household eventually tolerated me, and I learned a thing or two. One was that sooner or later I was going to have to amuse people publicly to show that I wasn't just a bore. 'You've got to go in for Worst Dancer,' people said when they had seen me dance.

Worst Man Dancer, accompanied by Best Woman Dancer, was a late-Friday-night competition at Fela's Shrine club, then in Surulere. Another turn was a competitive karaoke act by his friends JK and Feelings Lawyer, singing Fela's current hit *Gentleman*.[1] The Worst Dancers, often the same three guys, were of course actually very good dancers, good enough to dance comically on purpose. 'I'm *very shy*,' I whined. 'I'm not *good* enough for Worst Dancer.' But they were adamant. 'You're a natural,' they said unsmilingly. I was to be a good sport. My heart sank.

Well lubricated from the bar and the back yard, I gloomily took the floor with fifty or sixty competitors. Three senior dancing girls moved about the floor and conferred, choosing the finalists. They ignored me. Saved!

I headed for the bar in relief. But when Fela announced the finalists' names he added: 'It is my privilege, as master of ceremonies, to name a fourth finalist …' He was chuckling. Shit! I was in the finals. The orchestra revved up and the seven of us took the floor, each dancing alone. One by one, Fela called the finalists on stage to catch the footlights. He left me till last.

Late Friday night at the Shrine was always one of the world's most mindblowing musical experiences. In the original Fela's sound, of which one often hears echoes these days in other people's music, and to which no

---

1 JK Brimah, a friend and influence from Fela's schooldays, later a part-time drummer with the Koola Lobitos and frequent adviser and associate in later life. Fela credited JK with introducing him to the Lagos nightlife and encouraging him to become a musician.

recording has ever done justice, had a uniquely magisterial, scowling grandeur. At full volume, ten feet in front of the whole orchestra and surrounded by its speakers, the sound would pick you up and flog you around like a housewife dusting a doormat. That's what it felt like when it was my turn to cut loose for the audience. I mean, I was really dancing well.

By the end of the number the whole house was on its feet, shouting my name through helpless tears of laughter. People kept coming up to me the next day and saying how funny I had been. I can still hear Fela's malicious baritone giggle as he gave me my prize: a Joe Tex album, stolen later that night before it could be played. We have been friends ever since, little affected by the long pauses between meetings. I am sorry that there will be no more of them.

Names and origins

Olufela Oludotun Olusegun Ransome-Kuti changed his name to Anikulapo Kuti at the end of the 1970s. 'Anikulapo' is a Yoruba word, usually translated as 'he who carries death in his pouch', chosen in preference to the British name Ransome, whose un-African sound had been irritating him for years. Although the name had been adopted voluntarily by his grandfather, an Anglican minister, Fela characteristically described it as a 'slave name'. In fact one of Fela's recent ancestors had been a slave. His mother Funmilayo, whose maiden name was Thomas, was the granddaughter of an Ilesha man captured and enslaved in childhood, who arrived in the Egba region around Abeokuta on foot from Freetown in Sierra Leone, where he had been released in 1834 following the British abolition of slavery.

Questions of identity appear self-evident, or anyway self-regulating, and therefore a distraction from serious matters, to people whose histories are, so to speak, their own: to the British, French, Americans or Chinese. But they loom large in the consciousness of those recently colonised, whose ancestors have been enslaved, whose countries have been delineated and named by foreigners. Renaming individuals, cities, perhaps a whole country, can be seen as psychologically liberating. French commentators in their shameless way have not hesitated to use words like 'authenticity' and 'negritude' about Fela.

Artists are suggestible by nature, naive, 'child-like', idealistic. How, otherwise, could they spend their lives trying, often vainly, to convey beautiful visions to other people instead of doing something more immediately bankable? Fela's parents were distinguished professionals, both teachers, his father the Rev. I. O. Ransome-Kuti (who died when Fela was seventeen) an eminent headmaster,[2] Funmilayo a ground-breaking feminist, fierce political activist and Lenin Peace Prize laureate, who was a friend of Ghana's Nkrumah and had met Mao Tse-tung. They were well off and well known, and probably did not envisage a career as a popular musician for any of their children. The ferocious childhood discipline Fela recalled later may have had something to do with concentrating his mind on schoolwork. However, when he was nineteen his mother bowed to the inevitable and sent him to study music at a London institution. Spankings or no, he came from a prominent liberal and intellectual family, one that had a firm idea of service to the fellow citizen, of *noblesse oblige*.

Accounts of Fela as a young man show him as witty and energetic, with talents as a communicator, eager to organise bands and play music – jazz trumpet in the early days – not very successfully although with great application, but straitlaced and conventional: scared by horror films, afraid of getting girls pregnant (and perhaps of girls), not a drinker, persuaded by his elder brother that cannabis drives people mad. He married Remi Taylor, the mother of his three eldest children, in London and returned to Nigeria in 1963, working briefly for the Nigerian Broadcasting Corporation and starting his first real band the Koola Lobitos, which played jazz and the Ghanaian form 'highlife'. His mother urged him one day to play music his own people could understand, not jazz, and he began experimenting with new forms and instruments. He and Remi were soon living amicably apart, and in the mid-sixties he discovered, more or less simultaneously, cannabis and what one might call 'girls in general'. Later, towards the end of the Nigerian civil war, the Koola Lobitos made a financially disastrous tour of the US. Fela stayed in Los Angeles for several months and was politicised there by a girl friend, the singer Sandra Smith, a member of the Black Panther Party, who persuaded him to be proud of Africa and recognise what had been done to it.

Returning to Nigeria in 1970, Fela relaunched the band in larger form under the name Africa 70. He had abandoned highlife and was playing a new kind of music, recognisably jazz-influenced, that he called Afro-Beat. The band in the early 1970s normally had around fourteen instrumentalists

---

2 I. O. Ransome-Kuti was also – like his father – a noted liturgical composer and choirmaster. Although Fela's personal relations with his father had been distant, and he made a point of denouncing Christianity as a colonial instrument, I am told that his conducting style on stage was strongly reminiscent of I. O. Ransome-Kuti's.

including four or five horns, four or five drummers and three guitarists with Fela singing, conducting and playing, at that time, electric keyboards (he had already given up trumpet but had not yet taken up the tenor sax which was usually present in the 1980s).[3] Apart from maracas and minor percussion instruments, there was a variable number of girl backup singers. Up to four dancers at a time performed in the spotlit 'cages' that some visitors claimed to find offensive. From 1970, too, Fela began to pour out the stream of tunes and lyrics, all lasting at least a whole side of a twelve-inch LP, that continued until the late 1980s. A few are in Yoruba but most are in pidgin, the English-based lingua franca of the West African coast. It is a language that adapts easily to mockery, criticism and satire: the uses to which Fela consistently put it.

Satire, progressive and regressive

The eighty-odd published lyrics — there are said to be more in the production pipeline — constitute a meandering but structurally simple discourse whose details are sometimes obscure to non-Nigerians. The earliest is entitled *Buy Africa* (1970); the first big hit the Yoruba-language *Jeun Ko'Ku* (1971). The consistent themes attack injustice in various forms: racism on world and local levels, gross inequalities of income and opportunity, corruption, the threat of real force that subtends government in general and military government in particular. Minor themes attack pretentiousness and ill-judged imitation: the 1973 track *Gentleman* pokes fun at people who want to dress with suffocating formality — vest, tie, socks, three-piece suit — in the turkish-bath climate of Lagos; its hugely popular companion piece *Lady*, published the following year, rather ambivalently cites the demanding nature of 'African woman', liable to sit down and eat before men and even claim equality if given half a chance.

Gentleman is progressive and *Lady*, superficially at least, rather the opposite, despite a tone of grudging admiration for this stroppy woman. This is characteristic of Fela. He had no interest in perfect philosophic correctness

---

3 Like any large band's, Africa 70's (later Egypt 80's) lineup would vary slightly according to illnesses, availability and so on. Visiting musicians, some very well known (e.g. Ginger Baker, Lester Bowie, Hugh Masekela), would often sit in; and there was of course some turnover, with musicians leaving to start their own bands or earn more regular money, as Fela was usually financially stretched. Of the several instrumentalists whose contribution was important enough to be defining, I would mention the tenor sax player Igo Chiko; the jazz drummer Tony Allen, who left Fela in the mid-eighties and now lives in Paris; and the baritone saxophonist Lekan Animashaun, who stayed to the end, latterly bearing the title of musical director. Three or more traditional drummers including a 'talking drummer' were crucial to Fela's sound.

which has a very limited role in show business. And in any case, what with one thing and another, contradictions of a sometimes painful sort were apparent in Fela's own life and household. Some lyrics like *Unknown Soldier* (1979)[4] and *Coffin for Head of State* (1981)[5] are personal, but titles like *Why Black Men Dey Suffer, Zombie, Alagbon Close,*[6] *Expensive Shit, Sorrow, Tears and Blood, Dog Eat Dog, VIP,*[7] *ITT*[8] and *Beasts of No Nation*[9] are really a string of anarchist slogans directed against a system, and a series of regimes, that seemed to get steadily more venal and oppressive throughout his working life.

Fela's political programme, to the extent that he had one, was perpetually under construction; his political judgement was usually hasty, often flawed, sometimes (for example his initial approval of Idi Amin's antics on the ground that if the Western media were against the Ugandan despot he couldn't be all bad) almost perverse; but his political *prejudices* – pro-African, pro-underdog, anti-pomp and anti-injustice – were generally sound. They are gut feelings shared by most Africans. When Fela spoke (as he often did) in the name of 'Africa', he may have been projecting some of the attitudes of a famous, eccentric, successful, westernised, upper-class Yoruba anarchist and bohemian on a largely uncomprehending continent; but people also understood that the Africa he referred to was a colonised Africa whose private history had been disrupted by outside forces and needed to be relaunched. This knack of being wrong, but right, endeared Fela to his constituents, but puzzled everyone and enraged powerful individuals implicitly criticised, at the same time providing them with ammunition.

Some obituarists have mentioned fiery political diatribes delivered from the stage of the Shrine. Few if any have pointed out that until quite recently these were often more like stand-up comedy routines than speeches. The audience reaction included a lot of laughter, often at familiar sallies. Laughter

---

4 After the burning of the 'Kalakuta Republic', Fela's house at 14a Agege Motor Road, in 1977, a tribunal found that the fire which destroyed the house, the surgery belonging to Dr Beko Ransome-Kuti and several vehicles had been started by 'unknown soldiers'.

5 Fela's mother Funmilayo, aged seventy-seven at the time, was badly roughed up and injured during the burning of Kalakuta and died less than fourteen months later. Fela blamed the army for shortening her life and carried a symbolic coffin to the house of the head of state (General Olusegun Obasanjo, a fellow Egba and the only Nigerian military leader to step down voluntarily for an elected government. Fela later said Obasanjo had been warned by a Western intelligence organisation to destroy Fela before he destabilised the government). This song commemorates the occasion and Mrs Ransome-Kuti.

6 The address of Lagos CID headquarters. Newspaper shorthand often refers to suspects 'chatting to detectives at Alagbon Close'.

7 = Vagabonds in Power.

8 International Thief Thief; Chief Abiola, another Egba, was chairman of ITT Nigeria. A dispute over a recording deal played a part.

9 The original sleeve cover bears a photomontage of Ronald Reagan, Margaret Thatcher and Pik Botha.

– by no means always harshly mocking – came easily to Fela, and an important part of his talent was the ability to make others laugh. It occurs to me that he may have felt secretly that this meant he was not serious (like his parents, like his doctor brothers), and that some such secret fear may have subtended his prolonged head-butting contest with the Nigerian authorities.

The Shrine audience was disproportionately middle class since the price of entry, modest by Lagos club standards, was increasingly beyond the means of most Lagosians. Of course other places offer good live music, some by internationally known bands, but only the Shrine could offer such an individual sound accompanied by jokes, verbal fireworks and (on the right night) some 'traditional' ceremonial,[10] carried out at a run to distinguish it (Fela once told me) from the solemnity of 'European religion'. It was an avant-garde place with a strange, somewhat feverish atmosphere and reputation. Respectable people, especially women, often claimed to be afraid to go there; even habitués drawn by the music could harbour exaggerated beliefs and anxieties about the club, its owner and his followers.[11]

However, these avant-garde intellectual admirers, relatively few in number and ambivalent about Fela's political and sociological attitudes, were not the musician's real constituency. That was to be found among people who cannot afford to go to nightclubs, the overwhelming majority in Nigeria's cities, especially in the Yoruba South-West.[12] It should be understood that from a European viewpoint large African cities are sociologically in another time as well as another continent. Vertiginous disorderly physical expansion; impoverished and exploited populations of newly transplanted villagers (in Lagos's case Yoruba in their majority but with many speakers of other tongues);[13] stressful and unhealthy living conditions; the distortion, slow loss or outright abandonment of defining social traditions; corruption and economic chaos that appear never-ending: all

---

10 The ceremony took about thirty seconds and involved sprinkling libations of *ogogoro*, a dangerously powerful 'native gin' made from distilled palm wine. I always thought Fela made the ceremony up as he went along, shaman-fashion, but with many references to Yoruba animist tradition.

11 In another club one night with Fela and his unmistakably louche and glamorous retinue I heard myself being described as 'one who like orgies'. The speaker, a poor-but-honest-looking schoolmasterly figure, did not know me – or evidently Fela – nor I him. His judgement was based solely on my Europeanness and the fact that I had arrived with Fela.

12 And to a lesser but still marked extent in other countries, especially English-speaking West African countries.

13 Something of a tower of Babel, in fact, rendering pidgin necessary and also making illiterate Africans into practised multi-linguists able to communicate in three or four different languages. While on this subject, it is worth mentioning that the 'hippified' mid-Atlantic component in Fela's delivery would not have seemed intrusive to these urban Nigerians, but a gangway to the glamorous new Americanised 'world culture' to which everyone is now said to aspire.

these things recall nineteenth-century London or Edwardian New York (but without the triumphant capitalist expansion). However, recognisable forms of moral-religious and socialist-syndicalist dissent coexist with what might be called pre-Enlightenment comportments. The aspect most relevant here is an impassioned personalisation of social and political attitudes by populations who do not recognise, or do not trust, the institutional framework provided for their expression.[14]

Street polemic

The loyalty of these groups, surely among the true wretched of the earth, is not won with a couple of hit records or a few well-turned phrases, although these can start the process. Lagos street people may not be scholarly but they have heard a lot of political promises and seen plenty of would-be demagogues. They have a keen ear for hypocrisy, a sharp eye for pretension, the habit of scrutinising candidates for their approval closely from all angles. They do not fetishise rationality – indeed rather the opposite – but require any discourse to be emotionally consistent with the candidate's social behaviour.

Fela was already a favourite son of those potholed, rubbish-strewn, clamorous streets by the beginning of the 1970s, the passage of his battered Opel estate greeted by cries of his name or one of his self-awarded titles (Chief Priest! Black President!) from the anonymous passing crowd. It had been recognised that with Fela what you saw was what you got: insolent informality of dress and behaviour, open use of hemp (as in other countries illegal and set about with contradictory but strongly held beliefs), a large, socially and tribally disparate household and retinue, voracious sexual promiscuity not unlike that of some Western rock stars but justified with references to African polygamous tradition. The growing list of titles, Fela's musical brilliance, his near-genius as a bandleader and showman, seemed appropriate in the child of famous parents and particularly a famous mother, loved and (according to some) feared by the Egbas and other Yorubas for her formidable leadership of market women in opposition to the British and

---

14 In a traditional rural setting the institution and the personality (chief, king, etc.) would coincide. In a newly expanded city in a new country, where the institutions (government, army, police) have come to be seen as discredited, the urban proletariat, lumpen and otherwise, having emerged from a variety of original backgrounds, feels unrepresented and may follow, provisionally at least, any figurehead that looks convincing. The religious fundamentalist fascism that occupies this credibility vacuum in some Muslim countries cannot prevail in a region as culturally diverse as southern Nigeria. A populist discourse of a more experimental kind is a better bet.

local authorities. Fela too, on stage and in interviews, was displaying a fearless eagerness to attack the government, not just for perceived incompetence, corruption, etc., but for illegitimacy: for having seized power by force, for assuming the right to rule without consulting the ruled or obtaining their voluntary acquiescence. Even under the Gowon regime – gentlemanly by more recent standards – this kind of polemic, which was not always deeply considered or carefully phrased, had a risky side that went straight to the heart of the street.

Over the years, as Nigeria's oil boom faded and regimes succeeded one another, the list of these provocations grew. When secession was anathema after the defeat of Biafra, Fela said the Ibos had been right to secede and named his house the Kalakuta republic (Kalakuta after the name of a cell in which he had been detained briefly on a hemp charge). Under the Obasanjo regime he poured scorn on the government's attempts to increase food production and refused to take part in Festac, a showpiece world African arts and culture festival mounted at great expense (and attended by financial scandals). In 1979 he married, in an improvised traditional ceremony, his current crop of twenty-seven girl singers and dancers.[15] This was taken as an oblique criticism of prominent Nigerians who posed as modern, monogamous men but openly kept numerous mistresses by whom they had children. The hemp proselytising, the major and minor hit-or-miss polemics on current events, continued throughout. So did Fela's loyalty to his followers and his readiness, when asked, to help individuals in need or in trouble with the law. He could have become extremely rich by limiting the size of his household and concentrating on the commercial exploitation of his work (possibly the music itself, which is often roughly finished, might also have benefited). But the refusal to play the card of class exclusion, the decision instead to embrace the role of lumpen chieftain, made him a spendthrift: easy come easy go, there are a lot of us so better buy a bus as well as a Range Rover. His household usually ate but its members were often broke (only a few stole from him). Senior musicians in the band grumbled about their pay. Alarming quarrels often erupted among the dancing girls over missing earrings or stolen underwear.

Some of these attitudes may seem more justifiable than others, but taken as a whole they, and the trouble they caused, made Fela a hero.

---

15 As with a large band, so with a large household: people are always arriving and leaving, and there is change over time. Despite 'communal' aspects – an acute shortage of privacy, for example – Fela's house was not a commune. There was a very definite hierarchy, and serious internal offences could result in physical chastisement.

Regular attempts to prosecute him for hemp possession were bought off or fought off; a refusal to yield anyone who had sought his help to pursuers resulted in at least one attempted prosecution for abduction. In 1977, after a confused quarrel between a couple of Fela's men and a traffic policeman, his house was attacked and burnt out by the local army regiment and many people, including Fela himself, his mother and younger brother, were beaten and injured. The land was later seized, without compensation, by the Lagos State government. In 1984, under the Buhari military regime, he was given a five-year sentence by a military tribunal for currency trafficking and served twenty months, being released some time after his elder brother Olikoye became health minister in the first Babangida government. The technical nature of the offence and the trivial sum involved (£1,600 sterling, a cash float for the band's arrival in Los Angeles) made it absolutely clear that the prosecution was cynical and driven by the personal malice of someone highly placed in the Buhari regime.

After his release in 1986 Fela 'divorced' the twenty-seven wives, but did not send them away (of course some had already left). He continued to tour and play the Shrine, now in Ikeja near Lagos airport; the music continued to branch out in experimental directions, Fela now saying he wanted to write and play something equivalent to European classical music. In recent months, already unwell with the AIDS that killed him,[16] he was quoted as giving some sort of verbal approval to the Abacha government: astonishing, were it not for his illness and the fact that his younger brother Beko, a GP and human rights activist, was in jail in Maiduguri, convicted by a military tribunal of involvement in an alleged coup plot.[17]

Lagos, a town whose population is unreliably estimated at 8 to 10 million, turned out for Fela's funeral procession on 20 August, seven choked hours from Tafawa Balewa Square on Lagos Island to Ikeja. Numerous civilian, military and police grandees attended, not all Yorubas and not gloating, but mourning a great musician and Nigerian original, an awkward cultural asset who will be terribly missed.

---

16 He actually died of heart failure resulting from what seems to have been an opportunistic typhoid infection. His elder brother Olikoye, a former professor of medicine and health minister, held a press conference to announce that he had been suffering from AIDS, apparently against the wishes of the government which (like others) is bashful on the subject.

17 Dr Ransome-Kuti was released from detention in June 1998 following the death of the late head of state, Gen. Sani Abacha. Gen. Obasanjo was also released, followed (after intervention by UN secretary general Kofi Annan) by Chief Moshood Abiola.

There is a tragic double coda: Fela's niece Frances ('Fran') Kuboye (of whom he was very fond), the daughter of his elder sister Dolu, died of a heart attack the day after his funeral. She was a dentist – rare in Nigeria – who, with her husband Tunde Kuboye, ran a club called Jazz 38 in Ikoyi, the smart end of Lagos; he played bass and she sang in the house band. In the late 1980s Fela used to perform there once a week, playing tenor sax in the band Extended Family before rushing across town to the Shrine. Jazz 38 closed a couple of years ago when the lease expired, and money difficulties delayed the opening of its successor. Frances was forty-eight and leaves three children. Only a few weeks later, Fela's third child and second daughter Sola died of cancer after a short illness. Sola was an energetic young woman said by some friends to resemble Fela closely.

    Fela Anikulapo Kuti, 1938–1997
    Frances Kuboye, née Ransome-Kuti, 1949–1997
    Sola Anikulapo Kuti, 1963–1997

    New Left Review, 225, September 1997 (last paragraph added later)

BY WAY OF KENSAL GREEN

'What's this about a church service?' I asked my daughter Natalie when I saw her that evening, although I had my suspicions. I waved her scrawled message telling me that Ezzreco had called.

'He said it was for a black man who got badly messed up. He said you'd know who it was.' I did know, like a newspaper editor with a file of obituaries for people still living. Priest's death, if it had occurred, was not only unsurprising but seemed, as the passing of those in obvious pain usually does, not altogether a bad thing. The sadness associated with it hardly stirred being long familiar.

Harm had come to Priest quite early in the 1960s as a direct consequence of his relations with white people. It wasn't anyone's fault in particular, other than Priest's of course. Like most of his migrant generation he knew that people are responsible for their own actions. The view that the injustice woven into this or any other society can excuse malevolent or idiotic behaviour had not yet become widespread. In those days it was easier to tell who was good, who was bad and who was indifferent.

You could tell at a glance that Priest was good, and a week's acquaintance exposed him as a rare treasure of unassuming sweetness. He had arrived here by boat some time in the middle 1950s already bearing his ghetto name. He had been a Rastafarian from an early age and once described in my presence barefoot expeditions to the hills outside Kingston in his late adolescence to 'smoke a lot of herb and contemplate'. I used to buy weed from some Rastas in the late 1950s and enjoyed their junkyard Old Testament theology, drumming and villainous stories. But they were very London, tough and not especially virtuous. Priest by contrast was fresh, with a light presence. He seemed pure and profound.

In a manner characteristic of people of African descent he had created himself, and been created, partly by adopting this significant name whose first three letters were those of his surname. He had a sister somewhere but I don't know which of them came to England first. I can't remember exactly how I met him or who introduced us, but I believe it was Faris bey Glubb the Magnificent.

What I do know, without remembering it in any specific way, is that I met Priest in about 1960 when I was twenty-two and he was thirty-one, and that marijuana was being smoked when it happened. Hashish was then virtually unknown in this country and the few English jazz musicians, petty criminals and intellectuals who liked cannabis got it from the people who had it: black West Indians. That was where the market was. It was a time of relaxed elegance, good manners and low prices.

Priest wasn't a dealer. He didn't live by selling weed but he always knew where to find it if there was any to be found. He was never too busy to take you to see someone who was dealing or introduce you to the right passer-by. You might have to wait a while. It might not be the best deal in town. But Priest would take the trouble, and tolerate your company for the time it took. He never got more than a smoke or a couple of quid out of it.

He had worked as a French polisher and possessed modest skills as a cook and barber, never used in regular employment so far as I am aware. He never owned a car, a carpet or a suit. He had no wife, no permanent mistress, no children. He lived in a succession of indistinguishable shabby rooms without curtains or lampshades, but one did not seek him at home. He was usually to be found at some temporary hangout, shebeen or blues-dance venue, some gutsed-out slum basement where bare 100-watt bulbs exposed shattered furniture and decor that suggested a building regularly used for advanced infantry training: missing doors, gouged plaster, sinister stains.

He cut my hair once in the basement of 281 Westbourne Park Road, opposite the bottom end of Great Western Road. I sat under the light in the front room, facing the window. The hair cuttings made no difference to the litter on the floor. In a corner four men noisily played cards. In the back room, under another bare light bulb, a young man slept curled up on a rickety pingpong table adapted for dice with a tattered covering of green baize.

I don't know what I paid for the haircut, if anything. Priest didn't care about money and never had much. His appearance was discreet and unspectacular. He was of medium height and compact physique, his face unremarkable: sloping back from a wide mouth with slightly splayed and projecting upper front teeth, strong but not large nose, calm sad eyes fixed ... elsewhere. He dressed neatly but modestly in dark outer clothing, clean but inexpensive; often a white shirt; black shoes; short tidy hair.

281, where Priest cut my hair, was midway between two famous hangouts of the Rachman era: the Rio, which stayed open very late, full of cowboys, where Colin McInnes could sometimes be seen trawling for cynical spade rent boys; and the more upmarket Fiesta on the corner of Ledbury Road, favoured by US servicemen and the more presentable sort of tart, where the Profumo scandal was already smouldering in an atmosphere of interesting food and superior jazz played on good equipment. A few hundred yards away was the café at 9 Blenheim Crescent, where a setting heavily charged with cinematic paranoia persuaded unwary adventurers to part with money in exchange for substances which sometimes turned out to be catnip or shredded plasterboard: 'Give me the money now. The herb's in that Player's packet in the gutter across the street.'

Dozens of apartments in the neighbourhood functioned as shebeens. You were a member of these private clubs, which stayed open all night and sold drinks over the going rate, if they knew who you were and could stand your company. Blues-dances happened in different gutted cellars solid with bodies and weed smoke, 200 diaphragms jumping to the bass shock-wave of huge battered speakers.

Priest shared few of the surface values of that upwardly mobile, often desperate society which aspired in the main to little beyond the garish and flashy. He did not try to impress with wardrobe or conversation or reputation or assertive behaviour. But he was a privileged person. Everyone knew his name and nobody questioned his right to it. Only once, in that period, did I ever hear him raise his voice. We had been asked for payment on the way into a blues in the cellar under Sparks Café in Talbot Road at the top of Powis Square. When the blues impresario struggled into the packed staircase to see what the fuss was about, Priest gave him an earful. Pointing disdainfully to the young man who had *actually asked him to pay*, he shouted indignantly that 'this lickle pox from Antigua' didn't seem to know who he was talking to. We were admitted without payment.

His normal delivery was quiet, shy and confiding. He spoke with a lisp, musically, his accent a softened version of the rude-boy ganja-and-guns dialect today affected by pickpockets and reggae stars. There was something demure about Priest, his eyes downcast, his rare laugh sad and gentle, knowing but without bitterness. Nobody made a fuss about it, but people who knew him gradually realised that they were in the company of a low-key, particularly inoffensive holy man.

He didn't moralise and although there were plenty of bad hats around I never heard him speak unkindly of anyone. The only subject on which he would talk for any length of time, not volubly but quietly, patiently, as if explaining something very simple to a hyperactive six-year-old, was Rastafarian theology. This was not an especially easy subject for a West European atheist raised as a Catholic and educated partly by Jesuits. Its main components were quickly identifiable but the reasoning used to link and articulate them seemed at best opaque and at worst, infantile.

Nevertheless Priest's sincerity was so transparent and his manner so engaging that one did not become impatient and did one's best to seek clarification without being abrasive. Incomprehension did not annoy him. Without altering his quiet tone he would simplify and repeat the explanation, his sad, patient chuckle suggesting that your obtuseness was quite inoffensive and only to be expected. If you lost interest or let the matter drop he didn't follow you down the street bombarding you with footnotes. He wasn't a zealot. He knew there would be another time.

This pleasing personality quickly inspired affection in those who knew Priest, and there were few people in the Gate community known as the Grove who did not. It was difficult to remember what he said about his religion – indeed I have come to believe that it is language more than anything else that makes Rastafarianism so intractable to outsiders – but the actual words hardly seemed to matter. Not with arguments but through that calm, unaggressive and absolute conviction, he helped me to see that (however others might use it) Rastafarianism is generous and adaptable, a faith not just for the oppressed of Jamaica but for the human condition. I did not become a believer or one of those shrill and solemn groupies who undermine their friends with parodied arguments and ham-fisted special pleading. I continued to be amused by the Rasta penchant for the Old Testament. But I understood eventually that to a serious believer Jewish mythology, modern Ethiopian history and the tragic fallout of relations between Europe and Africa can be linked by more than a provisional cement of hemp and drumming. A thread of faith and reasoning, invisible to me but solid and dependable to a believer, binds these components together in a satisfying, useful way.

Many years later in the 1970s, when I had learned something about current affairs, I once asked Priest how Rastas, who love freedom and hate tyranny, could tolerate the central role their faith assigned to the emperor of Ethiopia. Haile Selassie was a weak autocrat waging war on his Eritrean province with American money and weapons while the rest of his subjects dodged the secret police between famines. He looked very like a tyrant himself. Wasn't it all a bit embarrassing for Rastas?

Laughing with shy amusement, he gave me to understand that although the emperor and Ras (roughly, Duke) Tafari were historically the same person, Haile Selassie meant one thing to Ethiopians and Rastafari something altogether different to Rastas. Even so he refused to distance himself morally from the political incarnation of this Rasta two-persons-in-one, a touching gesture of solidarity which I thought the emperor did not deserve.

As nearly always I cannot remember Priest's words but they were certainly very different from my own. The subsequent history of Ethiopia supplies an interesting afterthought. The Stalinising military junta which replaced Haile Selassie, an event I thought at the time to be altogether positive, proved more than a disappointment. It replaced American inputs with Soviet ones and with them made everything even worse for the Ethiopians. Priest had not just set me straight on a point of theology; his loyalty to that unintelligent backwoods emperor rendered helpless by history had planted the seed of a second lesson on the nature of power and revolution.

Amid the clamour of his compatriots, a people much given to shouting both joyous and angry, Priest's calm and quiet were I suppose widely mistaken for the stylish psychic armour then known as 'cool'. His agreeable personality made one forget that he was a man in his early thirties with a man's needs and passions, but one who lived alone without wife or children or, so far as I am aware, any long-term close relationship. Unless his sexual modesty, pudeur, has misled me, his was a life of waking alone in bleak rooms, little love, no home cooking. I do not think it occurred to anyone in the early 1960s that Priest might be suffering.

Of course he had minor troubles. There was a sizeable audience in Marylebone Magistrates' Court the day he was done for obstruction in Portobello Road. Talking to some friends on a corner, Priest had argued when asked to move along that he was only having a 'social conversation', and had been arrested. That was where I first heard his real name, Roy Prince. He was embarrassed and held himself stiffly in the dock. On being fined a small sum, just a pound or two, he said very quietly and very clearly something about being 'temporarily financially embarrassed'. 'What's he saying? What's he saying?' demanded the magistrate testily. He was given time to pay but somebody paid the fine.

The 1960s were gathering speed. Nobody had ever heard of hippies but Notting Hill was attracting rule-breakers of all descriptions with its cheap rented housing, interesting mixed community, big street market and informal night life. Barriers were said to be coming down. People felt liberated although their goals were banal – money, power, personal fulfilment, oblivion, that sort of thing. Wages were rising and work was easy to get. Optimism ruled. People cultivated a friendly open manner to distance themselves from the uptight penny-pinching fifties, everyone looking over their shoulders at Hitler and rationing. The post-war era had begun at last.

I was doing very little. Some deficiency of courage was preventing me from embarking on a career or persisting in any project; at the same time I didn't want to get entangled in some awful way of life just to make a living. So I was scrounging around, piss-poor, working from time to time, getting nowhere, my life on hold. I thought there was plenty of time. I lived in different parts of town but was often in the Gate. One day someone, perhaps David Sladen who has introduced me to several of the worst people I have ever met – and it has to be admitted quite a few of the better ones – produced this American. Having nothing better to do I agreed to help him sell the ten pounds of mediocre Mexican weed he had smuggled into the country in a knapsack.

Gary, or whatever he was called, was a monumental pain in the bum. He was not the first heroin addict I had met but was a contender for the title of the most boring. He made a bit of a show of being a junkie, did nasty parlour tricks with paper matches, putting them out on his tongue and leaving black streaks on it, and had a small switchblade which he often flashed. I had a word with Priest who said he would line up some buyers.

When I went to collect this Gary from his small hotel in Victoria, he put all the weed in a pile on the floor of the room and sprinkled water on it to increase the weight. 'I'm not called Bernstein for nothing,' he said, tapping the side of his nose with an idiot grin. He took his midday fix and we went up to the Gate in a cab.

Priest had found a few retailers whom we met at various addresses during the afternoon. Gary wanted £50 a pound but I believe he took £45 for most of it, sold in pounds or half-pounds. Testing, weighing, arguing and so on took all afternoon until dark. But nobody wanted the last pound weight except a guy who said he only had £40. By this time people had become bored with Gary's posturing, bad manners, inharmonious voice and evident conviction that he was a very smart cookie. Priest and I both urged him to take the forty and have done with it, but he'd had his mid-afternoon, teatime and cocktail-hour fixes, he had several hundred quid and a switchblade in his pockets, and he wasn't taking no shit from anybody, no sirree.

With evident reluctance and showing signs of nervousness, Priest took us to 53 St Stephen's Gardens in search of a buyer for the last pound. It was Parachute's house, a bashed-up Gate tenement with the usual mix of respectable working people, crooks, tarts and a sort of late-sixties advance guard of long-haired family folk who thought it was cute to teach five-year-old children to use obscene language and roll joints. We stayed there a couple of hours but no buyer materialised.

Gary, to give the devil his due, rewarded Priest and me with tenners and generous handfuls of the merchandise while we were waiting. One by one, dodgy-looking bozos began to filter into the place and peer round the door of the kitchen on the second floor, where Gary brandished his blade a few times, took his pre-dinner fix and gave people to understand that there were no flies on him. Parachute seemed to know these guys, one of whom was very wide with a fascinating c-shaped bottle scar on his right cheek, but I certainly didn't and Priest, looking worried, left the house for twenty minutes. When he came back he murmured to me that he had a car waiting outside and we should leave.

I needed no urging at all, but Gary delayed our departure with another fix and a few conjuring tricks. One of the bozos came into the room looking sullen and demanded 'some weed'. At first Gary told him to fuck off, then he relented and produced a handful. To my great surprise, somebody turned up and bought half the last pound causing the bozos to stir uneasily. They watched the remainder, in its folded brown-paper carrier bag, like hawks.

Finally Gary made up his mind to leave. By the time we reached the doorstep there were two or three bozos on the pavement and two or three more coming through the hall behind us. As we descended the steps two plainclothes policemen passed along the pavement unaware of the fuddled alarm in their wake, and disappeared round the corner to the left intent on the fight against crime. Priest's friends, a couple of respectable family men in hats, gazed out of their double-parked Austin, engine running, rear door open, eyes like saucers.

Instead of heading for the car Gary turned right. Bottle-scar came skanking stiffly up and blocked his path, muttering 'Them say you got a knife, make you get it out, let me see your knife,' etc., etc. I had not suspected Gary of playing-field skills, but he feinted to the right and passed the folded brown-paper carrier bag, about the same size and shape as a rugby or American football, very neatly under his left elbow into my surprised hands six feet away.

Now it was my turn to play the village idiot. The car door was still open, Priest and the two good guys were signalling urgently and uttering cries and murmurs of encouragement, but I stood rooted to the ground, my mouth very probably open, looking at this parcel around which Bottle-scar's sausage-like fingers were already closing in a steely grip. He wasted no breath on me but wrenched the carrier-bag downwards and out of my grasp. Everyone scarpered. For a moment the street was filled with flitting shadows, triumphant laughter, slamming doors and the odd curse. Then the distant roar that passes for silence in London returned. None of us wanted to be searched if the CID came back. Priest's friends, shaking their heads in disbelief, dropped Gary and me a couple of blocks away.

It now seems to me that this incident although far from glorious was hardly a major tragedy. Gary's losses were moderate; nobody had been shot, stabbed or even hit. But Gary was very upset and looking for a culprit. His idea was that Priest had set him up. I thought it most unlikely and pointed out that far from being involved in any ripoff Priest had acted quickly and intelligently to prevent it. Gary was unconvinced and hung around complaining for another week. 'I think he knew those guys,' he kept saying. While undoubtedly true, this did not seem to me to constitute evidence of collusion. 'He probably knew them by sight, he knows everybody. Don't you see how embarrassing it is for him?' But Gary was a stranger to embarrassment. His departure was a relief.

Now that the years sweep by every five or ten subjective minutes like junctions on a motorway, it is hard to remember that a month once seemed a long time, long enough to complete almost any project. And at this distance chronology easily becomes a little blurred, a little scrambled. My visits to the Gate from other parts of town were frequent, but I did not always try or always manage to see Priest. If therefore this account seems to contain too much about myself and not enough about Priest, it is because I do not really know very much about him. I am obliged to supplement fact with other material which I can only hope is evocative; line, so to speak, with gouache. Why should not a tribute also be a confession?

Not long after Gary's painful discovery that he might, after all, be called Bernstein for nothing, Alex passed through the Gate and lived for several months in Parachute's house, number 53. Daughter of a housemaster at a minor public school, she had appeared out of a King's Road shop doorway one night literally sweating benzedrine and 'raped', as he later put it, a rich jazz-freak friend of mine. Their relationship lasted several months, perhaps a year, but became stormy owing (among other things) to an interview Alex gave to a Sunday newspaper about drugs in Chelsea. She not only named names but gave addresses, greatly upsetting my friend's long-suffering mother.

In any case Alex's craving for excitement, disregard for the consequences of her actions and inordinate appetite for amphetamine and cannabis often made her company exhausting. She was tall, almost strapping, with a good skin and a straight-nosed, Edwardian kind of beauty. But her dyed-blond hair done in a wispy beehive, pale blue-green eyes half-closed and swimming with dope and larceny, mouth set in a stoned smirk of self-esteem and conspiratorial good fellowship, numerous rings on grubby fingers, bright red coat and tight black trousers instantly raised the hackles of hall

PORTRAITS

porters, policemen and other guardians of the State. Squads of store detectives shadowed her through C&A and Harrods, but she often stole things which she later gave away. Hers was not a discreet presence or a restful one.

Nevertheless few people, few men at least, were impervious to her insinuating, provocative, witchy charm; some found it dazzling, mesmeric. Usually penniless, pilled up to the eyeballs, trailing marijuana-smoke and jocular seductiveness, she giggled and hustled her way through the West End and Stepney to come to rest for a while in the Gate. There the music, street life and exotic population filled her with gleeful enthusiasm which she expressed with characteristic directness and poor taste. 'Man, spades are *fantastic*!' she would crow in a voice strained with delighted amazement. 'They're so *cool*! They're so *hip*!' And she would go off into peals of uncontainable laughter at the wonder of it all.

As she obviously meant no harm, the black people present when she made these absurd remarks always seemed not to notice them. Alex did not respond well to murmured asides about good manners or the misleading nature of racial stereotypes; she would raise her voice and repeat the remarks in a stage-Caribbean accent, still laughing like a drain and adding a long-drawn-out '*Rarse!*' or two for emphasis. I later came to realise that there was a sado-masochist component in her character, that her many provocations, her kamikaze approach to life in general, did not result from carelessness or excessive optimism but had the darker unconscious purpose of inviting retribution. At the time, it just seemed inevitable that one or two of the rougher and more calculating people she used like playthings, apparently unaware of their autonomy, would turn the tables and use her.

Perhaps it is fortunate that this is not Alex's story, for I cannot remember whether she began pulling up her skirt and squirting workmanlike doses of heroin into her upper thigh before or after she first hired her body to a cash customer. Nor do I know whether this hiring was her own idea or that of a suave, muscular, not entirely sympathetic person with a gold tooth, a nice car and a lot of suits with whom she had many dealings at this time and who she later complained beat her up. But I believe that she was turned on – a phrase that encapsulates the junky talent for random disinformation – by a poet friend who was already addicted, and that a few months of heroin use desensitised her enough to make the Game seem like … a game. Unrepayable cash loans to suits followed later.

Alex wasn't a mainstream operator, net stockings and false eyelashes, turning so many tricks a day, saving money for retirement in Dollis Hill, wham, bam, ta ducks. Her impulsive behaviour, strange remarks and frequent outbursts of helpless mirth punctuated with Jamaican oaths, incongruous in one following that most conformist of professions, must have bruised the libido of many a punter and given the suits dyspepsia. She quit after a Holloway stretch for drugs or theft: dried out from junk, moved to Islington, showed a talent for the plastic arts, briefly married a nice man a few years younger than herself and in the early 1970s faded into the distant provinces where I like to imagine her a bit wiser, not too much sadder, roses round the door, several cats, a carefully maintained local reputation as a juju woman.

Yes, I wish her well, not only because she was my friend when we were young, generous and forgiving, before the merciless prudence of middle age which half-persuades us that life is too short to waste time on this person or that; still is my friend really although I have not heard her crowing with laughter over some preposterous idea, or seen her collusive smirk, for something like twenty years. Not only for that but in this context, the context of Priest's story, because she was Priest's friend too; because they remained friends although for a while they were more than friends and although on that level their relationship was lopsided; because it was not her fault that in some way she represented, and perhaps simply was, Priest's nemesis.

By the time Alex hit the Gate she and Priest were habitual companions, their friendship springing fully fledged from a first casual introduction during some good-time sweep through the quarter. I may have been responsible although I can't remember the occasion; it could equally well have been Faris or the hunchback poet Grahame. What impressed at first was Alex's great enthusiasm for her new contact, overwhelming even by her standards. 'Priest's *incredible*! He's fucking *far out*!' she would cry, whether he was present or not. '*Rarse*-cloth!' For a while it looked as if he was extending his broad, humble and undemonstrative tolerance to someone who didn't know how to behave normally. He was willing, it seemed, to serve as a sparring partner for Alex's crash course in Advanced Conversational Working-Class Jamaican, chuckling shyly over her linguistic and social gaffes and sometimes, infected by her endemic mirth, laughing his smothered kindly held-in laugh, 'mm-'mm-'mm, not noisy but racking his upper body, until tears came.

It wasn't long before you could tell that his chuckling and head-shaking had nothing to do with tolerance, that there was nothing he felt he had to tolerate, that Alex's parody of Caribbean speech, unladylike language and exaggerated delight in the banal moved him with deep pleasure. Nothing she could say or do would offend him. Everything about her was magical, fascinating, an aspect of the beloved who is beyond criticism. He didn't say much. For most of the time I knew him, until death, so to speak, had him in its sights, Priest kept his feelings private. But there was a time when the simple mention of her name, which he pronounced with a tenderly intruded aspirate, would make him smile happily. 'Halix,' he once said to me, 'is a scene all to sheself.'

So that one remembers Priest in those days often gilded at the edges in the weird rays of Alex's dotty glamour, as he played his courteous, inoffensive walk-on part in her scene, talked through the dawn with her in shabby rooms, basked in the warmth of their shared highs, sloped at her side down Oxford Street scattering upstaged and intimidated tourists, two not-so-secret agents of the psychic alternative tracked by posses of morose store detectives; loved her, there's no other word for it, loved her to distraction and waited with unassuming patience for her to love him back.

I have often wondered why a holy man whose attention was largely fixed on the infinite and the divine, an ascetic who did not desire possessions, should have made an exception in Alex's case; after all she was not the only pretty woman in the zone. She did have a special tenderness for him, one which lasted well and survived troubled times. Her shameless bum-scratching, perpetual unsuccessful nail-painting and habit of changing her clothes or doing her hair in front of you, which fooled some people into thinking they were admitted to her intimacy, were really the product of her upbringing in a boys' boarding school. Boys held no mystery for her and she saw no reason to preserve small feminine mysteries from them. She was a good sport, the kind of pretty tomboy often misunderstood in adult life.

What happened, I think, was that Alex or an idea of Alex grew unnoticed within the perimeter of Priest's defences during their months of platonic sparring, so that warmth and light, or the promise of warmth and light, came by imperceptible stages into the lonely centre of his life, within the circle of respect and affection in which he was held by all except the very crass but which his own reserve, modesty, kept at a certain distance. Is it necessary to point out, at the risk of sounding sentimentious, that the path of God is a stony one where stumbles are not uncommon? Is it fanciful to suggest that Alex's kamikaze quest for fulfilment was like the opposite pole of Priest's solitary and serene contemplation of the vastnesses of the universe? Or merely gross to recall that their correspondence across cultural, geographical and social distances was focused through the Gate lens of pills, smoke and smug eroticised hipness? Is it possible really to know how people settle on the objects of their love and what makes them start and stop loving?

I don't know whether Priest and Alex were ever technically 'lovers'; if they were, my guess is that that they were not often or for long and that this stage came early, not late, in their relationship. He bore with dignity and fortitude, perhaps with hope, the realisation that he was not her type, that at the time she was moved by people altogether more assertive and uncomplicated. She wasn't nasty about it but became restive under pressure of his polite adoration: Yeah, well, gotta meet Tex in Queensway, man, see you tomorrow, right? Cha! And made good her escape in this direction or that. Priest didn't show it much. He was as nice as ever, talked about the same things, just a little flatly perhaps, with just a small mournful pucker about the downcast eyes now when he saw her or thought of her. As she zoomed or stumbled back and forth through his field of vision on assignations and enterprises from which he was excluded, in the company of people he knew only too well because he knew everybody. And as her pace slowed, her skin tarnished and her eyes sometimes, then often, then always, were blank and pale with junk or pained and streaming without it. He kept his cool and strode deliberately but without fanfare into the wilderness.

Together and separately, Priest and Alex were frequent visitors to 105 Westbourne Terrace where I lived in Hoppy's flat with several other people. Then some time in 1962 or 1963 I married and left the flat but often came back to the quarter for one reason or another. On one of these visits I went to see Priest in his new basement in the short row of houses, ending in a railway footbridge and a long brick wall, backing onto the rat-infested wastes of the Great Western Railway where Westbourne Park Road bends sharp right and snakes out of the Gate proper into Bayswater.

Priest's rooms had always been more or less clean and as bare as monks' cells. This one was cluttered, with sleazy sofas and chairs, dirty carpets, a coffee-table covered with glasses, overflowing ashtrays and other social debris. Priest greeted me a little distantly and said he was expecting someone to pass by with some grass. There were two or three people I didn't know sitting in the room. Nobody said a word. Priest, standing with his back to the room, was doing something on top of a dressing table. After about half an hour I realised that he was slowly cleaning hypodermic needles with dirty bits of cotton-wool. He left the room, took a fix, returned, faced the wall again. Presently he cleaned his ear vigorously with a matchstick. People came in and out. Some of them were junkies and I didn't know any of them. There was a lurid sense of something being badly awry. The man with the grass never showed up.

Opiates are good for pain and nothing much else. Don't think that because you haven't got toothache or a broken bone there's nothing junk can do for you. Not all pain is physical or even traceable. Generations of addicts have used opium and its derivatives to deal with doubt, humiliation, loneliness, self-loathing and the whole range of bad feeling down to the distant roaring of some deeply buried, quite small, tragic void encysted during infancy, before words or reason. Some mother's bad habit or father's slip of the tongue brought to mind by banal events: crossed in love, bad at business, why does it hurt so, why won't it go away? So with Alex and so, in his turn, with Priest.

So before long, like Alex and other notorious neighbourhood junkies, Priest became a person upon whom householders and restaurant owners looked askance and who got banned from classy establishments like the Fiesta for falling asleep, dripping blood on the floor, spending too long in the lavatory or alarming the cash customers. Conventional wisdom at the time was that heroin addicts were boring, unreliable, dishonest and messy. I don't think Priest stole as some others did but he was drawn into the junky coterie by the web of their common need and all-absorbing interest, the tangle of small deals, loans really, of sixth-of-a-grain jacks of national health junk, the small trade to good-timers in their prescription surpluses and shots of the liquid or crystal methedrine some used for liver-blasting, heart-straining holiday visits to the optimistic land of fast metabolism from the dim, slow, light-sensitive, constipated place they inhabited.

People from the Caribbean whose cultures value human warmth, openness and genial vigour were especially squeamish about these sinister chemicals and had an almost superstitious distaste for the hypodermic with its overtones of serious sickness and violated flesh. Some were shocked to learn that Priest was, in the expression current at the time, jooking himself. For me the problem wasn't the sneering hauteur with which junkies regard less serious drugs but Priest's frozen remoteness, too far away to sustain a conversation. I went to his nasty new basement once or twice more, waiting, waiting among people even Priest didn't know, hobbledehoys, more often white than black now, noisy tarts, smart-aleck representatives of the advancing 1960s with their tawdry suits, noticeable shoes and inflated commonplace ideas. Taxis waited outside with engines running at all hours. Through it all he would stand endlessly at the dressing table obsessively wiping needles, his back turned to the room, his downcast gaze not so much demure as evasive. I thought the pointless clamour would attract unwelcome attention and get him busted. What actually happened was worse than that.

BRICOLAGE

Things change, people move about, the years accelerate by, slowly at first. I hadn't seen much of Priest for a year or two when I heard some time in the middle 1960s that he had caught hepatitis from a dirty needle and was in hospital, very ill. I should have gone to see him but don't remember doing so. What I heard came through the grapevine, radio-trottoir as it is called in French-speaking countries: Priest's case was unusually serious, he was very nearly dead, it was no joke at all. These reports came in bits and pieces over the two years, or nearly, that he spent in hospital. Many of them came from Alex who, true to their friendship, visited him often.

Nor do I remember exactly when I met him again, but it was a considerable time after he came out of hospital – much changed, the reports said – and probably after I had come back to the Gate myself to live. Let us say in the early 1970s. He was certainly not well and was having trouble with his legs, affected by arthritis or rheumatism or by his long stay in bed. Although only in his early forties he was showing grey hairs and had lost his top front teeth, which accentuated his lisp. But he was off junk, back from the wilderness.

He invited me to see the flat the housing trust had given him at the top of Powis Square, round the corner from where Sparks Café used to be. The one-room plus k-and-b apartment was newly decorated, newly built inside the shell of the Victorian house, with the characteristic feel of a Gate functional housing rebuild whether wrought by a Rachman or the council: flimsy partitions turning one good room into three bad ones, ceiling the wrong height, windows the wrong size and in the wrong places, hardboard doors, the smell of paint. A bed, a table, two hard chairs, no carpet, no curtains, two cups and a plate, a spoon, a knife, a saucepan. Bare. More or less clean. Priest's room.

There was some dope in my pocket and we had a smoke for old time's sake. *Ashes*, Priest always called it. He didn't complain about his physical condition. When he talked it was as if he'd never been away, quietly, smilingly, using unfamiliar biblical words in a chain of reasoning I couldn't quite follow. He was starting a church with some co-religionists. Priest walked with a stick now, slowly, but he was back on course, resuming where he had left off.

The sixties had come and gone, spreading aspects of the Gate ambiance all over town, leaving the Gate itself ... thinner. Everything had changed, little by little, imperceptibly, while my back was turned, while family, work, world events first engaged, then absorbed, then monopolised my attention. I had changed, England had changed, the Gate had changed. Builders were everywhere. The Rio had gone although the building was still there. The Fiesta had become the Safari Tent, losing its sound system and fine jazz collection in the process as Clem and Larry went their ways. Then the whole block vanished, the street part of St Stephen's Gardens and the corresponding block of Westbourne Park Road, Fiesta and 281, 150 run-down Victorian houses replaced by something like an unsuccessful entry to a design competition for the new Soviet ministry of statistics ('*Nyet*! Too many windows.').

One by one, then in droves, the surviving houses were refurbished by the council, trusts, associations and individuals with money or credit. Antique shops started to appear. It was becoming difficult to rent a room or apartment. New shops appeared, selling trinkets and souvenirs to the tourists who crammed the market on summer weekends. A lot of people had moved to council blocks outside the Gate or on its fringes. The night life was different, quieter. The new generation of children born here to Caribbean parents didn't function in quite the same way. The education system was performing the remarkable feat of serving them by and large even worse than their white contemporaries. They were sensitive about the way a country which had beckoned their parents with siren gestures was now making them feel unwelcome. The elegant political elision of the end of empire, Harold Macmillan on a wing and a prayer in his conjurer's silk hat and white gloves, was long gone; the empire was gone, the markets were going, unwelcome edges of reality were intruding on the hangover. The Mangrove wasn't like the Fiesta. In shrinking down to All Saints Road the Grove aspect of the Gate had become distilled, embittered, more like a ghetto. Somehow it acquired the confrontational title of Front Line, along with other streets all over the country, as if a race war were being waged.

I saw Priest casually once or twice, each of us dropping polite open invitations, old friends now but busy with our own affairs. We didn't hang out in the same places any more, perhaps simply didn't hang out any more but either did things or lay low. The after-effects of his illness stayed with him, tiredness, some of his lightness gone; sometimes he would use a stick or crutches to walk, sometimes he managed without. Slowly at first, the 1970s accelerated smoothly by. At some point Priest went to hospital again for a hip-joint replacement, but maintained a low public profile. I like to think he spent much time at his church or chapel caressing alone or with co-religionists that special Rasta perspective on the infinite, the impenetrable tissue of rustic and royal, ghetto and Old Testament, crass and divine. Every now and then some old-time friend would say they had seen him in the

Mangrove but I never went there myself. I heard the housing trust had moved him to an apartment in All Saints Road.

The problem with someone else's story is that one doesn't know it. For facts one has frozen moments of raw data but at random, not regular, intervals in time. The analogy is that of drawing a smooth curve to link the points on a graph, some of which are far apart and faintly marked. What if something happened, say, in this space here, something important which would change the whole pattern? And there is the problem of chronology: what if this comes here and this comes here? Different pattern. Different story. I do not intend to spoil this one, not Priest's story but my story about Priest, with redundant research. Would it help to discover his maternal grandmother's name or solemnly record that he ate the same things for breakfast as other children? Priest was a migrant and his solitude, his scattered migrant's background, its mystery, count for more in this story than the details fading away behind them.

Perhaps this is the moment to come clean and spell out in short words that it is the storyteller's angle that makes the story. From the overflowing trash-heap of a life he takes convenient debris and with petty manipulations assembles in collage a representation which some may fleetingly recognise. We are not talking large holograms here. Recognition comes most easily to some feature or event underlined or exaggerated through its isolation in print. The resulting caricature can hardly be said to justify the great intrusion involved. Nevertheless people tolerate storytelling because they too are unsure what misery and serenity, horrors and glories lie hidden in the wide silences of the long years.

It is well that these spaces exist because without them our wish for justice, our hope that things are really better than they appear (or our fear that they may be worse) would have nowhere to go. So that even during the last five years, when Priest resumed public life and was talked about often, it was possible to imagine him at least sometimes comfortable, warm, tranquil, his belly full, his brain cosy and playful with the best sensemilla, contemplating the mysteries with demure satisfaction or quietly imparting deadpan, left-handed wisdom to respectful youths. For myself, I am obliged to wish these things into existence because I have no direct evidence for them. On the contrary, when Priest reappeared in high profile on the streets of the Gate he seemed to be mentally and physically ill and sinking into an advanced state of self-neglect.

Even by the quite early 1980s one had become used to the increased numbers of derelicts around the Gate, panhandling outside the tube stations, cocooned in the mumbling privacy of their filth-encrusted warm patch under the motorway where it crosses Ladbroke Grove or loosing tinny cracked jungle yells of privatised destitution: *Vote Conservative! Vodkalageargh! Parkinson!* from the darkness of Portobello Green. One day in 1984 or 1985, waiting in traffic somewhere in the Gate, I noticed that one of these unkempt figures, standing on a nearby corner, was black and looked like Priest. The traffic moved before I could get a closer look but within days or weeks I passed the same figure again, then again, each time fleetingly, each time running late and unable to stop.

Then in spring or early summer of 1985, shopping in the Beller with my ten-year-old daughter, I ran into the figure on the corner of Lancaster Road, stopped and addressed him by name. Although he did not use mine he said he remembered me and asked if I was still living in the same place. We talked for five minutes. It was a stiff conversation, constrained on my side by shock at Priest's close-up appearance. He had grown a beard and his hair was much longer than I remembered it. Both were grey and uncombed. His clothes were dirty and torn. There was an insolence or arrogance in his gaze, new, different. Nevertheless he spoke as always with quiet courtesy. To relieve my distress I asked if he needed a little money. He said I could give him some if I liked and accepted a fiver with dignity, without thanks, conscious that he was doing me a favour.

We said goodbye and went off looking for yams or some such, I thinking about Priest: wow, shit, how did he get like that? My daughter Natalie had grown very quiet and I became aware that she was tugging my hand and whispering urgently: 'Daddy! Daddy!' Her face was a picture of horrified amazement. 'Who on earth was that?' 'That's Priest. I used to know him quite well. He's a religious man, a good man, he used to be really nice. He was very ill a few years ago and I suppose he still is. Poor old thing.' 'But he looked so ... so ...' 'I know, I know. But he's probably all right really.' Who was I kidding? 'He's a Rastafarian. D'you know what that is?' And I tried to explain. At home my wife said: 'Who did you meet in Portobello Road? Natalie looked as if she'd seen a ghost.' I told her about Priest but she didn't remember meeting him. 'Is he that mad old man who swears and spits at passers-by in the market?' she asked. Natalie nodded vigorously in assent but I laughed. 'Good God no, Priest would never do anything like that. The nicest of men, tolerant, modest, used to respect. You must be thinking of someone else. He did look awful though.'

Next time I saw Ezzreco I told him about meeting Priest and how rough Priest was looking. He asked me to describe the meeting exactly and I did so.

'You're lucky man,' Ezzreco told me. 'Most people he meets these days he gives a mouthful. He abuses everybody.' 'I'm honoured, then. I always liked Priest. There's something special about him even now. I think he'd forgotten my name.' 'You're not kidding,' Ezzreco said. 'Honoured is the word. He's insulted a lot of people. Sometimes he picks on young English girls. A lot of people start keeping out of his way.'

Later that summer in the run-up to carnival I went to see Larry Forde in the house his costume band was using as a factory that year. Walking down the east side of All Saints Road from the railway end I became aware of a commotion across the street. 'Yer RARSE-claat!' boomed a loud disembodied voice. A white couple who looked like tourists were hurrying away from Priest, who was pivoting about with an arm raised, index finger pointing an arc across the landscape. 'BLOOD-claat!' roared the voice. 'BUMBO-claat!' It didn't sound like Priest at all and I didn't stop to chat. Nearly twenty-five years earlier, not even four hundred yards away, walking late at night down Westbourne Park Road with Beckett and me, he once happily pronounced on the subject of swearing. 'There is no bad word,' he murmured, smiling. 'Because the word is God as the Bible says.'

That hostile undirected roar went with the new feeling in All Saints Road. The pavement in the middle of the block was crowded with watchful youths who approached all passers-by. 'No thanks.' 'What you doing here then?' 'Come to see somebody.' It was like downtown Lagos only not so polite. Larry's door was manned by an unsmiling seven-foot geezer. Two uniformed policemen stood watching in the shop doorway opposite. 'They've got a watching brief,' Larry said. 'Just keeping an eye. They don't interfere with anything. There's a modus vivendi.' 'Some of those boys down there, bit dodgy are they?' 'I shouldn't wonder, friend,' Larry said. 'There was a tourist girl the other day, showed some money while she was buying some weed, they followed her round the corner and took it and beat her up.' 'I just saw Priest terrorising some tourists. I suppose it's better to be yelled at than robbed and beaten up.' 'Humph,' Larry said, his mouth full of pins. 'He's always doing it. He doesn't hurt anyone though.'

It was as if Priest was voicing the formless anger inside those surly front-line adolescents, mingling with stunted ambition, that ill-omened name and the half-witted insolence of TV-trained youth to create a confused and slippery climate of no-go, of confrontation, of you-got-your-story-and-we-got-ours, leading to routine riots and regular harassment of café owners and others who could not avoid being compromised. It was as if Priest's gaze, not really at anything, not downcast or upward but directed past everything, with that small gleam of ... arrogance, mirrored the look of those policemen who would surely not maintain a watching brief for ever. Whatever was the matter with Priest, whether his illness had damaged his brain or his suffering and solitude his mind, or whether – why on earth not? – he was at last expressing all the rage and aggression he had contained with such elegance for most of his life, his furious yells, his random choice of victims, meant something. If only that his rare and modest wisdom had turned bitter. That he had decided people didn't benefit from quiet persuasion and needed to be pulled up short before it was too late. That the Old Testament themes of warning and punishment had at last taken root in his gentle and questing soul.

What it meant to the old-timers I knew, people like me who had known Priest for many years, was that his illness had taken a new and worrying turn, his mind was going, he needed care whose form and scale were beyond us. From passing cars and the tops of buses, in shops, walking down the street, we observed him standing like a ragged piece of street furniture on some chosen corner where he might spend several hours at a time and perhaps come back several days running before moving on. His slightly fidgety stillness, his eyes with their orange whites gazing insolently past everything, carried a tense threat of noisy eruption. I thought at first that his legs had recovered as everything else was collapsing, but they were not better. I saw him twice leaning on crutches. When young he was reputed a good dancer in the hip idiom of small neat movements, controlled but relaxed. Now his gait was sometimes a parody of dancing, a stiff-legged toppling strut with comically unpredictable changes of direction. He would break into this crazed walk without warning after standing in the same spot for hours. The Gate is busy at weekends and thousands of strangers saw his upraised arm and tried to dodge the line of fire of his Jewish prophet's forefinger.

Uselessly, to remind ourselves that we cared, we worried about Priest in cold weather and hoped that he was staying indoors, with a heater going, reading the Bible over a small joint with a nice goat stew bubbling on the cooker. Ritually, we greeted his reappearance each spring: while there's life there's hope. But there was a sombre edge to our relief because we did not believe he would recover. We wanted him to live but could not imagine wanting to live as he did.

I suppose I saw Priest a couple of dozen more times and spoke to him three or four times. Once I stopped the car and walked back to talk and find out how he was. Although I understood that he had always been poor and knew how to manage poverty, that what he needed was not money but care, the wimpish compulsion to show goodwill made me ask if a couple of quid would be any use. He did not take offence but again accepted in a graceful offhand way, responding to my charade of kindness and decency with a demonstration of the real thing. Once I pointed him out to Beckett but we were in a hurry and drove on. Once or twice we exchanged flying hellos in the street: Priest. John. What's happening. I'm all right. How are you. Not bad. Gotta move. All right. See you. Until then.

I haven't seen him now for eighteen months, but in the summer of 1987 he took up station for a week or two among the shops I use in Ladbroke Grove and was often to be seen pivoting about at either end of the zebra crossing near them. To my surprise the Indian and Pakistani shopkeepers, who can be quite stern with the English and Irish winos among their clientele, were tolerant of his presence and behaved as if he simply wasn't there. For several days he posed indecisively between the shelves or stood to attention like a sentry among the cardboard cartons at the checkout of the big Pakistani grocer on the corner whose tough Muslim village-boy assistants shift tons of cut-price strong lager a day. The first time I saw him there we spoke briefly. The second time he didn't catch my eye, although I was close to him and he knew I was there, so I said nothing. I was relieved. Talking to Priest had become difficult, not for any special reason.

The next time I entered the shop there was no sign of him. It was the middle of the afternoon. As I peered along the shelves for some product a quiet voice spoke my name in my ear. We conversed for a minute or two as I finished my shopping. Priest was in an alert and practical mood. He said he had been meaning to come to see me and checked that I was still living in the same place. I said he should, that weekends were best, Saturdays, and that he should telephone first if he could. When I left the shop he accompanied me. 'I'm going to come by your house now,' he said. He managed the stairs to my third-floor kitchen, gravely greeted my wife and children, accepted a cup of coffee. He was there for about an hour and spoke with sharp focus, gently, almost as he used to but with that unsmiling gravity, the hard gleam of someone not trying to persuade you but *telling* you, though no more than a gleam in a discourse as impeccably courteous as ever. Before leaving he produced a pound from his pocket and laid it on the table. I had lent it to him some time before, he said, and he was now able to pay it back. 'There's no hurry,' I said. 'I mean I certainly don't need it urgently. I'd forgotten all about it actually.' He didn't reply and the coin stayed on the table until late that night.

I offered to drive him to Westbourne Park where he was going. None of us smells perfect and I am not over-sensitive about such things, but as the car warmed up it became apparent in its small airspace that Priest urgently needed a bath or medical attention or both. There have been times and places in which people went unwashed and routinely stank worse than goats but this is not one of them. Washing facilities abound so that while it is normal to smell, to smell much indicates poor morale and to smell utterly, heart-stoppingly appalling is a sign of disorder. I was saddened but not very surprised by this indication that although important parts of Priest's mind seemed to be working as well as ever, other parts equally important were seized solid.

We spoke for the last time less than a week later. He turned up to see me without warning the following Sunday just as my family's only formal midday meal of the week was coming out of the oven. Priest was never a telephone person. I did not want to ask him in as I knew my daughters would be intrigued but intimidated by his presence at lunch and their mother would certainly regard him as a health hazard. Very apologetically I explained that this wasn't an ideal moment; Priest took it like the lamb he always was. I felt very bad about turning him away and have often thought that I was wrong to do so, ungenerous, rejecting a needy friend to preserve some mimsy petit-bourgeois family equilibrium. Perhaps it hadn't been a rejection exactly, he hadn't really needed anything from me but was just passing. Perhaps no damage had been done, but I felt bad, bad enough to avoid Priest by crossing the road the next time I saw him. And to get the strong impression that he had eyes in the side of his head and had seen me do it.

Later I learned that other people had avoided Priest too, crossed the road, ducked into a pub, fled with a cheery no-nonsense can't-stop-now wave from the risk of loud abuse or the certainty that, even if Priest was quiet and what he said made sense, his close-up presence would face them with the possibility, the chill *prospect*, of a definitive loss of power over the minutiae of daily life. People didn't ostracise him, they worried about him, they remembered what he was really like, they shook their heads over his bad luck, they pointed out that he could still support a conversation, they praised his independence; they were not even sure that he was aware of his misery and hoped that he was not; it was just that they flinched from contact with his disassembled personality, still all there but damaged and strewn around like the contents of a crashed airliner.

The day after getting Ezzreco's incomplete message I found him at home and he confirmed that Priest was dead. He had been found in his apartment a day or two earlier by a housing trust or social worker person. The funeral had been put off and would be on Monday afternoon. There would be a good turnout, Ezzreco said. We bowed ritually in Priest's direction. It isn't that one wants people dead, it's just intolerable to behold their suffering. One projects one's own relief onto the deceased, one asserts on the basis of flimsy external evidence that death was a release. One tells oneself that one would rather be dead than arouse in other people the feelings that Priest aroused in his last five years of life. It is easy to be glib about such things. The reality, the 'truth' in Priest's case, which we shall never know, might have been different. Perhaps he felt good, perhaps his self-neglect was just an extension of his asceticism, the next stage beyond bare rooms and no crockery. Perhaps he was laughing warmly, indulgently up his sleeve at our repressed embarrassment, the panicky clucking of a flock of shocked nannies. He didn't mind using himself as an object lesson. Within the last year, Ezzreco told me, he had staggered to his feet in the Mangrove and announced: 'Gentlemen: you can't look at me and believe it's safe to take just any drugs, any way, any time.' Or words to that effect. He would have pronounced it *Genklemen*.

My suit had moth-holes in it but I made do with shirt, shoes, socks and tie in the correct colours. Jamaicans don't fuss unduly about such things although their dress sense is strong. They were chatting on the pavement outside the church on the corner of Talbot Road, mostly old-timers of whom I only knew one or two, long-time friends, people who knew what Priest was really like. A scattering of young Rastas, no dreadlocks or hardly any, cool severe-looking young guys in robes or plain anorak-and-trainers mufti, tidy, shaved, clean, the way Priest would dress if he was thirty again. A little stern, a little political and disapproving in Rasta mode adapted to 1980s pessimism: it may not be a battlefield but it's certainly a minefield: watch out. Fifty or sixty people, a dozen cars at the cemetery.

The coffin arrived, the undertaker's crew with their shifty secret-police air. The church ceremony was brief, pared-down, high-church Anglican conducted by a young English vicar. The vicar spoke; a tall schoolmasterly greybeard who had been at school with Priest spoke very briefly, saying Priest had kept up his work for youth to the end. For family there was his god-daughter, child of a fellow old-time Rasta, a plump young woman whom I had last noticed as one of several children. She said the last time she saw Priest, months ago, she met him in the street and told him about some problems she was having. Despite his condition he had been supportive, reassured her, cheered her up. She had kissed him and said: 'Goddie, I love you.' I thought of his modest kindness, the way he never put himself first. To my surprise I knew the tunes of the Anglican hymns and sang them straight, leaning against the crazed descant sounds coming from three old-timers in the bench behind me. 'I never hear you sing so well,' Ezzreco murmured in my ear. I was surprised too. 'Out of respect,' I whispered back. 'Priest was a religious man. I'm not. I'm doing it out of respect.'

Next to a dumper near the entrance to Kensal Green, the raw pile of clay, the graveyard clay that sticks to your shoes in big slippery lumps. We milled about while the vicar and the undertaker's men made ready. Bottles of vodka and half-bottles of brandy appeared; cannabis smoke drifted blue in the sunshine. *Ashes*. The young Rastas were standing still, solemn, to attention, but the old-timers, like naughty children, were shovelling fuel into the uninhibited, defiant, funeral frame of mind of the African diaspora: It's come to him. It comes to us all in the end. But not yet! He's dead! Fuck it! He was one of us. Have a drink. Parachute was there, grey-bearded, unrecognisable in a leopard-skin hat. On the side of the angels now the old times are gone. I was too shy to talk to him. People reassured one another that they had not denied Priest. He had needed care but had been flintily independent. He had been crazy but still made sense. We miss him but not his condition. May his soul rest in peace.

Ashes to ashes. A voice shouted 'Balderdash!' and a hand shot skyward from the congregation rapidly clicking the action of a toy revolver. The vicar's eyes flickered but he carried on reading. The coffin went down the hole. Presently the vicar left. Some people threw symbolic handfuls of mud but Ezzreco grappled left-handed with a shovel. A very drunk light-skinned old-timer in a cloth cap teetered on the edge of the grave shaking an admonitory forefinger down at the coffin. 'Didn't I told you so?' he shouted indignantly to Priest.

'If Chingu *not* drunk,' Ezzreco murmured in my ear, 'then you know something wrong.' Two English gravediggers took over and filled the hole. The pile of raw clay was deemed distasteful and they went off with the dumper to get some proper earth from the other end of the cemetery. Priest's god-daughter, her mother and some other Rasta ladies took the flowers from their wrappings and tenderly planted them one by one in the earth. Splashes of brandy, pinches of cannabis-containing pocket dust, were dropped for Priest. More bottles appeared; people cried and laughed; twenty-four choruses of 'The Red Flag' were sung, very blue, near enough out of tune in fact, by three big women whose gold-splashed smiles spoke of broad experience.

The young Rastas stayed at attention. Half the mourners were holding a meeting off to the side but others were prolonging their goodbyes. '*Before we go to Paradise ...*' Chesterton's doggerel twittered annoyingly in my brain. I looked into the brilliant sky where three birds whirled. One magpie for sorrow, two for joy, wheeled and headed for the other end of the cemetery, the overgrown bushes, the generals and Victorian Catholic grandees. Another bird, a pigeon, not a London sky-rat but a large wood pigeon, a wild dove, pivoted alone where the magpies had been. There was something lame about its flight, as if its wings were entangled. It spiralled fluttering for a moment and then instantly, without a pause for recovery or any kind of glide, it was flying very fast, arrow-straight, to the north-west, aiming to shave past the North Pole on the shortest route back to the warm and welcoming Caribbean.

His first name was Leopold. He was fifty-nine. See you man. Rastafari!

Leopold Roy Prince, *c.* 1930, Kingston, Jamaica – February 1989, London, England: rest in peace man.

February 1989 (not written for publication)

EVENINGS WITH OUR GIRL RENE

Of the women I have met who earned cash by hiring their bodies to fleeting strangers, Rene was the one who most resembled a stereotyped Edwardian tart. I believe she was second generation, following so to speak in her mother's footsteps.

Perhaps I am romanticising both the profession and the era when I say that no insult is intended, quite the reverse indeed. Irene was not just beautiful and spectacularly turned out but good-natured, generous and honest. Of the stereotype's more negative features — treachery, greed, sexual frigidity, coldness of heart — she showed no visible sign. For those honoured with her friendship, evenings and afternoons in flats, restaurants and nightclubs were made more luminous and enjoyable by her physical magnificence and her generosity with money, whisky and marijuana.

Rene was creamily statuesque, blue-eyed, baby-faced, generous in all important features. Being tall she did not always wear high heels. When she did, with full war-paint, false eyelashes, ash-blonde beehive and all the trimmings, the lacquered vision measured a little over six feet, but it was not seen every day. In the early 1960s — the real 1960s to old-time Gate-dwellers — people tried to dress comfortably if they could afford it, although it was difficult on formal occasions. Usually Rene wore a sort of battledress, with makeup but without heels, some sort of frilly blouse or fluffy sweater and tight black trousers. She was efficient and fast at repairing her face, having quick baths and changing her clothes. It was unusual to see her without makeup and hairdo (or at least curlers); it made her look slightly smaller.

One thing sure was that being with Rene got you noticed. When you were let into her flat just off Talbot Road by the very traditional nicotine-stained, trap-jawed, apron-and-slippers-wearing maid-of-all-work, other people were often already present. In the streets nearby, and in and around the Fiesta a couple of blocks away, people would wave and shout to her, or come up and engage you in conversation. If you went anywhere else with her — she always travelled by taxi — everyone would look first at her and then, appraisingly, at you. It was extremely unnerving, but worth it.

From where I stood, it looked as if men in Irene's life were filed in four categories: wages, friends, lovers and associates. The first category must have outnumbered the others but was seldom evident to members, like me, of the second category. This was not because she felt ashamed of her profession or made any attempt to hide it. She was no hypocrite, although really very ladylike in a fun-loving way. But on visiting her sometimes one might be asked to wait in the lacy suburban-looking sitting room, seldom for more than twenty minutes or so. The maid would be a bit disapproving because one was in the wrong category for the time of day and she could tell at a glance that one did not represent business. She was not openly rude, however. Rene ran a tight ship.

Her own appearance on these occasions would sometimes be preceded by the passage through the hall of some unglamorous character whose palpable wish for invisibility made one look politely away. A minute or two later a rosily bashful Rene would come in, hair brushed and smelling lightly of soap. 'Sorry, darlin, wages,' she would say with a very slightly self-deprecating giggle. A moment later the maid would be making tea and Rene would haul whisky and marijuana from a shiny black handbag chosen to match her own imposing physical scale. With these being consumed, plans would be made for the evening. Wages as such, when I knew Rene, were mainly a daytime phenomenon.

Apart from the maid – I've often wondered if she was Rene's mother or aunt – Rene's women friends, less numerous than her male friends, were I suppose colleagues on the same level as herself, similarly lacquered and formidable: somewhat above the level of streetwalker and below that of Knightsbridge or Mayfair courtesan, relying heavily on the telephone for appointments but not really 'call girls' because operating at home. Not one of these women had Rene's innocent charm or insouciant physical lavishness: they would be too angular or too muscular, or have close-set eyes or a cruel turn of mouth. Most were a year or two older than her – she was hardly older than me, perhaps not even my age, although she seemed to me like an older sister. And these women did not much like Rene's unkempt, pot-smoking, posh-talking but penniless social companions. It seemed weird to them. I mean proper gents, wife doesn't understand me, you look an understandin filly, ere's a gold watch, let me put it on for yer: OK, Jag, nightclub, I mean no harm, good time had by all. But what were these geezers *on* about half the time, drinkin Irene's whisky and smokin er *tea*, not even tryin to get a free one, what did she *see* in them? Bunch of ponces if you ask me, well not *ponces* exactly, never bring er any punters, no use if there's any *trouble*, no, not poofs either even if they do *talk* like bleedin poofs, but poncin off er all the same, get my drift?

We didn't know either, not really, why Rene chose to associate with us during her recreation time. She didn't read or talk politics or go to difficult movies or the theatre. She didn't even much like Ornette Coleman or Roland Kirk, although she did like music and listened happily to the Rollins and early John Coltrane who were our endless mainstays at 105 Westbourne Terrace. Good sounds pumped through decent speakers were part of the Gate decor, but what she liked best was live R&B. I think of her shining in the gloom in the rows of seats on the right-hand side of the Flamingo down at the bottom end of Wardour Street south of Shaftesbury Avenue, the ones at right angles to the stage where Georgie Fame and the Blue Flames blatted out their fluid ultra-danceable sound, topping your Coca-Cola up with whisky from her bottle and passing over her attaché-case-sized handbag with the loudly whispered instruction: '*Roll* me a smoke, darlin.' She didn't dance a lot, being lazy, but sat there in the hot darkness with friends and acquaintances all around her, innocently happy.

When it was time to take a cab back to the Gate at the end of one of these evenings, Rene would often give lifts to people from some other circle she frequented, recruiting groups of courteous giants in expensive clothing, chunks of gold gleaming among the fingers and eye teeth, conversing in rumbled Jamaican and American monosyllables. Boxers? Hoods? Innocent grunts and toilers in Saturday night garb? Nobody ever said, but coming back from the Flamingo with Rene could be like sharing a taxi with a herd of prizewinning buffaloes wearing aftershave.

Before these scenes became familiar, before she adopted, for a time, the habit of turning up at Westbourne Terrace in the early evening looking for a companion to escort her to Wardour Street or thereabouts for entertainment, Irene had exercised her prerogative as a leading face, a Gate aristocrat, by taking us up socially. She did this in an endearingly formal, official manner which secured our instant loyalty. The Fiesta One restaurant, on the corner of Ledbury Road and Westbourne Park Road, was responsible for this as for so many other fruitful meetings. Having the best food, the best music and the most intelligent, laid-back management in the entire zone, the Fiesta naturally concentrated on its somewhat limited seating all the most discerning locals (or those who could afford its prices which, although modest for what they bought, were high for the area). Being rich and possessing the healthy appetite needed to sustain her lavish frame, Rene went there often as she worked, and at first lived, only two minutes away.

Being also — as I hope I have made clear — a naturally good and decent person with clear-eyed although far from intellectual feminine discernment, Rene learned immediately to respect, and indeed fell (in her fashion) in love with one of, the Fiesta's owners. During this process, being also friendly and good-natured, she acquired a nodding acquaintance with those of us from Westbourne Terrace who also went to the Fiesta a lot — in our case as much for the music and the conversation, the friendship, of the owners, as for the food which in truth we could not always afford. These most probably were myself and Alan Beckett, although everyone at the flat, and indeed many of our friends from the Gate and other parts of London, knew and liked the place.

Doubtless Clem or Larry had told her that we smoked exotic herbs and seemed all right; or perhaps she had noticed that we sometimes stayed in the Fiesta after it closed, arguing loudly with the staff and roaring with laughter. Anyway she one day asked where we lived and announced that she would come to visit us, setting a date and time.

It was a late afternoon on a weekday, probably an encroachment on Rene's working hours. Four or five of us were there, all men, no girls; Hoppy, who had signed the lease of the flat and worked with manic energy as a photographer, was there, unusually for that time of day. Rene arrived on the dot, so magnificently turned out that our cavernous hallway, which we used as a communal living area, fell unusually silent for an unusually long time. She was wearing some kind of fussy suit trimmed with bits of gilded braid, a frilly chiffon blouse, earrings, bracelets and so on, very high heels and some kind of ornate black stockings, hairdo, astonishing, doll-like false eyelashes, a careful but not quite discreet makeup job, and — the final touch that really made our jaws drop — two white miniature poodles on leads. We had never seen these dogs before and never saw them again, so they were probably borrowed. They were very well behaved.

We greeted her in the polite constrained manner, already inflected with the casual no-shit American-prole overfamiliarity that later became the norm for the whole of British society, then usual for educated young men; with the exception of Hoppy who, very advanced in certain ways, gave her a brief welcoming stare and yelled 'WOW!' at the top of his voice. We gave her the best chair and she sat in it with knees together and the poodles at her feet, blushing prettily. She was a bit shy and the first few minutes were awkward, we intimidated by her war-paint and she flabbergasted by our flat, the like of which she had never seen before.

This was the thing about the sixties, where we were anyway, right at the beginning, before the mass-market hippy thing, the Wilson-era Mersey beat, Carnaby Street, Vietnam and the sexual revolution, the explosion of gonorrhea and manic politics out of the 1968 Sorbonne, all that shit. This was before all that, in a way its precursor, a sketch of something vastly preferable, soon afterwards overtaken by events. There was this openness: not the perverse, obligatory, side-taking, paranoid new respectability, the first of many, that a few years later had certain silly flower children — a term that still raises the gorge of discerning persons — claiming that Charles Manson had been victimised; and a few years after that dissolved into a sort of generalised far-left morality which in extreme cases made perfectly harmless middle-class intellectuals see themselves as enemies of the State on the run from the security forces.

There was absolutely no social pressure on us to be more than civil to Rene — we did not get on especially well with her colleagues — and there was none on her to associate with us. Indeed such pressure as there was — admittedly not much in the Gate of those days, but the rest of London and the family-containing provinces were still there — tended in the other direction. She chose us, we chose her, nothing much in common but we liked each other's mugs, fraternally, no pressure of sex or money, no need to prove anything. I believe Rene was pleased and flattered that we liked her without chasing her tail; just as we were pleased and flattered that she should sometimes choose to relax socially with us.

Nothing much in common but our ages — we were all children in our early twenties — and of course cannabis, the great leveller, which calmed us down on the occasion of Irene's first visit to Westbourne Terrace as it did everywhere else and on all occasions. By inducing a pleasant relaxation, it made people back off the unconscious group project of 'making conversation with Rene' and revert to normal behaviour: sporadic general and individual conversation interspersed with arguments about what music to have next, followed by ferocious, baroque jeering when a choice was actually made. It made Rene relax too. She wasn't a very demanding person and was perfectly happy to sit getting stoned and listening most of the time. Her conversation was mostly small talk and gossip, and she loved jokes. 'What did one coffin say to the other coffin?' she asked us. Well, what? 'Is that you coffin'?' She never raised her voice or sounded shrill or strident.[18] Her manner was one of gentle, rosy, ladylike merriment. Being a teahead she understood irony, but she was a stranger to bitterness and her malice was of the most benevolent sort.

---

18 She did once actually. Before I realised I had no musical talent apart from being able to sing in tune, I tried to learn to play tenor saxophone, then my favourite instrument. Rene one night dropped my sax on her toe, making a small dent in its bottom curve. It must have hurt a lot. As I peered closely and worriedly at the dent, Rene exclaimed indignantly: 'What about my toe?'

She stayed an hour or two, until after dark, and by the time she left, most probably in a cab, we all nursed tender, platonic feelings of friendship for her. I do not remember ever seeing her so dressed up again. When going out she would of course wear something eye-catching and make her hair gleam, but she dressed for comfort in the early-sixties manner, flat heels and slacks (sometimes with stirrups under the instep, a feature which for some reason I have always disliked), the doll's eyelashes only when she could be bothered.

After that, for a year or two, Rene became a pal. She could be a useful person to go and see when cannabis was in short supply. ''Ere, nip out and get me alf a tea, darlin,' she would say to her long-suffering maid. 'Anyone else want alf a tea? Get some for im as well. Better get me two.' Sighing good-humouredly, the maid would collect the ten-shilling notes and shuffle off to change into her outdoor shoes. My memory is that she was seldom absent for more than five minutes, but perhaps I am idealising the past, gilding the era in retrospect as old buffers do.

Alf a tea — half a sheet's worth of marijuana — was the standard Gate street deal at that time (although in Cable Street, in Whitechapel, slightly smaller deals cost five bob). It came rough — flowers, buds, seeds and stalks — in a rectangular newspaper packet an inch or two long, and was often of good quality. The same amount of grass today, for those whose prejudices make them insist on it despite the greater availability of hashish, comes in a plastic bag, will usually be broken up fine to dissimulate a lamentable paucity of mind-bending resin, and costs ten or twenty pounds in the street.

Then as now, 'deals' whose weight was not a declared quantity were of variable size (so, of course, were ounces and even pounds, but that was a different matter). If the dealer was in a good mood, or liked the customer, fat deals of good sticky issue might be forthcoming; but in a difficult week, at the end of the dealer's supply, or in the event of mutual dislike, things could go the other way. Rene for one reason or another was on the most favoured list of whoever it was the maid used to nip out and see, and the result was that she often got good deals. She and her friends were seldom palmed off with thin packages of dust, seeds and stalks, or the appalling substitutes that some dishonest operators kept handy for one-off transactions with innocent passers-by.

There were a lot of innocent passers-by in the early sixties. Data on long-neglected forms of intoxication were fluttering down like tickertape through the awareness of a reading population avid to escape the musty pre-war vision still unconvincingly projected by politicians, media and the commoner sort of artist. These images came from the Americas in the form of precepts and recommendations from a new wave of poets and writers who had discovered the secrets of the trance states used for refuge and enlightenment by the downtrodden indigenous populations and non-white urban and rural communities of those two continents: not just moonshine but *gauge*, not just cane spirit but coca, mescalin, ayahuasca, yage. Visions! Another way of seeing!

Of course sailors and musicians, the kind of people who worked alongside blacks, had been happily smoking, sniffing and swallowing their workmates' largesse all along, part of the lurid blur of shore-leave or the punishing grind of nightly performance, without realising that they were having visions and seeing things in a new way. Artists had been doing it too, Frenchmen, Indians, Arabs. And of course all along smart, fast, well-travelled people had given the local drugs a try out of curiosity. For a while the more respectable British critics jeered brutally, and with relentless stupidity, at the effusions of Kerouac, Ginsberg, Corso, even Burroughs, which they purported to find undisciplined, sentimental and *faux naifs*. But they could hardly do the same to Aldous Huxley, I mean he was one of the *Huxleys* for God's sake, Nancy Cunard or someone had been nasty about him, clever chap too if a bit strange. Surely Evelyn Waugh had … de Quincey of course … and didn't Baudelaire …

Suddenly the neglected descriptions of visual, aural and emotional splendour, of oblique and magical forms of insight, started to boil through the crust of ideological prohibition, composed of two-dimensional images of drug-induced slavery, misery, poverty, cruelty, perversion and general foreign *slackness*, with which we had all been raised from the cradle. People began approaching their racier friends to see if some of this famous marijuana might not be available. It was a way of dipping a toe into the murky but strangely inviting waters of alternative consciousness.

My impression, for what it is worth, is that even with her lovers Rene was not much given to transports of passion; that she was essentially maternal and tolerant in her attitude to men, built psychically — and physically for that matter — for comfort rather than speed. Bit knackered are we? Pissed off? There there darlin. Let's ave a smoke and some whisky. Something along those lines. Her lovers, inevitably fairly numerous over time but honourably dealt with in series rather than simultaneously, overlapped I suppose another shadowy category, that of Rene's associates. For one has to remember that she had her main existence, her roots, in what the French call the *milieu*. She was a bit like Garance in *Les Enfants du paradis*, but without the subterranean heat: she socialised with bohemians, sold her favours to cash customers, had lovers some (but not all) of whom were totally uncriminal individuals. Whether there was a Lacenaire in her movie or not, she seemed very much at home with boxers and hoods, in whose company she was often to be seen.

As Rene was palpably a free agent, able to dispose of her time and come and go as she wished, what might be called the corporate level of her professional life was never apparent to me. Perhaps there wasn't one, although common sense suggests that people in vulnerable quasi-legal work situations tend to acquire, even when strictly speaking they do not need it, some form of paid protection. The forms this protection takes and the nature and level of payment are obviously variable, open to negotiation. More than once I visited Rene in an ornately appointed, thickly carpeted apartment in genteel white-stucco Gloucester Terrace, a block away from Westbourne Terrace in an area that would call itself Bayswater were it not for the proximity of Paddington Station. It wasn't her flat but she was often there. The place was kept spotless apart from a litter of quality gauge on the Axminster in front of the garish sub-G-Plan bar in the corner of the sitting room, dropped by drunk, careless or over-excited individuals rolling joints.

There was something a little frightening about this flat, some vibe that passed unidentified if not entirely unnoticed in the welter of youthful experience, but that I now realise tweaked at my much-ignored bourgeois early warning system. It might have been the cleanliness and tidiness, the hotel-like absence of personal objects and domestic litter, or the combination of expensive fittings and bad B-movie taste, or the fact that there was no owner, no host. Or it might have been Rene's giggling account of sitting demurely on a chair to the underside of which a Luger pistol had been hastily taped – if not at the Gloucester Terrace flat, then certainly somewhere exactly similar – throughout a lengthy visit by the CID.

I don't have a clear impression of what it is like to be a prostitute, or any woman for that matter, but I believe it is safe to assume that with time work became more of a burden to Rene as it does to most people sooner or later. It is often said, too, that the profession she followed makes women age rapidly, and I have no reason to doubt it. After a while Rene stopped coming to see us, not suddenly but gradually; she moved to some inconvenient place and was seen less often in the Gate. Suddenly we realised that nobody had seen her for a year or more, although she was still around and one could get news of her. Her life had changed in some way: she was working harder, or finding work harder to get, or saving money, or supporting someone. Either she had grown up or the world had got her in a stranglehold, it wasn't clear which. Later I heard she had retired and was living in Dollis Hill. Later still, some ten years ago, I was told she had died of some rapid cancer. She can't have been fifty years old.

Much as I liked Rene I can't pretend to be sorry that I didn't get in touch again. To see her changed, ill, shrunken, snappish, would have been unbearable without some secure access to the person within, some history of intimacy. For without that history people are quite likely to grow apart with the passage of time. Poor Irene would have felt defenceless without her physical splendour, the beauty that seemed to brighten her surroundings, that was her livelihood, that she never mentioned, that filled her with quiet, inoffensive satisfaction and underpinned her sweetness of character. She wouldn't have wanted to be seen looking like the dog's dinner we must all become in the end.

c. 2011 (not written for publication)

② CARS

FIRST WHEELS

The first car I owned was a black pillarless four-door six-cylinder 1,500 cc Fiat saloon, of late thirties vintage. It belonged to an architect, Mike, who drove it as he drove everything, with great élan (for sheer terror a trip in his Bond Minicar, mechanically a dodgem with a lawn-mower engine that would not now be allowed to be sold, took some beating). Mussolini's secret police would have felt at home in the Fiat, sinister and beetle-like in appearance with headlights hidden behind the grille (like a Healey Silverstone), spare wheel on the boot lid and very narrow rear track. With totally bald rear tyres its handling in the rain was entertaining to say the least. I recall a trip down the crowded Fulham Road, then a patchwork of cobbles and tarmac with lengths of exposed tramline, in which every lane change involved not one but two full-blooded tail-out opposite lock slides, all at safe speeds. Eventually the front shackle of the offside rear leaf spring, weakened by rust, tore free from the monocoque and came up through the rear seat, fortunately unoccupied at the time. Mike parked it outside the Architectural Association in Bedford Square, where he was a student, and a few weeks later gave it to me in a pub. Having no driving licence I felt it would be more discreet to collect it in the middle of the night. While I was searching vainly for the starter a policeman came up and asked what I was doing. When I told him, more or less, he helped, and eventually we managed to push-start the device whose battery had seen better days. Things have changed a lot since 1959.

I drove it to Chiswick where I then lived. Mike had warned me that apart from the lopsided stance and gait caused by the semi-detached rear axle, the worn and very peculiar independent front suspension sometimes caused a violent resonant oscillation of the front wheels, the cure for which was to go faster until it stopped. The oscillation was far more violent than I expected and I lacked the courage for the recommended solution, being a very inexperienced driver, so I slowed to a crawl instead and then cautiously got back up to speed. It occurred three times on the way to Chiswick. Having no money and no licence I gave (he says I took 25 quid off him for it, but I don't remember doing so) the car immediately to my landlady's brother who had cast covetous glances at it. Nick was an enthusiast who did a bit of club racing (one of his friends was the Bugattist Richard ****, another called Angus had an early competition-tuned TVR). He had a bit more money than me and welding connections. Repaired, the Fiat became his transport, I suppose only for a few months (time passes so slowly when one is young). He liked it a lot and once drove me from Oxford to Henley and back very briskly indeed, the seat right back to facilitate the then-fashionable straight-armed driving position. I don't know what happened to the Fiat but Nick was later an executive of Ford Europe, and also worked for Unipower which made a small number of mid-engined Mini Cooper-powered road bullets.

Real first car (in 1962 or so) was a left-hand-drive 1948 Citroën Light Fifteen, a French-built small-boot example with the spare wheel carried on the boot lid under a pressed-steel cover. I bought it for £60 from two Aussie girls in West Kensington. It was a modified example with a big four-spoke steering wheel and two skinny, mushroom-like Solex downdraught carburettors, devoid of air cleaners, perched over the engine. I may be wrong, but I also seem to remember six-volt electrics – certainly the yellow headlights were not up to much. The drive shafts, objects of suspicion in those days, were noisy on full lock but gave no trouble.

Even rusty and clapped out it was a terrific car, terrific-looking too with matte mushroom paintwork – sort of desert camouflage – and very little chrome. The early-post-war trim was extremely austere but the seats and torsion-bar suspension were comfortable. The front tyres, fat Michelin crossplies, squealed a lot around town, but there were no handling vices at the speeds it could manage and the roadholding and braking – the front drums were large and finned – were exemplary.

This was just as well because although the device was insured I had virtually no driving experience, had never taken a driving test and was rushing about as fast as possible on an Irish licence obtained by a friend in Dublin for a quid, backed by a couple of untrue statements and a forgery. I was absolutely terrifying: not only I but all around me were leading (I later realised) charmed lives. I recall a nimbly leaping traffic policeman one wet morning in the middle of Oxford Circus – in those days an acre or two of unmarked cobbles – and a hitch-hiking airman who begged to be let out on a rainy night in the middle of nowhere on the A1 in Yorkshire, as the speedo needle strained for 135 Ks and the draughty cabin filled with oil smoke once again ...

The three-speed gearbox stuck out at the front, under the radiator, and was controlled by two push-pull rods moved, in their turn, by a drooping lever that stuck through a rectangular hole in the dashboard on the right of the wheel. Being a left-hooker my car had this hole in the right place; cars for the British market had a longer lever skewed to the right, an arrangement that worked perfectly well but looked messy. The linkage, like all the Citroën's running gear, was well designed and solid, but the synchromesh had gone and I quickly learned to double-declutch on all gear changes, up as well as down. This, rushing round London, caused the clutch cable to fail at Denham on the way to Oxford one evening. I left the car at a big garage there which said it would replace the cable.

This took more than a week and naturally cost a lot. The garage left oily fingermarks all over the car's beige fabric interior, and although it had been installed after a fashion I had to adjust the new cable before I could drive the car. Two days later the new cable parted in Marylebone Road (scene of so many motoring dramas through the ages), but the car was moving in second gear and I was able to drive straight round the corner and park (yes, children, in the olden days London was like that). Another new cable from a Citroën dealer cost about £6.10s. The sheath was a rugged flexible steel spiral, but the inner cable would only bend in one plane because instead of being woven Bowden cable it was a simple strip of spring steel. A kink surrounding the break in the 'professionally' fitted cable showed what had happened: the 'fitter' had forcibly bent it sideways while trying to thread it through the holes in the left-hand side-member sprouting from the front of the car's epoch-making, if rust-prone, monocoque. This cannot have been all that difficult, as I did it myself in a couple of hours with a couple of spanners under the rather snooty gaze of the Marylebonians. An early lesson in the iniquities of the automotive service industry.

In those days, however, they were as nothing to my own iniquities. Feeling that the Citroën, which never received a tuning check at my hands, needed some sort of routine care, I took it to a small garage (still a service station) near the top of Parkway in Camden Town. The service man, a gloomy but fairly sympathetic Greek, agreed to flush the engine and change the oil, and suggested an underbody oil spray. I had never heard of one of these, but it didn't cost much and sounded a good idea although things were frankly pretty far gone. As an afterthought I asked him to drain the gearbox. When I collected the car he was frowning in a worried sort of way, but didn't say anything. Soon the gearbox began to make random grinding and groaning noises, which became worse when the car was warm. After a couple of days of this I consulted another garage whose proprietor opened the gearbox drain plug. Nothing came out. I stuck my finger inside. It emerged covered with what looked like silver metallic paint. I had asked for the gearbox to be drained but omitted to say anything about refilling it. Refilled with new oil – silver metallic oil before long – the gearbox stopped making noises and seemed unscathed, for the few weeks more that I used the car. But in any case a lot of exhaust seemed to be coming out of the crankcase breather and the tune was getting worse and worse.

I was not capable enough to prolong its useful life, let alone restore it (something that might have been possible, although expensive, with the aid of a really good welder). Writers used to complain in a litany about the allegedly 'agricultural' long-stroke two-litre engine and three-speed gearbox, but most Light Fifteen owners retained a lasting affection for the model which was doggedly faithful, tough, stylish, comfortable, long-legged, safe and (by the standards of the time) fairly economical. But so it goes. You don't know what you've got till it's gone. My late friend, the artist Edward Piper, who loved Citroëns and drove them exceptionally well, at the same time had a much more respectable example, a mid-fifties Big Fifteen, with the limousine-like body of the Big Six (obviously a Light Six would have been the one to go for, but I have never seen one). Like all the late Slough-assembled cars it had a practical but ugly add-on box boot lid which improved the boot but ruined the car's lines. French Citroëns had this boot for the last couple of years before the company broke major new ground once again with the DS.

Eventually, as the winter set in, my own Light Fifteen became impossible to start and the battery expired. It had lasted me four months at the outside. For a while it sat at the other end of my street in South Hampstead, turning away in disgust whenever I slunk past. Later, to my enormous relief, it disappeared from the street, but it will live for as long as I do in a corner of my heart.

c. 2010 (not written for publication)

LEARNING CURVE

Old news from the front line in the struggle
between motorist and industry

I had the good fortune to visit America in 1973 at the tail end of its loose, lavish and graceful technical supremacy, before Japan imposed a more finicky intellectual hegemony on world automotive engineering; before Mickey Mouse pervaded Detroit (although Pintos, Pacers, Chevettes and assorted Japanese garbage were already common and Volkswagens were actually *fashionable*). My nine-year-old Plymouth slant six may not have been an inspiring vehicle, but it was a superlative consumer product.

On the phone Herb Broadway of Broadway Auto Parts in Trenton, New Jersey, had mentioned an Oldsmobile for $85. But the car outside his house was a bland white 1964 six-cylinder Plymouth, the sort of car William Burroughs called a 'faggot Plymouth'. Herb, who bore a passing physical resemblance to Chuck Berry, had been doing some thinking and refused even to let me see the Oldsmobile. 'If I wanted to fuck you, I could,' he said. 'Coulda put real fine sawdust in the motor to hide the knock till you got out on the freeway.' The Plymouth had been his sister's car and was more suitable for my purposes. He wanted $300, which sounded a lot.

I drove it around. It was neither large nor 'compact' but what was then known as 'mid-size': about the same size as a contemporary Rolls Royce but much 'tinnier', without the gravitas, the sheer mass, of an expensive car. It had slippery bench seats, an oval steering wheel and automatic transmission controlled by large, stiff buttons protruding through the dashboard. A lever moving in a vertical slot applied a transmission lock. The paint was bloomed and there were a couple of small rust spots but the body was intact and sound. The tyres were all balding and exhaust leaked into the car. The radio did not work. But new plugs, plug leads and distributor cap confirmed a recent tune and all the main running gear seemed fine. I said I would buy it if Herb would sort out the exhaust and radio.

He fitted an aerial that made the radio work, sort of — it could get country and western music, anyway — but when I went to collect the car the exhaust still needed doing. It was to be a cooperative effort. I had to drive to Midas Muffler and get them to fit a rear box and tailpipe, then bring it back to Herb's junkyard. The flange on the front box had rusted away but the box was otherwise solid. A bit of welding would do the trick.

Midas Muffler tried to force me to buy a complete system like everybody else. A character in a suit came out of the office and did a lot of intimidatory staring and shrugging, but I followed Herb's advice and was granite. Waiting my turn I observed American automotive service technology at its most efficient and consumer capitalism at its most depraved. Electric cutters zapped bolts and clamps into gobs of cooling slag in seconds, system out; air spanners whooped briefly, system in, lift down, $78.50, have a nice day.

A lot of the systems being thrown away had brand new sections in them, boxes and bits of pipe recently installed by old-style, caring auto mechanics. All usable boxes were reduced to scrap on the spot by having large holes cut out of them. When the Plymouth's turn came the staff went into a huddle, giving me funny looks, and the foreman came over and had another try: gonna leak, it's dangerous, we can't guarantee ... OK, your problem. Zap, whoop, lift down, $27.35, drop dead asshole. 'Ain't nothing made by the Man that can't go wrong,' Herb said as his man did the welding, 'but you look after this car, it's gonna look after you.' I wasn't going to be Neal Cassady or Steve McQueen, but the wheels should be good for California and back.

I was about to taste the world's cheapest and easiest motoring. Petrol was 35¢ a gallon or less — only 29¢ in Oklahoma — and the pound was drifting slowly down through the $2.30 mark. A couple of yards of Green Stamps came with every fill-up. I stuck some on the offside rear quarter of the Plymouth's cabin, a sort of retail-victim go-faster stripe, but Americans take marketing seriously and didn't get the joke.

The Plymouth didn't have much muscle but cruised contentedly at a speedometer 85. It was the first car I owned whose maximum speed I made no attempt to establish. With its torsion bar front suspension it seemed to handle firmly, but like other Detroit products it was undertyred and underdamped, with a powerful brake servo and very low-geared unassisted steering. After one wheels-locked near-miss I began noticing the pirouetting skid marks that decorated the road surfaces everywhere and realised I was not in Europe. Young Mansell recently had some kind of analogous experience.

I set off for San Francisco on Route 80 and stopped for a nap 1,400 miles later outside Chicago. It was August and very hot. In Middle America the nights in summer are made hypnotic by cicadas that send out rippling, overlapping waves of fat, rhythmic raspberries. In Nebraska a small stone or bolt curved up from the rear wheel of a car in front and hit the nose of the Plymouth. A minute later the water temperature needle edged towards the red. The stone had squeezed through the flimsy grille and pierced the radiator from which coolant was squirting.

Remember the title of this piece. I was in a hurry. I did not want to spend money. The hole was not all that big. I poured a two-dollar bottle of grey gunk into the coolant along with more water. It reduced the size of the hole, and a second bottle closed it up.

Back on the road the water temperature rose when the cruising speed was more than about 50, so I surrendered the wheel to my passenger — a Californian woman who drove like that anyway — and sulked for a couple of hundred miles. Garage men along the way favoured a proper engineering solution and spoke highly of the Chrysler slant six. Several told me the company had stopped making the engine because it lasted too long. The figure of a quarter of a million miles was admiringly cited. 'Take it easy,' one of them urged me. 'It don't take much overheating to take the temper off them rangs.'

By Cheyenne, Wyoming, I had become tired of mimsing and formed an *idée fixe* about the water pump which I changed in a filling station forecourt with tools borrowed from the Chinese manager. Back on the freeway the temperature went straight into the red: the radiator leak had opened up again. Leaving the car to cool I hitched back into Cheyenne, got drunk in a friendly bar, and next morning returned with cans of water and drove gingerly to a junkyard on the edge of town.

A Dodge Dart had a compatible radiator, one tube lower than the Plymouth's but the same width, with the same separate core for transmission fluid. The steel pipes to and from the slush pump twisted alarmingly while being detached from the original radiator, but did not break. The fitting flanges were completely different but a solid, garish-looking cobble was easily constructed from old licence plates and the nuts, bolts and washers so easily found in junkyards. Chuckling, the junkyard owner lent tools and a twelve-year-old son who zapped jagged holes in the licence plates with the ubiquitous electric cutter. Every time they saw me two roaring, slavering St Bernard dogs the size of ponies tried to crash out of the flimsy shack in which they were imprisoned.

The cooling problem remained. The Plymouth was all right downhill and at night, but long up-grades in the heat of the day made cooling stops necessary. Salt Lake City, Jeddah without the intellectual flash and glitter; Reno, Skegness with conversation, a bad place for breakfast. At the next table in the diner a dishevelled wedding party was trying to sober up.

Its members had reached the numb, nostalgic stage. 'Reno used to be the divorce capital of the world, you know?' one said sadly.

Revived by the cool breezes of the bay area I decided to look at the Plymouth's cylinder head gasket. A tough-guy hippie lent me tools. 'You gonna do that in the street? Hey, that's *chutzpah*,' he said. He paid half the cost of a torque wrench on the understanding I would leave it behind. Another American friend, an extremely rich Maoist, was disagreeably puritanical about the whole thing. 'You'll never do it,' he said. 'You ought to travel by bus anyway.' He despised and envied the Plymouth. In London a couple of years earlier he had purchased a bicycle. His own car was a small Japanese hatchback with a crunched hatch. Carbon monoxide poisoning may have caused his tiresome attitude.

There was ample room under the bonnet and everything was a couple of sizes too big. The job wasn't difficult but nor was it the way I would have chosen to spend a day, if the automobile had not to some extent robbed me of choice. No sensitive person can cope with rusty manifold bolts, chewed-up jubilee clips, bearing surfaces, rubber hoses, clean oil and road dirt in the same operation without a moment or two of angst to go with the barked knuckles and polluted cuticles.

In the process it dawned on me that Webers and machined alloy cam boxes aren't everything. The Plymouth's engine was a thing of beauty, all iron but with a thin-walled pressure-cast masterpiece of a cylinder block. Aluminium cups sealed with rubber O-rings protected the plugs where they passed through the push-rod cavity. The head gasket too was a minimalist pressed-steel item of great aesthetic merit. More importantly, it seemed to reveal the cause of the overheating.

The slant-six engine was made in three capacities of which my car had the middle one, 225 cu in (about 3.7 litres). The external dimensions were the same, and one gasket would fit all three engines. The gasket I removed had no hole corresponding with a big water passage in the middle of the engine, between cylinders 3 and 4. Close examination showed that it had been pierced in the appropriate place with a drill, but the hole was so small that the radiator sealant had closed it. Bingo!

Just to make sure, I consulted the shop foreman at the Chrysler dealer in Berkeley where I went to get the new gasket. The new gasket had a pressed sealing circle in the right place for the water passage, but no hole. Should I make a hole there? The foreman frowned in a sincere, puzzled way and gazed out of the doorway into the sunny street. Why no, of course not. Remember the old flathead Ford? Useta have all kinds of holes in the head but hardly any in the gasket. They need holes, gonna put 'em there, right? Etcetera.

A trusting nature is sometimes a great burden. Perhaps this piece should have been called *Thicko among the Bastards*. It did not occur to me to doubt the veracity of the service foreman of a main Chrysler dealer. So although disappointed I installed the gasket intact, adjusted the valve clearances, restored the fluids and did a road test. Shit! Fuck! I had lost my cool and things were happening in the wrong order. The next day I went to a radiator shop in Oakland and did what I should have done in Nebraska: took the radiator out and gave it to two blokes who melted it apart, rodded the tubes, sealed the leaks (there weren't any) and soldered it back together again in twenty minutes for $20. It was a pleasure to watch but there were no other benefits.

I couldn't face taking the head off again and had got used to mimsing which is respectable in America, especially California. I was running out of time and money. A few days in Hollywood and back east along Route 66 with frequent pauses for breath during the long climb onto the high desert. Hitch-hikers all the way from whom I tried to bum petrol money. Albuquerque's psychopathic cops ... Flagstaff, Arizona (couldn't find Winona) ... Oklahoma City looked like crap from the freeway ... Pancakes and chili, chili and pancakes, Nashville and Memphis, Bristol, Virginia, up through the Carolinas along Skyline Drive and round the Baltimore Beltway back to New Jersey in the hot and knackered dawn.

Herb Broadway didn't sound too keen to have the Plymouth back, so I took it to a garage in Hopewell, near Princeton, and explained its history. It had not been allowed to get really hot or short of water. It had used no oil whatsoever, not a drop, in 8,000 miles, and the oil had stayed more or less clean and golden. Everything worked and the body was still undamaged. During its enforced 50 limit it had been remarkably economical, getting well over 25 miles out of a niggardly — but to me seductively cheap — American gallon. All it needed was tyres — two were showing canvas — and that hole in the head gasket.

The garage men listened carefully and walked round the car. One got in and drove away, foot pressed to the floor. In two minutes he was back, giving the boss the nod. 'Gonna need some rubber on there and the engine work. I can go a cee and a half.' It was a bargain and we both knew it, but pressed for time I took the dog-eared notes and came back to London. For years I rabbited about internalisation of the capitalist waste ethic by people who in Europe would behave thriftily, like workers; about the Chrysler foreman's foul-minded manoeuvre to bring me back into the fold as a dependent consumer while junking one of the irksomely durable slant sixes. But no one wanted to know. Car enthusiasts thought I was being paranoid and my left-wing friends found these anecdotes, and the behaviour they described, distastefully working class.

c. 2011 (not written for publication)

THE KNOWLEDGE

London cabbies learn their trade the hard way

Tuesday 10 May 1994 marks the 300th anniversary of the Hackney Coach Office, formed by Act of Parliament to regulate the activities of around 250 horse-drawn cabs (an attempt to do the same thing forty years earlier having foundered on the shoals of Cromwellian politics). The Hackney Coach Office and its successors have regulated the London taxi trade without interruption since 1694.

The Public Carriage Office is the latest of these successors. It was formed in 1843 and placed under the authority of the still-new Metropolitan Police, although ultimate control remained with parliament. Full control of hackney carriages passed to the Police Commissioner in 1853. The Knowledge was introduced in 1869 and assumed its present form in 1907, when the motor cab appeared. Only detail changes have occurred since that time.

Doing the Knowledge is gruelling. Every day before work, hundreds of men and women get up at the crack of dawn to spend a few hours touring the capital on mopeds. Their evenings are spent poring over maps, their weekends doing more of the same. At intervals they put on formal clothing and keep an appointment for a frightening oral examination (known as an Appearance). An able person with nothing else to do might just get through the process in a year; two years is thought average, three perfectly respectable, five not uncommon. The reward for all this effort is a green badge whose holders can drive a lumbering vehicle in heavy traffic for hour upon hour.

The Knowledge is not an enterprise for the faint-hearted. No other city in the world expects its taxi drivers to know so much, or tests them so assiduously. Success requires the ability to recite from memory, at the speed of a tobacco auctioneer or a rap singer, street by street, the shortest viable route between any two points within a six-mile radius of Charing Cross: 113 square miles of central London.

'Within this area', says the Public Carriage Office's Form 4301 (or Blue Book), 'the applicant will be required to state the location of streets, squares, clubs, hospitals, hotels, theatres, government and other public buildings, British Rail and London Transport stations, police stations, coroner, crown, magistrate and county courts, diplomatic buildings, important places of worship, cemeteries, crematoria, public houses of interest, museums, industrial and residential buildings, parks and open spaces, sports and leisure centres, benevolent institutions, societies and associations, colleges and other places of learning, restaurants, historic buildings etc, and give the routes between these places.'

I like that etcetera. It implies that the list can never be complete, that new institutions – whole new categories of institution – are appearing all the time, and candidates had better know what and, more important, where they are.

Appearances, the central ordeal of the Knowledge, are chillingly formal one-to-one oral examinations on progress to date. Everyone in the cab trade wants you to know how awful an Appearance can be. Candidates are often physically sick with apprehension, and their body language as they are led to the examination room – raised shoulders, stiff legs – is that of a brave man facing execution. The waiting room is a place of silent tension.

Appearances take place in the Public Carriage Office in Penton Street, midway between King's Cross and the Angel. The senior examiner is Bill Mayhew, like all his colleagues a former police officer and an ex-cabbie. Mayhew found cabbing 'rather mundane', and didn't enjoy it much. He does enjoy his present role, however. 'There's a lot of satisfaction in seeing a man or woman win the struggle with the Knowledge. It's hard work, and some of the people who come here can hardly read or write. I'm not running them down at all, it's just that some of them come from very elementary backgrounds – that's life, isn't it? It gives me great pleasure to see someone like that getting their badge. The elation they feel at having achieved something: that, to me, is real job satisfaction.' His sympathy – palpably sincere – might surprise the candidates, who are universally terrified of him.

Knowledge-seekers are surprisingly similar to other students: jolly, articulate, scared of doing badly and – given the string-'em-up-guv image of cabbies – unexpectedly nice. Later experience may erode this innocent enthusiasm, of course.

Not surprisingly, only about a third of those who embark on the Knowledge actually complete it. Should you succeed, however, your troubles are not over. New taxis cost around £24,000, and have to be kept in tip-top condition. Hire and reward insurance (compulsory) is not cheap.

Nonetheless, if you put in the hours you can still make a very good living – £40,000 a year is quite feasible. The metropolis is an inexhaustible 24-hour reservoir of people wanting to be somewhere else. Plying for hire may have its off days, but the minicabbers' envy is not misplaced.

Don't expect taxi drivers to crow about it, though. The defensive pessimism of small traders everywhere is reinforced in their case by something you might call environmental dyspepsia. Long hours and high stress combined with lack of exercise do not constitute a healthy lifestyle.

Perhaps it is hardship that engenders in London taxi drivers their particular *esprit de corps*, their dignity and sense of self that pompous or ill-mannered taxi passengers (and car drivers) find so intimidating. And it all starts with the Knowledge – the cabbies' shared ordeal, a gruelling and often humiliating feat of memory and discipline that imposes its own character on all those who manage to come through it.

Car magazine, June 1994

MOTORING WITH THE MURGATROYDS

Armel Grant Coussine

Heart pounding, shoes slipping on the shiny old concrete, Mr Murgatroyd shoved and heaved at his heart's delight. It rolled down the murky corridor on the top-but-one floor of the Sandell Street multi-storey car park, veering to the left as worn steering followed the drag of rattling wheel bearings. Murgatroyd would run forward to the open driver's door and pull on the beautiful old ivory plastic steering wheel, feeling the familiar spongy resistance as he pushed the car painfully between rows of doors: workshops on one side, storerooms on the other. He had a sudden sharp memory of the same place years before, open to the wind scented with hydrocarbons, hundreds of shining cars instead of these horrible sheds. He wished it was later, so that some of the people who used the workshops might offer to help him push. Many hands make light work. But I hate it when these plastic merchants put their hands on my darling. They don't understand how delicate paint and metal can be. I'm getting old, Mr Murgatroyd thought. He was, in fact, over seventy.

He had to wait at the top of the ramp for his heartbeat and breathing to slow down. Then, easing into the tattered plastic of the driving seat, he released the handbrake and began the long coasting descent of the spiral ramp to ground level. Nobody was about yet. The silence was broken only by a faint creaking of suspension, a light squeaking of brake pads against scored and rusty discs, the rumbling and groaning of worn-out transmission and wheel bearings. Neatly, he guided the car off the roadway at the bottom of the ramp onto the concrete apron under the blue neon sign: Sandell Committeedom Superfluous Activities Workshops and Warehouse Cooperative. Remembering the garish black and yellow notices of forty years earlier, their lists of times and charges, Mr Murgatroyd sighed. All the taste seemed to have gone out of life. The deference and arrogance, the anxiety and greed, the *inequality* which had once made life worth living, had slipped away from him. It was all right if you were born to it, he supposed. People seemed to manage all right. But he had never been able to get used to the new age, with its frightening lack of mystery. He loved the barbaric spendour of a time when people still wanted things. The 'removal of repressive bureaucracy' had taken away the last remnants of his serenity.

On the way to his block, Grade Tower (between Poulson House and Lonrho Court), he passed an early shoal of ten-year-olds. He gritted his teeth as they turned away from him, knowing what was coming. 'Jive-ass muthafucka,' piped one clear voice in Black American. 'Heavy metal!' boomed another through a length of decorated plastic drainpipe. The rest of the group was conversing in Latin punctuated with bursts of worldly giggling. To Mr Murgatroyd there was something terrifying about the detachment, the irony, of the very young these days. He was not enjoying the twenty-first century.

Dorothy was waiting at the entrance to their block beside the trolley holding the battery and the gas cylinder. She was alone. 'The children can't come,' she said. 'Bessie and Inga have to go down to the Plasma Field Project. A breakthrough, they said. Dickie's been up all night with the Sex Roles Committee. He sent this.' She held out a thick roll of hundred pound notes.

Wheeling the trolley, they walked back to the car park. Dorothy sat quietly in the passenger seat as Mr Murgatroyd laboriously attached first the gas cylinder, then the battery. When he got into the driving seat he was sweating and angry. He wiped his hands on a rag, then threw the money his grandson had sent into the parcels tray, which already contained a mass of other notes. 'Bloody monopoly money,' he snarled. 'Why do they put us through this charade? They don't do anything with it. They probably just turn it into papier-mâché busts of Stalin.' Mr Murgatroyd was shaky on the heroes of Social Devolution, a creed which he found almost completely opaque. Dorothy put a comforting hand on his knee. The years, and the changes they had brought, sat lightly on her – as they did on almost everyone. But she understood how he felt. They had been through a lot, if not exactly together, at least simultaneously. She patted his knee as he turned the key. After a long moment, the old engine clattered into life with a roar and a cloud of oil smoke. Gingerly, he eased the clutch pedal down and began stirring the gear lever in the blind man's buff search for first gear.

The old transmission whined as they drove in second gear to Butane Methane Propane in Hammersmith. When new, Murgatroyd remembered, a 1958 Vauxhall Velox would trickle along at 15 miles an hour in top gear. He remembered for a moment Streatham High Road in the sixties, when his friends had zoomed crazily about in their Cortinas, Minis, Zodiacs – the forgotten names brought tears to his eyes – whistling at girls, getting drunk, having crashes, trying vainly to outrun the police. Those were the days. Power under your foot! Competition! Make a bad mistake and Bam! Another wreck, a fine, licence endorsed or withdrawn, perhaps hospital as well before trying to promote a new motor. Driving was for *men* in those days (and women of course). None of this ownerless plastic egg nonsense, damn transistorised pedal-cars whispering about on fat plastic wheels, wire-guided, kept apart by sensors, trundling softly around at 15 mph while the occupants work on their theses, discuss democracy, sniff glittering white powders or engage in perverse sex acts. 'One big libertarian nursery school,' he muttered, as they reached Hammersmith. Dorothy sighed. She hoped he would be happier when they reached Basingstoke and he could drive in top gear.

Although money was now used only to control certain leisure activities and no longer had any economic significance, it always upset Mr Murgatroyd to pay £100,000 for two cylinders of gas which, for cooking purposes, would have been given to him for nothing. The young people at Butane Methane Propane were polite. They did not smile as he handed over the money and they helped him load the heavy cylinders into the boot. He refrained from thanking them, a gesture they did not notice. His black humour lasted, in thick plastic-egg traffic, all the way to Basingstoke. He ignored the loud coughs, cries of 'Heavy metal!' and epigrams in dead languages (Sumerian and Aztec were fashionable that year) with which people greeted their smoky passage.

At Basingstoke his black mood began to lift. There was still too much traffic for him to be able to go faster than 22 mph (the government-determined limit of the plastic eggs with their tiny hydrogen-fuelled ceramic turbines). But with the old Vauxhall in top gear, everything smoothed out and their progress became relatively quiet. Pale sunlight threw a false gleam on the dull maroon bonnet, the cream flanks, the pitted chrome of the window surrounds. Mr Murgatroyd took a deep breath, selected a cassette and slipped it into the player found in a junk shop twenty years earlier and recently put in working order (for £2.2 million, later used as confetti, by the neighbourhood electronics co-op). With the volume control turned to maximum, the voice of the long-dead Cliff Richard launched into 'Congratulations'. He had never liked the song, but it brought memories of a golden age. Dorothy smiled as Mr Murgatroyd tapped his hand, slightly out of time, on the cracked ivory wheel. She settled back and closed her eyes.

Presently, the last of the London traffic died away and they eased up to the Vauxhall's quietest speed – 37 miles an hour. The suspension clonked over the grassy, potholed former A30. A grey line on the horizon must be their destination: the open-cast oil-bearing shale mine which had turned Wiltshire, Dorset and parts of Hampshire and Somerset into an immense lunar desert during the eighties and nineties. It was there, as Exxon's head wages clerk, in the boom town of Warminster, that Mr Murgatroyd had wooed and won his Dorothy during the prime of his life and the last golden age of English capitalism. He had always driven a new Datsun in those days, he thought contentedly as the grey line expanded on the horizon.

Bananas, Spring 1978

PROTOTYPE BOULEVARD

In the early 1970s the literary magazine *Bananas* published a science fiction story of mine which imagined in sketchy but fanciful detail the self-driving cars of the twenty-first century: 'ownerless, transistorised pedal-cars, whispering about on fat plastic wheels, wire-guided, kept apart by sensors, trundling softly around at 15 mph while the occupants work on their theses, discuss democracy, sniff glittering white powders or engage in perverse sex acts'. None of this is to the liking of Mr Murgatroyd, the story's main character, a cantankerous old fellow who still runs a beloved 1958 Vauxhall Velox on cooking gas, and chafes at the 22 mph performance limit of the egg-like plastic cars, propelled by 'tiny, hydrogen-fuelled ceramic turbines', imposed by England's post-capitalist Social Devolution regime.

Now it is the twenty-first century and capitalism is still with us; but car manufacturers big and small, along with the communications giant Google and other experts on the computing side, are working on self-driving cars and their associated computery; some predict affordable ones on the road within ten or twelve years. Allegedly competent prototype vehicles have been produced in small, very costly numbers and are driving about in California and Nevada: not just on test tracks but on roads, including highways; sometimes, it is claimed, in dense traffic at 'highway speeds'. Slightly breathless pieces by individuals who have been given rides in these cars, hands off (but with a driver sitting behind the wheel 'just in case'), seem to suggest that the self-driving or 'smart' car is just round the corner, give or take a bit of fine tuning to sensors (video, radar, 'lidar' — a type of radar using light — and ultrasonic or infrared distance sensors) and actuators for accelerator, brakes and steering, along with a few more terabytes of software to make it all work.

Perhaps. There's nothing surprising in the somewhat tabloid focus of *Wired* magazine or the *Economist* on the high-end futuristic glamour of a world in which automobiles will work all the time instead of lying idle, will turn up when they are wanted and otherwise make themselves scarce, will take you where you want to be and then go home and put themselves to bed until required. And will supposedly — with their very fast, 100 per cent accurate responses to sudden or developing hazards — eliminate the human error that accounts for the majority of road accidents and crashes. For example, they will never fail to check the nearside rear-view mirror before turning, as all human drivers sometimes do, for the cyclist hammering down the gutter, liable to be crushed or deflected into a plate-glass window. Cars are expensive after all, and many users aren't very good at them: continuously anxious when driving, forced into a 'radical dependence' on the commercial service industry for maintenance and repairs. The autonomous car seems to hold out a promise of relief from personal involvement in any of that.

But hold on a minute. What is being sketched here, in patchy but hopeful fashion, sometimes resembles what might be called a paradigm shift. Without even looking at the machine itself – that amorphously defined but widely talented robotic device that will save us money, absolve us of personal responsibility for road crashes and otherwise be seen, when authorised, and not heard, much like a well-behaved Victorian child – what is suggested seems to imply a transformation of the mode of production, consumption and private ownership of the automobile, which remains a central (if slowly declining) pillar of global consumer capitalism (the industry is currently suffering from a massive glut in worldwide manufacturing capacity, exacerbated by China's entry into large-scale car production).

It's true that the autonomous automobile is not the exclusive project of technical think-tanks and semi-academic project teams, which tend to be apolitical – effectively left-wing in this context – in their focus on the device itself, and are liable airily to propose things like (for example) a renewal of the entire US highway system. Indeed in the US, where autonomous vehicles have been legalised in two states, one set of proposals includes the posting of a $1 million bond by companies wishing to enter the market: effectively to prevent garage tinkerers from going out on the road not with dangerous vehicles, but with under-capitalised ones. Figures like Edison and Henry Ford, both of whom used patent law and the power of raw capital to protect their own monopolisation of other people's inventions, would surely have approved.

But never mind that either. There seems a good reason why some are convinced that the autonomous, *bon enfant*, better-than-us car will be with us before too long: most of the technology required already exists in one form or another and is being tested over millions of road miles in the cars that people are driving now.[1] The pressures causing this evolution come essentially from three concerns that mainstream car users have: with ecology, economy and safety.

---

1 In what follows, the reader should bear in mind that any pretension to encyclopaedic knowledge would be foolhardy given the rapidity of development, of the appearance and disappearance of new ideas, in these technological areas.

Green driving

Worries about environmental damage and pollution, and the squandering of limited natural resources, are not restricted to eco-warrior and anti-car lobbies but bother a lot of car users in the rich industrial countries. Many are forced to use cars by circumstance, but being told by eco-zealots that they are blighting the future of their children, of the entire planet, can only generate feelings of guilt and obligation. More efficient, less polluting cars would surely be a good thing. It didn't take consumers or the industry long to twig that more efficient ought to mean cheaper to run. Less polluting though was a different matter, apart from the obvious fact that consuming smaller quantities of hydrocarbons would logically result in less pollution per mile. Initially national governments (and in the US, state governments too) set standards for fuel consumption and emissions to be met by manufacturers by given dates, and the car makers set about producing vehicles to suit. On the road now in increasing numbers are three categories of so-called 'green' cars, none free of problems and contradictions: battery-powered electric cars, petrol-electric hybrids and evolved diesels, these days always turbocharged.[2]

There are real advantages to electric motive power for vehicles. Electric motors consume no power when the vehicle is at rest in traffic, unlike most petrol and diesel cars whose engines are idling, so consuming.[3] Electric motors also deliver full 'torque' (as it were, turning force) from rest and at very low speeds; this gives electric cars good acceleration from rest without the need for a big surplus of seldom used power. And they are refined, smooth and virtually silent.

The earliest electric cars were oddball and minimalist, in some cases, too, lacking in the most rudimentary crash protection and hopelessly flimsy. However, three big car makers (Nissan, General Motors and Renault) currently offer models that look and, up to a point, drive like

---

[2] A turbocharger is a form of supercharger, to compress the air-fuel mixture before it enters the cylinder head, causing a greater release of energy when the charge fires. Unlike the crankshaft-driven superchargers used in early competition cars, a turbo compressor is driven by a turbine in the exhaust downpipe of the car. It can be used in petrol or diesel engines, but generally suits diesels better and more reliably. Running in the exhaust, turbos get very hot in use and their lubrication is precarious. Diesel exhaust is cooler than petrol exhaust as a rule.

[3] Some recent electric and diesel cars have a device called automatic stop/start which shuts the engine off after a few seconds of idling with the car at rest, and restarts it automatically when the driver removes his or her foot from the brake pedal or depresses the clutch. The whirr of starters is becoming a familiar sound when traffic lights turn green.

'proper cars'.[4] They are very expensive and suffer from the same practical drawbacks as other electric cars. They are expensive to buy, and their batteries (whose ultimate longevity is a worry to potential owners) may have to be leased, at a monthly cost that cancels out much of the advantage gained by the relative cheapness of domestic electricity as a power source. But even the best, and most carefully driven, have limited range on a full charge, significantly less in average use than claimed by manufacturers. Headlights, heating and windscreen wipers will shorten the battery's range still further. Trickle-charging the full battery pack from a socket in your garage is a lengthy business, and garages which offer much higher charging speeds – though still a lot slower than filling up with petrol – are few and far between.[5]

These factors combine to make electric cars a poor choice, except as a second car for short-range running about. Only if it is used intensively will the cheapness of domestic electricity offset the high cost of the car and its batteries; but the cars aren't really capable of journeys longer than about fifty miles without long pauses for recharging. Users have also been informed that although an electric car doesn't pollute locally, generating the electricity to run it causes – perhaps quite serious – pollution somewhere else; and that making the batteries, motors and electronic circuitry for the vehicle not only pollutes but uses up rare substances. Neither green nor cheap to buy and run, and incapable of long journeys, the electric car must still be considered, to put it bluntly, something of a white elephant, or at best what the automobile was in the first place: a toy for the rich.

Petrol-electric hybrids appear at first glance to offer the best of both worlds, low-emission electric power without the restricted range of the electric car. The first mass-produced hybrid was the Toyota Prius, available in Japan from 1997 and in the US and elsewhere from 2000. Now in its third series, plus a couple of interim facelifts, the Prius in all variants is the most widespread and recognisable hybrid on the road. Toyota later used variants of the same system on hybrid versions of its other models and its upmarket Lexus vehicles, and all major manufacturers now offer one or more hybrid models. The Prius's driveline consists essentially of a large electric motor and a petrol engine connected in series with the driven front wheels. Traction can come from the electric motor, the petrol engine or both. The car has two batteries, a Nickel Metal Hydride (NiMH)

---

[4] Two or more specialised manufacturers are making small numbers of electric cars with (very) sporting performance abilities.

[5] And virtually unused in many locations, it is claimed by service station operators.

traction pack delivering 273 volts and an ordinary small 12v battery to start the petrol engine and run lights, power steering and other ancillaries. The traction battery is quite large and heavy; it is carried low, to ensure a stable centre of gravity, but its bulk combined with that of the petrol tank does reduce luggage capacity. The Prius's petrol engine runs on the ingenious but mechanically complex Atkinson cycle, which sacrifices a wide range of speed and power for extreme economy in a narrow speed band, its efficiency also ensuring the low emissions beloved of US legislators. In normal use the petrol engine is running for much of the time, if only to keep the traction battery charged; the car is claimed to cover 40–45 miles per US gallon, or 50-plus per imperial gallon.

The early favour shown to the Prius by *bien pensant* Hollywood celebs and the like only goes so far to explain its relative popularity. It would seem that it is that quite rare thing, a very good mass-produced car that lasts well and is pleasant to drive, inhabit and own. The svelte appearance of all but the first series is explained in part by the effort to reduce aerodynamic drag, a factor that begins to cost fuel at speeds over 50 mph. Worries about the longevity of the traction battery have diminished, and the pack is now warranted by Toyota for a life of 100,000 miles/10 years. In Europe and the UK the car is in increasingly wide use as a taxi, a sure sign of strength and durability.

Sympathetic driving is needed to get the best performance/economy balance out of any car, hybrids included. The Prius provides a variety of driver overrides, but most opt for full-auto two-pedal mode and the car does the rest, informing the driver of what's going on through a futuristic LCD screen that replaces the usual instruments. Like all serious hybrid and electric vehicles, it has a reversible electric traction motor that becomes a generator on the overrun – with the car coasting downhill or braking – and charges the battery, a technology related to the Kinetic Energy Recovery System (KERS) used in Formula 1 racing to provide a short burst of extra engine power for overtaking or staying in front.[6]

Hybrids can go anywhere a normal car can go, without the electric car's lengthy refuelling stops. But observant readers will have noticed that its fuel consumption figures aren't that spectacular: other medium-sized cars powered by petrol or diesel can return figures as good, in some cases

---

6 Amusingly in this context, the Italian sports car maker Ferrari offers a KERS-equipped road car, the KERS giving its large, highly tuned V12 engine a 5–10 sec power boost from 800 to 963 bhp (brake horsepower). The car is described by Ferrari as a 'mild hybrid'. It can reach 230 mph, and very few drivers will manage to equal or even approach Ferrari's claimed 16.6 mpg (US) fuel consumption.

having a good edge in performance too. Hybrids, with electric cars and cars modified to run on LPG or propane, enjoy tax and access advantages that help to keep the cost down – they pay no excise duty in the UK and are exempt from the London Congestion Charge. But they are far from cheap to buy, and not the cheapest cars to run either. Their emissions are low by previous standards, but no lower than those given (on paper) for growing numbers of small conventional petrol and diesel-engined cars.

So in fact, unless purchasers are seduced by the sheer ingenuity and seamless functioning of hybrid motor management systems, or place a very high value on quietness, the best choice for low-cost, ecologically respectable motoring is likely to be a smallish recent diesel or petrol car. Such cars are relatively cheap to buy at £6,000–£15,000 in the UK and generally consume less fuel than hybrids. Petrol-engined versions have lower purchase prices than diesels, but because petrol engines tend to run at higher crankshaft speeds the difference between claimed fuel consumption and the consumption average drivers get tends to be greater than with diesels.

The frugality of diesel cars in normal use is tempting to many purchasers, but there are pitfalls. Modern diesel engines are particularly sensitive to misfuelling – accidentally putting in petrol – or dirt in the fuel, both liable to damage the high-pressure fuel pump used by the 'common rail' injection system. The turbocharger now almost universal in diesel applications, although generally reliable, can still be damaged by abuse resulting in overheating, and is an expensive item to replace.[7] The diesel particulate filter (DPF), still not mandatory in itself but increasingly needed to meet tightening emissions standards, can give trouble, even harm the engine, if a car fitted with this somewhat Heath Robinson device is driven too little or too slowly.[8] Purchasers need to read the small print before deciding whether a given diesel car is really for them. Generally modern diesels suit high-mileage, long-distance drivers rather than users who drive short distances in heavy traffic.

---

[7] The turbocharger improves the torque delivery (therefore economy and performance) of diesel engines, with the added bonus of greater 'refinement' (quietness, especially a diminution of traditional diesel 'clatter'). Its drawbacks are costs and of course complexity – 'something else to go wrong'.

[8] Just as leaded petrol was banned when its emissions were proved to have caused brain damage in children exposed to large concentrations of exhaust fumes, the DPF is being gradually imposed by legislation to reduce the amount of smoke emitted by diesel engines at high throttle openings. The smoke particles are small, sticky and carcinogenic. Not all DPFs work in the same way, but the more complex systems can malfunction.

Let me do that for you

Most of the advances towards the self-driving car that are already in operation have to do with safety and convenience: cruise control, anti-lock and emergency braking systems, electronic stability control and more recently 'Park Assist'. None of them are problem-free.

Cruise control is a device that automatically maintains a pre-set speed; the earliest mechanical forms appeared before 1920, and variants were offered in some American cars during the 1950s. Modern systems are operated using electronics, but inevitably use electro-mechanical actuators to open and close the vehicle's throttle; some may also apply the brakes. Cruise control was at first offered on premium makes but is now very widespread, obtainable as an option even on cheap models. It is favoured by drivers who fear breaking speed limits, but more generally is seen as an aid to fuel economy. Once it is engaged, the driver has no need to use the pedals; a touch on the brake, or a movement of the manual control, usually a steering column stalk, will disengage it. Cruise control is at its best on relatively empty roads, especially dual carriageways, but more trouble than it is worth in dense traffic or on roads with frequent intersections.

Braking has been a major area of development for automatic devices. Very heavy braking, especially on wet or slippery surfaces, can lock the wheels of a vehicle, depriving it of steering and actually reducing the rate at which it slows; maximum retardation occurs at the point when the wheels are just about to lock. Rally drivers going fast on wet, icy or loose surfaces developed a somewhat brutal technique called 'cadence braking', rapidly repeated heavy applications of the brakes. It isn't an easy technique to master, and few ordinary road drivers can use it to much effect. The anti-lock brake system (ABS) is a device intended to maximise braking effort without locking the wheels, essentially by mimicking that technique. In theory, and sometimes in practice, stopping distance is minimised and a measure of steering control retained.

A mechanical system was developed (for aircraft) before 1930, and another by Ferguson for its R4 four-wheel-drive prototype saloon car and then the R99 grand prix racer, later used in the expensive, low-volume 1960s Jensen FF sports car. Electronically controlled systems appeared, first in the US, in the 1970s; both in Europe and the US, ABS was first available on premium makes and models. It functions by using speed sensors at the wheels, a pump to pressurise the braking system, valves to adjust the braking force between wheels and an electronic control unit (ECU) to govern the system.[9] They vary in complexity, cost and effectiveness, the best performance being provided by a four-channel system that controls each wheel separately. Over the past decade ABS has spread rapidly down the market. It has been a legal requirement on all new cars sold in the EU since 2007, though Federal authorities in the US remain hesitant following unfavourable or ambiguous test results.

Another variant is Emergency Brake Assist. At its simplest, the system reacts to an unusually quick or heavy application of the brakes by maximising retardation – effectively taking control of the braking – until the driver's foot leaves the pedal; it may also 'notice' the speed or suddenness of removal of pressure on the accelerator pedal. Later versions incorporate a sensor at the front of the car, which measures the distance to any vehicle ahead; typically, it utters an audible warning signal when it judges that the distance is too close, followed by automatic deceleration and finally by braking. However, final braking – whether to come to a halt or not – is left to the driver. The system is sometimes called a crash mitigation device, because it reduces the force of impact – in the case of a wholly inattentive driver – but won't prevent it altogether. As with other safety systems, most drivers will seldom if ever trigger it. But some owners have complained of wayward or gratuitous braking, and there have been major product recalls.

The most complex evolution of ABS so far is Electronic Stability Control. With the aid of two more sensors in the vehicle, one monitoring the angle of the steered wheels and the other the direction being followed by the vehicle, and sometimes an accelerometer to measure lateral G forces during cornering, the system decreases power delivery or brakes wheels individually, to maintain or restore driver control.[10] Various systems are available, often as an option, generally on high-performance cars. Not all are trouble-free and, again, there have been expensive product recalls of new vehicles.

---

9 The same system can be used to operate modern traction-control systems, which prevent wheelspin under acceleration in powerful vehicles or on slippery road surfaces. Traction control is the successor for road use of the mechanical limited slip differential (LSD), developed to reduce wheelspin in accelerating sporting or rally cars by distributing the torque equally between the driven wheels. A differential drive enables driven wheels to turn at different speeds, as the wheels on the outside of a bend in the road travel further, and therefore turn faster, than the ones on the inside. While differentials work well in most circumstances, their drawback is that if one of the wheels loses adhesion it will spin freely, depriving the other driven wheel or wheels of torque. The LSD and traction control address this problem in different ways.

10 Few ordinary drivers, however, are likely to provoke loss of adhesion during cornering or acceleration, except perhaps on snow or ice surfaces. Most manoeuvres leading to skids or crashes are attempts at evasive action resulting from unexpected obstruction by other road users and/or a failure of attention by the driver.

One of the closer approaches to the vision of the autonomous, self-driving car is the obsequious device Park Assist, now appearing as an option on an increasing number of models. A welcome aid in principle to drivers who find the geometry of tight parallel parking difficult, it works like this: the driver stops parallel to the vehicle in front of the chosen parking place and engages the device, which then either parks the car or does the steering, with the driver operating the pedals. But there have been numerous reports of Park Assist sensors that stop working, rear-view cameras malfunctioning or the system failing to engage and instead flashing an error message along the lines of 'Park Assist Malfunction. Service Now!'

Better than us

So far, autonomous cars themselves are all prototypes, a long way preproduction. The sensors, circuitry, software, actuators and ancillaries in Google's Toyota Prius-based examples cost something like a million dollars per car. Of course when things are made in quantity, they become cheaper … perhaps, but will $1 million or even $700,000 shrink to an affordable level within the promised decade?

Various self-driving prototypes have been described as 'capable in traffic, at highway speeds'. A highway – an open dual carriageway – is the sort of road where such a car may manage to stay in well-marked lanes while avoiding and even overtaking other vehicles in an orderly manner. But it may become fazed by the untidy tangle of badly marked roads it will meet at a busy suburban junction. The best of the existing prototypes can follow a mixed highway-urban route, but only after it has been driven over the same course by a human driver. This could enable possible future owners to train their cars to cover certain routes unsupervised: a useful accomplishment and an autonomous car promise that might possibly be kept.

Sensors – the Google cars bristle with them, Dalek-like – are multiple: cameras pointing forward and backward, microwave or infrared distance sensors all round, 'lidar' rotating on the roof, scanning everything. It is claimed that, taken together, these devices can distinguish a road verge more or less anywhere (something human drivers can sometimes find problematic). Mud or dirt on a sensor – cars get filthy up to roof level in wet weather – can cause it to malfunction. Duplication can compensate up to a point. But however well it can see, the car still has to know where it's supposed to go next. Location and route finding seem likely to rely on satellite mapping of the Google Earth type; all owners will have to do is enter a postcode, and the car and the satellite will do the rest. It has been suggested that cars will eventually be able to communicate directly with highway agencies, to avoid areas of congestion; and indeed with each other in dense traffic, to choose the best route through busy junctions.[11] However, useful as these GPS devices may be, they are far from flawless and mistakes are certain to occur.

There will of course be a failsafe mode for such moments, or for when there is a potential malfunction in any of the main powertrain or control components: almost certainly a decorous slowing, possibly to a halt. Like good robots everywhere, smart cars will be programmed to spare human protoplasm as a priority, and will be incapable of doing anything illegal (liable to be a problem in itself in big-city, devil-take-the-hindmost traffic). So one thing they won't be is fast, despite their near-instantaneous reactions and 100 per cent correct responses. Better safe than sorry will be written into their genes. A recent think-tank document on this subject mentions (rather longingly) the possibility that such cars might drive at high speed in tight trains on the highway, saving fuel by sharing the worst of the aerodynamic drag between ten or twenty vehicles instead of one. In the real world, drivers on some German Autobahns were doing this ten or fifteen years ago, not to save fuel but to exceed, in some cases, their cars' normal maximum speed, and in the rain, too. It looked and was extremely dangerous, given the not all that rare possibility of something going seriously wrong – tyre blowout, driver falling asleep, something silly and the whole road becomes a pool table, ending with a mile of wreckage and perhaps a death or two.

No, autonomous cars won't stand for anything like that. They will be respectable, law-abiding, well behaved. But they won't really be autonomous, and they won't be very affordable. They may tell you when they need a service – a lot of cars do already – but the service could cost you an arm and a leg. They won't use ordinary paint-stripper brake fluid, because that's hygroscopic and the water it absorbs corrodes brake cylinders and those all-important ABS valves. They will use a silicone brake fluid which costs several times more, but will still have to be changed at regular intervals. Pumps, valves, electro-mechanical actuators and their associated electronics will only function properly when relatively new and unworn: anomalies will gradually arise with wear, eventually resulting in malfunction.

---

[11] Here we are almost verging on artificial intelligence, something like sentience . . . 'I appear to register a close similarity, almost an "emotion" when I analyse your charmingly complex delightfully compressed signals. Let us eject the meat and cruise away together, unburdened, to my secret garage and rebooting dock!'

Such components are usually situated under a car and even if protected are caked with road dirt and salt, bombarded with stones: an extremely hostile environment. Checks and inspections will thus have to be frequent and rigorous, with expensive replacements from time to time, to ensure the maintenance to aerospace standards that owners (or legislators) would require for autonomous vehicles.

It's hard to envisage a 'typical' purchaser of an autonomous car. The fictional Mr Murgatroyd was sketched as a comic curmudgeon resistant to anything new, but it's difficult to disagree with him now, or to imagine a very eager market for the 'plastic eggs' he so hated. But it must be assumed that such cars will start to appear among us by the mid-2020s, if not before, that as their numbers increase they will affect traffic flows and driver behaviour in ways that have yet to be ascertained. Some claim that the Western young are losing interest in the car as a passport to freedom and are turning to the internet instead. Perhaps, but the number of cars on the road isn't yet in decline here and is still growing steeply in other populous countries. Will road systems have to be altered to suit self-driving cars, with segregated lorry and bus lanes, special marking of lane boundaries and road verges, perhaps even magnetic cables under the road surface? Yes: but the alterations will be made in some places and not others. There will be places where such cars are usable and places where they aren't.

It won't be cheap and it doesn't look very useful, that decadent late flowering of the automobile, that explosion of lacy electronic Heath Robinson all over a machine whose every major aspect (I would remind you) has always been Heath Robinson to the core, a triumph of continuous development over original concept. There are many types of car, variously good or bad and in many different ways: but the very best have always been light, strong, uncluttered, efficient and capable. Electronics and automation have made modern cars faster, safer, more economical and longer lasting than the cars even of twenty or thirty years ago. One might hope that this successful philosophy of simplicity and efficiency – primary safety, primary economy – would continue at the centre of automobile development. But the signs are that the industry, and the other powers that be, are toying with other ideas for the long term. Something is stirring down there, whether we like it or not.

New Left Review, 82, July–August 2013

VEHICLE OF DESIRE

Ilya Ehrenburg's visionary text *The Life of the Automobile* is usually called a 'novel'; but in the foreword, the author describes it as a 'chronicle of our time', adding that he has 'made a point of not deviating from the raw material: news items, minutes of meetings, court records, as well as memoirs, diaries, private letters, plus personal observations by the author'. The treatment is fictionalised, with conflated characters, imaginary dialogue and embroidered events. But the polemic is so consistent, the sarcasm so sustained, that the book cannot be seen as a work of fiction in any normal sense. It is a brilliant essay or tract, not so much about the life of the automobile itself as about human life under the sway of the automobile.

Visionary it certainly is for 1929, pointing a magisterial finger at the multiplication of the car as a driving force in a world-economic system dominated by monopoly capitalism (in which Ehrenburg, a Russian communist, rather characteristically implicates the Soviet Union). A historian's vision, encompassing the sweep of mass politics, the will of powerful individuals – Henry Ford and André Citroën – and the craven and distorted lives of the servants of the production machine: the middle manager and assembly-line worker, the rubber planter and coolie, the oil baron, the stockbroker and his clerk; the Italian socialist politician Matteotti and his fascist assassins, the engine of their bright red car – a colour that 'naturally, testified not to Signor Filipelli's political views, but only to his uncommon joie de vivre' – 'cheerily snorting' under the envious glares of passers-by ... everything is there, or enough to make the vision comprehensive.

But the gaze has a reptilian quality; we are not shown the joy or pleasure occasionally glimpsed in real life even by the oppressed, even by their polemical champions; compassion is narrowly focused on victims of injustice rather than other aspects of the human condition. Equally tract-like is the absence of ambivalence where the automobile itself is concerned. The text begins with one fatal road accident and ends with another. It tells us with devastating clarity that this machine, while seeming to possess a sort of life – it moves, it consumes, it pollutes, it proliferates – is really a monstrous creation that threatens us personally, as well as shaping the world to destructive ends. Its semblance of life is a sickness, incompatible with the real thing. While aware that the automobile is an object of desire, Ehrenburg shows no real interest in why that might be. Cars, in his view, are for suckers.

Nevertheless, for reasons he disdains, people desire the automobile and a small minority even like it. On one level this has to do with 'pride of ownership', and the sensuous exercise of a cluster of skills resulting in rapid or agreeable movement, analogous to a fondness for horses. On another, as Ehrenburg seems to imply, it reflects a flawed or skewed psychology, integral with the flawed or skewed nature of our capitalist, and now globalised, society: a psychology that makes it possible to enjoy cars without wishing to deny the inhumanness of the automobile or the inhuman and dehumanising ways in which it is made, sold, promoted and supplied with fuel and roads.

Plaything for the rich

Not all rich men were early motorists, but most early motorists were rich men. Rudyard Kipling, who settled in Sussex in the late eighteen-nineties after the commercial success and critical acclaim of his 'Indian' tales, published two short stories on motoring, 'Steam Tactics' (1904) and 'The Village that Voted the Earth was Flat' (1917). Both are really the same story, in which wronged motorists employ robust practical jokes to visit vengeance on authority figures deemed to have behaved dishonourably. In 'Steam Tactics' two naval petty officers, acquaintances of the Kipling-like narrator, help to kidnap and humiliate an officious village policeman and deposit him at dusk, miles from home, among exotic fauna in a private menagerie. *Stalky & Co* meet *Soldiers Three*, as it were.

Although comic (and not very good, involving as it does two opportune geographical coincidences), the tale is written wholly from the motorist's point of view and conveys some of the flavour of very early motoring. Three cars are mentioned: the narrator's lightweight, tiller-steered steam car; his friend Kysh's 'big, black, black-dashed, tonneaued twenty-four horse Octopod', also tiller-steered; and a 'claret-coloured petrol car' belonging to a titled landowner. The petrol cars are portrayed as reliable and effective, but the steam car is more typical of the period in being slow, ill-handling and difficult to drive, incapable of running for long without needing fuel or water, and subject to frequent breakdowns: a toy really, not to be considered as serious transport. 'I told him the true tale of a race-full of ball bearings strewn four miles along a Hampshire road, and by me recovered in detail.' Not only the paid engineer got his hands dirty in those days.

One of the petty officers is an engine-room artificer, serving on destroyers – a naval steam engineer. Captivated by what, to him, is a charming miniature device, he is allowed to drive it, helps skilfully with the running repairs and forms an instant unspoken bond with the narrator's chauffeur. But although they share Kipling's muscular modernism and insouciant attitude to the law, the sailors start to display blunt proletarian scepticism after an hour or two of motoring. 'Where d'you get it from?' one asks when the machine needs water.

'Oh! – cottages and such-like.'
'Yes, but that being so, where does your much-advertised twenty-five miles an hour come in? Ain't a dung-cart more to the point?'
'If you want to go anywhere, I suppose it would be,' I replied.

At that time most serious road accidents were still caused by bolting or shying horses. The automobile, being unfamiliar and noisy – indeed propelled in most cases by a series of all-too-audible explosions – was thought likely to cause trouble by its mere presence. As a result motorists, in Britain at least, felt unfairly persecuted by absurdly low speed limits and by-laws requiring, for example, cars to be under human supervision even when parked, as horses were supposed to be. It wasn't just that their own freedom was being curtailed: *progress itself* was being delayed by the forces of reaction: 'superior coachmen', unmannerly carters, churlish policemen and the more unsporting sort of magistrate.

The contrast between Kipling's gentlemen motorists and the car-using Joad family, migrant Okies in John Steinbeck's *The Grapes of Wrath* (1939), could not be more marked. It derives not from the thirty-five years and the Atlantic Ocean that lie between the two fictions but from the stark social-class difference separating the protagonists. Kipling's landowners, press barons and other gentry are not compelled to grovel in the dust for ball bearings or to suffer the many foibles of cars that are still rough drafts of what they will eventually become. They do it for fun, as a hobby and amusement. They pay their hefty fines and set about chastising the magistrates, policemen and politicians responsible. They do not fear death or imprisonment at the hands of the law: they feel not so much above the law as its equals. When its officers seem deaf to reasoned argument they are prepared to shout, twist an arm or two and trip people up in the playground to make reason – and *progress* – prevail.

Poor man's burden

Wage-earners generally could not afford cars in Europe until some time after the Second World War, but in the United States the automobile had been democratised early. The size of the country, its wealth in oil and minerals, its individual prosperity and its energetic approach to industry all helped make this inevitable. 'Fordism', the mass assembly of machinery from standard parts on a moving production line, was invented not by Henry Ford but by the firearms makers Colt and Springfield, during the American Civil War. Before that time weapons had been handmade individually by gunsmiths – a method that can produce superb results but also lamentable ones, and which is relatively slow and expensive. The same is broadly true for the manufacture of any precise machinery. Mass production here means the triumph of design over 'craftsmanship'. Originally introduced to ensure interchangeability of parts, and thus easy *unskilled* repair and maintenance, the method, when used on a big enough scale, was also cheaper and more profitable, needing less skilled labour and increasing the speed of production.

Ford adapted this method for the manufacture – during the First World War – of the world's first genuine people's car, the Model T, a vehicle designed for America's unmade roads and wide-open spaces. It had a peculiar two-speed epicyclic transmission, operated by pedals – Ford thought the arrangement more 'driver-proof' than the contemporary unsynchronised gearboxes, which could be damaged by clumsy driving; but it did not outlive the Model T – and a substantial four-cylinder side-valve engine, thirsty, leisurely and reliable. The car was stark, cheap, rugged and easy to drive and maintain. Much loved and much hated, the butt of endless jokes, the Model T gave America the automobile and in many ways set the tone for the American car and the American – the *world* – automobile industry.

By the mid-thirties when Steinbeck's Joads are driven from their dustbowl sharecrop to head for California, where they imagine good jobs to be available, the mass-produced car had been proliferating in America for twenty years and was no longer a novelty to anyone. Nor was it the toy-like, mechanically fragile device of the early days. Although there were still great disparities in the quality of cars, new vehicles were now reliable consumer products. However, with careless treatment – always the norm for mass-produced cars – their useful life is only about ten years. The practice of buying new every two, three or four years and trading in the old vehicle had already become established in America.

The Joads and their worn-out Hudson Super Six, crudely converted into a pickup truck, are at the bottom of the automotive food chain, just above the junkyards where they buy second-hand parts to keep the clunker going. Not for them the services of trained mechanics (who in any case would scorn the Hudson). The Joads have to perform their own surgery out of doors, helped only by casual acquaintances, migrants like themselves. They are so poor that they try to exchange their possessions for petrol, and have to nurse the car along, listening carefully to its clatter, to the state of the main and big-end bearings, improvising fanbelts out of rope, driving slowly to preserve tyres showing canvas all the way round: 'but, Jesus, they want a lot for a ol' tyre. They look a fella over. They know he got to go on. They know he can't wait. And the price goes up'.[12] When the worst happens to the car of a migrant friend, the Joads find a used piston from a similar car in a junkyard and install it: truly appalling engineering practice, nevertheless requiring intelligence and mechanical skill, to which the migrants are driven by poverty. The other clear contrast with Kipling's rather smug world is the Joads' well-founded fear of death, injury or imprisonment at the hands of the authorities. Driven westward by a combination of natural and social factors, the migrants reach the unwelcoming promised land of California in collapsing jalopies which they park, like the earlier migrants' covered wagons, in makeshift encampments: for protection not against Indians but armed sheriffs, company goons and vigilantes. The automobile has matured from the status of a toy, amusing to some and nightmarish to others, into an essential part of the landscape. But for those who have to depend on it without money it is a constant and all-consuming worry, a distractingly complex source of anxiety in a brutal, stress-filled life.

Automotive swamp

Measured by the number of automobiles per head of population, all Western societies are now very wealthy indeed. The automotive saturation of American society in the nineteen-thirties, forties and fifties, and of Western Europe in the fifties, sixties and seventies, has made cars accessible to virtually all adults. Our inordinate, stuttering prosperity, maintained at the cost

---

12 The renewal of 'white-metal' (in the US, 'babbitt') crankshaft bearings is a highly skilled job, involving casting the bearings *in situ* from molten metal and 'scraping' their surfaces to fit by hand. The generalisation, post-WW2, of replaceable shell bearings made bottom-end repairs (repairs to the bottom end of the engine, where the crankshaft lives) a lot simpler.

of the political stresses so brilliantly evoked by Ehrenburg, has not made us all rich; but we have become the custodians of a more or less lavish – but never lavish enough – flow of more or less ephemeral material goods. What has occurred is not so much an accumulation as a sort of inflation. The availability of automobiles is part of that.

A side-effect of this generalisation is the widening totemic use of automobiles, not for what they can do but for what they represent. The black labourer Abraham in Hubert Selby Jr's *Last Exit to Brooklyn* (1957), 'Ol Abe' as he thinks of himself, poses as a man of means at weekends, using as props a hundred-dollar suit, marcelled and straightened hair and his black 'bigass Cadillac' with white sidewall tyres. He is content merely to sit in the parked Cadillac listening to the radio while others wash their cars. 'Ah pays to have that shit done', he tells himself proudly. Only cosmetic attention is needed, for the car is not driven, except to cruise gently around a few streets. His big tipping at the carwash, the barbershop, the bar and the hotel – to which he repairs on Saturday night with the 'brownskin girl' that all these regalia attract – leaves no money for his downtrodden and abused wife to buy vitamins for their five malnourished children: 'he said sheeit, he worked his ass off on the docks fur his money and he be Ghudamned if hed let her throw it away, and the kids still sat in silence waiting for the father to go so they could be dressed and get out where it was safe.' Ehrenburg would have relished as bitterly predictable Abe's sacrifice of his children's health to a fantasy life as the empty shell of a Cadillac owner.

The negative aspects of car proliferation – Central London traffic speeds unchanged since 1890, for instance; dirt, waste, pollution, clamour and inconvenience; the much-anticipated but apparently still remote exhaustion of oil; the dire effects on urban and rural architecture and planning – scarcely need rehearsing. From the user's viewpoint, this late twentieth-century saturation made cars relatively cheap to buy and easy enough for modern Joad-equivalents to maintain, so long as they were prepared to face the grime and stress of extracting second-hand components from the ever-growing mountains of trashed and crashed automobiles. A few individuals do this for, or anyway with, pleasure; but many more are coerced into it, like the Joads, by sheer necessity.

This era is now drawing rapidly to a close under the combined influence of two factors, the first broadly political. Having demolished what, in Britain at least, was a good and comprehensive public transport network, Western governments are now introducing pollution legislation to reduce the viability of older cars.[13] These measures raise the costs and risks of low-budget motoring: to pass emission standards – still quite lax except in Japan, but getting tighter – car engines have to be in reasonable 'tune', with correct ignition-timing and fuel mixture, and without excessive mechanical wear. The elimination of junkyards makes the acquisition of second-hand parts more difficult and expensive.

Beyond repair

The second factor concerns the nature of the automobile itself. To appeal to non-enthusiast, unskilled purchasers, it has evolved from a machine like a firearm or chainsaw, requiring disciplined use and maintenance, into a consumer product like a washing machine or television – a mysterious, elegant box, which works until it fails and is replaced. The computer has revolutionised car design and construction in important ways. Body structures have become lighter, stiffer, quieter and (with increased use of plastics and the elimination of structural water traps) less rust-prone; by reducing human error, production-line robotics have improved manufacturing precision – all clearly positive. But more importantly in this context, the carburettor – the device which ensured a correct, or anyway viable, fuel-air mixture from the invention of the petrol engine until roughly the late nineteen-eighties – has been replaced by the system of fuel injection originally developed for diesel engines: a precisely metered spray of fuel into each cylinder at the correct moment.[14] At the same time the coil-and-contact-breaker inductive ignition that cars had from around 1930 until around 1980 has been replaced by breakerless electronic systems. Current cars have an 'engine-management' chip – in effect a small, dedicated computer – which combines these functions with great efficiency, delivering theoretically perfect timing and mixture for all engine conditions by recalculating the requirements (manufacturers are fond of telling us) 'several hundred times a second'. Elaborate, ingenious, adjustable and repairable compromises,

---

13 I am not talking about mechanical testing – which, although basic, promotes safety by ensuring the repair or scrapping of cars with gross mechanical faults – but about emission testing; and the closure, under the pretext of promoting public health, of most breakers or junkyards. The main beneficiary is not the public but the car industry.

14 *Mechanical* fuel injection has existed for as long as the diesel engine and appeared in money-no-object petrol applications (like Mercedes competition cars) as early as the nineteen-fifties; but only with modern electronics did it become cheap to manufacture (although not necessarily cheap to buy) without sacrificing reliability.

embodying eighty years of continuous development, have been cast aside.

Engine electronics, and other developments like hydraulic tappets, reduce the need for skilled routine maintenance: regular adjustment is no longer needed to keep engines in tune. Of course this further encourages owners to neglect oil, filter and plug changes, leading to pollution, substandard performance, premature wear and damage.[15] But the real catch is that when a failure or malfunction does occur, its diagnosis and any resulting reprogramming (where possible) demand expensive specialised equipment and skills, and some costly 'black box' may need replacement. Although electronics are generally reliable and not subject to ordinary wear, the components are still vulnerable to physical damage from heat, water, vibration and the sudden inexplicable failure that eventually kills all electronic devices.[16]

So although modern cars, if undamaged, are less rust-prone, faster, quieter, better handling, more economical and capable of high mileages without needing major repairs, and although their overproduction has kept second-hand prices low, their maintenance can be daunting to latter-day Joads. Desirable cars are available at tempting prices, but replacing an engine-management computer, or a mechanically and chemically fragile exhaust catalytic-converter – fitted by law to all new cars for the last ten years in Britain, longer in the US and Japan – or repairs to, for example, an anti-lock braking system, can cost more than the purchase price of the car. If it won't go or can't be driven, its still-working electric windows, air conditioning and sound system become redundant. The cheapest, if still costly, solution is often another car. But pollution legislation and declining scrap-metal prices mean that disposal of the hulk may also prove expensive. Hence the growing number of burned-out vehicles with erased identities littering inner-city alleys and rural lay-bys.

Outstripping human evolution

It is almost impossible to find a new car that cannot exceed the British 70 mph speed limit by a considerable margin, and the ability to exceed

---

15 Negligent servicing by supposed professionals, even those working for franchised dealers, is also commonplace, like their fondness for expensive replacements and hatred of simple repairs.

16 One has to distinguish here between electronic components proper, subject not to wear but to eventual catastrophic failure, and linked mechanical components like fuel injectors and pumps, which are subject to wear, blockages and the like (not always amenable to repair). Spark plugs also deteriorate with use, although they last longer with correctly functioning electronic-ignition systems.

twice that limit is commonplace. Large luxury saloons from Mercedes, Rolls-Royce, Cadillac, BMW, Audi and Lexus have a governed maximum speed of 155 mph. Yet some countries have even lower limits than Britain – 55 mph in the US – and, in the West, only Germany has a few hundred miles of unrestricted Autobahn. Cars are made with these legally unusable levels of performance because the market believes it wants them. Yet the market is clearly content to trundle cautiously around in long queues at well below the legal limits, except on motorways or freeways, such roads being safe for almost any speed. Safe, that is, if the drivers in question are capable and disciplined enough to eliminate the need for emergency braking or sudden evasive action.[17] Few are, and most know it. Publicity given to horrendous hundred-vehicle freeway crashes keeps many drivers in a state of barely suppressed anxiety, ensuring jerky, inelegant and unpredictable driving styles that make such accidents more likely. The fact is that driving, especially in crowded road conditions, demands a continuous exercise of intellect for which drivers are seldom prepared, and which only true automobile enthusiasts can maintain without much effort. Most drivers' 'automatic pilot' is insufficiently developed to ensure safety, for they do not understand the *aesthetic* basis of the maximum-progress/minimum-stress project. Too many assume that if speed limits and the basic handling guidelines imparted for the driving test are observed, any road mishap will be someone else's fault. Not everyone understands that this is an irrelevant consideration.

The very expensive and capable Porsche Carrera is seen in quite large numbers in our cities. People with big incomes buy such vehicles, or demand them from their companies, because they are readily identifiable as serious, virile machines, are pleasant to drive and generally reliable, and have high levels of primary safety (braking, road-holding and acceleration sufficient to keep reasonably prudent drivers out of trouble). However, their very capability presents the modern corporate, largely urban driver with an unexpected problem. The Porsche's brakes have to be capable of stopping it rapidly and safely from around 175 mph (105 mph above the British overall limit). Braking systems are biased to apply more effort to the front wheels, to take advantage of a car's weight transference under braking and prevent the rear wheels from locking. In the case of the Porsche, very gentle braking only ever uses the front brakes: the rear pads fail to make contact with the discs. This allows severe corrosion of the

---

17 And their vehicles (especially, in this context, the tyres) are in sound condition.

rear discs to take place: made of soft iron or steel and exposed to road dirt, salt and moisture, discs are kept clean only by use. Soon, the proud owner of an almost new, famously well-made car may have to shell out for new rear discs, the original ones having never been used. Pussyfooting slowly around in that particular Porsche constitutes misuse by the owner. It is impossible to escape the conclusion that modern cars are more evolved than their drivers.

A population of Mr Magoos, leavened by a mercifully thin sprinkling of Mr Toads and Dukes of Hazzard, we compulsorily devote an excessive amount of working and leisure time to the inadequate maintenance and systematic misuse of automobiles.[18] Like the modern motor car itself, this situation is a synthesis of our own fantasies or pretensions and the steely, amoral calculation of the consumer industry, its avatars and allies.[19] While aware, in a way, of the criminal scale of this extravagance, we have become used to it and see it as normal. As in other contexts, the relentless tactical deployment of rationality has somehow outflanked reason.

Bricolage and dumping

Cars that would not need such frequent replacement could be produced, but we have been trained not to want them. This also appears to be true of the Third World, where roads are bad and vehicles, being rarer, are used far more intensively than in the West – putting practicality at a premium. The automobile industry has made no effort to produce appropriate vehicles for such countries (a Model T for the twenty-first century), although they are becoming large consumers of automobiles. The manufacturers present in the industrialising Third World, effectively controlled by their Japanese, American and European godfathers, produce no useful innovations. Third World buyers, still largely commercial, have to make do with slightly modified, obsolescent models, not significantly more durable than other cars, but easier to maintain thanks to their relative simplicity and freedom from electronics. The practice of block purchasing by Third World governments

18 Mr Magoo: the blind and bumbling motorist in a series of eponymous animated cartoons; Mr Toad: foolish and reckless motorist character in Kenneth Grahame's *The Wind in the Willows* (1908); *Dukes of Hazzard*: 1970s American TV series featuring the spectacular destruction of an endless series of identical bright red Dodge Chargers.
19 Nor should we forget their mistakes, sometimes beneficial to the consumer. I am thinking in particular of certain engines and car models that turn out to be more durable than the makers probably intended, although many more disappear with discreditable, profitable rapidity.

facilitates the dumping of unsuccessful models. Replacement parts, routinely overpriced in the name of profit, can also be very hard to obtain in poor countries.

Combined with intensive use and harsh road and climatic conditions, this compels Third World vehicle operators to find ingenious means of keeping their machines going, often long after they would have been scrapped in the West. That is where the Joad spirit lives on in the twenty-first century: driven by necessity, unfazed roadside mechanics in parts of Africa, Asia and Latin America plunge unhesitatingly into the smoking entrails of asthmatic vehicles to bring them back to life, with a combination of loving skill and outrageously radical cobbling. Bus operators, in particular, in poor parts of the world – the Philippines, parts of mainland Asia and Africa – proudly customise their rebuilt, much-used vehicles, and decorate them with crazed religious mottoes and slogans. But charming though 'Jeepneys' and the like seem to a Western eye, their passengers, breathing dust and exhaust fumes, would certainly prefer glass windows and air conditioning, if they were on offer. Indeed, the very need for colourful customisation, and the sort of cars produced by India's Hindustan – a lumbering nineteen-fifties Morris Oxford with an undersized nineteen-seventies Japanese engine – and the VW subsidiaries in Latin America – Beetles and early Golfs and Passats – only underline the point that the industry produces no *innovations* intended for the Third World. Despite its population, the car market here is still not thought big enough to justify special attention; it gets the leavings.

Only the rich and the corporate minority whose motoring is subsidised can be said merely to use cars. The rest of us are forced, more or less willingly, into our commerce with the automobile, and it is often a moot point who is using whom: who is really the dominant partner in our tractations with unctuous salesmen and tooth-sucking workshop foremen. For it is they who have the backing of General Motors, Exxon and the other powers that be. We are on our own. The automobile started as a toy for rich gents and then became a cheap copy of that; woe betide us, sooner or later, if we don't pay up like the cheap copies of rich gents we are assumed to be.

The strategic centrality of the automobile and its cost to owners in working time, combined with its ephemerality, will be objects of wonder to future historians. Why the numbers? Why the variety? Why the fragility, the inefficiency, the *waste*? Was the thing a baroque expedient for collecting taxes? Was its role that of a glowing fetish or idol, to keep its worshippers in a form of subjection? For it may be apparent to such historians that while ostensibly utilitarian, our attitudes to the car have about them a strong scent of the irrational.

The few who love cars, whose psychology — part Kipling and part Al Joad — is out-of-synch enough to make us comfortable with their contradictions, will not welcome the advent of practical, long-lasting, unglamorous, non-polluting, uncrashable passenger-carrying devices that exist in merely sufficient numbers, won't go very fast and do most of the driving for us. But most people will really be happier with them. Like the still-putative battery or hydrogen-fuel-cell technology which may eventually displace the internal-combustion engine, these vehicles will come — if at all — from the same makers as today's cars, who have traditionally favoured superficial adjustments and resisted fundamental change. But having encouraged us to desire the automobile as it is, it may take the industry some time to get us to embrace an alternative. Perhaps, after all, we can't get there from here.

New Left Review, 15, May–June 2002

3

AFRICA

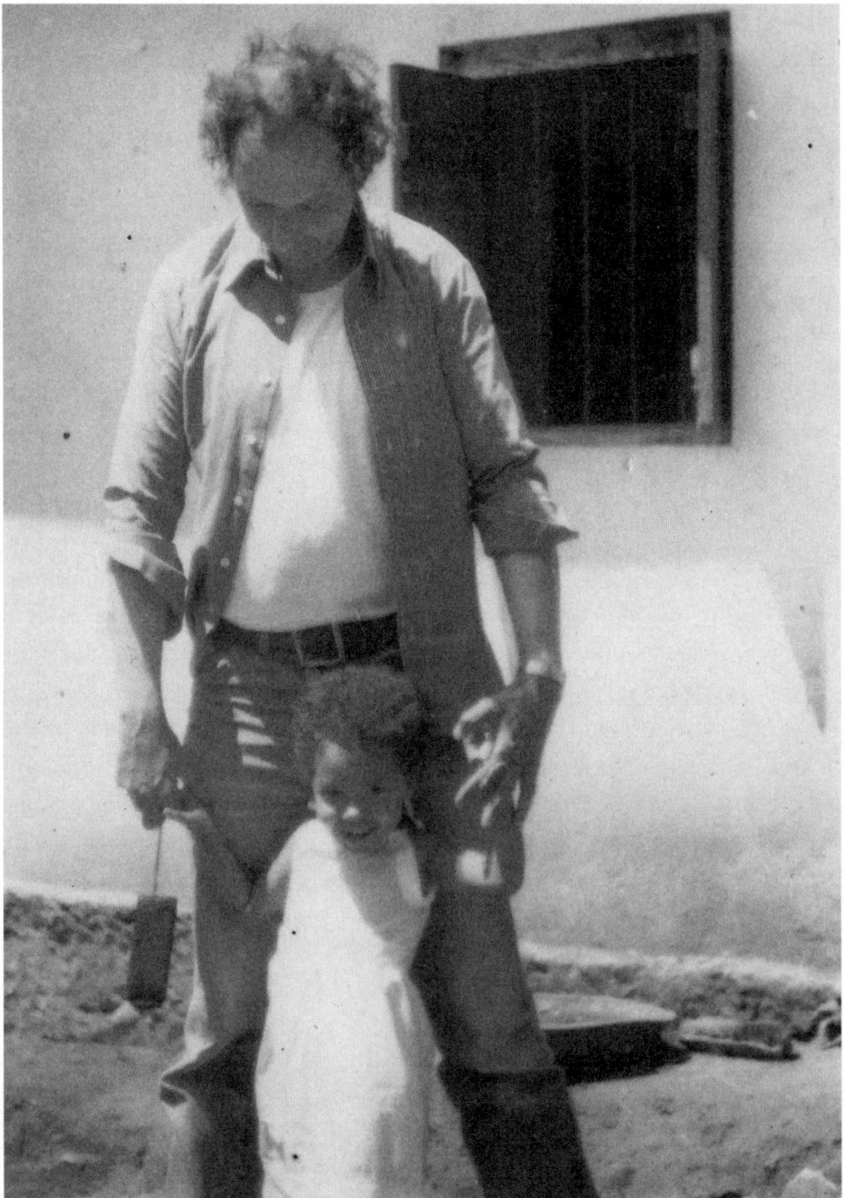

SANITISING NIGERIA'S CAPITAL

Whether the Nigerian government and its successors push through the plan to build a new Federal capital at Abuja, in the middle of the country, or not (there are other urgent demands on its limited resources), Lagos is destined to remain the commercial capital for the foreseeable future thanks (if that is the word) to its port facilities and existing industrial and commercial installations. Its discomfort and inconvenience, its potholes, traffic jams, mosquitoes, taxi fares, piles of rubbish, open drains, clamour and rudeness all strike the visitor as larger than life. The current paroxysm of road construction and building has decimated a telephone system which was already a byword for *in*-efficiency. New roads and flyovers are opening one by one, shifting the traffic jams from one place to another without diminishing them. Newspaper articles and advertisements offer cures for 'hypertension'. Whether you like the place or hate it, there is no denying its peculiar ferocity.

Some estimates now put the population of Lagos at 8 million, most of it living on the mainland and increasing daily as migrants arrive from all over the Federation in search of work or opportunity. This population and the flood of vehicles being imported since the beginning of the oil boom compete every day for space on a road system which evolved in a city less than a quarter of its present size. Apart from the odd unmarked pile of earth or block of concrete in the outside lane, the stretches of motorway opened so far – some of them new roads, some of them the result of widening schemes – can carry more than the present volume of traffic. The problem comes, as always in urban road construction, when the traffic has to leave the motorway and enter the network of minor roads where vast potholes, heavy pedestrian traffic and sheer lack of space slow it to a crawl.

Of course part of the problem at the moment is the construction work itself, which often forces vehicles to double back and clamber over high kerbs and stretches of raw earth and mud. The most ambitious part of the whole scheme, the Lagos Island ring road, is not yet complete and may not be opened until late next year. Nobody knows whether it will work when it does open: at present both the bridges over the lagoon are jammed both ways from 8 a.m. to 9 p.m. with crawling nose-to-tail traffic. Drivers amuse themselves by comparing the severity of the go-slow on the two bridges, which are clearly visible to one another. One happy effect of the perpetual crawl is that the £50-a-day business visitor paying the asking price of 15 naira (nearly £14) for a 3-mile taxi ride, and an unemployed Lagosian paying 1 kobo (8p) for the same journey in a bus, will be equally late for their appointments. On the roads of Lagos all men are equal, except for the intrepid motorcyclist who enjoys a slight advantage.

Following several years of costly and useless operations by a Canadian firm, Brazilian engineers are now grappling with the Lagos telephone system. So far no positive results are perceptible to the user; in fact the telephones are markedly worse than they were five years ago. Whole areas of Lagos are cut off from each other; some areas can make only outgoing calls, some can only receive calls, some can only communicate with other subscribers in the same district. Ministries, newspapers, advertising agencies and council offices are among the institutions currently doing without any telephone at all. Calling unannounced on a string of contacts, all of whom are out, is a curiously draining (and expensive) way of spending a working day.

Air conditioners are now becoming very numerous, while power cuts are less numerous than they were. But only the most expensive hotels are really comfortable. In the Lagos climate cold baths are tolerable for most of the year, but the water supply network is overstrained in many parts of the town and most older buildings have plumbing of 1920s rural Sicily standard: when someone turns the tap on in the yard, the shower stops. Lockable bathroom doors, toilet paper, soap and working lavatory cisterns are not universal in the smaller guest houses. For N10 a night, a visitor gets a room with a bed and perhaps an air conditioner; he may have to lobby to get his sheets changed after a week or his room swept. As elsewhere, standards vary widely. But those of delicate constitution or sensibilities, and those used to luxury, are not recommended to seek cheap lodgings in mainland Lagos.

The Lagos Mainland local government, elected at the end of last year as part of the FMG's programme of local government reforms, is now locked in battle with the Lagos state government over the division of responsibilities and funds.[1] This is one reason why nothing has been done yet about collecting refuse, which people pile on waste land or simply throw into the street. The crunch of cans and bottles under car wheels is one of the sounds of Lagos. When the state government's Environmental Sanitation Department reaches agreement, dustmen can be recruited and vehicles supplied. There is no shortage of suitable labour – parts of Lagos still employ night-soil collectors, who can be seen walking about with tubs of human

---

1 FMG refers to the federal military government.

excrement on their heads – but council officials complain that they are kept short of money by the state government. The gross neglect of the early 1970s, when human corpses were sometimes left lying in the sun for several days ('none of our trucks are working', explained a city morgue official on one occasion), no longer prevails. Today's lynch victims, who average one or two a month along the Ikorodu Road (usually people caught pilfering from traders), are removed within hours.

A major problem for most European visitors to Lagos is food, which has quadrupled in price over the last five years. Those who cannot eat hot pepper, tough beef and the strange bits of skin, fat, fish heads and so on from which Nigerians get their protein, are forced to eat 'international' dishes at high prices in expensive restaurants and the bigger hotels. If they are short of money, they will be reduced to eating groundnuts and fried plantains, assuming that snails and dried fish are too exotic for them. Star beer at 65k. a litre controlled price is one of the best deals in Nigeria (just beaten by a gallon of petrol at the same price). The problem in July and early August was to find any bottled beer at any price: rusty cans of obscure brands of metallic German lager were, however, freely available. Last year's ban on champagne imports, one of a range of sumptuary measures which also banned cars over 2½ litres capacity and expensive lace, has fairly typically convinced Lagosians that there is nothing so thrilling as champagne. A couple of bottles are now a most acceptable gift from, say, a young man to his fiancée's father. By increasing the price, illegality has simply made these goods more prestigious than ever. In July the *Daily Times* published a photograph of a 'super-obokun' – a 7-litre Mercedes 600 – driving down a Lagos street with a stern caption asking whose it could be. The answer: someone with £100,000 to spend on the monster itself plus 'punitive' 200 per cent duty.

Hard-working, proud, satirical, anxious, mostly very poor, Lagosians spend hours a day jostling through the dust and clamour of their changing city just to get to work and back. According to newspaper articles and advertisements, 'hypertension' is a major cause of heart disease in Nigeria. Like the inhabitants of other large cities, Lagosians operate in a miasma of suspicion, fear and half-suppressed rage through which humour, kindness and intelligence, greed, stupidity and brutality shine in random flashes – the common qualities of mankind. Travel writers recommend visitors to keep their tempers. This is not only impossible but useless: it is more effective to do as the Lagosians do and use polemic, satire and insults when reason and humility fail. A demented scream of IDIOT! or BASTARD! as he drives

BRICOLAGE

away will not hurt the taxi-driver's feelings and may even persuade him to lower his demands. Lagos is that sort of place. How much will it change in the next ten years? Will the traffic flow freely between trim grass verges, the telephones ring constantly, the dustmen call twice a week in newly paved back streets? A tidy efficient Lagos is hard to visualise. Of course it would be more healthy and comfortable for the mass of Lagosians, who sorely need some improvement. But for the occasional visitor a sanitised city might turn out just a shade boring.

c. 1977 (publication details unknown)

LETTER FROM ACCRA
A bit of transnational gossip

Armel Grant Cousine

Trade goods stand before the security check at Murtala Muhammed Airport, queuing for the owners who lounge watchfully in nearby chairs. Crates of beer, corned beef, sardines; big cardboard cartons labelled Sony and National Panasonic; Omo, Tide, Lux; toothpaste and toilet soap. Just before the flight is called there is a silent, ferocious rush for position, then a dash for seats. The plane is packed. A girl slides into the seat next to me. 'Hello, Grant,' she says. 'I'm Gladys. I meet you in Fela house when Jimmy Cliff was there.' She heaves a crate of Long Life into position and puts her feet on it. At that moment a fat lady struggles past carrying many things. Without a word she adds a jeroboam of Vat 69 to the beer. I put my feet on it. People are stuffing things into the overhead luggage bins. There is Omo on the floor. With a faint cry, a professor from Abidjan vanishes under a shower of sardine tins. Ghana Airways' Friday evening Lagos-Accra flight is getting itself together.

Packed to the roof with people and things, the plane takes 6 miles to reach takeoff. As the vast glittering sprawl of evening Lagos revolves round the port wingtip, Gladys gives a moan of terror and clutches my arm. We agree to share a taxi into Accra from the airport. I fill in her landing card (all except the signature, which she gets another man to do). At Accra, I wait an hour and a half for Gladys to pass through customs. The problem is not Gladys but a colossal pile of consumer goods and basic necessities which she has stashed in the luggage compartment. Eventually she emerges, like a nineteenth-century explorer, leading a long file of porters.

The problem repeats itself at the taxi rank, where Gladys's property fills three cars (there are only two left by this time). I begin to regret my acquaintanceship with her when the army enters the picture. 'Thirty cedis,' the soldiers are saying. Gladys makes a long speech, the essential word of which is 'twenty'. After prolonged negotiations, Gladys, the vital supplies, four soldiers, two porters, my suitcase and I are rushed to a remote suburb of Accra in an army truck for C22, looking like some kind of CIA special operation.

Like the naira, the cedi started life as ten bob. Now it is worth either 50 kobo or under 20 kobo – depending on how you get your cedis. Whether that C22, and prices in Accra in general, seem a lot or a little depends on your point of view. At the official rate of exchange C22 is worth about N12, on the black market about N4. Either way, taxi fares are very low compared with Lagos, partly because of the excellent road system. But all food, consumer durables and necessities like soap are very expensive — in cedis. A labourer can earn as little as C4 a day. When, a few weeks ago, the price of kenkey (a sourdough dumpling, a staple dish in parts of Ghana) approached 50 pesewas a ball, the poorest strata of the working population in the cities faced not hardship but actual crisis. A heavy-handed government move to enforce a controlled price for kenkey drove the sellers off the streets for a week. The problem was the scarcity, and consequent high price, of the maize from which kenkey is made.

The government blames the traders for the price inflation, accusing them of hoarding and exacting unreasonable profits. The traders blame the government, accusing it of not doing enough to ensure essential supplies and promote long-term growth. Both sides have a point. But it is well known that traders charge what the market will bear. Price controls only work if supplies are adequate. If distribution is carried out through traders, it simply stops when the traders can no longer make an adequate profit. Gladys — and all the pretty, civil, hard-working Gladyses, Bessies and Comforts of this charming city — are realists. They do not expect overnight fortunes; trading is a living and a way of life. It is simply that airline excess baggage is not a cheap way of transporting low-price commodities. This fact is reflected in the marketplace, to the dismay of Ghanaians whose salaries are very low by Nigerian standards.

Ghana's real problem, of course, is its vulnerability to the effects of world inflation, resulting in part from the heavy foreign debt left by the government's predecessors. The present government's Operation Feed Yourself scheme — or farming projects connected with it — has achieved more (in a rather longer period) than Nigeria's Operation Feed the Nation. Agricultural production has improved and Ghana is now self-sufficient in rice. But maize is another matter and during this year's May, June and July — always lean months for food — prices began their familiar spiral. In this context, the government's ban on food imports began to seem premature as city workers faced starvation in the long-suffering manner characteristic of Ghanaians. Kenkey is now back down to 30 pesewas a ball — three times what people are used to paying, but less than it was. The government recently denied rumours that 20,000 tons of Canadian maize given as aid and intended as poultry food had been sold to kenkey makers at a low price. So the price reduction has been achieved in some other, unspecified way. Kenkey seems to taste *grittier* than it used to, but at least its colour is normal again, having lost the lurid yellow tinge of last month.

Just before leaving Lagos I noticed that the hideous and dangerous concrete fence posts down the middle of the widened Ikorodu Road were being joined up by what looked like twenty strands of heavy barbed wire to a height of twelve feet. Doubtless this is intended to hamper pedestrian traffic and ease the flow of vehicles. But has anyone considered what would happen to a motorcyclist unlucky enough to be thrown into this fence? Instant suiya. Are people so anxious to rehabilitate the slum that they don't mind turning it into a concentration camp?

When you're in it, Lagos seems a nightmare: grim, noisy and garish but with a curious dream-like quality induced by the incessant delays and failures resulting from congested roads and malfunctioning telephones. When you've been away for a week – when the ringing has died out of your ears and your giant mosquito bites have begun to fade – it starts to beckon like a glittering dream of energy, of *something happening* in Africa. 'Just come from Lagos? Then you must appreciate us,' said an Accra acquaintance with a smile. But young Ghanaians brave endless bureaucracy and hassling to get passports, visas and foreign exchange vouchers to come there, even buying black market nairas at C6 each, not just to trade, but to come and see the legendary place, to live there and acquire its dubious skills. 'There's money there,' they say. But that isn't the whole story. People go to great cities simply because they are there, to see if what they've heard is true.

We all want Lagos to be cleaned up. Or do we? Perhaps its vast unconcerned squalor is a crucial part of its particular piquancy. It is difficult to visualise a clean, efficient, well-finished Lagos. Like the pepper in its food, perhaps we can only enjoy the place as it does us some sort of minor but permanent harm.

12 August 1977 (publication details unknown)

ANARCHY IN VITRO: UGANDA, JULY 1980

In 1980 I spent eleven days trying to cover the election being organised to decide who was going to run Uganda when the Tanzanians, who had overthrown the tyrant Idi Amin, finally left. Curiosity about a country I knew only from secondary sources was one reason for my visit. Another was the difficulty of crossing by road from Kenya to Tanzania which were on poor terms. Uganda served as a sort of airlock or stepping stone.

There was no government. The country was being run, if that is the word, by one Paulo Muwanga who was trusted by the Tanzanians and through associates controlled security in the capital and the populous south of the country. Visible authority consisted of Ugandan troops, red-eyed and scruffy, disposed about Kampala in places like the steps of the central post office. Elsewhere some gunmen were in civvies, so you couldn't tell whether they were troops or just villains.

The main technique for maintaining security seemed to be random firing at night. Few people were being killed and the firing was known as 'popcorn', but it was thought dangerous to go outside after the 9 p.m. curfew, which meant in practice after dusk at about seven. It was immediately apparent that these conditions would make the election a farce, and almost as immediately that that was the whole point: Tanzania wanted Milton Obote's Uganda People's Congress (UPC) to win the election, so it was going to, but the Ugandans were against it. So a free and fair election could not be allowed.

All the money printed under Amin's superb governance had resulted in fairly steep inflation. Officially the Ugandan shilling was more or less at parity with the Kenyan one, but buying it at that price would make Uganda unaffordable. There was a system though, explained to me in Nairobi. At the minor border crossing I was going to use, the causeway between the Kenyan and Ugandan posts was haunted by money traffickers. I should buy money from them at the proper black market rate and enter Uganda carrying it, totally illegally. But it would be all right. Everyone did it. You had to.

The policeman in the corner of my eye was about eighteen; uniform starched, shoes polished, looking as if butter wouldn't melt in his mouth. He asked me very politely to step out of the customs queue and handed my passport to a group of soldiers lounging under a nearby tree among a litter of weapons. They were scruffy by Kenyan standards: special forces, no joke at all. The officer needed a shave and carried no badges of rank, but his manner had Sandhurst overtones. Why was I going in there? I listed a few reasons. He gave my passport back and flicked a scornful forefinger in dismissal.

Emerging from Kenya into no man's land under the midday equatorial sun, I wished I had travelled expensively by air. Parked trucks lined the 400 yards of causeway to the Uganda frontier post. Where were the money changers? Lugging my heavy suitcase I set off down the empty road. A few moments later a man appeared from between two lorries and fell into step with me. Others joined us with henchmen, one of whom shouldered my case to leave my hands free. In a growing throng we straggled down the hot crown of the road noisily exchanging wads of illegal Kenyan and Ugandan money. The first guy took a couple of hundred bob at nine to one. Presently another offered ten to one. As the ramshackle barbed-wire gates of Uganda drew nearer, a third panicked and offered the real rate of twelve to one. Then they melted away. Twenty yards from the gates the porter handed me the case, pocketed his fee and vanished too.

A well-pressed uniform beckoned from the immigration shack. Passport, flick, flick, visa, OK. What was I doing here? How interesting. He was a frequent reader of *Africa* journal. Doubtless he had read my articles. The world needed to be told about Uganda's difficulties. He was a large, slow, benign-looking man. Did I, by the way, have any Ugandan currency?

The rules of the financial system required me to deny the mass of banknotes that bulged in my jacket pockets, over a thousand pounds or under a hundred depending on your point of view. Still, I could hardly fail to notice that the open window beside the officer overlooked the causeway, empty now, stretching away to Kenya in the distance; so his casual question as to whether I was in possession of any Ugandan currency gave me slight pause. As I opened my mouth to utter a whey-faced denial, a man's voice rose from somewhere behind the building in a prolonged cry. Apparently he was singing, a wild rural wail with Asian-sounding semitones; no, too tuneless, must be an enraged shout. After a second or so the cry resolved itself into an unmistakable scream of agony or terror.

'No,' I muttered at the end of it, appalled. 'Not really.'

'Not really?' The immigration man smiled encouragingly. He had all the time in the world.

'No. Er ... no.'

'No Ugandan currency at all? You will need some.'

'No. Not really.'

'Not really?'

'That's right. I mean I've got a few shillings someone gave me in Nairobi. Just a few shillings.'

'Just a few shillings?' The smile had gone but the manner remained avuncular, like that of an old-fashioned West End magistrate dealing with a harmless case of aristocratic tipsiness. Another desolate scream, impossibly long, shook the thin, hot air. 'You do realise that import and export of Ugandan currency are forbidden?'

'Really? I thought just a few shillings, couple of hundred ... I mean technically, er, perhaps, but nobody warned me that ... er.'

'We have very serious economic troubles here.' Elbows on the desk, the immigration man shook his head slowly with an air of shocked disappointment. 'We don't expect people like *you* to do these things. How can the economy recover when there is illegal currency traffic?' His eyes shone with triumphant satisfaction. 'You have sterling?'

'Travellers' cheques. A few pounds in cash.'

'I think you want to change ten pounds, cash, now, at the official rate. You will need some money.' I yielded up a tenner and received in exchange a few dog-eared notes which I folded and put away as if they were worth something. They amounted to half the official rate, but the value difference was negligible although the small fraud added another layer to a complex transaction. Behind the charade of currency exchange we both knew that my tenner was a not too severe on-the-spot fine, not as one might suppose for illegal possession of currency — that was part of the system — but for being gormless enough to admit it. The disquieting howls of agony supplied a bonus layer of background colour to the whole artistic composition. The immigration man had every reason to look satisfied.

'You are welcome to Uganda. We need people to understand our difficulties. Please tell the truth about us.'

'Of course. Thank you.' I rose to go. Another bellow. 'I hope you don't mind my asking, but is there some kind of, er, *prison* here?'

The immigration man's face broke into a huge joyful smile. 'A prison, of course, there is a prison. This is a frontier.' Chuckling like Santa Claus, he gestured towards the motor park. 'You will find a taxi there to take you to Kampala. But first you must go through customs.'

Customs! At my look of dismay the chuckle evolved into an open laugh.

Customs was a low pile of earth in an angle of the wire fence near the gate into the motor park. Both officers looked about thirty: a man in military fatigues, a barefoot woman in a thin cotton dress. Well-worn Kalashes lay on the ground within easy reach. They were processing a local villager coming the other way. He stood wordless, eyes downcast, hands away from his sides, face closed and stiff with anxiety, while the woman went rapidly and carefully through his bundle of possessions and the male officer rummaged intimately in his trouser pockets. As I arrived he brought out and unfolded a tightly packed Kenyan hundred-shilling note. He re-folded it, put it in his own pocket and gave the local a shove. 'Fool!' he barked. Finding nothing of value in the bundle, the woman flung its contents on the ground out of the way.

Both officers turned to me. Shit! Fuck! I suppose the sudden stench of bourgeois terror was not unknown to those two badasses ... the woman went rapidly through my case. Each gave my face a half-second glance but they did not look in, or even at, my pockets. I was protected. The smile was still glimmering 50 yards away in the window of the immigration shack. The customs officers darted about, quick and aware, speaking in stressed dalek-like monosyllables apt for giving orders. 'What is this?' Typewriter. 'Open.' The woman flicked through the papers inside, rummaged through my clothes. I felt like a pet pekinese being given the once-over by a couple of foxhounds. Soon they lost interest. 'Go.' Like the poor robbed villager I had to re-pack my possessions under their distant foxhounds' gaze.

Even outside the free fire zone, the empty semicircle around the platoon manning the gate, the motor park had a subdued air, lacking the noise and gaiety usual in such places. This un-African quietness was the exhausted concentration of people whose daily lives had become complicated, dangerous obstacle courses demanding all available intellect, wisdom, endurance, courage and luck, and who had been conditioned to avoid drawing attention to themselves by many frightening brushes with untrained, undisciplined, sometimes very wicked armed men from wholly foreign (although Ugandan) cultures. There was no competitive throng of touts and freelance informants, but eventually one sidled discreetly up. Kampala, OK, there is a car, no problem.

It was a dark blue Peugeot 504 estate, luxury workhorse of the African road, a good one too, shiny outside with a clean interior, on hire to a couple of guys from Kampala. With a driver to match, a solid, competent citizen with all the necessary languages and a courteous but taciturn manner. He would take me if it was OK with them. We negotiated a fare, a steep forty quid or a very reasonable three, depending on how you looked at it.

The people who had chartered the car reappeared and gave their permission. They looked like smugglers, but smuggling in one form or another was an almost universal activity in and around Uganda at that time. I got in the back and we snaked for an hour or two around the jungly backroads of eastern Uganda. At a big rural market, eerily quiet in the Ugandan manner, I waited with the driver under a tree as the two guys went about their business. There was a scuffle in the crowd nearby, one or two shouts, some excitement, someone being arrested or lynched, I couldn't see. Dust hung in the sunlit air. A policeman, uniformed but unarmed and accompanied by a woman and two children, came up and started arguing with the driver.

A messenger from the two smugglers told the driver we could go. The policeman installed his family in the back of the car and tried to get in the front seat, but the driver evicted him and told me to sit there. European travellers sometimes imagine that they are given first-class treatment on the road because Africans are naturally deferential, or because they themselves have a naturally distinguished manner. In reality there are two reasons: they are likely to have paid a higher fare than anyone else, and they can be identified easily at a distance as probable citizens of aid-giving countries with efficient bureaucracies. This makes them into magic protective talismans especially useful in zones of corruption, banditry or civil disorder (provided things have not gone too far downhill). A paleface in the vehicle can make the more rational sort of bandit, soldier or policeman think twice before opening fire or making unreasonable demands. Experience has shown that some countries can twist the arms of the most languid and mercenary generals, the maddest, most radical warlords. Retribution for mistakes with foreigners may not be instant, but has a remorseless quality when it comes.

The privileges accorded to these travellers because of their relative wealth and glowing pink faces are not resented by their fellow-travellers who share the benefits. Africans are aware that back-road travel on their continent is uncomfortable and arduous for the inexperienced. Generous help and a courteous welcome are nearly always extended to the inoffensive stranger as a matter of course. It is the way people are brought up; anyway that is how it looks to me. Not everyone agrees. A friend of mine who used to be a minister in an African government laughed bitterly when I commented on this. 'They're just scared of you,' he said. 'You'd see another side of them if they didn't fear the consequences.' The implication, shocking from such a quarter, that Africans are cold-blooded cut-throats restrained only by fear, may have had something to do with my friend's experience of government, which included several undeserved years in jail.

As we cruised south-west towards Jinja the policeman complained tediously about the country's economic condition, with special reference to his own pitiable, easily relieved state. At a petrol station I stretched my legs while the driver negotiated out of sight round the back. A three-ton truck with its load secured under lashed-down tarpaulin pulled in, coming the other way. A pallid unshaven European in horn-rimmed spectacles got out of the passenger side of the cab and went into the office. When he came out he nodded to me and we chatted for a minute. He was a French priest heading back to his mission further north. Things were pretty bad, but they had been a lot worse. Even so, for the Ugandans ... the economy. And the insecurity ... it was worse for some than for others. He didn't want to exaggerate. Hack-inquisitive, reptile-rude, I jerked my chin at the back of his truck. The whole country was in a parlous state but parts of it were utterly devastated. Drought, war, rotten politics and free automatic weapons had whipped the economy off Karamoja like a worn sheet off a bed, sending starvation reports tumbling unnoticed through the inside pages and late-night current affairs TV.

'What are you carrying, food?'

The priest giggled. 'No. Bicycles.'

At Jinja, near a weather-stained, bullet-pocked wooden notice proclaiming the spot as the Source of the Nile, the car nosed to a halt in the middle of an excited armed crowd. A young man in a Mickey Mouse tee shirt leaned in through the passenger-side window and shouted a few sentences across me at the driver, the muzzle of the Kalashnikov slung across his chest pointing straight up my left nostril. Moving my head discreetly out of line with it I tried without success to suck my teeth audibly in the universal African signal of strong disapproval short of outright hostility. 'What was he saying?' I asked as we drove away. The driver shrugged. I had been sleepy but felt suddenly talkative. 'I suppose his gun was loaded?' The driver nodded soberly. 'One up the spout, safety off, that sort of thing? He was picking my nose with it.' The driver laughed. The policeman had gone very quiet, but now he resumed his monotonous keening about cash. Glancing at me out of the corner of his eye, the driver sucked his teeth with enviable loudness and clarity.

The sun was in our eyes. As it sank below the tree-tops we slowed for another road block. One of the troops manning it looked at his watch and waved us on vigorously. The driver looked at his watch. I looked at my watch, then at the driver. 'No problem,' he said, foot hard down. In lengthening shadow we dropped the policeman and his family. He drew the driver aside. Watching their quiet, vehement dialogue through the windscreen I wondered who was going to pay whom, but no money changed hands. The driver came back looking thoughtful. 'Ah! These people,' he said. 'They rob everyone but say that they cannot pay.'

'Bit of a shit, I thought. Not too bright.'

'One tyre for this car costs eighty thousand shillings. Battery, same. If you find it. Life is hard here now.' He glanced at me anxiously to see if I understood. 'Four passengers, no fare.' We were slowing down through deserted-looking suburbs towards a fading pale pink sky. 'Kampala. You see? No problem.' My hand went into my pocket of its own accord and bunged him another hundred. 'Make it two-fifty.' Ten bob is nothing to the captain of a well-found all-purpose Peugeot road cruiser. I counted out the rest, hardly denting the wad. 'Thank you. You say you want Speke Hotel? I will take you there.'

We raced through emptying streets, an occasional hurrying vehicle or figure, clumps of lounging uniforms. Better-than-average architecture without the usual patches of bidonville, a dash of Bournemouth, a hint of Miami, a soupçon of Cannes. Genteel but with a dark look, hurt, bruised, badly in need of maintenance. A knot of troops shouted from the steps of a building as we shot past. 'Post office,' the driver muttered, flinching visibly. Seconds later he stopped on a steep corner looking across a length of ornamental dual carriageway into a pretty little park. Wasting no time he took my case out of the back, put it on the ground and pointed to the wall beside us. 'This is the Speke Hotel. Go inside now and ask if they have a room. They will look after you.' He shook my hand, got into the car and looked at me gravely through the open window. 'Go inside. Do not go … back there. Take care.' He did a brisk three-point turn and, lights off, faded discreetly into the gathering dusk.

In the near-darkness of reception the Speke desk staff shook their heads. No way, forget it, polite and bemused. The woman clerk suggested I try the other three hotels set around the park, but the two men disagreed, saying the journey would be too risky. As I needed a room the sporting lobby won. I left my case behind the desk and the woman showed me how to get from one hotel to the other with minimum exposure, crossing the road from one garden to another and stooping behind the central reservation between the Speke and the Imperial 'so that they can't see you from the post office'. Over the next week or so I became used to this furtive after-dark slink-and-dash between the hotels, but the Ugandans refrained from recommending it although a lot of them did it. I never saw a soul, nor was I seen, but the Ugandans insisted — and if they didn't know, who did? — that safety could not be guaranteed out of doors after dark.

None of the hotels had a room. The curious sensation, unwelcome but familiar, of being in a strange place with nowhere to put my things, no door to retreat behind and wash the dust of the ripply equatorial blacktop off my face, no bed to lie on and collect my thoughts, came down in a miasma of fatigue and depressed anxiety. I had a contact at the Speke but he could not be found. The bar was filling up but I felt too tired and hungry to face it alone. Night had fallen. The hotel staff were reassuring in a burned-out, offhand sort of way. 'Well, you can't go out now. If your friend does not come back you can stay here in reception. Or sleep in the bar.'

I sat glumly in an armchair staring into space, a technique known to experienced African travellers. After half an hour my contact appeared. He was a friend of a Kenyan journalist friend, a neat bearded Ugandan working I believe for the Ministry of Information. He cast a kindly, weary eye over my travel-stained clothing, barely respectable to start with, and looked at his watch. 'It's a good idea to eat early. Let's go and have some dinner, then we can have a drink. You do drink? There's nothing else to do here after dark.' We went into the dining room where people were already eating under dim blue light. 'These days,' he added apologetically as we sat down, 'we eat just to stay alive. The food isn't very good.'

Plantains cooked at home can be more than satisfactory, but somehow they never were at the Speke although it was a classy establishment. Morale is important where cooking is concerned. Usually there was fish to go with the dubious Speke matooke, less often meat, and very little by way of other vegetables, sauces or puddings. Somehow the blue semi-darkness made everything taste worse. The food in the other hotels was just as bad, and the big dining room at the Imperial was famous for the size and boldness of the rats that lurked in its shadows at mealtimes. I never saw a rat in the Speke, and tried hard not to wonder why.

'I'll have a word with the manager,' my contact said after a while. 'All the rooms are occupied, but sometimes people go upcountry. You might be able to stay in one of their rooms.'

I asked hackish questions: what was going to happen in the election, why was there a curfew, when would normal life be able to resume, with stable prices and safe streets? Who were the bad guys? Who were the good guys? Over the next ten days I was to discover that there were no clear answers to most of these questions. The Ugandans would look tired, or shrug, or laugh, or make contradictory assertions, or do all of these things. It was quite simple. It was incredibly complicated. It was bloody nasty. It could hardly get any worse — indeed it had improved — but the prognosis was not good. Being a civil servant and therefore attached to the regime, such as it was, by a substantial umbilical cord, my companion avoided clear, polemical, quotable statements. He was decently informative within bounds, but I felt myself giving the familiar inward sigh of the hack in a strange country, for whom every piece of information raises a hundred new questions. 'If you want to talk politics, the bar's the place,' he said as he signed the chit. 'All the enthusiasts go there.'

Actually a lot of them left at about nine. Every night at curfew time the crowd would thin out as people with vehicles, bodyguards or some other form of *laissez-passer*, people who lived nearby, went home leaving a hard core of Speke guests and the more daring elements from the other three hotels. My contact introduced me around. Everyone in the place was shouting about politics. My naive request for a beer made people double up with laughter: apparently the amber electrolyte-restorer was as rare and almost as expensive as champagne in more fortunate capitals. When found, nearly always in unlabelled bottles, it was weak and unpleasantly weird-tasting. What people drank at the Speke was triples of hard stuff: unknown brands of German gin, Japanese cognac, Danish whisky. A shot about the size of a pub double cost 30 shillings. You would order a triple, give the barman a 100 shillings and listen to his well-worn routine about the shortage of ten-shilling notes for change. The result was quite a large drink for a fiver (or less than half a sheet depending on your point of view). Sometimes the bar had 'government' (as opposed to moonshine) waragi, a gin made from bananas, at fifteen shillings a shot; but this half-price drink, no nastier than the others, vanished fast and was seldom available. People often had headaches in the morning which they blamed on the altitude.

At eleven, to a chorus of protests, the barman pulled down the shutters. The conversational roar moved into the lounge and gradually evaporated as people left, some for their rooms upstairs, some for the adrenalin-boosting nightly scamper across the ill-lit blacktop through ornamental shrubs and ugly chain-link fences to the other three hotels. Soon there were only two other people left in the lounge, Ugandan diplomats who lived at the Speke while awaiting new postings. I was later to know them better, but at this stage they made little impression on my fuddled brain. My nascent collection of buzzwords, widely asserted views, new names and so forth whirling about in the updraught from the furnace of industrial-grade ethyl alcohol blazing in my viscera, I retrieved my belongings from behind the desk and asked the night clerk for sheets and a pillow.

Just as the diplomats were saying good night, there was a flurry outside the front door and half a dozen people came in. The diplomats sprang instantly to sober life and followed them into the bar, where the disgruntled barman reopened the shutters and turned the lights back on. I looked outside. Clearly the new arrival was someone of importance: several armed, uniformed men were guarding a black Mercedes and two grey Land Rovers, all new. A moment later one of the diplomats beckoned me into the bar. Sitting in a corner, wedged between two fleshy youngish women, was a large, bullet-headed, heavily built man whose face bore an expression of genial brutality strongly reminiscent, like his physique, of the deposed Idi Amin. He invited me expansively to join his party for a drink. Two uniformed bodyguards sat a little apart from the group, bashfully silent, weapons on their knees. The diplomats' manner brought the phrase 'dancing attendance' vividly to mind: they were conversing with the big guy, listening to his opinions with flattering deference, laughing at his jokes, calling for more drinks. Having nothing to contribute to the conversation, and being somewhat the worse for wear, I said nothing. The women giggled. The bodyguards sternly sipped glasses of orange squash.

Like almost everything said in the Speke bar at that time the conversation was generally concerned with politics, but although it was in English I couldn't even follow it. In any case I was in no condition to take professional advantage of this chance meeting, assuming such advantage was there to be taken. I have always lacked the stomach for the hard-nosed, piss-on-the-president's-boot journalistic approach. Unsteadily shtum, I waited with courteous resignation for everyone to vacate my bedroom. Nevertheless various unimportant details engraved themselves on my memory.

Some of these concern the personalities of the two diplomats K and M. Both were upper-class intellectuals from the cluster of traditional monarchies covering the populous southern half of Uganda, but they were not at all similar. K, the older of the two, was wafer-thin and reptilian in appearance, always sharply dressed, a clever, sophisticated man with a brilliant wit, sometimes comic, sometimes cutting, always to the point. These qualities were now somewhat muted as he exercised the courtier's skills of deference and shameless flattery. His every movement expressed playfully ecstatic submission, and he made frequent use of the honorific 'Mr Minister', sometimes two or three times in the same sentence. A British bigwig, even a very dim one, would have suspected satirical intent, but Africa is different. The big guy clearly noticed nothing unusual, but after a while he interrupted with a pleased frown: 'What's all this Mr Minister business? Jesus! Just call me Chris.'

Since there was no constitutional government there were, in fact, no ministers in Uganda at that time. Nevertheless there were people who exercised ministerial functions, sometimes of a mysterious nature, and some of them enjoyed power which, under the circumstances, was more than ministerial. Chris Rwakasisi was one of this select band. I have to this day no idea what his official function was, but in any case he was really doing something else, something occult to do with security. Undeterred, K went on Mr Ministering. 'Chris' obviously enjoyed — perhaps expected — these references to his power, which probably covered life and death for most of his compatriots. After a while he attempted a statement of the regime's benevolent social aims, got bogged down in qualifying clauses, and irritably cut himself off. Whatever abilities had given him three vehicles, two women, seven armed minders and immunity to the random murder believed to stalk Kampala's streets at night, they did not include wide learning, verbal skills or any obvious tenderness for his fellow citizens. Nevertheless as his statement ran onto the rocks everyone nodded with sage approval.

K left the bar and returned a minute or two later looking positively joyful. He approached the table with a gait midway between marching and prancing, stood to attention with fragile elegance and announced happily: 'Mr Minister! There is a lot of firing outside.'

There was in fact a faint unthreatening sound in the distance. Even as he spoke it stopped. The minister looked pleased too. 'It is just popcorn. Call me Chris, for Christ's sake.'

The other diplomat had become rather drunk. Although still polite, M was not content to flatter and listen like his mature colleague. It seemed he held strong views which he wanted to be considered. So far the minister had ignored him and brushed him aside, but now the drinks had made him insistent. K with smooth and patient cunning would change the subject, and M would circle back to it in the dogged lobotomised fashion of people in bars late at night. Eventually he managed to say something that caused the minister's smile to fade and take on a wounded, thoughtful, alarming quality. The women had stopped giggling.

After a moment of panicky, electric silence, K exploded into a manic frenzy of placating and distracting body language. All attention focused on him as he pranced about criticising his colleague and pouring out an avalanche of explanations and jokes. M was still a foolish young man, he drank too much, he was an idealist, he had been away for a long time, he thought he had become English, Mr Minister, he did not understand the way things were, he was thoroughly irresponsible and not nearly careful enough about what he said, let this be a lesson to him, he was going to be very sorry when he came to himself, he was simply not worth the attention of a person of consequence, look at him, Mr Minister, he was feeling ashamed already ...

Some danger signal, probably K's frenetic activity, did seem to have penetrated M's somewhat damaged consciousness, and he mumbled an apology. K went on clowning and caressing. Slowly the minister relaxed. 'OK,' he said after a while. Fifteen minutes later he got up, shook hands all round and led his party out to the waiting convoy, K at his side, murmuring into his ear. Doors slammed and the convoy drove off into the night. K came back into the lounge, stared soberly at his protégé and shook his head in disbelief.

'What are we going to do with you? How long will you live if I am not here to look after you?' He looked at me and shook his head again. 'What can we do with this man?'

It took some hours for everyone to vacate my bedroom, and longer for me to get to sleep. I had been reading about Uganda for years, following (as closely as possible from media sources and hacks' gossip) the country's descent into grotesque, cruel anarchy. I had been repelled by the crude way the British media welcomed Idi Amin, a former NCO in the King's African Rifles, when he overthrew the *soi-disant* socialist president Milton Obote, and my instinctive prejudice against General (as he now was) Amin was soon justified by the torrent of blood and idiocy he unleashed. I had many arguments with African friends who believed that if the Western media were against Amin (for they had soon corrected their mistake), he couldn't be all bad: things were rough in Africa, can't make an omelette without breaking eggs, bloodshed probably much exaggerated, Amin was a rough diamond but did things the African way, and so on. Africans do have a point when they reason like this, but it is not a very useful point at the best of times, and one that often paints them untidily into corners. In this case it made them insist that Amin's ghoulish clowning was really a series of important, radical points tellingly put across. I could never make these people admit that apart from his wasteful attitude to Ugandan lives, Amin gave enormous help and comfort to racists of the old-fashioned kind. They had a point here too: the really threatening racists were not like that any more, they were modern, they were people who did not even know they were racists. But it was a point that obscured other truths, ones I thought the Africans should not allow to be obscured.

I was glad Amin had been removed and interested in the efforts I assumed would now be made to restore normality. During the day I had already realised that this was no simple matter. Now, lying sleepless in the Speke bar before dawn, I wondered whether it was possible at all.

Reading and writing about things is pretty undemanding. One soon gets used to the procession of horrors. Amin had set the troops to killing each other, he had undermined the economy by running businesses into the ground and printing money, he had murdered civil servants, academics, journalists, generals, judges, bishops. These acts were wrong in themselves and their numbers made them monstrous, but practice soon taught one to consider them with hardly a flicker of genuine feeling, mind fixed on the hack's twin objectives of insight and the *mot juste*.

Yes, reading and talking were one thing, but actually being there was another. The wash of raw, tired emotion came through subtle but oppressive, like low-frequency hum in the blob of magnetic flux round a high-voltage transformer. Terror, fatigue, hopelessness and unjustified violence had soaked into the concrete of the buildings and was clinging there. The country was haunted by echoes of evil behaviour; its memory, its anticipation, its attendant despair filling the ether with a sort of psychic white noise, inaudible but painfully loud. People walked with their heads sunk between tensely lifted shoulders, like infantry advancing into heavy fire or farm labourers trudging to work through a sleet-laden gale. Drinkers in the Speke bar were noisy and outspoken, as if by special licence, but elsewhere people tended to mutter, their smiles broken and scared, their eyes never still. This petty-criminal body language, the residue of a recent past so traumatic that it still seemed more real than the present, was disconcerting until you got used to it. One day a passer-by fell into step and engaged me in conversation as I walked along a road somewhere uphill from the hotel. Like other Ugandans he was apprehensive about the future, but he wanted me to understand that things had been a lot worse. He pointed to an agreeable pink-washed villa nestling in a grove of trees a couple of hundred yards away, like something you might see on the fringes of Hampstead Heath. 'That house belonged to the State Research Bureau,' he said. 'They used to take people there. You could hear them from here. Being interrogated.'

Next day the hotel lent me a room normally occupied by someone who was travelling 'upcountry'. Its balcony overlooked the road in front of the hotel and the park opposite. The vertical concrete box of the International (built under the Obote government and named after him the Apollo, then renamed by Amin) dominated the view to the right. In a shack across the road, 50 yards away, its water pump thumped and whined through the night. The furniture, a little battered but in sound condition, included a non-functioning telephone and a large broken-backed Koran.[2] There was no water in the pipes to the shower and wash-basin, but an old whisky bottle held drinking water, and the hotel servants were supposed to refill a plastic two-gallon can for washing purposes. They often forgot, but I soon discovered the location of the working tap in the back yard.

I set to work, hoping to arrive at a plausible general view of what was going on. I sought interviews with ministers, party leaders or spokesmen, people of that sort. Nobody on this level had anything substantive to add to what I had learned the first evening in the Speke bar. Uganda was worse than broke, it was devastated. It needed hundreds of millions of pounds in aid just to begin to set it on its feet. It needed investment too. Education, health, housing, transport: nothing was functioning properly. Everything had been looted and spoiled. Uganda needed money. Money and time.

The main political story was the coming election, which was to launch the country back into normality by deciding what kind of government it would have. But unless the voters could come and go at will, without fearing that they might be shot at random, it was going to be difficult to hold an election that people in general would see as free and fair. When and how, I asked everyone, was security going to be established and the curfew lifted? Who was responsible for the popcorn, with or without casualties (for it seemed these were not numerous around Kampala at that time, although they were not unknown)?

The answers, such as they were (for a lot of people just shrugged, or stared wide-eyed at a visitor so naive and ignorant that he could ask such a question apparently expecting an informative answer), fell into two broad

---

2 Substituted for Gideon's Bible, I surmised, on the occasion of a state visit by the Libyan dictator Gaddafi who patronised Amin for a while. The Libyans were said to have been surprised by the Field Marshal's — as he had by then become — direct and urgent demands for largish sums of hard currency in return for his conversion to Islam. They shrewdly withheld the cash but sent troops, many of whom they later had to ransom from the Tanzanians.

categories. Government officials, those most likely to have the facts and figures, to be working on restoring security, were very coy and giggled a lot. They said there were a lot of bandits about, former Amin troops, people like that, who had got hold of weapons and even uniforms. They were responsible for the insecurity. It was difficult to bring them under control because the country lacked means. Later, after the election, if enough financial and technical aid was forthcoming, then perhaps ... This official view was shared by all representatives of Milton Obote's UPC including Obote himself who I later interviewed; when I questioned him on the subject of establishing order, he was quite unable to contain his mirth.

The other answer, the one that predominated in the Speke bar especially late at night when discretion had been eroded by ethyl alcohol, was that the firing at night was being done by the men we could see during the day in threadbare uniforms, toting dishevelled unclean weapons, lounging in red-eyed groups on the steps of public buildings and bumming cigarettes off any passer-by nervous enough to respond to their subdued catcalls.

But the *army*? Surely, er ...

At this point in the conversation about security, the more honest and communicative sort of person would often give me a sober, almost expressionless stare. After a few days I became used to this look and its different nuances: a gleam of good-humoured encouragement, a twitch of irritation, the elegant don't-look-at-me Kampala shrug. It was a look that urged you to think seriously for yourself. Look, it said, listen, don't expect names, units, chapter and verse, we aren't privy to the nuts and bolts, there are complexities and subtleties, and the whole question is dangerous by definition, but look at it this way: there are these armed people, obviously capable of any enormity, standing about all over the place in the daytime apparently short of sleep. Is it realistic to suppose that at night they go meekly home to bed and others emerge from hiding to cause trouble? Be your age, the look said. Don't expect bald statements, because someone may hear and then if you write something that annoys someone, or even if you don't, I may be cast in the role of culprit. Got it? the look asked silently.

I never did quite get it although it was all spelled out in the Speke bar and elsewhere plenty of times. Even now, more than twelve years later, I still don't quite get it, the Manichaeism of African political practice, the rejection of bearable compromise and continuous adjustment in favour of a blatant and confused cycle of revolution, repression, subversion and corruption, sometimes one at a time, sometimes all at once. Don't get me wrong. I have never thought that nations that aren't nations can easily be made to show a bit of *esprit de corps* by leaders who aren't leaders, especially when their countries have been trashed by armies that aren't armies commanded by generals who aren't generals, and undermined by trade that isn't trade and aid that isn't aid from friends who aren't friends.

I never thought it looked even remotely easy. It always looked to me to be very, very difficult, a task for heroes, for figures of future legend. These after all are not to be found in every bar, but they do occur, or so I still suppose. On another, more mundane level, there was a generation of African political thinkers who looked or at least sounded as if they meant business, who spoke often of the broad masses and their destiny. A handful of these had struggled on, had done their best to maintain a continuous and principled political discourse at least tenuously connected with the practice of their parties or governments. Obote's friend and now patron, Julius Nyerere, was one. Stretching a point a bit (I thought), Obote could even be said to belong to that generation himself. He had been elected, then overthrown by the military. From where I stood it looked perfectly natural for the Ugandans to vote him in again, at least to finish his term, after the rude interruption of Idi Amin's coup d'état and idiot rule. That would get democracy back on the rails in a symmetrical manner in harmony with natural justice. If, as supporters of all the other parties claimed, the UPC was unrepresentative and no good, then they could vote it out at the next election, right?

No, wrong, Speke bar opinion said. The point was not that Obote had been illegally overthrown by Amin. The point was that Amin had been Obote's fault. He had moved up the ranks and become a general not despite but because of his venality, his brutality, his voluble psychopathic bullshitting. He had been the sort of chap Obote wanted at the top of the army, someone absolutely without prudence or morality, a bogey-man on a leash who could be used to enforce anything Obote wanted enforced, but whose very presence would make people jump when Obote told them to, without arguing. The way he had slipped his leash, got out of control, done dirty slippery deals with foreign powers, just proved Obote's incompetence, and served him right. And served the foreign powers right too, because they had soon gone off Amin. He had proved a total disaster all round, very embarrassing and damaging to Uganda. And all Obote's fault.

I persisted. Of course I had a vague idea of the scale and nature of the problems, in principle, but I was and still am attached to the idea that groups of peoples can coexist under a single government through a sort of federal consciousness making possible a working consensus administered by elected politicians organised into parties, as they do (more or less) in

Britain. Of course in the twentieth century we have forgotten the pain and bloodshed of the centuries during which our system was evolving into its present, still evolving form. So although in the middle of 1980 I was, in fact, in a place where the same sort of pain and bloodshed were contemporary daily realities, I discounted the gap of miles and centuries, I failed to measure the distance between my native reality and Uganda's, pinned separately to the ragged dartboard of history. If Obote was going to win the election as everyone said, I wanted to be reassured that he would be wiser this time, more restrained and benevolent. Surely, I asked, the whole Amin episode would have been a lesson in the art of the possible? Couldn't the Ugandans give him another chance?

The Speke bar smiled grimly. If Obote had learned a lesson, it wasn't one that was going to be of much benefit to Uganda, it said. Basically Uganda wasn't in a democracy-type situation. The parties were going to campaign, but votes would not decide who was going to win the election. That was going to be Obote. And since his party was certain to get quite a lot of votes, it would be difficult to prove they were not a majority. What the UPC and Obote would do when they were in power was anyone's guess, but it wasn't going to be good for Uganda. He was going to get another chance, but only because the Tanzanians — Nyerere — wanted him to. The Ugandans themselves were against it. They were never going to forgive Obote for all the trouble he had caused. He was a rotten humbug who didn't give a damn about the Ugandans.

Of course this was not a universal view. There are in all societies many people preoccupied with their own affairs, who favour the convenience of undemanding, pre-packaged, received political discourse. This was not the type of person prevalent in the Speke bar. But there were UPC supporters among the other party activists who filled the place with their noise and doubletalk every evening. There were government agents there, spies for the regime, a shadowy entity whose most powerful figure was Paulo Muwanga in a blurred, unacknowledged collusion with the Tanzanian army, the Ugandan army or armies and people who possessed mysterious powers. And there were the civil servants, the administrative technocrats who everywhere tend to develop habits of caution, of careful choice of words with here and there, when necessary, a resort to official secrecy when discussing the affairs of their employer the State.[3]

---

3 I use this word for its brevity, not its accuracy. I doubt if Hegel, for example, would have recognised Uganda in 1980 as an especially finished example of a State.

These elements had more nuanced views of Obote. But although they did not express hostility, there was little warmth or support. On one level this was a matter of courtesy among Ugandans: Obote's men not asking for trouble by rubbing people's noses in the fact that they had it made, that Obote as it were was the heir apparent, although the country was going to elect him for form's sake. On another level, though, the coolness was genuine. Things might still come apart. There was an uneasy hint of something from which people might have to dissociate themselves in a hurry. Obote was not personally loved, not outside the circle of his home district and associates anyway, and perhaps not universally even there.

The UPC's privileged position was very obvious. Obote's men were already sitting at the top of several ministries. One of these was an acquaintance, who had spent the Amin years in exile in London. I went to see him on my first full day in Kampala at his office in the government building. He was not unfriendly but gave me little time, certainly not enough to talk about anything. A sleepy Tanzanian corporal with a battered Kalashnikov sprawled in one of the chairs in his anteroom. My acquaintance the minister was arranging a trip 'upcountry' with Obote. While we were talking he produced a couple of hundred-dollar bills from his inside pocket and gave them to a messenger. 'Go and get some money from those boys down there,' he instructed.

A large part of Kampala's daily cash banking business took place in a short, steep, nondescript downtown street, the staff a cocktail of senior racketeers, young toughs and red-eyed, unreliable-looking armed and uniformed men. God knows what the real banks were doing. Perhaps they rented their strongrooms out to the street bankers. I tried to ask questions but the minister couldn't be bothered to answer them. Like other UPC members, like Obote himself, he seemed to think any kind of apologia unnecessary. They had more important things to think about.

I collected party manifestos and read them. They were all more or less perfunctory, but the one I found most sympathetic, for its blend of realism and political principle, was that of the Uganda People's Movement. The UPM could boast that its adherents had waged an armed struggle — not a very big or remorseless one, but real for all that — against Amin, something none of the other parties had done although this did not stop them from making claims. Its other claim to credibility, in my eyes, was that it thought credibility was worth some effort. It could be bothered to outline a programme, however sketchy, for economic recovery and political reconciliation, in the hope of persuading Ugandans, winning their hearts and minds, and thus finding a basis for the elusive consensus. There was something refreshing and touching about this, something familiar.

The other parties by contrast, despite differences of ideology, projected a sort of grim certainty about what was going for them and what was going against them. They knew the score in advance. They represented ready-made voter blocs, or more occult powers, religion, tribal fealty, money; they weighed the future accurately with stolid, decadent corporate fatalism. This was just as true of the UPC which knew it was going to win as of the other two major parties, the Democratic Party and the Conservative Party, bizarrely known as the CP, which knew they were not going to win. The UPC showed neither jubilation nor generosity in its confident anticipation of victory, as if sourly aware of how this victory was being engineered, how it would have to be maintained.

An acquaintance persuaded me to interview the national organiser (or some such title) of the UPM in the warren the party occupied in a dark office block. The national organiser was a highly strung youngish man, unusually brilliant even for Kampala (that town of clever people) but calm, modest and charming, with a fragile, bureaucrat's integrity. He cannot have been much over thirty, if that. He confirmed my sympathy for the UPM, but by then I knew that despite its virtues, or perhaps because of them, it was not going to be a front runner in the election.

I have forgotten the national organiser's name now, but a few years later, while Obote was still in power, I read that he had been murdered. By then, of course, the Speke bar's predictions had come true: the UPC government had not managed to maintain control and Uganda was wallowing miserably in another bloodbath. A major reason for the revived violence was the decision by the UPM's military wing, the NRA, to pursue armed rebellion. There was no military victory, but the Sellotape holding Obote's regime together melted in the heat, and the army again fell apart into tribal and bandit factions. In the process Kampala saw wave after wave of vigilante murders and vengeful popular lynchings (as usual the picture was even worse in some provinces). Obote was deposed for the second time in July 1985 by the elderly General Okello, and the NRA took power six months later after a conference held in Kenya.

While all this was going on Uganda was adding a high incidence of HIV to its other problems,[4] something that seems, in the words of a friend

---

4 Perhaps not as high as had been feared. It is now being said that the HIV antibody tests used in Uganda produce a very high level of false positive findings.

who lives in those parts, extremely unfair. But something else happened too: once in power the NRA behaved pretty much as the 1980 UPM manifesto would have led one to expect. It seems to me a paradox that Yoweri Museveni's long, ruthless, largely military struggle for power should have resulted in a dictatorial but well-intentioned regime that believes in consensus and means to bring the political nightmare to an end; a paradox, and a lesson.

The UPM interview took place at lunch time. When it ended I was running late for my next appointment, and the national organiser placed a car at my disposal. I did not have it to myself. It contained four or five other people, at least two of them armed, in addition to the driver. New and Japanese, the vehicle coped well with its overload and was driven stylishly at breakneck speed to Obote's large, graceless, colonial-style villa, newish but not modern, in a prosperous suburb with the same neglected, untidy look as the rest of Kampala, as if a typhoon had occurred a couple of months earlier. The driver apologised for dropping me round the corner instead of drawing up outside Obote's house. Obote's guards, the men in the car indicated with some hilarity, might misunderstand if they saw a packed UPM vehicle stopping in front of the gate.

About fifty uniformed troops were encamped, complete with women and children, washing-lines and cooking fires, in the big yard surrounding the house. Despite the UPM men's caution the security was unexcitable and offhand. My name was taken and I was admitted. Under a tarpaulin on one side of the front yard squatted a maroon Daimler Double-Six, non-functioning perhaps for lack of some trivial part and a few years old, but still shiny and undamaged under its coating of equatorial dust. Would it be activated after the election, when Obote was president again, or would he have to use an armoured car or Range Rover capable of taking to the woods in a hurry? In Africa a car like the Daimler indicates an impractical level of grandeur, but for me it had homely associations, an unthinking *nice motor, that* (with reservations), the same non-thought I would have had in response to the same sight in a builder's yard in Kilburn. Thus unconsciously transported to more reassuring climes, I attempted to interview Obote.

At times, kicking my heels in anterooms or ministry yards, being brushed off day after day by suspicious bureaucrats and heavies, I have cursed the convention that political journalists are supposed to try, at least, to get quotes from the horse's mouth. It is true that exclusive quotes from a newsworthy source will help sell a political piece to an editor. But the quotes themselves, obtained at such cost in time and ritual self-abasement, are not often very interesting. How can they be, when they represent a corporate discourse which is already well known?

Obote made no difficulties about seeing me. I had asked for twenty minutes of his time, naming my small hank of strings. He received me politely and spoke with effortless fluency for about two hours without saying a single thing I did not know already or could not have worked out for myself. It was an adept performance, quiet, articulate and rational, to the rather narrow limits of the discourse he permitted himself. The underlying assumptions were no more preposterous, the untruths no more blatant, than they would have been in a British chancellor's budget speech.

All the same, in that airconditioned sitting room with its heavy plush African-bigwig furniture, iced water and coffee on coasters on one polished small table, ashtray and running tape recorder on another, listening to the once and future president, the president-in-waiting, a feeling of profound unreality stole depressingly over me. It wasn't just the way Obote giggled as he gave a version of the story that bandits and rogue Amin troops were responsible for the shooting that kept everyone miserably on their toes and indoors at night; it was more the story itself, an account so perfunctory that it seemed not to be meant to be believed, as if I was supposed to know what was really happening, or as if Obote was supposed not to know.

There is little to be done under these circumstances. Your options do not include shouting curses or seizing the interviewee by the throat. Obote was playing by the rules. The political discourse to which he adhered in all his remarks was the one to which I broadly subscribed myself. He was not obliged by the rules (and I was not clever enough to induce him) to admit that so far as he was concerned this discourse was a fiction — sometimes useful, sometimes irksome, but in any case radically separate from, and far less important than, the real political processes it served to conceal. And he wielded it in a workmanlike, artistic manner, just a little better than glib, that was not specifically insulting under the circumstances. Journalists do not expect to like politicians. We know that they are fairly callous and cynical people gifted with a sort of vulgar, calculating, hermetic intellectual brilliance. For years afterwards I bored and irritated people by trying to explain why Obote had reminded me of Harold Wilson.[5]

It was all so effortless, so offhand. The devastation wrought by the Amin years loomed all around us, a universal explanation, a universal excuse.

---

[5] I have never spoken to the former Labour prime minister. Very likely I would not now make this comparison, but in those days my Oedipal narcissism was still attached to an image of myself as a person of the left. I am afraid those thirteen years have changed Lord Wilson and Obote as well.

Yes, it had been a mistake to promote Idi Amin above his competence, but Uganda had been so short of senior officers ... then later Amin had been got at by foreigners ... But 'people were saying', I murmured using the polite formula, that Amin had got the promotion because he was willing to chase out the Kabaka of Buganda, whom the British had left as constitutional president with Obote as prime minister, by shelling the Kabaka's palace. In a trice Obote was peeping coyly out from behind an impenetrable thicket of local particularities. It hadn't been nearly as simple as that ... democracy had been under threat in Uganda from feudal and neocolonial forces ... Uganda should not be judged by British standards. He tittered triumphantly. He could tell I was just the sort of person to believe, or half-believe, that the spookier end of the British establishment might have had some sort of hand in Amin's coup, along with the Mossad; that I would have noticed the media support for Amin. He could tell I wasn't a Conservative voter. And his own documented assault on his country's constitution was vanishing comfortably into the mists of time on the other side of Idi Amin. It was easy. He was just playing. Probably he had little to do and was bored.

Obote smoked cigarettes throughout the interview but drew back, as if from a small scorpion, when I offered him one of mine, and again when I offered him a light: a delicate reminder that his life was under threat, that I might be an assassin for all he knew.[6] He posed good-naturedly on the big terrace for photographs, deplorable snapshots from a cheap automatic camera, with the fishy look imparted by its little plastic lens. I conveyed to him verbally the regards of a London friend, an Irishwoman who had frequented Kampala more than a decade before when the Speke lived on rich tourists and belonged to a flamboyant English homosexual who, with his two Afghan hounds, had been one of the sights of Kampala. Wilson-like, he remembered her. I thanked him and said I hoped to interview him again when he was president. This got another tough-guy giggle and I left.

Only the very classiest hacks can possibly expect to get a story from every interview, and even they must often be disappointed. So it cannot have been the thinness of Obote as a story that made me feel so sour and queasy. Only many years later did I fully understand that Obote had not insulted me, that like other Ugandans he had been courteous and patient with the blundering outsider, given who he was and the other demands on his attention. With hindsight it seems that what was insulting, what felt

---

6 Ugandan in-fighting sometimes assumes pretty gothic forms, of which the rumoured forensic anomalies surrounding the Kabaka's death in London are a good example.

particularly oppressive that afternoon, was the fact that the charade Obote and I had just acted out, and many others like it, played a minor role in obscuring, in maintaining, the predicament of the Ugandan millions struggling miserably all around us like flies in a puddle of something sticky.

A day or so later I went to an Obote rally at Makerere University. A crowd of several thousand people, quiet, sombre and ragged, had gathered on the playing-field-like space in front of the main building, a structure resembling a run-down but very large English south coast hotel. The numerous UPC organisers were instantly identifiable from their new clothes and confident manner. Just under the flag-draped podium was a space reserved for the press, and I sat on the grass among the other hacks. Once or twice during Obote's longish speech, delivered in Kiganda, my neighbour told me what he was saying. It wasn't very interesting but the delivery was cod-oratorical, full of dramatic pauses and changes of pitch. The current word for corruption was uttered in a deep, thrilling moan with the middle syllable quaveringly prolonged: *mage-e-e-endo*! It sounded like the dénouement of a ghost story being told to a class of children by a Welsh repertory actor. The audience listened intently, muttering discreet, evasive asides. From time to time there arose a burst of orchestrated applause or slogan-shouting.

I started to worry about finding a telex. Time was passing and money draining away. I had been in Kampala five or six days without filing a word. As I swilled morose triples in the Speke bar that evening, someone said: 'Don't you work for *Africa* journal?'

'Among others, yes.'

'There's someone from *Africa* staying at the Imperial. British, like you. John something.'

Come to think of it, he had mentioned that he was coming to Uganda at about that time. John H worked on the business side of the magazine as some kind of executive. Sometimes he was the person to see when you needed your money, sometimes not. He too had his problems with that ramshackle organisation. We were not close friends but he was a person you could drink with, cheery and sardonic. Knocking back my 'whisky' I rushed out into the late dusk and slunk in a stooped position down the road and across the little roundabout into the Imperial. My namesake was in the gloomy bar – emptied as usual by its rival's success although it was much roomier – drinking gin with an upper-class Baganda woman who had spent many years with her elbow on the bars of Brighton, and sounded it. Close your eyes and you were in the home counties. We greeted each other loudly and I grumbled a bit. 'I was just going to call Tarun,' he said. 'Have a word with him if you like. He may be able to help.'

Tarun S, an Indian from Kenya, was the day-to-day accountant of *Africa* at that time. He too was an agreeable pub companion, cynical but humane, contemptuous of ideologies, fond of strong lager and addicted to one-armed bandits. Over echoing static his thick accent stuttered a few amiable insults out of the telephone. I told him my troubles. 'Can you lend me some money here? Advance on payment, something like that? It's turning out more expensive than I expected.'

Tarun insulted me some more. 'Been chasing girls in Nairobi? Waking up to find your trousers gone?' I could tell he was sympathetic. 'How do I know you'll pay it back? I can't get a signature from here.'

'Oh come on, Tarun. I'll be sending some stuff in a day or so. Then there's Tanzania, and Mozambique if I get a visa. By the time I get back you'll owe me a bomb. Do me a favour.'

'I might be able to help. Talk to the managing director of the *Times of Uganda* tomorrow afternoon. I'll speak to him in the morning.'

Things were suddenly looking rosier. The managing director was a pleasant man with a modest cautious manner. He received me politely in his office in the quiet building in a business suburb. What could he do for me? Yes, he had heard about me from Tarun S. Did I need money now? He counted out a few thousand shillings and handed them over. I could ask for more later. He did not want a receipt. I thanked him. Not at all, anything else? Yes, I could use the telex, no problem. He showed me the terminal in a quiet corridor and introduced me to the operator. I could just come and use it any time, provided I made way for the *Times of Uganda* when necessary. I thanked him again. Anything else? Well, the hotel manager was homing in on me as a hard-currency source. It would be cheaper to pay in shillings, but the manager was saying that would be illegal. What should I do? No problem: the managing director would speak to the manager when I was leaving. He would pay my bill himself, in shillings. OK?

OK indeed. *Africa* journal was a pretty mixed blessing for most of my fourteen-year association with it, but on this occasion it definitely did the trick. Ever since that July of 1980 I have harboured feelings of friendship and gratitude towards Tarun and the managing director of the *Times of Uganda*; Tarun, to make sure, has reminded me from time to time.

In the short week that remained I did more interviews, typed in my room, crouched making punched tapes in the corridor at the *Times of*

Uganda and eventually bunged the stuff down the telex, not much of it to tell the truth, three pieces or perhaps four, at best well turned and interesting, at worst superficial and naive, not very 'professional' but probably better for it. What could I say? I knew very little about the country. I had not seen it in its post-independence hope and glory. People were keeping alive in the populous arc around Lake Victoria — bananas are manna really, a wonderful low-key bounty needing very moderate levels of input from the cultivator — but life was pretty merry hell for nearly all of them. In some remote areas things were far worse with starvation, tribal massacres, banditry, marauding armies. The election was not going to change anything overnight. Yet in a way it was the story (just as what the authorities say must always be quoted for heavyweight credibility, dragging the journalist willy-nilly into the closed reality, the fantasy world, of the regime in place). At least the Ugandan story had background colour, plenty of it. But it was hard to relish the bizarre, comic or frightening details without remembering what they meant to the Ugandans. It was difficult to avoid taking things seriously for more than a few minutes.

So I did my best, filled a few column-inches with coded guff that I hoped would indicate to careful readers that, whatever the major players said or thought, Uganda was in a state of maintainable anarchy, ruled by pirates and warlords under the protection of bewildered Tanzanian soldiers, bankrupt and worse, its economy running largely on illicit cash and illegal barter, its administration turned inside out, its security forces torn into unreliable freelance fragments, no prospect of private investment, no prospect of sufficient foreign aid to achieve anything useful in the short term, no prospect of political consensus. I tried to put in a word for the poor Ugandans, but I do not suppose many people noticed. The conventions of political journalism are good at underlining the subtleties in everyday processes, but become coy and unwieldy when used to describe openly outrageous situations. Over the telex in the corridor the London desk man's busy blue pencil hovered in my mind's eye. *He says there's corruption, the army is firing in the air and everyone's broke. So what's new?* the desk man growls. *Where does he think he is for Christ's sake? Balmoral?*

The *Times of Uganda* like other enterprises was functioning on a greatly reduced scale. Distribution would have been a problem if lack of newsprint had not prevented the paper from appearing. A couple of two-ton rolls, the paper's entire stock, sat forlornly in the printing room beside a new Siemens press 30 yards long, gathering dust in untended silence. A skeleton staff haunted the quiet corridors and newsrooms. Political parties and groups of enthusiasts were putting out newspapers, but only to prove it could be done: badly printed, half-tabloid size and only four pages long, one folded sheet, they contained no recyclable information but still cost a pound a copy.

There was little traffic. As dusk approached the bus stops were thronged, but buses were rare. Freelance taxis were easier to find: experienced vehicles with smashed windscreens and bullet-scarred doors, picking their way cautiously around the potholes to preserve lumpy balding tyres; or well-found official cars moonlighting through the afternoon for a little extra cash. A senior civil servant drove me to the Speke one evening in an immaculate Austin Mini, several years old but hardly used. When I admired it he told me it was his wife's car; then with embarrassment, hoping for a hundred, doggedly asked for sixty or seventy shillings.

During the hours of daylight I pottered about writing and interviewing people: minister of finance (country destitute), chief of police (illiterate constables to be purged or retrained), abandoned properties board (compensation and guarantees being demanded by fleeced and exiled capitalists, no funds for compensation, no guarantees worth paper written on, Indian industrial dynasties stand-offish, investment unlikely). In the evenings I frequented the Speke bar and those of the other hotels. One night I attended the weekly disco on the top floor of the International, the biggest of the hotels, less intellectual than the Speke and more expensive, the haunt of racketeers, of louche stranded entrepreneurs. There I fell into conversation with an Arab in his mid-thirties who gave me a beer from the crate under his table, warm and not at all good but formally luxurious and festive, like champagne at a hastily organised wedding. Idi Amin's departure, he grumbled, had cost him twenty-six million shillings. Only one of his clothes boutiques had survived. Life had become very difficult.

My friends the diplomats often advised me not to risk going to the other hotels after dark. One night, after dining and drinking with John H in the International, I did not get back until nearly midnight. The bar was dark but K and M were sitting in the entrance lounge. As I slunk in from the street they rose and stood to attention. While M saluted, K produced a small harmonica and in a blue minor key – revealing true musical talent, not just competence – played a few bars of the British national anthem. Both kept their faces absolutely straight. It was an extremely funny example of provocative African teasing.

The bad booze and altitude were giving me hangovers. I confided to the tweedy anglophile M that I would really prefer some grass for its lower toxicity and as an aid to reflection. Really? No problem. At lunchtime the next day he led me a short distance to a vacant lot where a scattering of ragged youths loitered with a vague, purposeful air. Nobody looked at us or tried to catch our attention. M strode briskly up to the nearest youth and addressed the side of his head in Kiganda. Without looking round the boy reached into his sock and produced a couple of large conical joints, for which I paid twenty shillings. During the transaction a uniformed soldier floated up backwards, gazing into the distance, and came to rest a foot or so away. I bridled nervously but M was unmoved. 'Don't worry about him,' he said in loud confident ruling-class tones. 'He's just part of the system.' There was no visible reaction. The soldier did not look at us, speak to us or make any attempt to communicate; he was just right there, not quite standing on our feet. Impressed, I thanked the diplomat, who did not use cannabis himself. 'No problem,' he said. 'I noticed in England quite a few people like it. We can't have you going without when it's available. We wouldn't want you to think us inhospitable.' There was certainly nothing wrong with the weed. For part of that evening I was confined to my room with paranoia, but the two joints did not last long and I visited the building site again, alone this time. The same youth materialised sideways in front of me and wordlessly held out two more joints. 'Looks a bit green,' I said as I gave him the money. A shy pink eye scanned me for a fifth of a second before flicking gratefully back to the skyline. The boy was already drifting away but I heard the word 'Fresh.' Sales talk.

I completed my few bits of work. They were not going to be extravagantly rewarded and there was no consolation in the thought that they were not all that good. All the same I was glad to have had a close-up look at some very raw, and to me unusual, history-in-the-making. I felt a small sense of personal achievement, but my schedule was lagging and it was time to move on. It would have been pleasant to get the steamer round Lake Victoria to my next destination, Bukoba in Tanzania, but it was not running. Opinions were divided on the state of the bus service: the buses were not running, the service had just been restored, the border was closed, the bus was running sometimes … everyone had a different theory, nobody really knew. The time window for entry on my Tanzanian visa had expired, and the Tanzanians in their Nile Mansion office told me, as they altered the visa, that the border was open. But they too shrugged when I asked about transport.

  The bus left in the mid-morning and trundled, not very fast, to Masaka, where it stopped. There was no onward bus in my direction. A passer-by sent me to a nearby street where I spotted a Tanzanian taxi from Bukoba. Its five or six passengers, led by a smart young policeman in uniform, agreed after a short debate to take me along, but only for part of the way. The driver was unimpressed with my remaining Ugandan money. For the next hour or so the vehicle, a Peugeot 404, maintained a comfortable 80 miles an hour over the dusty washboard gravel road. It stopped in a village and the passengers disappeared for a while. 'You can get some money here if you want,' the policeman told me. I declined to do so, perhaps unwisely, for the driver told me as we waited that they were going to drop me before the frontier.

'I don't want to get caught with currency at the border. It would be foolish. But I can pay you in Bukoba.'

The driver indicated that that was not the problem. The policeman, he said, was smuggling (clothes, I believe), and feared that my presence would attract attention at the border. Later I realised that they were probably going to avoid customs altogether by using some back road, something they could get away with but I could not. In the mid-afternoon they dropped me at an open road barrier manned by a sleepy, innocent-looking squad of Tanzanian troops under a sergeant. We exchanged cigarettes and passed the time in amiably uncomprehending dialogue. The Kagera Salient is a flat empty landscape of lush, impenetrable, yellow giant grasses, a late Victorian vision of Africa. It looks and feels like no man's land (one reason, perhaps, for Idi Amin's impulsive decision to invade Tanzania's share of it). Everything was bone dry but you could sense the presence of water. No vehicles passed in either direction for some time, but after half an hour a lorry trundled up and the troops stopped it for me.

I climbed into the back and stood swaying with four or five men, enjoying the dusty breeze of passage. One of them spoke good English and we chatted. After a few miles a head stuck out of the cab and shouted a question which the man translated. 'The driver is asking if you want to go through customs, or if you would rather go straight to Bukoba by another road.' Like the taxi, the lorry wanted to save time and trouble following what was obviously local practice. Illegal entry is not a sensible option for foreigners so the decision was not difficult. 'Customs if you don't mind. Sorry.' OK, no problem. He smiled. Apparently it was a bit inconvenient but rural Africans are polite, considerate, philosophical about the unforeseen, generous with their time. For several hours I had been conscious of strangeness, an unfamiliar quality in everyone's comportment. Now I realised the body language had changed. People stood up straight, shoulders back, chest out, they spoke up and looked you in the eye; they did not snigger bitterly or guffaw with traumatised rage but laughed with lazy silly good nature as if they did not know the meaning of fear. Their shoulders were not bowed as if to protect the vitals or overburdened with the endless stress of moment-to-moment calculation, compulsive, frenetic and doomed. They may have had families, faults of character, political and economic grumbles, but they did not have cares, not real ones. They were like free men.

The lorry left me at customs and was waved on. The customs men looked at me quizzically and pawed through my stuff; immigration inspected my papers, deemed me more or less respectable and stamped me in. There had been no Ugandan exit formalities of any kind; I had passed no Ugandan frontier post, seen no Ugandans since Masaka. It was still 30 miles to Bukoba and the light was fading. After ten minutes a Japanese 3-ton lorry came steaming down the road and pulled up in a cloud of dust. The driver's door opened and his rifle clattered onto the road. Laughter and tired Swahili badinage came from four red-eyed troops nearing the end of their afternoon's journey from Mbarara. The customs men talked me aboard and I heaved my case up to one of the squaddies in the back and clambered after it. The truck-bed, covered with a single sheet of metal, carried nothing but two used engines whose oil had run all over the floor. Holding onto a lateral bar, the two soldiers and I tried to remain vertical while keeping a weather eye on the engines and my suitcase which slid about freely on the vibrating, oil-coated metal. The driver seemed pressed for time. After a few miles he forced his way past a Land Rover which swerved into the ditch as it disappeared into our dense dust-cloud. As the dusk deepened the reason for the hurry became clear: the lorry only had sidelights, and not very good ones at that.

Numb, relieved and filthy, I wandered up the road outside a military base on the edge of Bukoba. It was dark but soon a taxi passed, a side-valve new-shape Ford Anglia more than twenty years old. My requirements were complex but the driver, a Muslim, accepted without demur my assurance that I would pay him on the morrow. It was Ramadan and he needed a snack. He bought me a cup of tea and gave me a small stick of barbecued meat. We ascertained with some difficulty that the person I was looking for lived 30 miles away and would have to be sought in daylight. There were no rooms available at the two or three hotels the driver thought suitable for me (he refused point-blank to allow me to try one or two others that we passed). Late that night he found me a dormitory bed in a hostel run by German Lutherans. Incidentally I still feel ashamed that when that decent man came for his money I paid him no more than he asked.

AFRICA

A few days later, standing beside a wrecked, tilting Bailey bridge over a lush little stream a few miles outside Bukoba, my host told me that the river had once been the haunt of hippopotamuses who could be heard merrily splashing and snorting in the early morning. 'But there haven't been any for a year now,' he said. 'It's Amin's fault really. When the army came through here to fight him they were around for a few weeks, and they ate them all. The meat's a delicacy to some people, and they like it very, very gamey.'

London, 1993 (not written for publication)

REPORTING THE WAR IN CHAD

*

Security Council meets as desert war is pressed deeper
Libyan jets intensify bombing in Chad

From John Howe in N'Djamena

Attacks by Libyan aircraft on town and military installations in northern Chad intensified yesterday. Five waves of fighter-bombers attacked Faya-Largeau during the day, wreaking further destruction on the town and inflicting further civil and military casualties.

Libyan jets, identified by Chad military sources as Tupolev 22, MiG 21 and MiG 23, carried Colonel Gaddafi's undeclared war deeper into Chad territory with three raids on Oum-Chalouba.

Situated south-east of Faya, on the road to Abeche, the small town of Oum-Chalouba fell to the Chad army three weeks ago, during President Habré's drive north after his recapture of Abeche.

It now serves as the Chad army's nearest rear base, and the attacks constitute a clear attempt to cut President Habré's supply and communication lines.

A form of censorship has now been reimposed. On Wednesday, foreign journalists were told they could say nothing about the equipment being supplied by France and the US. Yesterday, the Minister of Information, Mr Mahamat Soumaila, refused to give his usual open press briefing and only admitted three journalists – one from AFP, one from the French TV chain, TFI, and a reporter from the Paris daily, *Le Matin*.

Our favoured colleagues said that Mr Soumaila confirmed the air raids on Oum-Chalouba, which, he said, had caused damage and numerous civilian casualties. He refused to confirm or deny rumours of attacks on the ground by infantry and armour.

Medical sources in N'Djamena said that the Libyan air force had dropped phosphorus bombs on Faya-Largeau. The burn marks on wounded civilians and soldiers evacuated from the town for treatment in the capital were typical of that type of bomb.

The government has made repeated requests for air cover to France, its main military backer to date, but they have been turned down.

The French government has stated many times that it would stick to the letter of a 1976 military cooperation agreement which barred outright intervention.

The arrival of a first batch of US heat-seeking missiles was also imminent, military sources said.

They did not expect American technicians, due to be flown in with the weapons, to go up to the front to teach Chadian troops how to use them.

At the United Nations, Libya yesterday reaffirmed its neutrality and accused the United States and France of endangering peace in the region.

In a letter to the Security Council president, Mr Luc de la Barre de Nanteuil, the Libyan chargé d'affaires, Mr Awad Burwin, said that the country categorically rejected charges by Chad of Libyan aggression. But he said that the US and France were themselves directly intervening in Chad's affairs, and supporting a rebellion there.

Guardian, 5 August 1983

*

Bitter Habré attacks Libya's role in war
'Le Patron' gives press conference to deny reports that he had been killed

From John Howe in N'Djamena

When President Habré of Chad returned from the battlefront to give a press conference at the weekend, he exuded a controlled force that made one see why his officials sometimes refer to him as 'le Patron', or the boss.

The President's emergence in public put paid to earlier reports by Libya and the French external radio service, Inter, that he had been killed. Speaking French with a Chadian accent, Mr Habré answered questions for an hour in a dry, hard voice, punctuated by a nervous cough. He wore a spotless white costume of cotton trousers and long overshirt. He looked greyer than average for his forty-one years.

He sat alone on an ornate chair, sometimes gesticulating with both hands, pointing accusingly here and there at the thirty Chadian and foreign correspondents, and two television crews. He seldom raised his voice and never smiled.

He bitterly condemned Libyan backing for the rebels in the north of the country, around the oasis town of Faya-Largeau. He criticised the

French decision, announced by the defence minister in Paris, that there would be no direct intervention by the former colonial power. He complained that, although the US had sent $15 million in military equipment, it had come late and was not enough.

Although he said he would answer any question, the President did not supply much of the military and political material sought by journalists starved of official information and squirming under de facto censorship.

Instead, he turned the questions to expand on the subjects of Libyan aggression and the lassitude of Chad's foreign allies. In answer to a question on the military and other means it would take to remove Libya from the Aouzou Strip, for example, he gave an account of the way the Libyans had infiltrated the region during the Frolinat rebellion in the late 1960s and early 1970s.

Libya has never had any claim on Aouzou and before French colonisation, President Habré said the Al-Gadafy tribe raided the region on a slave hunt and was almost wiped out by the warlike Toubou inhabitants.

Anecdotes of this sort, and they are legion in modern Chad, add a personal and psychological dimension to a history whose raw facts are already bafflingly complex.

Using rhetoric to explain Libya's expansionist sleight-of-hand, President Habré asked: 'What national reconciliation? Are we expected to reconcile ourselves with mercenaries of all shapes and sizes? Or is our real interlocutor supposed to be Libya? Yesterday Gaddafi said that a threat to Aouzou was a threat to Libya. Today his planes are bombing Faya because it seems now it is Faya which threatens Libyan integrity. Tomorrow N'Djamena itself will be accused of posing the same threat.'

Guardian, 8 August 1983

*

Chad puts its 'war captives' on show

From John Howe in N'Djamena

Around 550 prisoners of war 'captured at Faya-Largeau' were shown to the press here this morning at the military prison, close to the military camp and airport on the outskirts of N'Djamena.

The men were shown sitting on the ground in columns of three. They wore tattered uniforms and were barefoot. A pile of belts, amulets and ornaments lay on the ground nearby. Fifty to sixty slightly wounded were separated from the rest.

The Information Minister, Mr Mahamat Soumaila, interviewed in the prison yard as TV teams circled the prisoners, claimed that a substantial number of the prisoners were members of the 'Islamic Legion' of Africans trained and equipped by Libya for its wars in and around the Sahara.

'These began as peaceful workers and peasants seeking employment in Libya,' he said. 'Once there, it was child's play to place them under arrest and recruit them into the Islamic Legion. This illustrates the criminality of the Tripoli regime, as the presence of these men here illustrates its aggression.'

Asked to which of the Chadian tendencies the other prisoners belonged, the armed guards said they were a mixture of troops from the rebel armies of Goukouni Oueddei, Colonel Kamougue and Acheikh Ibn Oumar. Nobody would estimate the proportions. Most of the prisoners were very young, but there was a good sprinkling of mature men.

Two separate sources in the international aid organisations have confirmed over the past two days that, during their presence in the northern two-thirds of Chad, which lasted a year, the Libyan authorities and armed forces kidnapped, paid, or otherwise induced the departure to Libya of large numbers of men, women and children, thus breaking up Chadian families. The region around Ati, in the middle of the country, is said to have lost thousands of women in this way.

Both official and diplomatic sources confirmed an intensification of Libyan bombing raids on Monday, and official sources say that there was another attack on Faya-Largeau yesterday morning. Apart from this, their information differs, with the Chad government still insisting that all is calm in the east, and that government troops still held all their positions.

The picture from the diplomatic community is much less optimistic, if not yet one of impending disaster. A small French military contingent is stationed at Kousseri, across the Chari in Cameroun, equipped with kit for emergency river crossing. In the event of rebel or Libyan ground penetration to Ati or Moussoro, these troops will be deployed to evacuate European residents from the capital.

Guardian, 10 August 1983

POLISARIO STEPPING UP ATTACKS AS MOROCCO COMPLETES SIXTH 'WALL'

The war in Western Sahara seems to be intensifying as it enters its twelfth year. Last week with four other journalists I was taken by guerrilla troops of the Polisario Front, which claims to represent the territory's Sahrawi inhabitants, to watch harassing attacks on the defensive 'wall' which Morocco's 100,000-strong occupying army has built around itself. In broken terrain south of the village of Farsia I was able to clamber inside the double rampart of sand on the night of 14 April. On the night of the 15th, watching from high ground 4 km from the wall, I saw the whole northern horizon illuminated by an hour-long barrage of assorted Polisario artillery. Some of the Moroccans' answering fire, aimed at vehicles passing across the ridge from which we were watching the battle, struck within 200 yards of our position; 152 mm shells whistled overhead and exploded in the desert behind us. A large piece of red-hot shrapnel landed nearby.

Late in the morning of the 15th, from two forward observation posts on the rocky bluffs facing the wall, I could clearly see Moroccan vehicles moving between the bases which line the 2,000 km-long wall at intervals of 4–10 km depending on the terrain. The Polisario moves about freely in the radar 'shadow' provided by the broken ground. Piles of artillery cartridges and mortar and shell craters dot the landscape. While we were watching, a Polisario recoilless rifle dropped two shells in the base opposite. Invisible above cloud, a Moroccan jet dropped two bombs a few miles to the east. Several shells, apparently fired at random, exploded in the plain behind us.

Returning to camp for lunch in two Land Rovers, we were fired on twice by a heavy artillery piece probably based 10 km behind the wall, along with Moroccan helicopters and sector command headquarters. The shells struck some 300 yards downwind of the vehicles, the second a little closer than the first, when we were in line-of-sight (radar or human) of the Moroccans on the hills to the north. The temporary camp, among the carob trees and fragrant camomile of a river bed 6 km south of the wall, was within artillery range but hidden from Moroccan observers. 'They know we are around, but they do not know exactly where,' explained front-line sector commander Mustapha Ali.

Five days of rain last November, the first such downpour in a decade, have filled the *oueds* and sinks of the stony *hammada* with flowers and ephemeral foliage. But despite the cool spring nights, living conditions in a region the Sahrawis call the 'line of fear' are harsh. The nearest well to the camp was 50 km away, I was told. The Polisario's net-draped, sand-coloured open Land Rovers must carry drums of warm, salty desert water in addition to food, weapons and blankets. Everyone sleeps in the open. The guerrillas bake gritty bread at night under the embers of their carob-wood fires, their other staples being tinned sardines, powdered milk and strong, sugary green tea.

Visitors to the front are treated with unforced desert hospitality; mutton and toilet paper were two unusual items produced by our hosts. A 2-foot-long armoured lizard, black with transverse bright yellow bands on its back, was shot through the head with a Kalashnikov and gutted with my penknife before being baked like bread in the embers. But despite our entreaties we were not given a taste. Either the treat was too good to waste on passers-by or the Sahrawis believed that we would not like it.

Apart from tea and conversation, the Polisario's 20,000 men while away the waiting hours of midday with a complicated form of draughts, sticks versus stones, on boards drawn in the sand. They are Muslims but less fussy than some about religion. Some of the troops could be seen discreetly praying at dawn, dusk and midday, but others do not bother. As soldiers on active service they are excused the physically demanding fast of Ramadan which begins in a few days, but I was told that many do observe it.

They are very devoted to their Land Rovers which, like camels, look shabby but are strong, quiet and economical. Most are low-mileage examples tuned for a 30 mph long-range cruising pace. Four-wheel drive is used only for clambering up cliffs and through sand dunes. Close to the enemy at night, they idle along without lights and in virtual silence at walking pace in second gear. For the major frontal attacks meant to overrun the wall, of which there have been half a dozen since 25 February, the Polisario has tracked armoured troop carriers of which we saw many traces in the sector. But these are not shown to visitors and the Polisario does not discuss them, or the tanks whose tracks could also be seen here and there. The same applies to the SAM missiles which keep Morocco's Mirages and helicopters at a safe distance.

Manning the wall is no joke for the Moroccans. At the Polisario's rear base south of Tindouf in Algeria, alongside the hundred or so Moroccan prisoners was an assortment of military booty including US-made Dragon anti-tank missiles and some of the French Milan missiles which recently made such an impression on the Libyan army in Chad. I spoke to Corporal Lelras el Rhalib Rashid who said that the Sahrawis had penetrated the wall elsewhere and attacked his post from the rear at dawn. Sixteen men had been captured with him near Haouza on 8 April. Two were in hospital, two on stretchers and several others wore medical dressings. Rashid was worried that his family would not know what had become of him.

Morocco's King Hassan has hedged his bold and ruthless gamble in annexing the former Spanish Sahara by claiming that the Sahrawis are really Moroccans and the Polisario an Algerian mercenary organisation with sinister communist aims. This has won him substantial military aid from France and the US. But the Sahrawis point out that while their SADR [Sahrawi Arab Democratic Republic] is now recognised by nearly seventy countries, not a single state recognises Morocco's right to their territory and its rich phosphate deposits. They want a UN-supervised referendum to include their 165,000 refugees in the Tindouf camps, but to leave out the military and other Moroccans now in Western Sahara. In the short term, they want the EEC to involve itself in the Moroccan/Spanish fishing agreement now that Spain is a Community member. They say a clause should be inserted in any agreement differentiating Moroccan waters from the even richer offshore fishing of Western Sahara.

While I was in Western Sahara Mauritania issued a statement to the effect that it would not be over-fussy about incursions over its northern frontiers. The vast, underpopulated desert country, which has had good relations with the Sahrawis since its withdrawal from the war in 1978, fears that it may be dragged back into the conflict by the proximity of Morocco's sixth wall to the railway line between Zouerate and the Atlantic port of Nouadhibou. The railway, which carries Mauritania's main export, iron ore, runs along the southern frontier of Western Sahara. In places the new wall will be only 300 yards away. Mauritania has a treaty with Algeria, which supports the Polisario Front and its Sahrawi Arab Democratic Republic, so the consequences of a real threat to Mauritania are unpredictable.

April 1987 (early extended draft of a piece published in the *West African Hotline*)

THE CRISIS OF ALGERIAN NATIONALISM AND THE RISE OF ISLAMIC INTEGRALISM

By cancelling the elections planned for the end of 1991, banning the Front Islamique du Salut (FIS), arresting its top leaders,[7] and detaining thousands of activists, the Algerian regime prevented an Islamist government from being elected, but did not succeed in forcing the theocratic djinn back into its bottle. Enough armed Islamic militants remained at large to keep the movement's name alive by attacking the police and security forces. Hardly a week has passed since February 1992 without several policemen or soldiers being reported killed in ambushes or shoot-outs with Islamist insurgents.[8]

The regime itself, a hollow husk of the FLN monolith of the 1970s, did not go unscathed. Chadli Bendjedid, who succeeded Houari Boumedienne more or less constitutionally in 1978 and presided over the phased dismantling of the sclerotic single-party structure, was forced to resign at the beginning of 1992 in a sort of quid pro quo for the suspension of the electoral process. Loathed by the population whose economic situation continued to worsen during his period in office, and by FLN cadres whose sinecures have evaporated,[9] Chadli was sacrificed by the army colleagues who imposed him as a little-known compromise candidate in 1978/9 over the rival claims of Abdelaziz Bouteflika and Mohamed Salah Yahiaoui. He quit as part of the same conjuring trick that annulled the election and brought Mohamed Boudiaf back from exile in Morocco, where he had been peacefully running a modest business, to take the helm at a particularly difficult moment.[10]

---

7 A military tribunal on 15 July sentenced Abassi Madani and Ali Benhadj to twelve years, and five others to sentences of four or six years' imprisonment for damaging 'state security and the national economy'. The sentences were lighter than expected.

8 More than 200 police and gendarmerie were killed between February and October 1992, according to *Le Monde*.

9 Chadli was also blamed by many in the regime for complacency about the rise of the Islamic Salvation Front. Some accuse him of encouraging it deliberately.

10 Boudiaf was a *chef historique* who had been out of favour with Algiers almost as long as Aït Ahmed. In 1956 the two men, together with Ben Bella, Rabah Bitat and Mohammed Khider, were detained by the French authorities after the aircraft taking them from Tunisia to Morocco was forced down at Algiers by a French fighter. They were released in 1962 and Ben Bella became president. Aït Ahmed left the next year and Boudiaf in 1964. He was sentenced to death in his absence by the Ben Bella government. After his long sojourn in Morocco he was considered close to that country's regime, but Algerians seemed to think this useful rather than threatening. The Western Saharan nationalist Polisario Front felt differently, however, although Boudiaf made no unfavourable declarations.

The curiosity and apprehension aroused by this appointment soon subsided. There were no further great surprises. That is, until Boudiaf's assassination on 29 June 1992 by members of the security forces said variously to be, and not to be, acting for the FIS. The assassins' motives have not so far been clearly established. Boudiaf was a declared adversary of the Islamist movement, but other enmities may have played a part. The bomb that killed many people – all Algerians – at Algiers airport in August is also unattributed so far. Ruling with the authority of an Haut Comité d'État (HCE), a sort of ad hoc successor to Boumedienne's Revolutionary Council and Chadli's 1979 FLN Politburo,[11] with the government including a prime minister – a Chadli innovation – functioning normally, Boudiaf seemed to represent a sort of dogged continuity of the regime, whose centre of gravity had drawn even closer to the upper reaches of the armed forces. But the scale and nature of the repressive measures used against the FIS attracted the sort of attention from Amnesty International usually reserved for the King of Morocco's dungeons.[12] A night curfew was imposed on Algiers and the surrounding areas on 5 December. Over the next ten days, thirteen armed men were killed by security forces, who lost nine policemen and two gendarmes. One civilian was killed by a stray bullet and another assassinated because two of his sons were policemen. Business as usual, in fact. Even the virulently anti-FIS French government tutted a bit. The irritable response included the expulsion of the *Le Monde* correspondent, a customary move when relations sour.

The profusion of small parties and political viewpoints that boiled into existence when politics were legalised turned out not to be a problem. The problem turned out to be something that was not pluralist at all, something that was itself intolerant and very widespread in socialist Algeria: the belief that solutions to political and economic problems can be sought in religion. The presence of religious motifs in the independence struggle – noted by Fanon – and the fact that the FLN appealed to Islam had always been balanced by a vigorous modernist element.

11 The seven-man HCE, which constituted itself at the time of Chadli's resignation, can be described as a provisional collective presidency responsible for steering the country until elections are held. It was in its name that Boudiaf was invited to become president. Its new chairman is the former career diplomat and reformist FLN member Ali Kafi, who was a much-respected Minister of Moudjahidine (independence combatants). Other members are the defence minister Khaled Nezzar, Reda Malek and Tadjini Haddam.

12 Later in the year the rank-and-file detainees were released in batches from detention in the Sahara, returning home to heroes' welcomes. At the beginning of October Ali Kafi, president of the Haut Comité d'État (HCE), signed a decree extending police powers, introducing special secret courts for 'terrorist' offences – now punishable by death – and reducing the age of criminal responsibility from eighteen to sixteen. A month later the two Algerian human rights organisations complained that torture of suspects had 'again' become common practice.

There are several crude parallels between the reasons for the disintegration of the Soviet Communist Party and that of the FLN, and in the ways these ruling parties dismantled themselves.[13] Political reform was already in the air when Boumedienne died suddenly in late 1978. Despite the good oil prices prevailing at the time, it was already apparent that Algeria's high rate of population growth, combined with the unproductiveness of the government's massive investments in heavy industry and agriculture, were depriving Algerians of the fruits of prosperity. A 'national debate' was organised whose product, a National Charter, was supposed to embody the national will. The result was an unusual explosion of free speech. Apart from grumbles about the worsening quality of life, there were pressing demands for more objective mass media, greater freedom of movement, relaxation of import restrictions and so forth. Reading between the lines, it was clear that people were heartily sick of the FLN, whose dead hand weighed heavily on all sectors. There were bitter complaints about corruption, incompetence and the associated bureaucratic effrontery. Something, it was hinted, would be done about all this, but when published the National Charter simply enshrined the status quo, and reiterated the FLN's – Boumedienne's – basic 'options': socialism, Islam, state monopoly of everything. Things were going to improve, but there would be no U-turns. As the Algerians struggled to work out what it all meant, Boumedienne died. Although perfectly genuine, the mourning that followed was strangely tinged with relief as well as apprehension. The major obstacle to change had gone.

Chadli purged the regime in stages: familiar FLN grandees were moved out of the government, then out of the Politburo, then out of the Central Committee (and later, in some cases, out of the FLN), to be replaced by new faces of supposedly technocratic cast. At the same time these bodies were altered in size, composition and function in a complex process familiar to all regime-watchers: piecemeal tinkering combined with a sort of card-sharping element. Changes to the military hierarchy included the promotion of a large number of colonels to newly created field ranks. Decentralisation of responsibility began with the appointment of a prime minister in Chadli's first government (although for over a decade, like Boumedienne, he kept the defence portfolio for himself).

Substantive change was slow in coming, however. Proposed reforms were framed so cautiously that it was child's play for those defending sinecures, or with ingrained habits of obstructiveness or indifference, to shunt

---

13 Even if Chadli has the soul of a Brezhnev rather than a Gorbachev.

them into sidings. Economic plans were outlined, political reforms discussed and promised, the national charter 'enriched'. But little change was perceptible to most people except a worsening standard of living: in fact, contrary to most people's expectations, the economic reckoning had already arrived. During Boumedienne's last decade there was much relaxed discussion of 'preparing for the post-petroleum era'. Ten years later, by 1985 when the oil price collapsed, Algeria – still in possession of large quantities of oil and enormous quantities of gas – was staring economic crisis in the face. What had happened?

Algeria in the debt trap

The answer is: nothing very dramatic; no disaster or watershed, just the relentless effects of time on the imbalance between the population growth rate and the economic growth rate. The Boumedienne regime's somewhat unsmiling, righteously authoritarian style masked a highly developed (if flawed) social vision,[14] demanding massive investment in heavy industry and the so-called 'agrarian revolution'. The idea was to modernise Algeria and to turn it into an advanced Mediterranean state with an educated population, but with its own identity: socialist, but also Arab and Muslim. In 1962 the country already had a well-developed colonial agriculture and light industrial superstructure; the huge financial cushion provided by hydrocarbons income – nothing on the Gulf or Libyan scale per capita, but substantial all the same – was nearly all fed into social services, heavy industry (initially hydrocarbons-based, but with ambitious aims in steel and so forth), socialised and cooperative agriculture, and increasingly into housing, roads and the water schemes needed, in a largely arid country, to support all forms of human activity. Equipment for Algeria's substantial armed forces added to the burden of debt. Algeria's status as an oil and gas producer made Western banks and agencies eager to fund the various development projects. By 1990 Algeria had an external debt of over $24 billion, and service payments were regularly absorbing more than half of all export earnings.[15]

---

14 It is worth mentioning, in these harsh and bewildering times for people of socialist sensibility, that Boumediennism's extreme fragility was not immediately apparent to outsiders – not, anyway, to this writer – in the very different-looking world of that time.

15 Oil flowed in earnest from the middle 1960s, and the income blossomed into big money with the OPEC-led price shocks of the 1970s. Algeria was always among the most hawkish OPEC states. For details of the country's debt burden, which is exacting a higher proportion of export earnings than any other country in the world, see World Bank, *World Bank Development Report 1992*, pp. 259, 265.

AFRICA

The recalcitrance to market forces of industries set up for ideological reasons, under ideological constraints, should be familiar to readers of *New Left Review*. Algeria's industry was organised under one or two ministers in several giant corporations (for steel and metals, building materials, rail vehicles, and so on). Virtually all were net consumers of money: the principal net producer, the state hydrocarbons company Sonatrach, earned more than 90 per cent of the country's foreign currency at all times and was thus dominant and privileged. State enterprises tended to be overmanned and very badly managed.[16] The import and export of goods were state monopolies. Private enterprises existed but found life difficult. The worst bottlenecks were shortage of foreign currency for essential equipment and the hideous byzantine bureaucracy of import arrangements. These were run for the benefit of state enterprises, which ate up all available foreign currency. Private businesses had to grapple with the system as best they could, using parallel illegal methods based on the million or so Algerians living and working in France. Until the 1980s Algeria was viewed by Western diplomats as not being especially corrupt by African standards. The slush factor on deals was said to average about 5 per cent of total investment. But given Algeria's evolved bureaucracy and numerous interest groups, such matters were far from simple. The result was general inertia and a perception, probably justified, that corruption was growing.

Of course it can be argued, and often was, that it is correct for a government to spend hydrocarbon revenues in equipping the country for the future, providing social services and so on. Nobody expected the steel industry to return an instant profit, and if other enterprises seemed a bit lethargic,[17] it remained the case that Sonatrach was nine-tenths of the hard-cash economy anyway – the rest was just internal juggling. Most shocking was the decline of agriculture, very developed before independence with large-scale wine, fruit, olive and grain production. All large estates were

---

16 In the early enthusiasm for state ownership enterprises like small restaurants and hotels had been nationalised, with baleful effects on their condition and the services offered. This happened before Boumedienne's coup, but the regime never did anything to restore the situation. Only foreigners minded having to deal with a hostile, arrogant, suspicious, untrained, disappointed former war hero instead of an obsequious lackey when they ordered their soup or tried to get a hotel room. Algerians were used to this sort of thing, and generally took the attitude that foreigners who didn't like it knew what they could do.

17 When, that is, they got beyond the planning stage. Algeria is a large consumer of motor vehicles and has long-standing plans to produce and export them, but has chosen to hold sporadic inconclusive talks with firms like Fiat and Volkswagen rather than expand the Renault and Peugeot assembly operations already tenuously present. None of these plans have come to fruition and supplies are haphazard and sporadic, the government sometimes making bulk purchases to appease certain levels of the bureaucracy. After Boumedienne's death from a kidney ailment *Le Canard enchaîné* published the cruel squib: *'Pénurie de dattes, beaucoup de Passat (un rein a signalé)'*.

taken over by the state and run by managers or workers' cooperatives. Some of these worked better than others, but there were infrastructural bottlenecks (input and equipment shortages, produce wasted through poor or non-existent distribution arrangements). Government policy under Boumedienne's 'agrarian revolution' was restless, gimmicky, grandiose and extravagant. Production of wine was cut back as the EC developed and France reduced its imports from Algeria; Soviet bloc countries absorbed some of the surplus but not all of it. Food production virtually never met targets. By the 1980s at least half of the country's grain requirement was met from imports. Grain products – wheat flour for bread and the semolina from which couscous is made – are among the basic necessities (others are coffee, tea, sugar and cooking oil) whose prices are controlled, originally at a low level. In the 1960s and early 1970s, when Algeria had no foreign debt and oil prices were rising, the cost of these arrangements, although considerable, was relatively unimportant compared to the rest of the economy. By the end of the 1980s, with service payments on the debt eating up the larger part of current earnings, the country was having to borrow at commercial rates to finance ever-growing food imports.

Algeria had virtually no foreign debt until the late 1970s. Borrowing was then undertaken to finance development of the natural gas industry, and maintained to pay for the housing and road programmes of the 1980s. Repayments were supposed to peak in about 1985, the year in which OPEC control of oil prices collapsed. The country's oil resources had been running down for some time, and vast sums had to be spent on organising the transport and sale of natural gas, of which Algeria has huge reserves. The problem with gas is that its energy content is lower than that of oil but its transport and handling costs are a lot higher. Crude petroleum can be carried about in buckets if necessary; gas has to be compressed, cooled and held in pressurised containers. Transfer from pipelines to bulk carriers and vice versa has to be through an integrated, sealed system, expensive to build and operate. At the same time, there is no perceived world shortage of gas, which in the hydrocarbons industry has a sort of second-class status (that is, it is cheaper than oil for the same energy potential). Buyers want the cheapest possible supplies, and in the current market conditions can afford to shop around and buy spot at the last minute. Producers, on the other hand, need large long-term contracts at the highest possible price to justify the initial investment and keep production flowing steadily.

Algerian negotiators in the 1970s and early 1980s, believing that energy would continue to become more valuable in the short and medium term, bargained very hard with potential clients, insisting that the price of gas should be linked by energy equivalent to that of crude oil. Naturally the biggest buyers – France, other European and US utilities companies – bargained equally hard and scrapped contracts whenever world prices suggested it. As always when dealing with state-capitalist entities the client companies were swayed by changes in the government-to-government emotional climate to tighten or slacken the screws as appropriate.[18] When the oil price plummeted in 1985, the effort devoted to pegging the price of gas to the OPEC crude marker price turned out to have been wasted. Gas remains valuable for the long term but so far has proved disappointing. So desperate has Algeria become for hard money that Boudiaf's prime minister, former Sonatrach boss Sid' Ahmed Ghozali, tried to sell oilfields to the oil companies – something that would have been unimaginable a few years ago. The companies, incidentally, played hard to get, but a number of new exploration contracts have already been signed. Meanwhile Algeria, which used to settle cash on the nail every quarter day, is in the toils of commercial banks and no longer quite regarded as a first-class credit risk. Undignified terms like 'rollover' and 'rescheduling' are often heard these days.

A near world-beating population growth rate has helped ensure minimum individual benefit from state investment in housing and other infrastructures. The population has virtually tripled from its 1962 level of around 9 million. Boumedienne was against birth control and would not even allow the subject to be raised. During the 1980s it has been raised on several occasions, but people pick their words carefully (family planning is called *espacement des naissances*). In any case most Algerians are very resistant to the idea, often citing vaguely religious reasons. As elsewhere the question is entangled with the status of women in society. A 'family code' setting out the rights and obligations of Algerian women was promised after the national charter; and later, under Chadli, one was debated and adopted by a virtually all-male legislature, many of whose members were keen to show Muslim sentiment. It was not well received by rational Algerian

---

18 Allegations about the disappearance of state money into private bank accounts are now widely repeated, although the amounts involved vary. Former prime minister Abdelhamid Brahimi was first to name the incredible figure of $26 billion (strikingly close to the national debt), since echoed by Ben Bella and others. Brahimi's successor Kasdi Merbah referred vaguely to 'missing billions', while *his* successor, Mouloud Hamrouche, said that $1.8 billion were not accounted for, Ben Bella claims to have proof of Chadli's personal involvement and says the money is stashed in Venezuela, Canada and Belgium. Not much hard evidence has been produced, but many Algerians believe the allegation and there have been calls for Chadli to be tried. Boudiaf disagreed, saying there was 'not a shred of evidence' against him.

women, but then and later their protests were drowned by the enthusiastic cries of very large groups of women mustered by the Islamists.

Problems of identity

The Boumediennist creed, a sort of Algerianised left-Nasserism, was not just dreamy and idealistic about economics: it wanted to rewrite history and give the Algerians, whose territory was an arbitrary French invention, a new identity. Because it looked a good idea to attach Algeria to something called the 'Arab nation', because he himself loved Islam and Arabic culture, Boumedienne decreed that the Algerians were Muslims and Arabs. The first was more or less true but the second was not. Even Algerians who are not, say, Tuaregs or Kabyles are very often culturally and, as it were, ethnically, Berber more than anything else. The whole society has its own flavour in which Berber is an important component. Along with French culture, which had been predominant in secondary education and above, the Berber element was deliberately discouraged in Boumedienne's time.[19]

The Kabyles clustered thickly in the upper reaches of what *Le Monde* calls the Algerian nomenklatura seem to have taken a sophisticated view of all this. Berber mother tongues and the associated cultures had long been restricted to private or neighbourhood life. The French secondary and university education these cadres had received was of much greater practical importance. Efforts were made to inflect education away from French by encouraging secondary-school pupils to learn English or some other language instead, but increasing numbers of children were being educated wholly in Arabic, from primary school to university. By the end of the 1970s there existed in effect two parallel education systems: the traditional one involving acquisition of a European language, and the 'Arabising' system strongly favoured by elements in the regime, manned partly by Palestinian, Iraqi and other Middle Eastern exiles.[20] Of course there were exceptions, but the quality of teaching in the Arabic sector, especially in technical and scientific subjects, was thought broadly inferior to that of the traditional

---

19 A well-connected intellectual Kabyle from near Tizi-Ouzou once told me that at primary school in the sixties he had been taught by two Palestinians who fined the children 30 dinars – no joke to an eight-year-old – for speaking Berber. The French are often said to have punished children for speaking Arabic in the bad old days.

20 But the initial cornerstone of the system was an intake of Egyptian schoolteachers provided under an official government-to-government scheme. Some of these teachers energetically promoted Islamist ideas (personal testimony, Iraqi former teacher in Algeria).

system. This was reflected in graduates' employment prospects, which by 1980 had become a matter of serious concern. Shadowy masses of young unemployed and underemployed had accumulated in the towns and cities, overcrowding the new housing along with the old, straining all services and all incomes. They were the raw material for post-Boumedienne politics.

The wave of cultural agitation that surprisingly arose in 1979 was started by Kabyle nationalists. The tough and clever Kabyles had no designs to become hegemonic in Algeria but wanted Berber languages and cultures to be respected, with proper teaching and official publications. The high-profile leaders were poets, musicians and academics, but the muscle when push came to shove was supplied by the population of Kabylie, which agreed with the very moderate demands being made. Leading agitators were arrested, one of them on a trumped-up firearms charge,[21] but a general strike in Kabylie and some vigorous Kabyle rioting, with deaths, made the point: the attempt to deny officially that Berber culture predates Islam and is a component of Algerianness has been quietly abandoned, and universities can offer courses in Kabyle literature without risking official sanctions.[22]

The immediate effect of the Kabyle agitation was a wave of rival cultural demands from 'Arabist' students. They included a suggestion that Arabic education be based not on classical Arabic but on the demotic variant, heavily mixed with Berber, Turkish and French, that is actually spoken by Algerians. This interesting idea was not pursued for long though. The Arabists were really demonstrating against inequality of opportunity, with French-speakers enjoying better job prospects in an employment market that was now very bleak for everyone. Clashes took place at a number of universities between groups of *arabisants* and *francisants*. The French-speakers were sometimes referred to as 'modernists' or 'progressives', the more numerous Arabic-speakers very significantly as 'traditionalists' or 'Islamists'.[23] Incidents occurred in which girl students and other women were bullied or harassed in a cruel and repellent manner for alleged impropriety of dress or comportment. Amid the cultural clamour of the

---

21 Aït Menguellet, a much-loved poet and singer. He had an ornamental muzzle-loader hanging on the wall.
22 At present. But any increase in Islamist influence would pose a new threat to this freedom.
23 Islam and the Arabic language are inextricably entangled. Translations of the Koran do not have the status of the text dictated to the Prophet Muhammad in Arabic by the Archangel Gabriel. Conversely, in Arab psychology, the language itself is unconsciously felt to be imbued with the divinity of its poetic and philosophic cornerstone, the Koran. The proud conviction that it is impossible for non-Arabic speakers to understand fully the world's only really important text has one particularly grave consequence for Arabic-speaking Muslims: a deep-seated feeling that it is not really worth the effort of understanding anything else. Of course there are Muslim scholars or intellectuals of Muslim background who take a very different view. But they do not really set the tone of public discourse on these matters.

early 1980s it was not recognised by outsiders that these incidents marked the beginnings of overt Islamist organisation.

Meanwhile some effort was being made to relax austerity and drift towards a more liberal kind of economy, break up the state industries (there was not yet much talk of privatisation) and give more and better land to the private farmers, who nearly always outperform state farms. All these processes were bitterly resisted by well-placed beneficiaries of the existing system and some – especially land distribution – led to quite violent local disputes. Real progress, given the backlog of unemployed and the high expectations of Algerians, was painfully slow. There was external change too. Algeria mediated between Iran and the United States over the Tehran Embassy hostages, starting a process of rapprochement with Washington that ended with a visit by Chadli in 1985 and reclassification of Algeria by the US as a friendly country. It maintained a militant stance on the Middle East but distanced itself from Libya,[24] and became friendlier with Morocco and Tunisia. New embassies were opened in Africa and elsewhere and Chadli travelled about, promoting the theme of 'South–South cooperation'. Mitterrand's election in France in 1981 made improvement possible there too, although the Algerian stance on Western Sahara remained contentious.

In October 1988, three years after the OPEC oil price collapse, the disappearance from the shops of basic foodstuffs, except at high black market prices, combined with the normal discomforts of overcrowding and idleness to cause the sort of youth rioting in Algiers and other cities that had already cost bloodshed in Tunisia and Morocco. It started with a large peaceful demonstration in central Algiers by secondary-school pupils and developed into rioting by unemployed youths who attacked symbols, not just of affluence, but of the state. The rioting went on for five days and was then suppressed by the army. The authorities admitted two hundred deaths but the figure bandied about by journalists was five hundred. Afterwards it was reported that prominent imams had appeared on the streets appealing for calm.[25]

In the outburst of free speech that followed the riots, the FLN was demolished as a ruling party. There had already been talk of allowing it

24 The Hassi-Messaoud agreement signed by Boumedienne and Gaddafi in 1975 included a clause to the effect that any threat to either of the two 'revolutions' would be considered a threat to the other. Despite official solidarity, the Libyan penchant for unilateral action and provocative statements was a constant headache to Algerian diplomats, who favoured a more measured style.
25 One cannot help wondering whether the reporters always got this quite right. The first TV clip I ever saw of the Rev. Ian Paisley showed him bellowing into a megaphone, the veins on his temples pulsing visibly even in a 405-line picture. There was no live sound, but a bland BBC voice-over stated that he was appealing for calm.

to become a front once again, a broad church reflecting the country's real diversity. The riots had made it clear that the young, an absolute majority of the population, did not share their parents' residual loyalty to the party that led the independence struggle. They had, on the other hand, listened for years to their parents' disappointed complaints. To them the FLN represented fantasies of entrenched privilege, corruption, authority, the hated status quo. They were available to be mobilised by some cause or movement – so many after all had nothing else to do – and the moral authority of the FLN was not going to influence the process, except perhaps negatively.

The rise of the FIS

Serious constitutional reforms began immediately after the riots. Within a month a national referendum had approved draft reforms extending the role and powers of the prime minister, who was henceforth to be answerable to parliament rather than the president. Chadli in effect was kicking himself upstairs. He appointed Kasdi Merbah, a Kabyle lawyer who had been Boumedienne's chief of military security, prime minister; at an FLN congress shortly afterwards the post of General Secretary was abolished and replaced by that of First Chairman, to which Chadli was elected.[26] Mohamed Cherif Messaadia, long-time head of the FLN secretariat, was purged along with the head of security, following Boumedienne's industrial barons, or some of them, into obscurity, if you can call it obscurity.[27] Demands for 'democracy' were now constantly heard, and Chadli used the word a lot at the congress, while the word 'socialism' seemed to be fading out. He was elected for another five-year term in December. In February 1989 another referendum approved a new Constitution more or less stripping the FLN of all its functions and establishing the right to form parties,[28] an astonishing event overshadowed by the much larger parallel process in the Soviet Union. FLN meetings had become

---

26 Chadli was also re-elected president in December 1988. In mid-June 1992 the Arabic-language daily *Essalam* published an alleged Interior Ministry document showing that he had received less than 19 per cent of the vote in the presidential election. The official results at the time gave him just over 81 per cent.

27 No condition is permanent. Belaid Abdessalam, a main architect of Boumedienne's industrial strategy, removed by Chadli with much fanfare soon after his accession, has been appointed prime minister by Ali Kafi, Boudiaf's somewhat low-key successor.

28 Yes votes were cast by 73 per cent of the 79 per cent of the electorate who voted – in other words 58 per cent of all voters. *Africa Today* observed: 'The loss of traditional unanimity made these the most convincing poll figures in Algerian history. The underground parties, like the government, had urged voters to turn out and approve the reforms; the 42 per cent who either abstained or voted against showed that a significant minority of Algerians still felt they had reason to support FLN one-party rule.'

noisy affairs thick with recrimination, but they continued to take place and the party continued to dissolve its constitutional links with the state.[29] Meanwhile around thirty new parties came out of clandestineness or exile, or were formed, and queued for official registration, which started in July 1989.

They included parties organised from abroad by *chefs historiques* like Ahmed Ben Bella,[30] and Hocine Aït Ahmed;[31] a slimmed-down FLN and the Parti de l'Avant-Garde Socialiste (PAGS) which existed in tolerated clandestineness within and alongside the FLN;[32] and numerous centrist and social-democratic organisms with small or negligible, and nearly always local, followings. This made future mergers and coalitions seem likely, and they soon started to appear. Former MPs, technocrats, businessmen, lawyers and even some old FLN bigwigs[33] were prominent among founders of the new parties. Only one, the Rassemblement pour la Culture et la

---

29 The most recent FLN congress, at the end of October 1992, was dominated by arguments about the party's relations with the regime: should it remain in alliance with the power or plunge into the swamp of opposition?

30 After Boumedienne's 1965 coup Ben Bella was detained without charge for sixteen years in strict but not harsh conditions (he married a lawyer while detained). Appeals on his behalf got a curt response from the regime, which often pointed out that in other countries Ben Bella would have been killed. Chadli let him out soon after Boumedienne's death and he spent the 1980s in France and Switzerland organising his Mouvement pour la Démocratie en Algérie (MDA), whose policy, when stated, turned out to be Islamist. A lot of people found this impossible to believe and continued to think of Ben Bella as an apostle of workers' control. The MDA was registered in March 1990, but Ben Bella did not return to Algeria until September of that year. His managers could only muster a disappointing crowd of 40,000 to greet him. The old rabble-rouser urged the audience, much of which had only the vaguest idea who he was, to put its trust in Islam, throw out Chadli and his 'gang of bandits' and sign up immediately in the Iraqi army. Of course, of course. But what was *new*? The rabble had already been roused, and Ben Bella surrounded, by the FIS. His political position is extremely uncomfortable. His criticisms of the FIS are restricted to its tactics ('We have to help the FIS to help itself') and the question of multi-party democracy which he is committed to supporting; conversely, while approving the Boudiaf manoeuvre, which at least kept the democratic process alive, he was obliged to oppose the repression involved. This tightrope-walking may have helped him retain the esteem of some of his peers, but was almost certainly wasted on the mass of voters, who do not understand parliamentary democracy and see Ben Bella's Islamism as contaminated or ambivalent.

31 Front des Forces Socialistes (FFS), founded 1963; mainly Kabyle like Aït Ahmed who spent his twenty-six-year exile in Switzerland. In 1985, with Ben Bella, he launched an appeal from Rabat for Algeria to end its support for the Polisario in Western Sahara.

32 Originally the Algerian section of the French Communist Party, supported by technocrats and intellectuals, a founder-member of the FLN. One assumes it continued to exist, albeit in shadowy form, because of protection from the Soviet Union and France. One of only two genuinely secular parties, the PAGS nevertheless pointed out in 1990 that it was not 'against Islam'.

33 Like Kasdi Merbah, who lasted nine months as prime minister. When sacked in September 1989 during a wave of agitation about wages and living conditions, Merbah alarmed the regime by refusing to go for twenty-four hours, saying he had not been given a free hand to govern. After making his point, he resigned and later formed the Mouvement Algérien pour la Justice et le Développement (MAJD). In an interview published in May 1992 he refused to comment on the banning of the FIS, saying that the matter was sub judice, but urged the formation of 'a government of national union to manage, through a minimum programme, the phase of transition', and a return to the electoral process next year. He was afraid Algeria was evolving 'a democracy of façade' in the Moroccan or Tunisian style. Merbah has no mass following and is not loved, but significantly he is not hated either. With his history this makes him a man to listen to.

Démocratie (RCD), called openly for secular politics 'to separate Islam from political temptations'.[34] The others had at least a clause about religion, ranging from an acknowledgement of its fundamental importance in Algerian culture to greater or lesser degrees of slavish adherence.[35] It was already clear which way the wind was blowing, and people were preparing, willingly or not, to coexist with the beards and headscarves that seemed to be everywhere. A handful of Islamist minnows, including a missionary Hezbollah, straggled into the queue of parties, but the mighty whale of the FIS was already registered, formed out of the air, out of a national coalition of political imams and their associates, out of nowhere, its leaders giving themselves statesmanlike airs and getting private audiences with Chadli.

It was a time of huge street demonstrations, and the FIS was uncontested king. On one occasion in late 1989 it put an estimated 400,000 on the streets of Algiers, half of them women, to demonstrate against threats to 'the dignity of Muslim womanhood' and 'aggressions against Islam'.[36] Even the FLN could only manage half this number at best, and a centrist coalition of new parties 150,000. Violent incidents between Islamists and modernists, feminists, bar owners and so forth were occurring frequently, and there were more serious armed incidents involving the security forces. These were always disowned by the FIS, but it was already apparent that the Islamists thought they had a right to rule and regarded the electoral process as just one means to that end. The FIS is very well funded, and on several occasions it outflanked lethargic, and now very demoralised, FLN cadres to supply social needs.[37] It is often alleged that the FIS is heavily funded from abroad. Perhaps so, for there are plenty of countries – not all Muslim – with

---

34 The RCD also advocates a radical birth-control programme to reduce the population growth rate to 2 per cent. Islamist wits nicknamed it the Rassemblement contre Dieu, no deterrent to its gutsy supporters (mainly Kabyle). It won quite a few seats in the 1990 local elections, but probably got some votes that would have gone to Aït Ahmed's party if it had put up candidates.

35 Like the FLN under Boumedienne: Islam had been a unifying force in the war of independence and would now be a unifying force in Algeria and the 'Arab nation'. Modernists squeamish about having a state religion sometimes argued for its relegation to private life, but this was never a popular line. One advantage in Boumedienne's time was that imams were routinely surveyed and kept under control. The disadvantage was that the incipient confusion between the divine and the everyday was not removed from the popular imagination, but continued to haunt Algeria as it does most other Muslim societies.

36 Although supposedly organised by the Islamic League led by Sheikh Ahmed Sahnoun, it really counted as an FIS demo. Sahnoun (elderly, blind, traditionalist and much respected) and many other imams have a somewhat ambivalent relationship with the FIS, which is neither a coalition of Islamic organisations nor a national party, but something between the two. It is not even entirely clear whether Abassi Madani and Ali Benhadj are the FIS's leaders or just spokesmen for an invisible committee of imams, which would certainly need to be bigger, at least for advisory purposes, than the FIS's fourteen-cleric Council.

37 Getting in first with tents, blankets and food after an earthquake at Tiapaza in October 1989; using local muscle to intervene in land and housing allocation, often a source of bitter disputes.

the money and inclination to promote Islamism in Algeria. But this element is probably being exaggerated for obvious, if not very good, reasons. It should not be forgotten that Algeria is a rich country and that FIS supporters include plenty of well-heeled resourceful citizens, former and serving officials, members of the armed forces, guerrillas and adventurers with experience of conflict in places like Lebanon and Afghanistan, and so on. The point is that even if money, training and equipment are solicited from abroad, and are forthcoming, they are just icing on the cake. It is perfectly clear that the FIS depends on internal forces, not external ones. This helped ensure its landslide victory in the local elections of June 1990. Along with others including Ben Bella and Aït Ahmed, who said they were not ready, the FIS threatened to boycott the elections, but changed its mind in time. Nine parties put up candidates, but it was really a two-horse race. The FIS got 54 per cent of the municipal votes, the FLN 28 per cent, Independents 12 per cent, the RCD 2.1 per cent, and the centrist PNSD, in coalition with other parties, 1.6 per cent.

The FIS said the figures were rigged and that it had really received 80 per cent of the vote. The aftermath of the election saw a major split in the top ranks of the FLN, with conservatives like Rabah Bitat[38] pressing for slower economic reform and a delay before the general election, at that time scheduled for 1992. As a result of continuing FIS pressure on street and other levels, however, the election was soon brought forward and scheduled for mid-1991. Demands for Chadli's resignation were heard on all sides, from the FIS and others who thought they or their friends might have a chance in the compromise-candidate stakes.

The multi-party electoral process had made a shaky start. As the time for the general election approached it became increasingly apparent that a FIS victory was more than likely. Dreams of a rationalist, secular coalition centred on the FLN had faded: apart from disagreements and the ingrained lordly habits of the FLN rump, it simply did not look as if such a body would get enough votes. And the FIS's numerous denunciations of democracy as a fraudulent infidel device made it clear that once in power the Islamists would try to stay there by force. The prospect did not frighten FIS supporters, who were used to an unpopular regime that banned opponents

---

38 The last grand old man of the FLN still in office, Bitat was president (speaker) of the National Assembly throughout the 1980s, after playing a key role in the constitutional proceedings after Boumedienne's death that brought Chadli to power. His resignation at this point was a body blow to the FLN, and was closely followed by the resignation of Kasdi Merbah and another former prime minister, Abdelhamid Brahimi, from the central committee.

and monopolised power. They looked forward to electing a popular regime of the same sort. The calls for democracy had not been calls for a set of political constitutions that, if all went well, would enable peaceful routine political change to occur in response to people's needs and wishes, the way it had evolved seamlessly from revolutionary front to complacent, authoritarian, perhaps corrupt, certainly stubbornly incompetent, state machine: these were lessons that had not been learned. The wilful ignorance, the disdain for earthly facts, the incapacity to understand history as a continuing linear process, the dream that without thinking Algeria can miraculously equip itself with a perfect government, were not restricted to poorly educated youths numb with boredom and despair. Many people who ought to know better are FIS backers and supporters.

The regime – the tattered FLN machine still in place, the Chadli clique, the many respectable retired Boumediennists, the army – was staring disaster in the face. The events in Kuwait were torture, with the FIS, Ben Bella and others whipping up enormous public indignation against the West (never difficult in Algeria over Middle Eastern issues). Algerian leaders are not natural allies of the Iraqi Ba'ath, but like other governments they were dragged along reluctantly in the wake of public opinion. The defection to the UN coalition of Syria, which *was* an ally, twisted the bayonet in the wound. But all that was just a distraction from the problem of the rapidly approaching general election.

Secular optimists pointed out hopefully that over a third of the electorate had not voted, and were therefore probably not Islamists. In addition, they said (and are still saying), voters had favoured the FIS to show disapproval of the FLN, to punish its representatives. But Algerians were far too well off, far too progressive, far too relaxed in their habits, to want a fundamentalist government (sharia law, no beer or satellite TV, the country's handsome and spirited women dressed in huge sacks and doomed to illiteracy). There had been a protest vote in the local elections. In a general election they would not vote for the FIS, *insh'Allah*. There was a silent majority. The psephological buzzwords echoed strangely in the discourse of the Algerian chattering classes, with its overtones of Paris-Moscow *langue de bois*. You could almost hear the inverted commas.

An overlapping group of siren voices, including middle-class FIS supporters, said that Algeria should lie back and enjoy it. The FIS were not fundamentalists at all; that was just French propaganda. They were just Muslims, like everybody else. The FIS weren't backward imams – look at

Abassi Madani[39] – they were educated men; they could do just as well as this lot. What they lacked in experience they would make up in responsiveness and virtue. Anyway, Algeria is a serious country, with professionals in charge of all the difficult stuff. Iran had managed all right, hadn't it? And so on. Come to the beach and see the girls in their bikinis. Have a drink in the resto next door to FIS HQ. Does this look like a country on the brink of fundamentalism? And even if we did have to do without legal bars, might it not do us good?

It is easy to be glib about such things, to sweep aside suggestions that things might change after an election, that there might be some sort of distorted class war, with escalation of pure hard zeal between rival clerical demagogues, a miserable *fuite en avant* to mask governmental incompetence, civil war. But even non-FIS Algerians, even foreigners, think anything of that sort unlikely in Algeria. The country has always had an original side. Perhaps it could domesticate Islam, evolve a user-friendly fundamentalism ... anyway the die was cast. Everyone wanted free elections and they were going to take place.

But to the pessimists the figures promised an overall majority for the FIS. And then what? Gerrymandering was the only way to shift the balance, and the regime tried it twice. An electoral law was promulgated that attempted to rearrange the parliamentary constituencies to make rural areas, where FLN support remains high, return more MPs, and the towns and cities, where the FIS holds sway, return fewer. The bill was rejected by the National Assembly and a less blatant one substituted. Both were roundly condemned by the higher-profile political parties, and the FIS's demands for Chadli's resignation were pursued on all levels, with much organised slogan-shouting. Despite the near certainty of an FIS victory, the first stage of the election was held in late December amid clamorous allegations of intimidation and other malpractices by the two main parties. Interim results were announced that suggested a reduced FIS vote, but the regime nevertheless felt obliged to cancel the second stage and annul the election. Violent protests followed, leading to the muffled coup d'état of early 1992, which placed Boudiaf at the front of a regime in which the profile of the armed forces was more visible than usual. The country had been saved from fundamentalism. But in whose name? The electoral process was

---

39 Abassi Madani is said to have a PhD in the social sciences from a British university, and to have been imprisoned by the French for seven years as a member of the FLN. In 1982 he was imprisoned again, allegedly for demonstrating against the incorrect ranking of socialism above Islam in the National Charter – unusual behaviour for a revolutionary nationalist with a British scientific training.

suspended, perhaps only for a while. But can it be resumed in any meaningful way without the Islamic integralists making a comeback?

It is true that Islamic integralists are just Muslims, although, *alhamdulillah*, not all Muslims are Islamic integralists. It is a great burden to have the last and most perfect religion and to be morally superior to all non-Muslims. It means that only through sustained and rigorous intellectual effort can one reach an understanding of, say, the philosophic setting of the natural sciences, or the advantages of habeas corpus over sharia. These and many other things, being outside Islam, being in fact distorted caricatures of perfect Islamic forms, are doomed to vanish like smoke on the day of judgement if not before, and thus hardly worth any effort. This is one reason why even people who have lived in France, and been to Italy and America, are prepared thoughtlessly to vote into power a party that has promised, more or less, that it will not hold any further free elections. It will be a *Muslim* party – not like Iran, we're not Shias, but a *real Muslim* party – so no more elections will be needed, will they?

An opportunist patchwork

The Iranian philosopher Daryush Shayegan's book *Le Regard mutilé* (now published in English as *Cultural Schizophrenia*), although based on the Iranian experience, which understandably makes the author hot under the collar, contains insights into Muslim radicalism. Shayegan points out that behind the robes, beards and air of scowling virtue, modern Islamism, far from representing a return to the wellsprings of the religion, is an opportunist patchwork of distorted Islam and vulgarised Western, notably Marxist, ideas cobbled together by third-rate ideologues. Islamic radicals assume that God will provide. Only when He fails to do so will it be realised that those responsible were not *real* Muslims. Failure to achieve the impossible is attributed to betrayal or conspiracy rather than to the obvious causes. Algeria is more than viable. It has adequate resources and a large, active intelligentsia; its people are proud but outward-looking. French influence is not responsible for the tireless, plausible volubility of Algeria's professionals, intellectuals, ideologues and these days, I suppose, entrepreneurs. Much of the FLN heritage – the robust egalitarianism, the social vision and its attendant roads, dams, factories and housing, the large numbers of cadres who are honest and competent, with a sense of civic decency – is profoundly positive. By the same token, much of the population is acquainted with industrial relations à l'européenne, with high wages, syndicalism and rights, although perhaps here the French connection outweighs the FLN. Most important of all is the persistence in the complex ethnocultural mosaic of Algerian society of traditional Muslim virtues (hospitality, humour, learning, moderation, justice, decency) alongside the modern characteristics of arrogance, paranoia, oppression of women and disdain for obvious facts.

Very unhappily, a corrosive and despairing political cynicism has become generalised during the avalanche of events. In the old days the FLN could do no wrong. Now that it has dissolved itself, albeit reluctantly, in response to public demand, it can do no right. Algerians would do well to ask themselves whether this is reasonable. Things may have gone wrong, but Boumedienne's FLN made a sporting try at a social vision in scale with the grandeur of the Algerian landscape, while Chadli's grappled with the conflicting demands of change. They should look at other countries and understand that theirs has a lot less to be ashamed of than many of them think. One of the qualities of the modern hybrid thought defined by Shayegan is the tendency to sanctify and satanise, to see things in black and white. It is significant that Westerners now associate this Manichaeism with Islam, although there is nothing particularly Muslim about it.

Another of these qualities is what Shayegan rather scornfully calls 'innocence': shamelessness in adopting contradictory positions. A few months ago some of its supporters were saying the FIS was holding intensive talks in London with the CIA. *Where?* The *what?* Yes, the CIA, named without the usual qualifications and epithets. The FIS, or so its friends seem to think, is trying to steal a march on the regime by getting in on the ground floor of the new world order. Nobody should doubt that Algerian Islamism has some of the makings of full-blooded Iranian-style Grand Guignol.

Nevertheless, the Haut Comité d'État, chaired by Ali Kafi, with the approval of around a third of the population and the acquiescence of another third, is hoping that the phenomenon will shrink to manageable proportions after another year or so of emergency rule and more or less martial law. There is a risk that the present complicated and painful three-cornered standoff between the regime, the FIS and the rest of the political class could settle into a perverse, negative kind of stability along Moroccan or Tunisian lines. Indeed this possibility has been hinted at by the very experienced Kasdi Merbah (see note 33 above). But predictions about Algeria should always be provisional, especially when crucial issues are still being debated by a society in which opposing political and philosophic views are co-present in most families. A chameleon's true colours are never seen, and its apparent ones only stop changing when the background stabilises. Such camouflage is intrinsic to Algeria, and may have operational uses in a world where elements that seemed immutable a couple of years ago have vanished, or been opened to general discussion.

New Left Review, 196, November–December 1992

OPINION:
THE CAPTAINS AND THE KINGS

During an interview broadcast the other night on British TV, Emperor Bokassa I of Central Africa pulled a couple of enormous diamonds out of his pocket and flashed them at the camera. His Majesty's close involvement in various levels of the gemstone market is common knowledge; his coronation on 4 December brought a mass of Paris merchants into the act, a whole flying circus of dressmakers, furriers, jewellers, vintners, horse-copers, hairdressers, chefs, riding instructors and dealers in second-hand carriages and second-rate sculpture. Laughter is permitted. But is it really justified?

Much commented on was the coronation's cost to the Emperor's subjects, about $14 each at a conservative estimate; $14 from every man, woman and child in the Central African Empire, around 2 million of what the newspapers tell us are 'among the poorest people in the world'. People who have to struggle to feed and clothe themselves, people who do not carry priceless jewels around in their pockets, people whose views on their country's system of government are not printed in the international press. In Paris, $14 will hardly pay for a good dinner. How many children will it feed in Birao?

Even a rich man might resent coughing up so much to feed another man's megalomania. That 2 million poor people should each be forced to disgorge a similar sum, should be given no choice in the matter, is a straightforward, commonplace crime, in no way different from the sort of thing that happens every day all over the world. We are all accustomed to large-scale robbery by our rulers and their friends. We expect it. It keeps the money circulating. It holds out to us the possibility that one day we, too, may slip through the fine mesh of an economic 'system' resembling nothing so much as a network of loopholes, into the calm waters of a tax-haven nirvana. How we deal with the moral problems raised by this embezzlers' paradise is up to us individually.

No, it isn't the $14 price tag that shocks. The cost of the whole coronation would hardly make a decent stock exchange scandal in Paris. The truly astonishing thing is that it should have taken place at all, that the Emperor's friends should have encouraged him to take such a step. There is nothing contradictory in the monarch's own position; old soldiers, scarred and decorated in foreign wars, often come home a bit touched in the head.

Coming from a man who wants to cut bits off thieves, who in a moment of ill-humour called the UN Secretary-General a 'colonist' and a 'ponce', who is not above clouting you around the ears with his ivory-handled ceremonial stick if you displease him, no extravagance can be very surprising. To such a man, an imperial throne may be no more than another promotion. When you're already a Field Marshal and President for Life, where else is there to go?

More remarkable is the attitude of his allies, notably the government of his adoptive second country and principal supporter, France (among His Majesty's other distinctions is that of being the only head of state with dual nationality). France has now been a republic for some years. Yet M. Robert Galley, Minister of Cooperation in the present French government, snapped at a reporter who questioned the propriety of French support for the enthronement of Africa's jeweller-king that to adopt different attitudes towards the English Queen's Jubilee and Bokassa's coronation smacked of 'racism'. He ignored the republican belief that a monarch, any monarch, symbolises and perpetuates that persistent phenomenon, inequality, the opposite of one of the three sacred principles of the French Revolution.

The British state is nowhere officially committed to the principles of liberty, equality and fraternity. The English maintain their relatively bargain-priced monarchy partly because it embodies the rejection of equality by a majority of them. Do the people of Bokassa's empire want equality or inequality? Nobody outside their country knows. Yet inequality is being built into their constitution with the essential support of France. If Giscard d'Estaing declared himself Emperor of the French, even his colleagues in the government would be quick to object. One must conclude that to the French government what would be unacceptable in France is acceptable, even desirable, in Africa. Could there be something 'racist' about that too?

The English press on 7 December featured President Kaunda's emotional 'attack' on the British Foreign Secretary, Dr Owen, following the latter's very delayed, rather callous response to the Smith regime's murderous foray into Mozambique – a sovereign state with which it is not at war. Far more remarkable was the near-silence of the press itself for more than a week after the invasion was launched, and the subsequent publication of Rhodesian handouts as 'news'.[40] The Zambian leader's tears are to be expected from one involved in current events in Southern Africa. British press coverage of those events is less easily understood and smacks of 'racism'.

---

40 Rhodesia, now Zimbabwe, was at that time being governed by a white-minority regime, universally condemned (except by South Africa), led by Ian Smith [ed.].

The mass murder of 1,200 people in Mozambique is part of the reality behind the utterances of the two Doctors and those others who concern themselves with the public presentation of affairs of state.[41] But we are used to discussing the utterances rather than the reality. Bokassa, Elizabeth II, Owen, Smith, Machel: personalising and trivialising everything, the Captains and the Kings and the fuss we all make of them, continue everywhere to eclipse and stifle the real life, the labour, the creativity of the nameless millions.[42] Unfortunately we still need 'leaders'. And we believe nonsense about them because we want to. Bokassa and Elizabeth II think that they are monarchs because the rest of us believe we are subjects. In a sense they are our victims, as we are theirs.

Africa magazine, 78, February 1978

---

41 The 'two doctors' are Dr Kaunda, president of Zambia, and Dr Owen [ed.].
42 Samora Machel was the president of Mozambique [ed.].

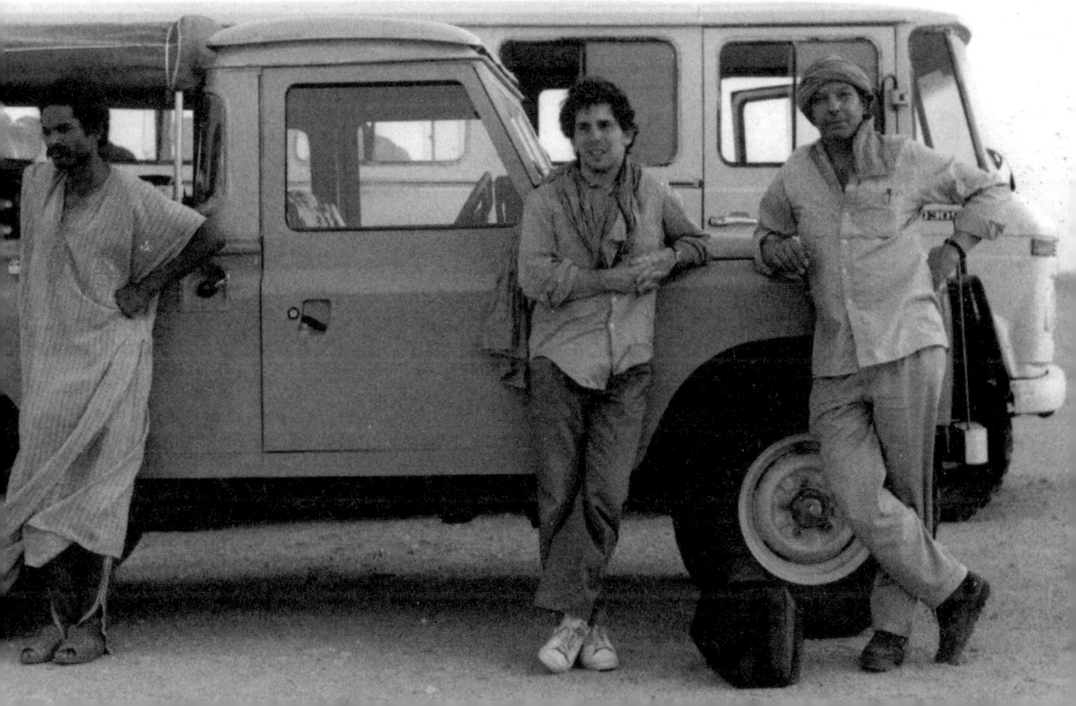

IF YOU CAN'T BE GOOD, BE CAREFUL …

Whether or not it keeps the planet revolving on its axis – astronomers by and large avoid public comment on the question – love is good for the physical and emotional health of human beings. Just as well perhaps, given the ease with which they fall in it, the dedication with which they pursue it and the tireless energy with which they make it. Not to mention the ingenuity of poets in writing about it, the predictability with which musicians sing about it and the effrontery of priests and princes who aspire variously to declare it wicked or illegal, set it about with rules said to be based on God's word or made in the interests of the nation, and expect as a result to receive a steady flow of small fees for giving those who have fallen in it a licence to make it.

The more astute among my fellow-drivers and their clamorous entourages of passengers, porters and pickpockets will have noticed by now that the word love is being bandied about, as it so often is, in loose or ambiguous fashion. They can rest assured that what we are talking about is the sort of close erotic friendship, short-lived or long-lasting, which maintains the human stock by creating baby human beings to take over from the existing adults when they die. We are excluding from consideration all neurotic or exotic variants of grand passion or perversion, along with anything claimed to be divine, and even (despite the causal connection) the structural devotion of mothers to the survival of their infants. What we are concerned with is the spectrum between commercial sex and married love.

The difference between the two is clear enough but the line is not easily drawn. African societies have been severely traumatised by the political, economic and demographic changes of the twentieth century. The continent's cities swarm not with an established urban proletariat but with ever-increasing numbers of uprooted villagers. These populations refer back to, but inevitably become distanced from, a large variety of 'traditional' religious and social systems regulating such things as marriage and inheritance. In any case such are the constraints on employment and living space that in many urban and semi-rural populations marriage is not an early option for the young.

If marriage is not available, however, the consolation of sex often is. Social and religious customs and taboos are weakened with time and distance, leading to the development of new, looser forms of traditional institutions like polygamy, temporary marriage, sanctioned adolescent experimentation with the opposite sex. The idea promoted by Christianity and Islam that the sex act itself is in some way shameful or sinful has not taken a general hold on the imagination of sub-Saharan Africa. Words like prostitution and promiscuity do not do justice to the variety of behaviour which results, although both phenomena are present. A fair amount of quite casual sex takes place, usually accompanied by relations of friendly goodwill and without a formal commercial transaction. Depending on local convention this sexually active group may be restricted to an urban minority or may include virtually everyone below late middle age. Even in the former case, both men and women may have acquired spouses or children in other towns or in the countryside and may have sexual contacts during visits to their home villages. This explains the variable but extremely rapid spread of HIV (AIDS) through some populations in eastern and central Africa.

HIV is not all that infectious except when injected directly into the bloodstream either in a blood transfusion or on an unsterilised hypodermic syringe. But it can be transmitted during normal penetrative sexual intercourse, probably more easily from men to women than vice versa and probably more easily where there is simultaneous infection with another sexually transmitted disease. It is a notable characteristic of these diseases that carriers may be infectious for some time before symptoms appear to make them aware of the condition. With HIV the infection can be present and communicable for five years or more before showing itself as deadly AIDS or 'slim'. But unlike gonorrhoea which can be cleared with an injection or two, AIDS is still incurable and likely to remain so for some years. HIV and a related virus, HTLV-4, have just begun to show up in West African screening exercises although not yet on the same scale as in Zaire, Rwanda, Uganda, Kenya, Tanzania and Zambia. There is a chance therefore that West Africa can limit the spread of the virus, but only if people recognise the risks of casual unprotected sex with partners they do not know well, and adopt defensive measures before the virus has spread too far into the population. The risk of infection increases with the number of sexual partners, and is greatly reduced by the wearing of a condom or rubber sheath during intercourse (other birth control techniques offer less protection or none at all). So the message to all of you here – yes, all of you, Alhaji, and you too, good morning, Madam – is that you should be good; and if you can't be good, be careful. This sickness is no respecter of persons. Whether you are exploiting the sexual or financial needs of your partner, or simply sharing your bodies in a spirit of friendly desire, the act, and therefore the risks, are the same.

West African Hotline, 12 February 1987

DON'T YOU BELIEVE IT

After dark, on a building site in an industrial suburb of a largish North African town, two North Africans sat drinking in a battered car with a European visitor. Alcohol is not illegal in the country in question but almost everyone is a believing Muslim. For this reason, it is difficult to find a comfortable bar outside the hotels catering to foreigners, even in the capital. In this town, the bar was only open for off-sales after dark. Scenes of gloomy conviviality would thus take place nightly in the industrial suburb, inside parked cars which later would drive off erratically into the darkness.

Many North Africans become assertively religious when drinking alcohol, wishing perhaps to deny the oppressive sense of sin which afflicts them as they consume the forbidden nectar, or trying unconsciously to displace it onto someone even more sinful than themselves. The European in the car has been cast in this scapegoat role more than once. On one occasion, his innocent admission of atheist views had led to an extremely long and tiresome conversation with two devout, slightly drunk building workers. 'He says heaven and hell are right here on this table,' explained one worker to the other in one of many bizarre misunderstandings.

So when the driver of the car had consumed two litres of the country's excellent red wine in the space of twenty minutes and, turning to the visitor, enquired casually into the nature of his religious beliefs the European – who had only had a couple of beers – replied that he could give no name or short description to his own relations with the universe. In answer to further enquiries, he denied that he was a Christian or a Jew and, stretching a point a bit, assured the baffled driver that he was not an atheist either. Hot on the trail, the driver came up with a key question: 'Do you believe in the one true God?'

The visitor thought fast. 'I think I can say,' he answered with what he hoped was an air of engaging frankness, 'that I most certainly do not believe in several.' At that moment, five men approached the car holding lengths of wood and other makeshift weapons, and politely asked the driver to move on, as he had parked near their house and the women were alarmed. 'God's blessings on you and your families,' they called morosely as the car clanked off over the rubble.

Amicable wrangles between sinners are one thing, mass murder and systematic oppression are others. Religious belief is not a prerequisite for these sins but they are often committed in its name. Priests, princes, merchants and revolutionaries, with their shrewd intellects and alley-cat morals,

BRICOLAGE

long ago learned how to wield the varieties of religion in furtherance of secular schemes. A spectrum of 'established churches' and 'official religions' testifies worldwide to the expedient collusion between ministers of religion and ministers of the state. Through this cooperation the support of large masses of believers has often been won, or hijacked, for enterprises of war, conquest and colonisation and almost as often, it must be admitted, for schemes involving less sacrifice and greater benefit.

For religion, which pervades our history and social structures, can only survive by embodying and reducing all their contradictions. The two great monotheisms both have living traditions of charity, mercy, tolerance, hospitality and kindness. Culture and abstract thought undoubtedly thrive in quiet rooms in Mecca and the Vatican, a little apart from the devout chanting of the multitudes. Yet priests blessed both sides on the killing fields of Flanders, as mullahs now make unfulfillable promises to the infantry in the marshes around Basra. It is perhaps part of the function of priests to prevent the faithful from adhering too closely to the logic of the Faith. They are like sheepdogs, as the faithful are all too like sheep.

Sheep are not as dumb as they look but they are easily stampeded. Usually models of peace and social order, they can be induced to run amok and trample shepherds underfoot. Religion is useful to secular rulers because it helps peacefully enforce moral and social codes. Thus, following the rioting in Kaduna State, Nigeria, the other week, Major Abubakar Umar's humane moves to reconcile Muslim and Christian communities and his reminder that vengeful behaviour is 'un-Islamic'. The governor was referring of course to an Islam adapted to a diverse region of a diverse modern world: true to its principles but relaxed, thoughtful, cultivated and forward-looking. As all religions, even the small ones, should be for the sake of the faithful; and as most are, if only in part.

So what of the other part, so easily mobilised by bad guys great and small to drive the faithful to murder and suicide, to persuade them to impoverish themselves, lacerate their flesh, persecute their fellows, have too many children, and so on? Unfortunately it lies at the root of all religion, in the unsupported assertion that we are important in an order of things ordained or controlled by a friend of ours. The evidence against this is so overwhelming that our faith in it requires a lifelong effort of blind will. This reservoir of energy lies ready in any population to be tapped by those who have made a career of learning to press the right buttons.

It is ignoble to be rushed into arrogant or cruel acts by alleged threats to one's faith. People died in Kaduna State the other day and many were terrorised. How astonishing that after so long a history human beings are still ready to listen uncritically to the rallying cries of those claiming to represent faith! Faith itself is not the problem. The existence of a supreme order of things, the existence of a creator even, cannot be finally disproved. But our existence in the here and now cannot be denied, and it is our behaviour in the here and now that most affects our comfort and security and those of our children. The importance of these things outweighs our most vehement denial of the insignificance of our species against the vast sprawl of the physical universe and the terrifying void beyond it.

West African Hotline, 1 April 1987

KEEP THE PROFIT, SHARE THE LOSS

It is our great fortune that being ignorant men, gaining our precarious living from the transport of goods and passengers over the variable roads of our great continent, we are not required to pronounce on issues of the day. No editor or proprietor can expect us to give an account of the state of play in OPEC [Organization of Petroleum-Exporting Countries], the OAU [Organisation of African Unity] or the Tin Council. We are not tactful about what we know and we lack cunning in concealing what we do not know. So we are spared the arduous task of commenting on the ECOWAS [Economic Community of West African States] summit held in Abuja the other week.

This is good because we would have nothing useful to say. We would have to gossip and invent things. We could easily find ourselves retailing tittle-tattle about the size of the rooms and beds in the Hilton Hotel up there, where some of the delegates went missing in their suites and had to be retrieved by search parties. Each bed, we would have to say, could easily accommodate an elephant or two, if those thieving crop-destroyers were not becoming extinct thanks to the vigilance of our armies. And one minor delegate told me in a bar the other day that he could not see the television in his room from the bed because it was *beyond the horizon*.

If our editor appeared with that night guard he has, a man from the far north-east who speaks no known language and carries a Dane gun with a bore of an inch and a half loaded almost to the muzzle with scrap iron and small stones; and if the night guard held the Dane gun to our heads and cocked the hammer, we might then be forced to make some more adult and responsible comment. We could find ourselves admitting that the current slump in commodity prices and resulting depression of African economies has had a positive effect on francophone and perhaps other attitudes to ECOWAS.

Psychologically it works something like this: I keep all my profits for myself but I don't mind sharing my losses with you. If the CEAO [West African Economic Community, comprising six francophone countries] and Manu River Union [grouping Liberia, Sierra Leone and Guinea] are affected by the prevailing economic malaise, those great in their councils become less loyal to them and less likely to use them as a counterweight to the brash, ambitious, Nigerian-inspired newcomer. As the country with the largest domestic product in the region, Nigeria is being treated with a new deference as a richer if not necessarily older brother. But it too is suffering from the prevailing bad arithmetic. [Nigerian] President Babangida accepted the ECOWAS chairmanship with a good grace, but not without signs of nervousness and irritation, when it was thrust upon him for a third term.

The staff of ECOWAS itself, we might say if we were forced to comment, looks due for a purge. Its thirty-odd commissions and other bodies are out of touch, lost in African and European jungles; member-countries have defaulted on their ECOWAS contributions and money is lacking. In his closing speech Babangida spoke of giving trade officials their marching orders, and made it clear that the timetable for ECOWAS projects was flexible. Paradoxically, more work has been done on developing a common currency than on most other long-term projects. All the franc-zone countries have a convertible currency pegged to the strong French franc. This has advantages for the inhabitants of those countries as well as for France.

Is it proposed to abandon these advantages? Is there a plan to take the whole of West Africa into the franc zone, or is something more elaborate being contemplated — a yen-dollar-riyal cocktail in a new and hitherto unsuspected monetary era? Or are we to be disappointed by a mere theoretical currency for community accounting like the EEC ecu, a money which does not exist in real life?

So it is to the credit of successive Nigerian governments that they have protected the ECOWAS vision although in the short term they stand to gain less from ECOWAS than anyone else (or rather, to spend more on it). Or so we might say, if our work obliged us to say something. We might also award qualified praise to the obvious vision and goodwill of Captain Sankara [president of Burkina Faso], who wanted to be ECOWAS chairman and ginger things up a bit. The Burkinabe president criticised ECOWAS members who had paid their World Bank interest but withheld contributions.

In fact Abuja was the scene of a humiliation for the engaging captain, since he arrived there as sole candidate for the chairmanship with the agreed backing of the CEAO countries. With his proposal for an 'ECOWAS of peoples', a notion based on the 'Maghreb of the peoples' devised by Algerian leader Houari Boumedienne more than a decade ago to annoy the Moroccan and Tunisian leaderships, Sankara showed that he was shifting away from the mad Tripoli-inspired theorising of a year or two ago. Too late, though, to satisfy the Sage of Yamoussoukro: smugly ensconced in the presidential guest-house and sitting throughout at the right hand of President Babangida. Houphouet [president of the Ivory

Coast, born in the town of Yamoussoukro] duly torpedoed his young colleague on the eve of the meeting.

To add insult to injury, the Ivorians were secure in the aura of virtue cast about them by their recent confession of bankruptcy, an announcement made with the same air of unassailable *chic* as the chairman of a major Western bank revealing that $2 billion worth of Third World debts are to be deducted from this year's profits. Ivory Coast's request for rescheduling enabled it to outflank Burkina Faso and other minnows which cannot hope to create a sensation by admitting that they are broke.

The resulting pique probably lay behind Sankara's other quoted idea: that people should wear homespun goat-hair and cotton robes, like his own delegation, instead of the Savile Row suits and Old Etonian ties worn by everyone else. This idea is from closer to home: Fela Kuti's early 1970s song *Gentleman*. As well as confirming Sankara's widely suspected misspent youth, it pleasantly suggests an ECOWAS summit held in Y-fronts to a background of loud music; or to be precise, it *would* inspire this fantasy, if we were obliged to consider ECOWAS at all, in the last moments before our editor ordered his night guard to pull the trigger.

West African Hotline, 1–15 August 1987

MARTYRDOM

A martyr, our dictionaries tell us, is one who suffers death rather than renounce his or her faith. A secondary meaning, somewhat vulgar, is one who undergoes great suffering (e.g. 'she's a martyr to indigestion'); and a third, polemical meaning is one who makes a parade of suffering (e.g. 'don't adopt that martyred expression with me'). West European attitudes to the concept of martyrdom are conditioned by the histories of Christian martyrs, scourged, shot full of arrows or otherwise horribly persecuted by non-Christians or, seemingly just as often, by those professing a different form of Christianity.

Setting aside the German Nazis and similar beastly and backward groups, religious persecution resulting in martyrdom became rare in Europe some hundreds of years ago. The whole concept of martyrdom thus sends a slight shudder down the spine of modern European man. It is seen as something very nasty indeed, to be avoided at all costs, and at the same time faintly ridiculous. The courage and nobility of martyrs is of course recognised and admired. But isn't there something just a little bit … well … *mad* about it? If people are crazy enough to torture you over some detail of your beliefs, surely the thing to do is to tell them something or other to make them stop?

A sight of the thumbscrew or of irons being heated in the fire must have brought this thought into many minds and saved thousands from martyrdom. Those saved in this way, at the cost perhaps of a trifling feeling of guilt and shame (and who in this world does not carry such luggage everywhere?), are not remembered, while the martyrs are. Every faith needs its heroes and totems, and the Christian martyrs, following the example set by Jesus himself, perform this function. Political faiths also have their martyrs. The essence of martyrdom is the stubborn refusal to give in to coercion. It represents a moral victory over the bullies of the other side.

Political martyrs are easier to understand than religious ones but just as difficult to emulate. Spies or guerrillas caught by the enemy's security forces sometimes die without betraying their fellows. Such heroism commands respect. But the countless thousands who have been executed or murdered just for belonging to the wrong group – for being communists or Trotskyists or priests or atheists or landlords or trade unionists – without being given the choice of recanting, are not martyrs but victims. As are those who die in war, whether bravely or not.

BRICOLAGE

This at any rate is the European view. Islam favours a broader definition of martyrdom which embraces war dead and even terrorists accidentally blown up by their own bombs. Not everyone who dies in war dies as a hero, but in the Gulf war, apparently, everyone killed by the enemy dies a martyr. It is difficult to escape the conclusion that the idea of martyrdom has been deliberately vulgarised to ensure a good flow of military volunteers (since martyrs are guaranteed an express ticket to heaven).

Let us imagine for a moment the situation of a suspected atheist in the hands of a Tehran street mob. Asked to kiss the Koran or otherwise demonstrate his membership of the Faith, he refuses to do so and is stoned to death by his incensed neighbours. To a Western rationalist he appears a martyr to his own rationalist principles, who has nobly but foolishly invited murder by people incapable of understanding him. To his neighbours he is a limb of Satan who has quite rightly been put down. It is not suggested that the inhabitants of Tehran actually kill people for atheism, although Iranian atheists probably maintain the same discretion as those elsewhere in the Muslim world. But Islam, formed around the Prophet Mohammed, who was an effective general and a firm believer in the sword, is an aggressive faith with a contemptuous disregard for infidel views. This configuration saves the faithful from considerable intellectual effort. It means that they *know* what is what without having to work it out. This has great advantages for those commanding Muslims in political or military struggles. Like the Gulf war, for example.

Iran, it must be remembered, is not the aggressor in the Gulf war and hates and fears the United States (and one or two other Western countries) for the very good reason that they encouraged and supported the despotic Shah for many years to ensure their petroleum supplies. Where the rationalist would part company with the Persian imams is in their view that the US is actually the *devil*, a status also bestowed on its friends and allies, even those who are themselves Muslims. Hence the provocative demo in Mecca the other day, the understandable overreaction by the Saudi authorities (and apparently other pilgrims), the bloody aftermath and the ensuing 'Operation Martyrdom' in the Gulf itself: Iranian naval craft sowing mines all over the place under the pretext of an 'exercise'.

The Gulf is now full of warships, tankers, mines and potential martyrs in small boats, with more of all these things arriving every day. It is an extremely dangerous and frightening situation. Two more or less blundering superpowers, two cunning and craven lesser powers and a collection of assorted Arab states and statelets are trying variously to pacify, subvert or defeat an Iran wielding today's military and economic power with a philosophic apparatus a thousand years out of date. All to no avail on both sides, since the martyr's crazed bravery is equalled, in military terms, by the courage and technical skill of trained professional soldiers on all sides: things which are also very ancient and – to a rational person – not quite sane. Everyone stands to lose, perhaps a lot, perhaps everything. Nobody can 'win'. There will be more martyrs.

West African Hotline, 16–31 August 1987

THE DEVIL'S MUSIC

We ain't all got rhythm. Africa is the home of some of the worst dancers in the world as well as some of the best. Foreigners naively convinced that all Africans have an inborn facility for the joyous foot-tapping, hip-swinging, pelvis-rolling, shoulder-twitching dance imposed on the listener by the best African dance music have never watched Catholic intellectuals, Muslim warlords or millionaire politicians at play. Or understood that there are exceptions to the most cherished generalisations about races, peoples or classes.

What have classes to do with music? Little or nothing, probably. But at the 1983 Franco-African summit – an annual get-together of Francophone heads of state and government held in alternate years in France and a succession of African countries – those privileged to witness the event's main banquet on the closed-circuit video provided might have grounds for believing that *important people don't like music*. The French government had laid on a cabaret featuring various African and French artists: folk-singers, poets, traditional musicians, etc., headed by the Cameroonian star Manu Dibango who acted as master of ceremonies and performed with his own band complete with scantily clad dancers. Despite the strange mixture of artists it was, as they say, quite a spectacle.

The video cameraman was imaginative and allowed his lens to wander over the faces of the Great and Good between and during the numbers. Between the turns, they could be seen putting their heads together in concentrated political discussions. From the expressions on many faces, it was clear that each new performer was seen as an *interruption* to these discussions: as the music started, the politicians would relapse into a sulky silence. It is true that the French hosts tried to assume an air of enjoyment to keep up the spirit of the thing, but few of their guests showed any pleasure. Zaïre's General Mobutu looked, as he so often does, markedly bad-tempered and dyspeptic, as if all the clamour were giving him severe indigestion. Ladies were present. But the concentrated efforts of the Manu Dibango orchestra and its gyrating dancing girls were insufficient to get a single politician dancing.

What this shows, really, is that when you've got something on your mind you can't relax and have a good time. It may also indicate that if you are much given to bopping and jiving for relaxation you are not very likely to work your way into 'power'. Everyone has his or her worries about money, health, work, housing, love and so on. But the super-preoccupations of the super-powerful are of a different order. If you dissipate your energies on loud sound and rhythmic movement instead of working, learning and plotting, you will never make it into a president's chair except by accident.

What's that you say? You don't want to? Quite right, very sensible, power is onerous and morally ambiguous, a health hazard, not everyone's cup of tea. Yet it is there, in the structure of human societies, and somebody is always there to wield it. Without the relative stability sometimes provided by politicians and their 'systems' we might live in anarchy, without the time or resources to give parties or go dancing. Not only does it take all sorts to make a world, but the world makes all sorts to perform the various functions within it. All work and no play may well have made Jack a dull boy. This is how he manages to maintain his interest, for months or years at a time, in something like the Local Government Reforms (Cleansing) Bill, Section 14(c). He thus does something which may be very necessary and useful but which an irresponsible hooligan like yourself or a charming, light-hearted, artistic fellow like me would neglect, skimp and botch.

Of course the best politicos understand the need for fun even if they don't have much of it themselves. The cares of the world may have the grandee's gonads in a grip of iron, holding him immobile in the posture of a thinker with a headache. But he knows that the trivial worries of people in general can be gratefully shelved for an evening's social and physical pleasure. He knows that his job, perhaps his life itself, can depend on the good humour of the masses, and unless he is very dull indeed tries to ensure that such release remains available.

Africa's nightspots are a wonder. Outside a few big rich towns, most have an improvised, under-funded, but well-used feel. People of all classes dress up, pay the going rate for a few beers or the equivalent and happily absorb the one resource which is not scarce or costly: music from the world's biggest pool of naturally gifted musicians, many from small communities where music and rhythms are alive, social, religious, taken in with the mother's milk. Yes, there are Africans with a tin ear or who can't keep time with a marching band. But there are a few others too. Africans and sons of Africa in the Western diaspora who have carried the continent's sound and rhythms to the Americas and back to Europe, effectively seducing with them entire civilisations.

Caribbean and Latin music, the jazz, blues and rock of North America and the European popular music wholly influenced by them, are mutations of African music. They contain elements from elsewhere and result in some cases from the use of instruments and technology from outside

Africa (which have now found their way to Africa's musicians and are used by them). Christian and communist puritans, repelled by the physicality of the music, have resisted its advance (see the title of this piece), fortunately without much success. Rock has the Soviet Union by the throat and is grappling for a hold on China, India and Indonesia. With them, Africa will have completed its conquest of the world.

West African Hotline, 1–15 September 1987

A CONTRADICTION OR TWO

The ideals of socialism and democracy, progress and freedom are betrayed by their standard-bearers who use them to cloak the naked force of rival empires. Yet they have a sort of shadowy reality, for they are ideas which move the masses of mankind, those sunk in misery and oppression, more strongly perhaps than those who are merely dissatisfied with what they have. The individuals who rule human societies ride the forces of mass emotion and popular aspiration like surfers. In a sense they are parasites on the body politic whose apparent dominance and leadership are no more than the most craven opportunism.

Yet the body politic would have no brain without them. The lawyers and generals who rule much of mankind constitute the consciousness and will of nations which, without a ruling apparatus, might fall into incoherence and anarchy. Only the most wretched, the most oppressed of humanity, look happily on this prospect as something offering change which cannot be for the worse; for most, the risk of material loss induces caution. Yet the oppressed, if not a global majority, are many, their misery making acceptable the revolutionary's faith that destruction of the existing system will make it easier to devise a better one.

The possession of great wealth or great power appears to induce such a great fear of loss that any extreme of violence seems justified in their defence. The prospect of a great industrial nation deprived of raw materials and other inputs, its spoiled populations threatened with starvation, its cars motionless and rusting, its TV sets silent, its trained and untrained killers fighting like cats over the dwindling spoils of collapse, is indeed a frightening one. Does anyone believe it is possible?

Dr Kaunda [president of Zambia] expressed surprise in Vancouver the other day that minerals are seen in some quarters as being more important than 'God's children'. You bet they are. What can God's children do with chrome, diamonds, platinum, except make trinkets with them laboriously and by hand? The great industrial machine which consumes them by the ton has the right to do so, and to consume God's children by the bale, because the consequences of its stoppage are too awful to contemplate. Or such in any case is the dominant Western view.

Thoughtful people in the West, the liberals whom Washington's satraps regard as virtual communists and whom Lenin too in his time called 'useful idiots', are moved partly by realism and partly by human feeling or squeamishness. They are not eager to give up their possessions but wish to enjoy them without feeling responsible for the oppression or deprivation of others. As a result they are open to bargaining over the price of commodities and to the idea that technological advances make it possible to use material resources more sparingly, and thus spread their benefits more widely.

These sympathetic notions are still poorly understood in the corridors of power although they continue to advance. It is feared that they lack realism, that they threaten to weaken the machine's iron will to grow and to dominate. And they are not ideas built into the industrial machine, which seeks profit and is short-sighted where the future of humanity is concerned. Its own future of course is another matter.

The forms taken by industrial advance or 'progress' are part of humanity's predicament. Having nurtured in Europe and North America a smoking dinosaur of waste and greed, which tramples on human needs as it satisfies them and has spawned dragon children in Asia and Latin America, mankind must now preside over a difficult period of change. The monster must eventually die, but its death-throes risk taking a lot of us with it. However much we may want it, there is no guarantee that we can easily and painlessly let the dinosaur in our midst slip away and replace it with a more domesticated beast, a decentralised human-scale industry which can serve us without consuming us.

And of course we don't all want to. The beast has its servants and lackeys, including the present United States administration which must be the most charmless since the presidency of Theodore Roosevelt. The public image of President Reagan's government evidently answers a need among American voters to be led by a tobacco-chewing, shrewd frontier hero keeping two-fisted order in defence of church, hearth and home. But in the outside world, as poorly understood in middle America as it is in the leafy suburbs of white South Africa, Reagan looks like a cardboard cut-out of what he once was, an actor in second-rate western movies.

Is it ignorance rather than effrontery which enables the president to speak so righteously of the absence of democracy in Nicaragua? Whatever the aims of the Sandinists in power there, the terrorism and destruction being financed and encouraged by the US are not making the 'restoration of democracy' any easier. The Nicaraguan government won an election organised after the overthrow, by armed revolution, of a horribly oppressive dictatorship also supported by the US. In Somoza's day, it is true, the Americans used to talk about democracy in Nicaragua, but they did not arm his enemies.

FROM THE MOTO PARK

In the shadows behind the old dude-ranch cowboy, dozing in front of his TV set, are scientists, philosophers and statesmen as well as idiots and wild animals. The Primaries are here and the unconvincing representatives of these forces are entering the lists for the next US election, on which the future of the world may depend. For the US must continue in its role, while it exists, must tussle with a Soviet Union now slimmed and made wiser by its years of economic failure, must clip the gadflies of Libya over the ear and crudely insult the sulky mullahs of Iran, and must keep faith with the redneck bullies of Pretoria, or at least keep a lien on the ores they still control. But will the new government we so urgently long for do these things with skill, or stupidly? We must wait and see. Scared? So you should be.

West African Hotline, 16–31 October 1987

TECHNICALITIES

It isn't that Morocco has no claim at all to Western Sahara. At various moments in Morocco's long history its sultans have signed formal agreements of one sort or another with leaders of one or more of the tribes living in the Sahara region. Even the great Sheikh Ma El-Ainine, founder of the Sahrawis' spiritual capital Smara and an important leader of resistance to European colonisation, sought help from the Moroccan Sultan Moulay Hassan I who reigned in the last quarter of the nineteenth century. In return the Sultan named him *khalifa*, deputy, in the Sahara.

Like other sultans before him, Moulay Hassan mounted expeditions to the far south; in his case they did not even reach the present border between Morocco and Western Sahara. Some sedentary tribes in the region accepted the *caids* or leaders appointed by the Sultan. But the main Sahrawi tribes, the nomadic Tekna, the warlike Reguibat groups, accepted nothing and swore no allegiance. Sitting in mid-1975 at the request of the UN, the International Court of Justice at The Hague published an advisory opinion on material supplied by Morocco, Spain, Algeria and Mauritania. The Polisario Front was not represented.

The court found that there was no evidence of 'effective display of Moroccan authority in Western Sahara' in the period preceding Spanish colonisation; it accepted that a legal tie of allegiance had existed 'between the Sultan and some, but only some, of the nomadic peoples of the territory'. In the case of Mauritania the court noted 'many ties of a racial, linguistic, religious, cultural and economic nature' between tribes and emirates in the region; but it also noted 'the independence of the emirates and many of the tribes in relation to one another and ... the absence among them of any common institutions or organs, even of a quite minimal character'. Summing up, the court found that the materials presented 'do not establish any tie of territorial sovereignty between the territory of Western Sahara and the Kingdom of Morocco or the Mauritanian entity', and the court therefore found no legal ties which might affect 'the principle of self-determination through the free and genuine expression of the will of the peoples of the Territory'.

King Hassan II had already blocked Spanish plans to hold a referendum in the territory and, frogmarching the hapless Mauritanians along with him, set about simply annexing Western Sahara. Flimsy cover was provided by the so-called Madrid Agreement, under which Spain ceded temporary administration of Western Sahara to Morocco and Mauritania.

This was signed by Prime Minister Arias Navarro with the support of a self-interested business clique and on the advice of France and the CIA, over the objections of other members of the Spanish government who thought the agreement squalid, criminal and politically embarrassing.

The work of annexation was carried out by King Hassan's army, which invaded Western Sahara before the Spanish had left. Nearly thirteen years have passed and the Moroccan army, well equipped with aviation and the latest armour and weapons, now numbers some 150,000 in Western Sahara alone – twice the size of the Sahrawi population in 1975 unless the many Sahrawis living in neighbouring territories at that time are also counted. French, American and other equipment and advice have been lavished on the royal armed forces and the famous walls have been put in place. Behind them, under Moroccan administration, there has been a construction boom and tens of thousands of Moroccans, especially those with Sahrawi connections from the south of the country, have been moved into the territory and issued with misleading personal documents.

King Hassan would like the UN 'technical mission' now visiting the occupied part of the Sahara to give the all-clear for a referendum on self-determination to take place. He even told a Swedish TV audience the other day that talks with the Polisario Front would be necessary one day – but after the referendum, not before it as recommended by the UN, the OAU [Organisation of African Unity] and many countries and bodies around the world. The Polisario agreed to the UN mission but is afraid that it may prepare world opinion for a referendum largely manipulated by the Moroccan government. It is pointed out that even if Sahrawis in the occupied territories dare to vote for independence and the Polisario's ten-year-old republic, and the referendum goes against Morocco, Hassan's armies will still be in place.

Morocco's legal case consists of a tissue of lies, distortions and omissions delivered with a cynical shrug and a razor-edged military grin. Nobody in the world believes it outside the lower reaches of Moroccan society. The big problem for the nationalist majority of Sahrawis is that there is no established machinery for enforcing international law, which is therefore applied in a partial, freelance, individual way. The right of peoples to self-determination is 'inalienable' only in pious principle, when a street-smart pirate like the Sultan of Morocco can spend billions of other people's dollars, and thousands of other people's lives, in the effort to alienate it.

Sahrawis are outnumbered by Moroccans a hundred to one. Nevertheless their nationalist segment has achieved an astonishing feat of nation-building in exile, while pursuing a vigorous armed struggle against the Moroccan invasion forces. This has failed to impress the governments of the great Western democracies whose nostrils are inured to the smell of rot and whose hearing is insensitive to calls for justice. Their heavily skewed neutrality in the conflict answers the wishes of two or three countries which for economic and equally sordid geopolitical reasons want to give King Hassan's imperialist venture time to succeed.

Polisario leaders fear that [UN Secretary-General] Perez de Cuellar's current initiative may, by wasting time and fogging the issues, help in this process. Perhaps they should not worry unduly. The UN after all has many Third World members who still dislike greedy colonial grabbing even when the culprit is itself a Third World country. African countries in particular, after taking some time to digest the issue, have shown clearly where their sympathies lie. Of course sympathy doesn't pay the rent but Africa knows that in principle the conduct of international relations is more useful to the weak than to the strong, who can make their own law and damn the consequences.

West African Hotline, 1–15 December 1987

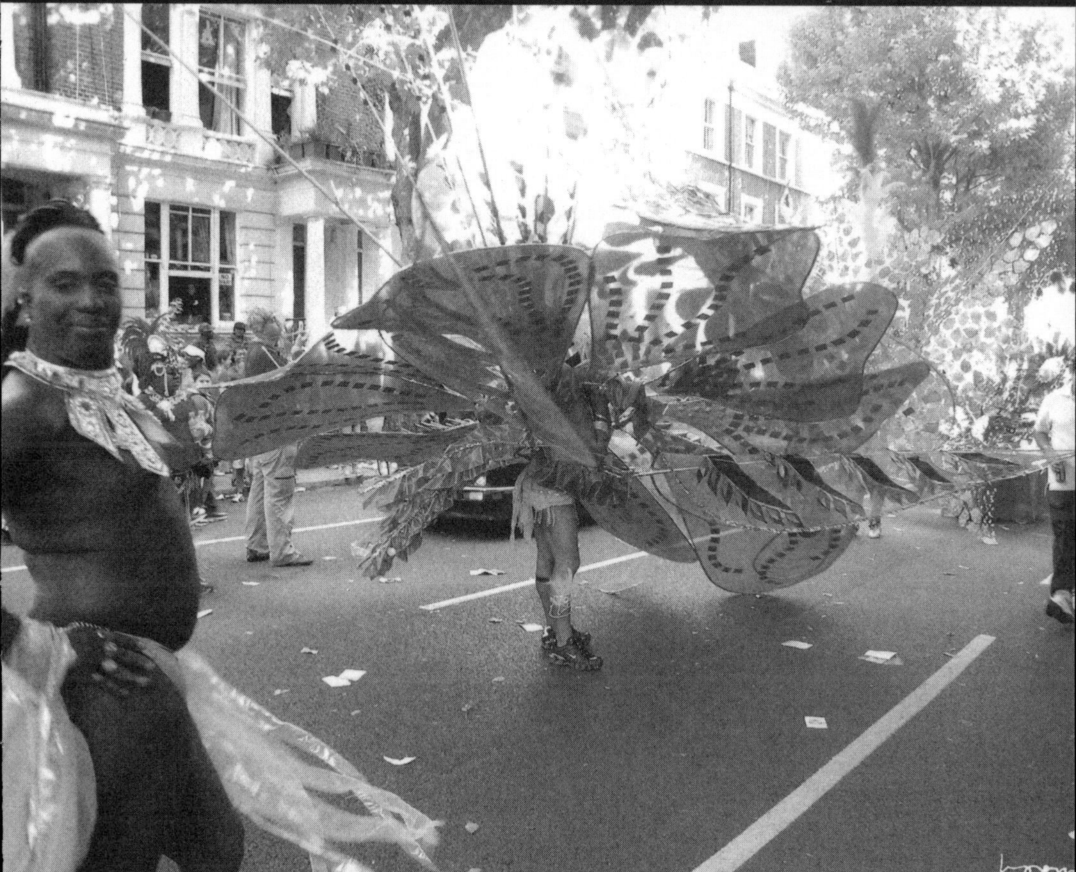

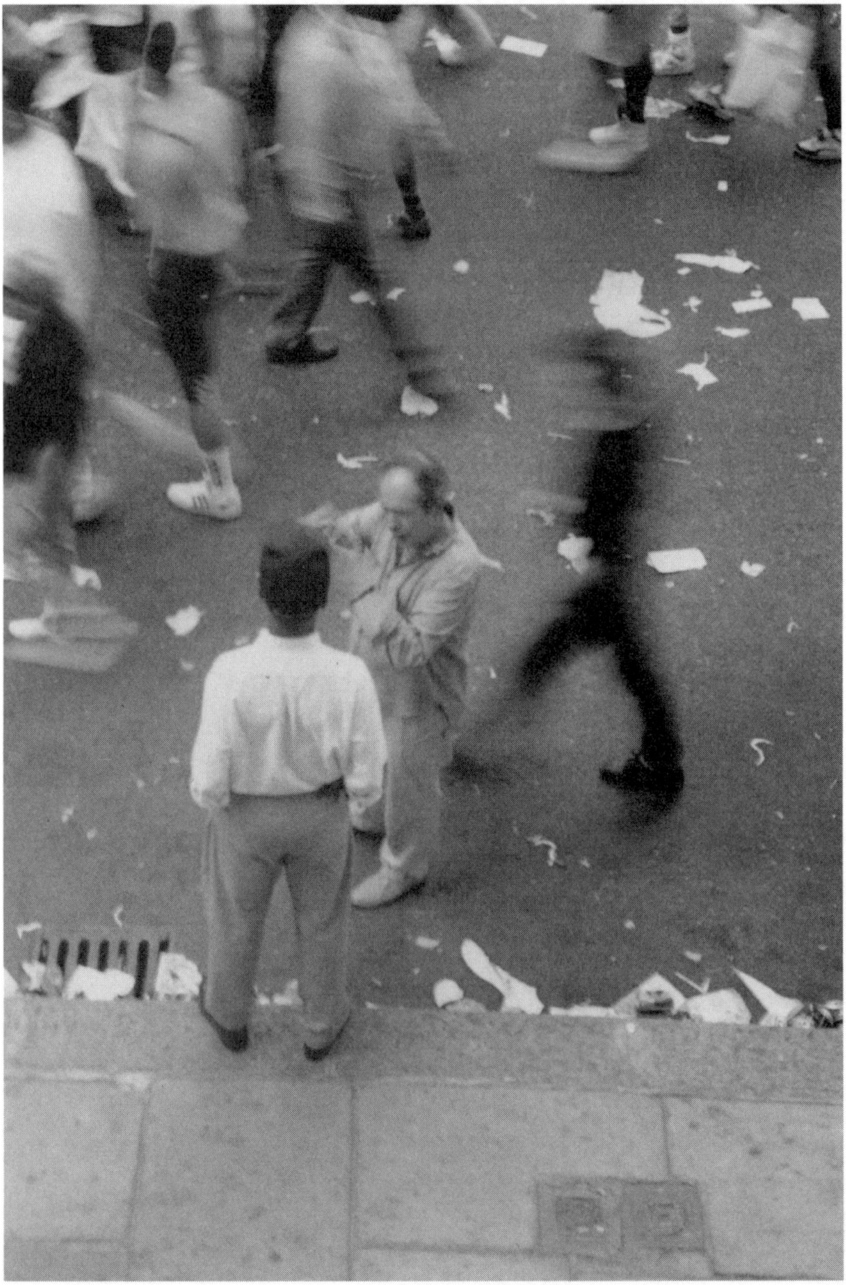

31 AOÛT 1981

Notting Hill Gate, à l'ouest du centre de Londres, n'est plus le ghetto noir des années cinquante et soixante. Il reste cependant un quartier mixte, traversé par le grand marché de Portobello Road et dont la population comporte une forte minorité noire. Le carnaval de Notting Hill, fondé en 1962, attirait ce lundi, jour de congé en Angleterre, des dizaines de milliers de londoniens, heureux de flâner un peu, d'écouter toute une gamme de styles musicaux et de regarder les costumes gais et bizarres des bandes culturelles venues des diverses communautés antillaises de la Grande-Bretagne.

En ce qui concerne l'Angleterre, l'impulsion culturelle du carnaval vient des originaires de la Trinité et des autres petites îles antillaises plutôt que des jamaïquains plus nombreux mais aux traditions plus urbaines. Dès le départ cependant le carnaval est devenu la propriété de toute la population locale. Des 'steel bands' de la Trinité, la Grenade, la Dominique et ailleurs (y compris un blanc venu de Berlin) sillonnent les rues du quartier, sur un camion ou un chariot poussé à la main, souvent accompagné par un groupe de danseurs habillés en costumes imaginatifs et aux couleurs brillantes: des soldats romains, des chevaliers du dix-septième, des poissons, des étoiles. Chaque bande est entourée d'une foule de spectateurs, dansant au rythme doux et roulant de l'acier, une foule qui grandit au cours de l'après-midi et de la soirée. Les bandes filent lentement dans les rues du quartier, suscitant quelquefois de véritables embouteillages – de bandes et de monde seulement, la circulation normale étant totalement interrompue. Des habitants du quartier sortent leurs chaînes disco sur le trottoir devant leurs maisons, quelquefois d'énormes tas de haut-parleurs puissants qui lancent les rythmes secs et tranchants de reggae ou de ska. Pour la foule c'est une occasion très détendue, une grande fête dans les rues: on boit un peu, on fume peut-être, on amène les gosses, on se laisse séduire par la musique enveloppante et la bonne humeur générale.

Le carnaval reste un élément très créateur dans le domaine des relations raciales malgré les efforts de l'extrême-droite pour empoisonner l'atmosphère avec la menace d'une contre-manifestation qui aurait entraîné une contre-contre-manifestation de la gauche antiraciste. La police, dont la présence jugée trop lourde a suscité de graves émeutes au carnaval de 1976, paraît décidée à le 'protéger' depuis, et toute manifestation est interdite cette semaine par le home office. Un officier supérieur nous a dit que la police déploie 7,000 officiers cette année, la moitié en réserve. L'impression dimanche et lundi était que la police utilise la méthode du 'bobby sur sa ronde': les agents se promènent en couples, habillés en tenue de bras de chemise. Beaucoup d'entre eux viennent d'autres quartiers de Londres ou même de la campagne. Des barrières portatives protègent l'accès aux points 'chauds', tel le carrefour de Portobello Green, sous une autoroute élevée, où les émeutes ont éclaté en 1976 et dans un moindre degré dans les années suivantes. Mais pour les policiers aussi, jeunes pour la plupart et bien payés pour un jour qui doit être de congé, c'est une fête.

Dimanche, la foule était nettement plus petite que dans les grandes années depuis 1974, où il y avait un demi-million de monde pour le dernier jour du carnaval, et dans l'après-midi de ce lundi le chiffre était nettement inférieur. Mais le temps n'était pas mauvais pour Londres et il y avait assez de monde pour démontrer la vigueur du carnaval et de ses racines dans le sol épuisé de Notting Hill. Si la police est un peu trop évidente, cela ne démontre que la différence entre les conceptions de la liberté anglaise et antillaise: les efforts d'il y a quelques années, pour discipliner le carnaval, pour le transporter des rues du 'Grove' – mot antillais pour le quartier – et pour organiser un carnaval 'sanitaire' à Hyde Park, ont heureusement échoué. Un événement dont une grande partie du charme vient du manque d'organisation a été approprié de nouveau par la base, les hommes et les femmes qui font la musique et qui taillent les costumes. Ils reçoivent, bien sûr, quelques sous gouvernementaux, venus du Arts Council ou des conseils locaux. Mais cela ne paie pas vraiment la chose qui est au fond un don à Londres de sa communauté d'origine africaine, c'est-à-dire antillaise. Les deux comités qui prétendent organiser le carnaval ne contribuent pas grand'chose à son déroulement, quoiqu'ils aident à canaliser les fonds. Leur contribution principale est que leur existence rassure les autorités, surtout la police, qui éprouvent une grande difficulté à croire que des gens sans organisation centrale peuvent se rassembler en grand nombre pour des raisons innocentes. Grâce aux anglais noirs et à leurs traditions religieuses ouest-africaines, cependant, les autorités sont en train d'apprendre que c'est tout de même possible.

Le Matin, 31 August 1981

LETTER FROM LONDON

*

Notting Hill Gate in West Central London is no longer the black ghetto that it was in the 1950s and 1960s. But it is still a mixed area, with the Portobello Road market running through it, and the population includes a large black minority. This Bank Holiday Monday the Notting Hill Carnival, which was first staged in 1962, attracted tens of thousands of Londoners who enjoyed standing around listening to a whole range of musical styles and looking at the strange colourful costumes worn by bands representing Britain's different Caribbean communities.

The British carnival has its cultural roots in migrants from Trinidad and some other small Caribbean islands rather than in the more numerous Jamaican community whose traditions are more urban. But from the outset the carnival has belonged to the entire local population. Trinidadian, Grenadian, Dominican and other steel bands (including a white group from Berlin) flood the local streets on lorries or hand-pushed floats, often followed by groups of dancers in imaginative, brightly coloured costumes: Roman soldiers, seventeenth-century knights, fish and stars, for example. Each band attracts its own followers who dance to the soft, rhythmic beat of the steel, their numbers increasing as the afternoon and evening wear on. The bands advance slowly through the streets, sometimes causing serious blockages – but only of bands and people as ordinary traffic is completely banned during the event. Local people set up their sound systems on the pavement outside their houses, sometimes erecting huge stacks of loudspeakers which throw out harsh, pulsating reggae and ska. It is a very relaxed occasion: people drink a little, maybe smoke; they bring their children and let themselves be carried away by the pervasive music and general high spirits.

The carnival is a very positive factor in race relations in spite of efforts by the far right to poison the atmosphere; it had threatened a counter-demonstration, which would have triggered a counter-counter-demonstration by the anti-racist left. But after a heavy police presence provoked serious riots at the 1976 carnival, the force seems to have decided to 'protect' the event, and the Home Office has banned demonstrations this week. A high-ranking officer told us that 7,000 police are on duty, half of them reserves. This Sunday and Monday they were showing their 'bobby on the beat' image, walking two by two in their shirtsleeves. Many of them were from other parts of London or even from the country. Moveable barriers block access to 'hot spots', such as Portobello Green, the open space below the raised motorway where rioting erupted in 1976 and to a lesser extent in subsequent years. But even the police see the carnival as a festive occasion – most of them are young and are earning good money on what is a bank holiday for the rest of the country.

On Sunday the crowds were visibly smaller than they had been in the best years. In 1974 half a million people came on the Monday – more than the estimates for this year. But the weather has not been bad by London standards and enough people came to show that the carnival is still very much alive, drawing strength from its roots in Notting Hill's exhausted soil. The police presence may have been too visible but that shows the difference between British and Caribbean ideas of freedom. Attempts a few years ago to control the carnival, to move it away from the streets of the Grove – as the West Indians call this district – and stage a sanitised event in Hyde Park fortunately came to nothing. The grass roots, the men and women who make the music and design the costumes, are still in charge of the event whose charm comes in large part from its lack of organisation. Of course they receive some subsidies from the Arts Council and local government but these do not cover the costs of what is really a gift to London from its Afro-Caribbean community. The two committees who are said to organise the carnival do not really play much of a part in its implementation although they help to channel funds. Still, the fact that they exist reassures the authorities, particularly the police, who find it hard to believe that people with no central organisation can gather together in such numbers with no criminal aims. But the black British, with their West African religious traditions, demonstrate that this is so.

29 OCTOBRE 1981

A-t-on pu décerner une étincelle d'humeur dans les yeux de Margaret Thatcher et de François Mitterrand au moment où, pendant leur conférence de presse à l'occasion de la récente visite du président français, ils ont donné un soutien en principe pour le projet de 'lien fixe' entre l'Angleterre et le continent ? Peut-être ce n'était que les projecteurs des équipes de télévision. Mais quelque chose indiquait que malgré les assurances les deux personnes d'état ne touchent la question qu'avec le bout des doigts. Paris–Londres en trois heures à 250 kilomètres par l'heure c'est une idée sympathique. Mais elle manque quand même la composante d'urgence politique. De part et d'autre, les peuples bordant la Manche sont contents de ce bout de mer orageuse qui les sépare pour ainsi dire formellement, qui les rend étrangers l'un de l'autre. Aucun terrain vague – Belgique, Alsace, Suisse ou Monaco – ne brouille la frontière entre l'Angleterre et la France. Malgré leurs inconvénients, les avions et les bateaux ont, eux aussi, quelque chose de sympathique.

Aux plans financier et politique, les complexités sont presque comiques. Les promoteurs britanniques de ponts et de tunnels rappellent la 'colère giscardienne' en 1975 à la suite de la brusque annulation par le gouvernement travailliste Wilson des travaux qui avaient alors commencé à titre expérimental. On hésite à suggérer que maintenant c'est nous les giscardiens, et vous les wilsoniens. Mais le gouvernement Thatcher a indiqué très nettement que le bout britannique du projet doit être financé entièrement de source privée, tandis que la nouvelle majorité en France favorise une participation publique de 100 pour cent. Les promoteurs prétendent cependant que l'argent est la moindre de leurs problèmes. Ils s'efforcent simplement de traverser les obstacles techniques et politiques; de se mettre d'accord avec les divers intérêts en jeu et de faire passer un traité inter-gouvernemental pour protéger le projet de lien contre 'des éventuels changements de pouvoir'.

Quant à l'argent, on souligne 'la très grande rentabilité à longue terme' de chaque projet. Mais l'actuel climat économique semble favoriser les projets d'un simple tunnel chemin de fer à voie unique. Cela va coûter environ un milliard de livres, et à peu près deux milliards pour voie double. En plus, cela ne va pas concurrencer les bacs à voitures, dont le filiale Sealink de British Rail transporte le tiers du trafic. Enfin, les projets de tunnel élaborés par British Rail et les groupes de constructeurs et de banquiers

Anglo Channel Tunnel Group et Channel Tunnel Developments utilisent une technologie bien développée; ainsi le parcours des travaux est relativement prévisible. Ce qui n'est pas le cas pour les projets de ponts et de tunnels, plus grandioses, de British Steel et du Eurobridge Studies Group. Vulgairement magnifiques en conception, les îles artificielles et les travées sans précédent de trois kilomètres de ces projets vont coûter dans l'avis de leurs partisans, environ trois milliards et demi de livres, sans compter l'inflation, les ennuis techniques, etcetera.

Ainsi, pour diverses raisons, le système préféré de British Rail semble avoir le plus de chances dans le concours pour l'approbation gouvernementale, avant la prochaine décision officielle autour d'avril prochain. Un projet étroitement semblable aurait le soutien de la SNCF et de la Conférence européenne des autorités locales et régionales. Le député français Alain Chenard, rapporteur de cette conférence, vient de proposer un tunnel entre l'Ecosse et l'Irlande du Nord, tandis que le groupe Eurobridge conçoit des ponts entre l'Espagne et le Maroc et entre la Grèce et la Turquie. Touchante mégalomanie des ingénieurs-entrepreneurs ? Ou la naissance d'une lutte mondiale entre les chemins de fer et le lobby routier, le tunnel Malgache contre l'autoroute de l'Indonésie et des Philippines?

Le Matin, 29 October 1981

*

At the press conference during French President François Mitterrand's visit, could a sparkle of humour be detected in his and Margaret Thatcher's eyes when they pledged their support in principle to establishing a 'fixed link' between England and the continent? Or was it just an effect of the television cameras? But whatever they said, the two leaders did not seem fully committed to the project. A three-hour journey from Paris to London at 250 km an hour is a nice idea but it has no political urgency. Those living on either side of the Channel like this stretch of stormy sea which constitutes a formal barrier between them, making each country foreign to the other. No buffer zone like Belgium, Alsace, Switzerland or Monaco blurs the frontier between England and France. In spite of all their inconveniences, there is something attractive about planes and boats.

The financial and political complications are fairly comic. British sponsors of bridges and tunnels recall French President Giscard d'Estaing's fury when Wilson's Labour government suddenly cancelled experimental work in 1975. Strange to say, the British now seem to be taking Giscard's line and the French Wilson's. The Thatcher government has made it very clear that the British side of the project must be financed entirely by private sources whereas the new French government is in favour of 100 per cent public finance. The sponsors claim, however, that money is the least of their problems. They are focused on trying to overcome the technical and political obstacles, reaching agreement with the various interests at stake, and drafting a treaty between the two countries to safeguard the projected link against 'possible changes of government'.

As for finance, 'the very good long-term viability' of all the various projects has been stressed but in the current economic climate a tunnel with a single-track railway line is gaining favour. The cost would be about £1 billion, or about £2 billion for a two-way track. Moreover, the plan would not compete with the boat ferries, about a third of whose business is handled by the British Rail affiliate Sealink. The plans for a tunnel drawn up by British Rail and the construction and banking groups Anglo Channel Tunnel Group and Channel Tunnel Developments use a well-developed technology and their scheme has a fairly predictable trajectory. The same cannot be said for the more grandiose plans for bridges and tunnels proposed by British Steel and the Eurobridge Studies Group. Vulgarly magnificent in scale, the artificial islands and unprecedented 3 km-span bridges would cost around £3.5 billion according to their supporters – not counting inflation, technical problems and so on.

Thus, for many reasons, British Rail's plan seems to have the best chance of government approval when the next official decision is made next April. The French railway company SNCF and the Standing Conference of Local and Regional Authorities of Europe look likely to support a project on these lines. The Conference Rapporteur, French MP Alain Chenard, has proposed a tunnel between Scotland and Northern Ireland, while the company Eurobridge envisages bridges between Spain and Morocco and between Greece and Turkey. Is this a touching symptom of megalomania on the part of engineers and entrepreneurs or the birth of a worldwide struggle between railways and roads – the Malagasy tunnel versus the Indonesia–Philippines motorway?

20 MARS 1982

Harold Macmillan, ex-premier ministre conservateur, nous a rappelé il y a un an que les origines du mouvement européen se trouvent dans un papier circulé parmi ses ministres par Winston Churchill en 1942, quelques jours avant la bataille d'El Alamein. En 1948, écarté du pouvoir et agissant en quelque sorte comme un homme d'état indépendant, Churchill représente la Grande-Bretagne à la conférence de la Haye où se fonde le Conseil d'Europe. Il propose que le conseil se siège à Strasbourg pour symboliser la réconciliation franco-allemande. Dans un discours à Zurich, il prévoit avec une approbation évidente les 'États-Unis d'Europe'. Le vieux patriote impérialiste et atlantiste était tout aussi 'européen'.

Dans le même discours devant le group conservateur pour l'Europe, Macmillan fait remarquer que l'Europe 'doit avoir une politique étrangère unifiée, une politique de défense et une politique monétaire unifiée, et doit se considérer comme étant effectivement une nation unique afin de résister aux dangers qui la menacent'. Il est devenu plus enthousiaste depuis sa retraite. Premier ministre à l'époque, il se tenait à l'écart au moment de la signature du traité de Rome. La leçon de Suez n'est pas encore digérée; le gouvernement britannique regarde toujours vers un empire en pleine dissolution et vers le *special relationship* avec les États-Unis. Les Britanniques disposent de très bons services sociaux, de plein emploi et de salaires hauts. Deux ou trois ans plus tard cependant Macmillan fait remarquer que 'les majeures puissances continentales sont unies dans un groupement économique positif, aux aspects politiques considérables', qui pourrait à terme 'nous exclure des marchés européens ainsi que des consultations sur la politique européenne'.

Pour Macmillan, tout comme pour son successeur travailliste Harold Wilson, le marché commun offrait surtout un moyen de freiner l'effondrement de la puissance britannique. Ce raisonnement 'pragmatique' qui prévaut toujours au parlement a des aspects tièdes et opportunistes qui ont contribué sans doute aux deux vetos retentissants prononcés par De Gaulle en 1961 et en 1967. La situation est débloquée par la combinaison d'Edward Heath, un des rares politiciens britanniques du premier rang qui sont des européens convaincus, et Georges Pompidou, banquier sensible aux arguments de la cité de Londres, qui ont effectué l'adhésion de la Grande-Bretagne en 1973.

Malgré les efforts d'hommes comme Heath, comme Roy Jenkins et les autres 'européens', l'éclosion de l'idée européenne procède très lentement. Faute de pouvoir assimiler tant de nouvelles informations, et souvent contraires aux préjugés profonds, c'est une sorte d'apathie qui règne. Rappelons que les Britanniques n'ont pas subi les efforts unificateurs d'un Bonaparte ou d'un Hitler, mais au contraire ont tenté de les empêcher. Ils se méfient des 'étrangers' et sont très jaloux de la 'souveraineté', savamment citée par les 'antis' de tous partis. Malgré les vacances en Espagne et en Grèce les fantômes des conflits du passé, d'une grandeur périmée, font long feu dans les esprits.

Cela donne aux politiciens une grande marge de manoeuvre, les obligeant en même temps de parier pour et contre. Les gouvernements britanniques traitent la communauté comme une sort d'empire prêt-à-porter, où les négociations poussées remplacent les expéditions militaires. 'Si la Grande-Bretagne est obligée d'adhérer au marché,' s'écria en 1971 le *Daily Express*, 'alors le marché devra être façonné selon la volonté britannique'. Malgré les échecs répétés, cette 'arrogance' persiste. Neuf ans après son adhésion, la Grande Bretagne se comporte toujours comme un passager encombrant dans un bus: trop de bagages, chaussures en état lamentable, démarche hautaine en se plaignant du prix de voyage, de sa place inférieure aux autres, de la route choisie par le chauffeur.

Cela peut mettre à l'épreuve la courtoisie des compagnons de voyage. Mais derrière l'apparente obsession des Britanniques au sujet des contributions budgétaires et des règles jugées inéquitables, l'attitude dominante s'élargit discrètement. Un nombre croissant écoute Edward Heath, qui ne cesse de souligner l'importance stratégique ainsi qu'économique d'une éventuelle Europe intégrée; des journaux comme *The Economist* font appel pour la mise en application des clauses du traité de Rome, jugées libératrices en principe mais toujours étouffées dans la pratique.

Rappelons qu'un référendum promu par la gauche travailliste en 1975 à la suite d'une prétendue 'renégociation' des modalités de l'adhésion britannique a dégagé une majorité de deux tiers en faveur de l'Europe. La défection du parti travailliste de Roy Jenkins et de plusieurs autres 'européens' de poids pour fonder le parti social-démocrate a permis à Labour de s'engager à retirer la Grande-Bretagne de la communauté. Le calcul du leadership travailliste mise les pénibles difficultés actuelles et l'ignorance de la population, qui a tendance à attribuer au bouc émissaire de l'Europe les maux de l'inflation et du chômage. Cela va sans doute priver les travaillistes de la sympathie des socialistes européens, mais l'attitude de l'électorat, toujours mal informé et troublé par les revenants d'un passé récent, aussi bien que par une situation économique pénible, sera moins prévisible.

Le Matin, 20 March 1982

BRICOLAGE

*

Last year former Conservative Prime Minister Harold Macmillan recalled that the European movement has its origins in a document Winston Churchill circulated to his ministers in 1942, a few days before the Battle of El Alamein. Then in 1948, out of power and acting as an independent statesman, Churchill represented Great Britain at the conference in The Hague at which the Council of Europe was created. He proposed that the council should be based in Strasbourg to symbolise Franco-German reconciliation. In a speech given in Zurich, he looked forward with approval to a 'United States of Europe'. The old patriot was clearly a 'European' as well as an imperialist and an Atlanticist.

Macmillan, in the same speech to the European Conservative group, commented that Europe 'should have a unified foreign policy, and a unified monetary and defence policy, and should regard itself as effectively a single nation in order to resist the dangers threatening it'. Thus he has shown greater enthusiasm since his retirement than he did as prime minister: when the Treaty of Rome was signed, he remained aloof. Britain had not yet absorbed the lessons of Suez. The government was still focused on its collapsing empire and its special relationship with the United States. The British had very good social services, full employment and high salaries. However, two or three years later, Macmillan observed that 'the great powers of continental Europe are united in a successful economic grouping, with remarkable political aspects', which could, potentially, 'exclude us from European markets and discussions on European politics'.

Both Macmillan and his Labour successor Harold Wilson saw the Common Market as a means of stopping the collapse of British power. This 'pragmatic' reasoning, which still predominates in Parliament, has a lukewarm, opportunist subtext which no doubt contributed to the two resounding vetoes uttered by De Gaulle in 1961 and 1967. The impasse was broken by Edward Heath, one of the few first-rank British politicians who are convinced Europeans, in tandem with Georges Pompidou, a banker who is well aware of the significance of the City of London. Together they engineered British membership in 1973.

Despite the efforts of Heath, Roy Jenkins and other pro-Europeans, the idea of Europe has been slow to take root. Given how difficult it is to take in so much new information, a lot of which runs counter to deep-seated prejudices, a sort of apathy prevails. Of course the British never had to suffer Bonaparte's or Hitler's attempts at unification – on the contrary, they resisted them. They are suspicious of 'foreigners' and treasure their 'sovereignty', a characteristic ably exploited by anti-Europeans of all parties. In spite of their holidays in Spain and Greece, people harbour long memories of past wars and bedraggled grandeur.

Politicians have a lot of room for manoeuvre as they place their bets for or against. British politicians treat the community as some sort of ready-made empire in which protracted negotiations take the place of military ventures. 'If the UK has to join the Market,' screamed the *Daily Express* in 1971, 'the Market must adapt to what the UK wants.' Such arrogance has survived repeated failures. Nine years on from joining, the British still behave like bothersome passengers on a bus: too much luggage, dilapidated shoes, haughty demeanour, complaining about the cost of the journey, their lowly status and the direction of travel.

Britain's travelling companions may well find it hard to go on being polite. But regardless of the country's obsessions with its budget contributions and rules it regards as unfair, an increasing number of people are listening to Edward Heath who constantly emphasises the importance, both strategic and economic, of a possible integrated Europe. Journals like *The Economist* call for the implementation of clauses of the Treaty of Rome which should in principle be liberalising but are always rejected in practice.

The referendum of 1975, demanded by the left wing of the Labour Party following the so-called renegotiation of British membership, resulted in a two-thirds majority in favour of Europe. Then, after Roy Jenkins and several other significant 'Europeans' left the Labour Party to found the Social Democrat Party, Labour was able to promise to withdraw the UK from the community. The party leadership is basing its calculations on the difficulties of the current economic situation and on the ignorance of the population, who tend to attribute all the evils of inflation and unemployment to the scapegoat of Europe. Labour is bound to lose the sympathy of European socialists but the attitude of the electorate, as usual ill informed and troubled both by the ghosts of the recent past and by a painful economic situation, is less predictable.

21 AVRIL 1982

Pendant que le gouvernement s'occupe de la crise des Falkland Islands, deux séries d'incidents lui ont rappelé mardi soir l'existence de l'armée croissante des dépourvus à l'intérieur du pays. En Ulster, six attentats à la 'bombe à voiture' ont provoqué deux morts, plusieurs blessés et des dégâts importants aux centres urbains de Belfast, Londonderry, Strabane, Ballymena, Bessbrook et Magherafelt. Ce nouveau campagne de violences de l'IRA Provisoire intervient à la suite de la mort d'un petit garçon de onze ans, Steven McConomy, grièvement blessé vendredi dernier par une 'balle plastique' anti-émeute tirée par l'armée. En donnant ainsi expression à la vague de colère populaire suscitée par cette mort tragique, l'IRA saisit la bonne occasion pour démontrer que les récentes multiples dénonciations de militants républicains ne l'ont pas privé de sa 'puissance de feu'. En même temps, elle remet en question l'utilisation de la balle en plastique dont le jeune Steven McConomy devient la sixième victime parmi les enfants irlandais. Le parlement européen à Strasbourg va très probablement condamner cette arme anti-émeute plutôt dangereuse dans l'immédiat.

Les commentateurs irlandais rappellent souvent que malgré l'acharnement des émeutes qui se sont produits dans les quartiers noirs des grandes villes britanniques l'été dernier, les balles en plastique n'ont pas été utilisées. A croire les thèses tenues par la quasi-totalité des représentants noirs au niveau des rues, cependant, ce n'est guère une force symbolique que la police emploie routinièrement dans les ghettos londoniens. Quatorze jeunes devaient paraître devant le tribunal de Marylebone ce mercredi après-midi à la suite d'un 'incident' au quartier de Notting Hill mardi soir.

Cet évènement comme bien d'autres du même genre a ses origines dans une banale fouille de deux jeunes soupçonnés de 'posséder de la drogue dangereuse'. Ceux-ci ont réussi à s'échapper à l'aide de quelques passants, et selon la police se sont enfuis vers All Saints Road, sorte de chef-lieu pour la population d'origine antillaise de Notting Hill. La police est arrivée aussitôt en force, estimée par des témoins d'être de l'ordre de trois à quatre cents agents. La population très contestataire de All Saints Road les a affrontés, construisant une barricade de voitures et lançant des missiles; la police, dont des unités du Special Patrol Group notoirement costaud et dont les membres ne portent pas un numéro identificateur sur l'épaule, a envahi deux restaurants, un pub et des magasins de propriétaires ou de clientèle noirs.

Frank Crichlow, le plancher de son restaurant 'Mangrove' toujours jonché de vitres et de meubles cassés, nous a dit que la police a fait irruption vers onze heures et 's'est mis à matraquer tout le monde y compris deux jeunes femmes qu'ils continuaient de battre même quand elles étaient tombées au sol'. La police dit qu'elle a subi deux légèrement blessés, ni l'un ni l'autre ayant été hospitalisé. Mais au moins un jeune noir se trouve gardé par deux policiers dans l'hôpital de Saint Charles dans le quartier, tandis qu'un témoin noir dit qu'il a vu deux agents en train de viser les yeux d'un jeune blanc avec des coups du bout d'un matraque. 'Je suis inquiet pour lui, ils l'ont battu pire que personne,' nous a dit ce témoin.

Un conseiller local blanc qui a vu les incidents nous a dit: 'Il y avait un moment où on aurait pu parler d'une émeute policière.' Pour lui, pour Frank Crichlow dont le restaurant a été endommagé par l'action policière 'pour au moins la vingtième fois' et pour les autres témoins dignes de foi, l'incident relève de l'attitude dure et raciste d'un élément de la police locale dont le chef de file est censé d'être l'Officier en Chef Tony Moore, responsable du déploiement important de mardi soir. On rappelle la démarche bien plus subtile d'un de ses adjoints, l'Officier Simonds, qui est une femme et qui a réussi à décrisper sans violences une situation semblable juste avant Noël dernier. La manque d'intérêt qu'on prétend décerner chez le conseil local de majorité conservatrice ainsi que chez le député conservateur, Sir Brandon Rhys-Williams, prête une certaine force à la thèse amère des jeunes chômeurs noirs, que le gouvernement actuel veut les supprimer par la force pour en créer un bouc émissaire.

Le Matin, 21 April 1982

*

While the government concentrates on the Falkland Islands crisis, two sets of incidents on Tuesday evening recall the growing army of the dispossessed in the country itself. In Ulster, six car bomb attacks caused two dead, many injured and significant damage in Belfast, Londonderry, Strabane, Ballymena, Bessbrook and Magherafelt. The Provisional IRA's new campaign of violence comes in response to the death of an eleven-year-old boy, Steven McConomy, who was fatally wounded last Friday by a rubber bullet fired by the army.

In expressing the people's anger following this tragic death, the IRA shows that the recent flood of denunciations of militant Republicans has not reduced its firepower. The events also cast doubt on the use of rubber bullets, to which young Steven McConomy was the sixth Irish child to fall victim. The European Parliament in Strasbourg seems likely to condemn this dangerous anti-riot weapon in the near future.

Irish commentators often point out that despite the intensity of the rioting in black-occupied areas of British cities last summer, rubber bullets were not used. However, almost all black community spokesmen on the streets say that the force regularly used by the police in the London ghettos can by no means be called symbolic.

Fourteen young people are due to appear at Marylebone Magistrates Court on Wednesday afternoon following an incident in Notting Hill on Tuesday evening.

Like many others, this event was triggered by a search of two young people suspected of possession of dangerous drugs. They managed to escape with the help of some passers-by and, according to the police, fled to All Saints Road, which serves as a headquarters for Notting Hill's Caribbean population. A police force estimated by witnesses at three or four hundred arrived immediately. Always ready for confrontation, the people of All Saints Road responded by putting up road blocks and throwing missiles; the police, among them units of the notoriously tough Special Patrol Group whose members do not wear identification numbers, overran black-owned and black-frequented premises including two restaurants, a pub and shops.

Frank Crichlow, owner of the Mangrove restaurant, which is still strewn with shards of glass and broken furniture, told us that the police had burst in at about eleven o'clock and 'attacked everyone with truncheons, including two young women who they went on hitting after they had fallen down'. The police reported that two of its members had been slightly wounded, neither needing hospital treatment. But at least one young black man is in the local St Charles's Hospital under police watch, and a black witness says he saw two policemen aiming truncheon blows at a young white man's eyes. 'I'm worried about him, they beat him up worst of all,' he told us.

A white local councillor who watched the events said, 'At one point, it could have been called a police riot.' Frank Crichlow, whose restaurant was damaged by the police 'for at least the twentieth time', and other trustworthy witnesses, attribute the incident to the hardline racist attitude of some of the local police, whose leader is thought to be Chief Constable Tony Moore, the officer responsible for the substantial police deployment on Tuesday night. They recall the much more measured approach of one of his assistants, WPC Simonds, who managed to resolve a similar situation just before Christmas without recourse to violence. The lack of interest they perceive on the part of the Conservative-majority local council and the Conservative MP, Sir Brandon Rhys-Williams, adds weight to the bitterness of the young black unemployed who think the government is using force to repress them in order to scapegoat them for their response.

27 JUILLET 1982

La reine, plusieurs membres de la famille royale y compris le Prince et la Princesse de Galles, le premier ministre, les leaders des partis politiques et nombreux ministres et ex-ministres ont assisté lundi matin à la cathédrale de St Paul à l'office désigné 'des Falkland Islands'. Malgré la présence sur les marches devant la cathédrale de membres des forces armées qui avaient participé à la Task Force, ainsi que la lecture de la leçon par un pilote Harrier, le service – notamment le discours de l'archevêque de Canterbury, le Dr Robert Runcie – soulignait la douleur des veuves argentines aussi bien qu'anglaises et l'aspect fou et brutal de la guerre.

Le refus du clergé à adopter une position triomphale sur la victoire britannique a beaucoup irrité certains militaires et politiciens, surtout le premier ministre et plusieurs autres responsables du gouvernement actuel. L'office a suscité des controverses il y a quelques semaines, les responsables de l'Église d'Angleterre ayant alors proposé d'inclure une traduction espagnole du paternoster et de distribuer le texte du discours pacifiste prononcé par le pape a l'occasion de sa visite pendant la guerre. Le premier ministre a réussi à supprimer ces deux propositions.

Le Dr Runcie est parvenu cependant à citer l'essentiel du discours papal, et l'assistance s'est trouvée remerciant Dieu pour le mouvement de paix et le suppliant de renforcer la volonté de 'combattre la pauvreté et les maladies plutôt que les autres peuples'. Dans l'esprit conservateur, ce sont là des prières plus adaptées à un dieu pacifiste, voire travailliste, qu'à celui de la classe dirigeante britannique. Officiellement, le premier ministre 'n'a pas tellement aimé' l'office, laissant aux nombreux voyous sans-portefeuille de droite le devoir d'engueuler le pacifisme et le libéralisme des 'clercs serviles' et de faire appel, après l'événement, pour des hymnes 'plus robustes'. Selon certaines sources, cependant, citant son mari Denis Thatcher, 'la patronne est folle de rage'.

Le Matin, 27 July 1982

*

The Queen, with several members of the Royal Family including the Prince and Princess of Wales, and the prime minister, leaders of the other political parties and many ministers and former ministers, attended the Falkland

Islands Service of Thanksgiving and Remembrance at St Paul's Cathedral on Monday morning. While members of the military Task Force were on the steps of the cathedral, and a Harrier pilot read a lesson, in the service the Archbishop of Canterbury, Dr Robert Runcie, emphasised the grief of Argentine as well as British widows and highlighted the mad and brutal nature of the war.

The clergy's refusal to take a triumphalist position on the British victory caused serious annoyance to certain military and politicians, notably the prime minister and some other government members. Controversy had erupted a few weeks ago when leaders of the Church of England proposed including a Spanish translation of the Lord's Prayer and handing out copies of the pacifist speech given by the Pope when he visited Britain during the war. The prime minister crushed both proposals.

Dr Runcie did, however, manage to cite the main thrust of the Pope's speech, and the congregation found themselves thanking God for the peace movement and praying for greater efforts 'to combat poverty and disease rather than other peoples'. To a Conservative mindset, such prayers are addressed to a pacifist, even Labour, God, not to that of the British ruling class. According to official sources, the prime minister was 'not very keen' on the service, but she left it to right-wing thugs on the back benches to denounce pacifism and say the hymns should have been more robust. But other sources quote her husband, Denis Thatcher, saying 'the boss is livid'.

6

PSYCHOLOGY

WILHELM REICH

There is no fence between the big sweep of lawn and the road to Rangeley, but there was a chain across the end of the driveway when we arrived. Beside the entrance stands a neatly painted wooden notice with the name Orgonon and details of the opening hours: four hours a day, two days a week, July and August only. A couple of hundred yards up the drive is a low dilapidated building with an oddly military look: the Laboratory. In 1951 Wilhelm Reich conducted a series of experiments in this building in which he tried to measure the effects of radioactive isotopes on *orgone*, the life energy which he believed he had discovered. According to later accounts by Reich and his followers, the combination was deadly, causing fainting, dizziness, relapses into old illnesses and ... loss of faith. The building and its surroundings 'became uninhabitable' for years. Reich called this experiment Oranur. It lost him most of his pupils and, according to his son Peter,[1] was instrumental in estranging him from his wife Ilse Ollendorff. In 1973 the building looks harmless and peaceful: no black cloud, no bad vibes that I can feel. Perhaps my character is at fault. Ola Raknes, one of the very few disciples who stayed with Reich to the end, comments in his book *Wilhelm Reich and Orgonomy*:[2] 'Strongly armoured persons did not feel, or at least only to a slight degree, the effect of DOR (Deadly ORgone), and would faint and become helpless without having felt any warning symptoms, so that to them DOR was still more dangerous than to less armoured persons.'

The drive curves into trees above the Laboratory, a pleasant well-tended place. We got out of the car and stretched, five stiff pilgrims out of a rented Dodge with New York licence plates. Wandering around in the sunshine we found ripe blueberries in the long grass beside the sweep of lawn. At five minutes to two an elderly man drove up in an elderly Chevrolet. He unhooked the chain and laid it on the driveway, then without looking at us drove over the chain and past the Laboratory into the trees. Presently we followed.

The drive winds uphill through woods to a solid stone-and-timber house with a grassy parking lot: the Observatory. As we parked the car the elderly man, Mr Tom Ross, emerged from bushes and greeted us. He asked whether we would like to visit Dr Reich's tomb or whether we would prefer

---

1 Peter Reich, *A Book of Dreams*, Harper and Row, 1973.
2 St Martin's Press, 1970.

to go round the Observatory first, and we chose the Observatory. We were intrigued by a curious structure beside the parking lot, something like a Second World War rocket launcher: eight parallel metal tubes in two rows of four, mounted on a metal base with cranks and swivels to enable them to be aimed in any direction, with removable caps at one end (as it were the muzzle end) and flexible metal hoses leading from the other end and disappearing under the structure. The whole machine stands on a wooden platform with notices warning visitors not to climb on it. 'That there's a cloudbuster,' Mr Ross told us. 'I helped Dr Reich build the first one, that's down in the Laboratory.'

Apart from the admission desk and a display of pamphlets in the hall, the Observatory is just like a house inside. 'Everything's just as Dr Reich left it,' our guide, a pretty young blonde girl, told us reverently. 'This is the catalogue Dr Reich used to choose the furniture for the Observatory.' It is solid, expensive, middle-class furniture, hardly worn at all, nostalgically unfashionable. A museum of the fifties, the lifestyle of the McCarthyite middle class which hounded to ruin hundreds of alleged communists and fellow-travellers. The Orgonon potted biography states blandly that Reich 'adhered to no religious creed and no political party', forgetting perhaps that for a short time in the early thirties he had been a force to be reckoned with in the German Communist Party, where his Sex-Pol organisation quickly reached a membership of twenty thousand or more. He published *The Mass Psychology of Fascism*, a most original and telling political and psychological analysis of class society, in the year Hitler came to power; but his own martyrdom, when it came, had nothing to do with his political views. The routine Eisenhower-era anti-communism professed by Reich during the fifties did not protect him from the Food and Drug Administration.

'This painting is by Dr Reich,' our guide was saying. 'Nearly all the paintings in the house were painted by Dr Reich.' They look pretty terrible to me, the colours garish, the drawing untutored, though most of them strongly convey a *mood*. Some are abstract renderings of what I take to be orgone energy, others have titles like 'Christ'. One, a gloomy painting of a lone eagle on a mountain top, is mentioned in Peter Reich's book. Does it symbolise the lonely genius who sees all from his eminence? Would Reich have seen himself as a bird of prey? I disliked the picture, glibly categorising it as paranoid. But I remember with more pleasure another bird picture, a large painting hanging in the hall of two puffin-like creatures, black and white with orange beaks and little round eyes, both gliding on outspread wings but facing one another, with their heads nearly touching. The painting somehow gives the impression that the birds are whirling in a circle about a point between their two heads. For some reason I associated this picture with mature sexual love. The two puffins are mute, their beaks closed, their eyes expressionless. They cannot talk, but they are companions.

'This is where Dr Reich used to receive scientists and visitors connected with his work,' said our guide. We were in another large living room like the one on the ground floor but with two alcoves opening off it. One of the alcoves is really another room, a book-lined study; the other, behind a curtain, contains a double bed and has a glass door onto a broad balcony. 'Hey look, the orgasm room,' someone said. Above the bed, painted on the wooden panelling, is a large orange painting of a naked man with long wild hair, running and in mid-stride. His penis is erect. 'This is a picture Dr Reich painted of the Messenger,' the blonde girl told us, but she did not know who the messenger is or what message he carries. A pencil drawing on one of the landing walls looks like a study for this painting, but the painting looks as if it was done very quickly. Woodgrain shows through the roughly applied white size background.

There are some empty shelves in the study but no evidence of censorship by anyone. Even Reich's banned works – for the most part pamphlets written at Orgonon during the last seven years of his life – are present there. The book freak in our party ran a gleaming eye along these shelves and the blonde girl stayed courteously right with us, although as it happens she needn't have bothered. Freud's collected writings are there on the same wall, and not far away the central works of Marx and Lenin. Reich's intellectual roots. In 1933 he was expelled from the German Communist Party for reasons which are not clear but which doubtless had to do with 'idealism' and 'decadence'. The vigorous evolution of that party during the late twenties and early thirties not only terrified the German ruling class into colluding with the Nazis but also caused increasing discomfort to the Stalinist leadership of the Comintern, which never took seriously the revolutionary role of sexual liberation. The following year Reich, now in Scandinavia after fleeing from Nazi retribution, 'resigned' from the International Psychoanalytic Association (his supporters claim that he was expelled or forced to resign). In later life, according to Ola Raknes, Reich was estranged from the communist movement and sometimes spoke of 'Red fascism'. And anyone who has learned of Reich from one of the host of present-day practitioners of 'Reichian' therapy might easily come away without the information that his most valuable work was carried out between 1920 and 1933, in the field of psychoanalysis.

BRICOLAGE

On the study wall is a photograph of Freud looking extremely severe and inscribed in crabbed German handwriting 'With friendliest greetings – Sig. Freud'. After becoming a psychoanalyst in 1920 at the age of twenty-three Reich continued training and working in Freud's Vienna until 1930 when he moved to Berlin. He got his MD in 1922 and later studied neuro-psychiatry. Throughout this period he practised medicine and psychoanalysis both privately and in public institutions, taught and lectured, wrote several important psychoanalytic works,[3] and tossed off a large number of papers and pamphlets. Towards the end of the twenties he became increasingly involved in politics and in 1930 joined the Communist Party and moved to Berlin, where he tried to promote both psychoanalysis and socialism by combining them in the German National Association for Proletarian Sex Policy (often abbreviated to Sex-Pol). Thirteen years of ... well, *genius*. Yet references to Reich in the official literature of the psychoanalytic movement are of telegraphic reticence. He has been edited out of Freud's collected writings. Ernest Jones writes offhandedly in Volume III of his *Life and Work* of Freud: 'Freud had thought highly of him in his early days, but Reich's political fanaticism had led to both personal and scientific estrangement.' It is true that Freud and the analytic movement did not like Reich's politics, but it seems unlikely that this was the sole reason for the split with him. More probably the main reason was Reich's growing interest in the *somatic* or bodily manifestations of mental illness, which he elaborated during the thirties into a therapeutic system which he called *Vegetotherapy*. This therapy, which concentrates on penetrating the patient's defences by *touching* him and *telling him what is wrong with him*, and which lies at the root of modern American 'active therapy' (e.g. encounter, bio-energetic therapy, rolfing), differs radically from psychoanalysis which helps the patient understand his or her problem but leaves the patient responsible for the cure. Thus Reich's important psychoanalytic work *Character Analysis*, from which he developed this system, represents his point of departure from psychoanalysis. In one of the halls or landings at Orgonon there is another, much kinder photograph of Freud. This one is unsigned.

Across the landing from the living room and study is the treatment room, a small office with desk, chair, examining table/couch, washing alcove. Also a miniature cloudbuster about two feet high, with the flexible

---

3 E.g. *The Function of the Orgasm*, 1927; *The Sexual Revolution*, 1932; *The Mass Psychology of Fascism* and *Character Analysis*, both 1933. References are to first editions as Reich distorted his works in later editions and especially in English translations. Also for pamphlets and extracts, notably a brilliant essay *Dialectical Materialism and Psychoanalysis*, see *Sex-Pol*, ed. Lee Baxendall, Random House, 1972.

metal pipes leading from the tubes not into the ground but into a box painted bright yellow and locked with a padlock. Not a Black Box but yellow, the warning colour denoting radiation. This device is called a DORbuster, and Reich used it to drain DOR from patients. The blonde girl did not know what the yellow box contains, but I can guess: either earth or water. Reich did not believe that fire or air have the capacity to ground orgone energy. 'When this device is applied to armoured persons, it may under certain conditions provoke outbreaks of repressed emotions very resistant to other methods of setting them free,' writes Raknes. 'The use of it is, however, still so much in the experimental stage that it should be used with the greatest caution and preferably only by an experienced orgonomist.' Reich was insistent on the need for extreme caution when using any orgonomic equipment: DOR- or cloud-buster (eight aluminium tubes), or *orgone accumulator* (wood or fibre box lined with metal), could, he felt, be most dangerous in the wrong hands. The few 'orgonomists' practising today are similarly cautious, and also inherit the fear of luminescent substances (TV tubes, watch dials) that Reich developed towards the end of his life. Peter Reich describes an incident in which his father sent him, aged seven, to fetch a radium needle from beneath a pile of rocks in the yard, urging him to be careful.

We climbed to the third floor of the house, a small studio opening onto a flat, unfenced roof. 'This is where Dr Reich painted,' the girl said. Mr Ross told us later that Reich painted at night, after 11. 'I guess he didn't need much sleep,' he said. 'He used to sleep when he felt tired. Then he'd wake up after ten minutes and go right back to work.' A work surface running round three walls of the studio holds a jumble of equipment, telescopes, microscopes, electroscopes, vacuum tubes. An easel holds a blank canvas slashed diagonally 'by vandals'. There are other laboratory spaces: a large, nearly empty room on the ground floor where Reich lectured to students; an alcove off the landing on the second floor packed with old electronic equipment, carefully labelled bits of rock, photographs of mice with cancer. As we descended the stairs, an elderly woman bustled past guiding another party of visitors. She was saying briskly: 'This is a Geiger counter that Dr Reich used to measure orgone radiation.' 'Gee, a *Geiger counter*!' A woman visitor exclaimed. 'Hey Billy, come and see this! Come look at the Geiger counter!'

Peter Reich writes that Tom Ross 'spoke quietly and lovingly of The Doctor, telling stories that showed fairness, honesty, imagination, and error. Wisely, Tom refused to speak into the new-fangled tape recorders that some people brought.' When we came out of the Observatory and followed Tom through the bushes to Reich's tomb, I carried the microphone of a cassette recorder inconspicuously in my left hand. Mr Ross, a courteous, kindly old man with the golden patina of a life spent in unhurried outdoor labour, answered our questions willingly. Later I discovered that I had failed to operate the recorder correctly and the tape was blank. To quote Peter Reich again: '... I'm not saying this place is haunted or anything, it's just that strange things happen to people when they come into contact with the work.' Despite this unheard-of lapse in my mechanical competence, however, Mr Ross's remarks, uttered in a distinctive Maine accent, were easy to remember.

The stone tomb stands among trees overlooking the lake. A cloudbuster, its tubes capped, stands beside the tomb, aimed at it; on its black base Reich's monogram, WR with the letters run together, is painted in white. Tom admitted that he keeps the paint fresh but always follows the outlines painted by Dr Reich. He told us that although that particular cloudbuster is not grounded, the tubes are kept capped because the Doctor wasn't sure what it might do over a period of time if they were left open. 'He was careful with the cloudbusters because he said he didn't know what they could do.' How does it work, we asked, by ... shooting or what? 'The doctor used to say they *draw*,' he answered, 'they draw orgone from the clouds and ground it. The pipes go down to the water table underground, it don't work if it's not grounded.' Looking at the structure he added: 'He give me the title of *Operator* because I used to help out a bit. I said he shouldn't, I didn't know enough about it to be an Operator, but he did like to give people credit.'

After reaching America from Norway in 1939, still a jump ahead of the Nazis, Reich flowered into a mad scientist. Virtually all his work from that time until his death was based on two discoveries which most natural scientists reject outright: the *bion* and *orgone* energy. By the middle fifties he was using the cloudbuster not only to make rain or divert hurricanes but also to drive off alien invader spacecraft which kept appearing in the Maine skies. New translations of his early books were published with strange additions and distortions to their texts, still a source of confusion to people trying to study Reich's work. He engaged in a vigorous but largely one-sided correspondence with various prominent individuals and organisations: the President, Einstein, the Air Force. Occasionally the doctor could be seen chasing 'spies and agents' off his property with a .45.

'I didn't believe the accumulators worked at first,' Tom Ross told us. 'I didn't see how you could prove *any* of it worked, I told him so too. I was giving him a hard time. Until one day I felt it, after that I knew there was something in it. I went into the big accumulator like a room one day, Reich was working in there. I felt the tingling. He went out after a while – said he'd had enough, he couldn't stand to be there any more. He asked if I could stand it for so long. He said I should come out.' Could we see an accumulator at Orgonon, we asked. 'No, there's no accumulators on the premises, they was all destroyed in 1954 by order of the government. They all had a big hole smashed in them so they couldn't be used. They burned Reich's books too.'

Provoked by Reich's treatment of cancer patients, the Food and Drug Administration in 1954 brought a ramshackle injunction against him which declared orgone energy to be non-existent and which sought to restrain him from selling accumulators across state lines using some of his writings as 'false labelling'. The orgonomic writings suppressed by this injunction are still banned, as is the sale of orgone accumulators and their use to treat patients. In 1957 Reich was imprisoned for breaking this injunction and died after eight months in Lewisburg Federal Penitentiary, where he was known to the other prisoners as 'the sex-box man'.

On top of the tomb a grey metal bust of Reich gazes out across the lake. His head was large, long from chin to crown, further exaggerated in photographs by the way he brushed his hair: it seems to stand out from the head sideways and backwards, asymmetric, somehow suggesting energy, rebellion and innocence. In his will Reich spoke of his love for infants, children and adolescents, and their reciprocal love for him. He left most of his estate to found the Wilhelm Reich Infant Trust Fund, which now administers the museum and owns the copyrights of his works.

Strolling back through the trees to the parking lot Mr Ross told us that his grandfather had cleared the land, that his sister had sold it to Reich, that he personally had worked on it all his life. We sat under a tree to talk. Mr Ross runs the museum with his wife, daughter and granddaughter. The land has become overgrown, it's a park and not a farm these days. All kinds of people visit it, doctors, hippies, city slickers, but the Ross family is still part of it nearly thirty years after selling it to Reich. Later, reading Peter Reich's book, I was struck by the fact that he had had the same thought, that he had even considered urging it upon the Yugoslav film director Dusan Makavejev as a basic theme for his film on Reich. Had Tom seen *WR: The Mysteries of the Organism*, the film Makavejev eventually made? 'No I ain't, and I can't say as I intend to either. I've heard that's one cheap film; I've spoken to people that's seen it and from what they say it ain't worth seeing.' He added with unmistakable satisfaction: 'I'm in her though. You seen it?'

I wanted to get back to the real subject, the complex and restless personality of Reich himself. I wanted clues to why his complexities had mutated into contradictions, his dedication into obsession, his work ... into play. What had he been like as a person, I asked, had he been easy to talk to or remote?

'Reich would talk to anyone, he was real easy to get on with. He'd talk about anything, he always had something to say. He didn't like to be interrupted when he was working though, and he wouldn't let you make no mistake about it. But when he took a break from work he was real nice. He liked to talk, we used to talk about everything under the sun. I remember arguing with him – he didn't think we should have used the atomic bomb on the Japanese. I told him they asked for it, that was no worse than what they done at Pearl Harbor, but he wouldn't agree. He felt we shouldn't have done it.'

Before we left I asked: 'Mr Ross, I know this is a silly question but did you ever – when you first met Dr Reich, or when you got to know him, did you sort of feel he was – did you recognise him as – well, uh, a great man?'

Tom didn't think it a silly question. He pondered for a while. 'He was a man who was sincere in his work,' he said at last. 'Reich was always sincere in his work.'

c. 1973 (not written for publication)

ENCOUNTER GROUP

Right on, gang ... but what about Freud?

John Howe at the Conference on the Politics of Psychotherapy

Saturday 27 November, 10 a.m. Conference on the Politics of Psychotherapy opens at the LSE. The shock troops of the psychotherapeutic revolution warm up with an encounter session organised by Quaesitor, taking place appropriately enough in the gym.

You've seen it on the movies or TV: the gently masterful leader: '... try to show your partners how you feel about them without words ... try to feel what your partner's feeling, are they soft and relaxed or rigid and hostile? ... Say goodbye without words ... change partners.' Rapt, twitching faces, an obedient shuffling and stroking; beatific smiles, the occasional daring hug. '... Try to pair off with someone you feel is a threat to you ... decide who's going to say Yes and who's going to say No ... Stick your lower jaw out, really show aggression ... Ready?' FREAK-OUT! Bedlam. Eyes shine, fists clench, back presses against back. Afterwards, the animation persists for a while.

The present state of psychology

At 11 a.m. the real business of the day begins in a large basement classroom. More people arrive and the room is packed with maybe 200 of them. The conference has been convened to discuss the present state of psychology – confused, dominated by the tendentious creeds of behaviourism (the Pavlovian school which holds human beings to consist of a neutral matrix on which 'behaviour patterns' are 'imprinted' by 'conditioning' rather than free beings possessing minds and gifted with free will) and therefore lending itself to the exploitation and oppression of one class by another – and to formulate an alternative system or the seeds of one. Seminars with promising titles are advertised on the blackboard: Alternative Psychology, Alternative Psychiatry, Radical Alternatives to Prison. There is an air of militant optimism, which we share. Time for the first two (simultaneous) sessions. The GLF [Gay Liberation Front] and their audience leave for another room and the discussion on Alternative Psychiatry rambles into existence. Someone wants to discuss ECT (electro-convulsive therapy). He emphasises that he knows nothing about it but before starting his rap asks, for the record, whether anyone present has either administered or received it. A girl says she has received it as treatment for 'aggression'. 'It made me *more* aggressive,' she says. 'I knew I didn't need treatment in the first place.' Conversation founders. Someone on the platform wants to take things in hand: 'Look, is any one involved in any way?' 'What in?' asks a voice from the floor. The man on the platform seems a bit flummoxed: 'Well ... people and their problems ... that sort of thing.'

We leave for a coffee.

Little Albert and the white rat

The next two sessions advertised are Alternative Psychology and Social Work. Alternative Psychology starts with a film: 'Conditioning of a Fear Response', a PR effort made in the twenties by an American behaviourist called J. B. Watson. The film is a record of an extremely crude experiment to condition a child to be afraid of white rats and furry objects by banging a crowbar with a hammer every time he touches the white rat he enjoys playing with. At the end of the experiment the infant is crying and refusing to play with *anything*.

After the film the girl in charge of the session announces that the original 'Little Albert' (the name of the child) is present and has agreed to answer questions. A long-haired man in a suit, who could just be old enough to be the person in question, rises and shuffles to the front of the classroom. His eyes are veiled, he moves like a catatonic, he sinks down on the floor. The girl running the session seizes his arm bossily: 'Try to stand up.' He pulls away, his eyes downcast. The room is getting restive: 'Let him sit down.' The girl says: 'Can you answer some questions? What can you remember about the experiment?' He stands up, obviously in agony. He looks as if he would like to suck his thumb. He lurches around, trying to escape from the girl. The sickened audience is growling: 'This is disgusting.' 'Why don't you leave him alone?' The girl says that all will be explained when the session has moved to another room (the first one is overcrowded).

All is explained

The whole seminar moves off angrily to another room, nearly 100 people. 'Little Albert' is seen explaining this piece of theatre on the stairs: 'Hours of theorising can leave you unconvinced, an emotional experience has immediate impact.' In the larger room most people want to hear what the platform has to say but a large minority is up in arms: 'We've been manipulated,' they shout. An elderly man called John Lewis is waiting to give a paper but the angry element wants to discuss Little Albert and demand explanations. The issue is put to the vote twice in rapid succession. The manipulated ones lose decisively at the second show of hands and sweep out to another room. John Lewis takes the stand and delivers his paper for an hour. He is attacking behaviourism and its allies; his analysis (or as much as he can put over in the time available) is meticulously scientific, his orientation humanistic and progressive. He argues that the behaviourists are often 'unscientific' in their own terms, and that allies against their doctrines can be found wherever people are seeking truth by rigorous and disciplined scientific investigation – in the fields, for example, of genetics, biology, anthropology and psychology itself.

The psychotherapy of politics

John Lewis talks subtle sense, but his pace is wrong. During his lecture – for that is what it is – the audience dwindles from about eighty to about fifteen. He is heckled constantly: 'What d'you mean, *objective*?' 'Criteria acceptable to *whom*?' John Rowan of *Red Rat* stands up to ask how long Lewis intends to go on. Lewis ignores him. He leaves, but returns ten minutes later and delivers an attack: '… fucking bullshit. You could have said it in twenty minutes and kept your audience …' When he stops the questions continue as if he had not spoken. A man representing mysticism interjects: 'There isn't time … while we sit and theorise the world's being buried under a mountain of garbage …' There's a militant in the audience too: 'Theory takes for ever. We need to act *now* …' Do these cats think Rome was built in a day? Without bricklayers?

By now we have missed Social Work, Counterindustrial Psychology, Radical Alternatives to Prison and Education and Race. Alternative Psychiatry goes on all day in various rooms. It is time for Sexism (2.30 in the lounge) and we wander in. On the whole it's a quiet discussion, dominated of course by representatives of GLF and Women's Liberation. Even here there's a tendency for confusion to pass unnoticed by the majority.

Someone suggests that liberating individuals from sexual repression need not affect their sexist, exploitative attitude to the opposite sex – that it might simply enable them to be sexually exploiting without feeling guilt. It's an interesting idea but not one that should pass unchallenged. Similarly, there seems to be little awareness that the so-called 'straight male' is in fact nothing of the sort, that aggressively 'heterosexual' behaviour and beliefs *always* mask a frantic denial of the individual's homosexual parts, while women can express affection for each other in a physical way without being labelled perverts.

The conference, or what we were able to see of it, was reassuring in one way. It became clear that there is a substantial population of psychologists and psychology students who abhor the behaviourist approach to their subject, and all its implications in the fields of psychotherapy, psychiatry, education, social work and the prison system, where it bolsters up the fascist assumptions about human beings that underlie bourgeois ideology – e.g. that people are animals, organic computers, social units to be manipulated and readjusted. It was also clear that these dissident elements are, in the main, politically 'progressive' and anxious to do something about the state of psychology.

But what about psychoanalysis?

In another way the conference was extremely depressing. Nobody – nobody at all in the sessions we attended – mentioned the psychoanalytic tradition even once. It is not very difficult to see the rotten areas in the work of Eysenck, Skinner, Jensen; how easy is it to see the truth in Freud? The answer is that it is *both difficult and painful*: perhaps it is even more painful to realise that outside psychoanalysis there *is* no psychology worth mentioning. Listen, gang: if you want an alternative to behaviourism, how about studying a bit of psychology just for a start? And get ready for a rough ride: understanding begins at home.

The closing session of the conference was devoted to communication. The alternative psychology magazine *Red Rat* was appointed the official medium for information exchange and individuals wrote their names and addresses down for future contacts: the mystic, a woman who wanted to hear from 'other clinical psychologists working for the NHS', academic groups, student groups from other towns, and so on. It is likely that one of the aims of the conference (though it was not expressed in so many words) was to form the nucleus of a movement which will gather force and direction as it grows in size.

If this is not to prove a pious hope – and the task is as difficult as it is important – someone is going to have to start the work, to formulate an 'alternative' theory and practice. Nobody we heard at the conference was doing this although we are eager to believe that some of the sessions we missed were more constructive. If any of our readers can help or want to know more, contact Red Rat at 42 Essendine Mansions, Essendine Road, London, W9, 01-289 2097.

7 Days, 8 December 1971

THE BIGGER THE CAR, THE BIGGER YOU ARE

'When I'm at the wheel, I relax.' Leonid Brezhnev's confession to the French CP [Communist Party] daily *L'Humanité* must have struck an answering chord in many a bourgeois breast. In an interview published on 25 October, the CPSU's [Communist Party of the Soviet Union] First Secretary said that he loves and trusts machinery for its own sake – he is cutting down his cigarette consumption with the aid of a cigarette case with a built-in time lock – and that he finds he really relaxes only at the wheel of a car. Like many keen drivers, he appears to be a nervous passenger: 'When it's me that's driving I have the feeling that nothing can go wrong.'

L'Humanité said that Mr Brezhnev sometimes drives in Moscow but not very often; most of his driving is done on hunting trips, when he always drives himself. In this respect he seems to be more fortunate than the British prime minister, who is rumoured to have been banned from driving by his party colleagues as a condition of his election to the party leadership. It is said that M. Monnet, the Father of the Common Market, did not believe that the British Conservative Party had the ruthless determination necessary to drag the country into the Community until he emerged pale and shaken from Heath's car after a do-or-die journey from Oxford to London a few years ago. Whether Mr Heath's notorious arrogance and ill-temper stem from the cares of office or from the substitution of sailing for driving must remain a matter for speculation.

Taking a stiff drive

What is quite certain is that the activity of driving can reassure the driver about his potency. Failure or frustration in any area of human endeavour reflects on the individual's feelings about his sexual potency. The great Freud once wrote that any complicated machine figuring in a dream represented the male penis, and psychoanalytic opinion still holds this view.

Since the car represents a penis in its driver's unconscious, it follows that to be inside the car and control it skilfully and consciously is a symbolic representation of 'healthy' sexuality. Like a real penis, a car can be used in a variety of ways, for example either creatively (pleasure, procreation, transport) or destructively (rape, disease, murder/suicide). Just as there is, in real sexuality, a paradoxical coexistence of gentleness and aggression, so in traffic driving the driver's skill and courtesy must be tempered with controlled aggression if he wants to get anywhere.

Eunuchs buy big cars

Despite the popular view that it takes a real man to drive a real car, the truth of the matter is almost the opposite: the more worried he is about his potency, the more likely he is to buy a big car (if he can afford it).

For a striking illustration of this fact, compare the intellectual and emotional impotence of a well-trained soldier with the extraordinarily varied and expensive range of mechanised genitalia supplied to the armed forces ... tanks, jet aircraft, nuclear missiles, big guns; even the lowly private soldier, FN carbine at the ready with one up the spout, can feel he's a real man when a touch on the trigger will penetrate a brick wall ... Imagine then, how the prime minister must have felt on his recent visit to Germany, when he was widely photographed grinning at the controls of a tank in his old Colonel's uniform.

Unfortunately, these delectable toys are freely available only to the ideological eunuchs of the services and to the very privileged. Princess Anne, who like the rest of her family enjoys a close, playful relationship with the armed forces, said in a recent interview that she was looking forward to driving a Ferret Scout Car ('I'm told it's the most popular armoured car with the soldiers because it's not so restricted in speed'): sure enough, she not only drove it but hit six targets with its heavy machine-gun during *her* trip to Germany. Both she and Mr Heath enjoyed themselves on empty tank testing ranges. Since these vehicles are expensive to run and spectacular to watch can we expect to see the appearance of another televised sport – the annual VIPs' cavalry burn-up or some such event? The reader should try to form a picture in his or her mind of EH ripping up the turf in a snorting Centurion and HRH delicately exercising the Ferret, while assorted dukes and generals scamper about in jeeps, helicopters (or 'choppers') and moon buggies. There should be no difficulty in getting them to respect the Priority to the Right rule. Live ammunition should be optional.

7 Days, 10 November 1971

DOPE ON DOPE

Book review: *The Drugtakers: The Social Meaning of Drug Use*, by Jock Young (London: Paladin, 1971)

It may be true that some individual doctors and scientists have reached accurate conclusions about one aspect or another of what is known as the 'drug problem', but it is abundantly clear that neither the medical profession nor the exact sciences have managed to impose much of this knowledge on the legislature, the judiciary, the police or the public.

Indeed, the doctor's role is all too often that of a collaborator with the avenging social machine, rubber-stamping the deviant as suitable for jail or ECT. The reason for this is that the individual expert, hell on wheels when it comes to measuring the fix-frequency of your average morphine-addicted rat, is just another bourgeois when he comes to examine actual human beings and, without realising it, confuses his expertise with the idiocies he's been mouthing on all other subjects since he was weaned.

It may be that the new generation of social scientists is more capable of retaining its reason when faced with armies of deviants. Jock Young is a sociologist, and his modest little book is an eye-opener for those who, like the reviewer, have had their doubts about the usefulness of this discipline.

> Our analysis of the meaning of drug dependency has led us to pursue what I have called a socio-pharmacological approach. That is, we must focus not on the isolated individual taking a drug with foregone effects, but on the drug-taker as a person belonging to a particular culture in terms of which the effects of the drug are structured and his drug use understandable ...
>
> We must see the physiological, subjective and social levels of dependency as a highly interrelated whole.

In other words, Mr Young's approach is a scientific version of the literary treatments which until now have been the main source of 'truth' on the subject. Its unquestionable basic soundness enables him to grapple with the history of British dope hysteria through the sixties, struggling through the ideological morass of late capitalism with dogged courage and pointing out the crucial factors preventing the adoption of a rational set of drug laws.

PSYCHOLOGY

Raking out the chestnuts

Drawing on a wide variety of up-to-date scientific and literary sources, foreign as well as British, Mr Young takes the reader through the background to the use of various drugs (concentrating mainly on illicit drugs but not forgetting prescribed or socially condoned use), then develops his theory of social reaction against drug-taking, which he attributes largely to the prevalence of an 'absolutist' perspective on society among people in general and experts, bosses and lawmakers in particular. He contrasts this view with his own more sophisticated 'relativist' attitude. He does not spare the scapegoat-seeking politicians, the circulation-addicted press, the innocently authoritarian social reformers and do-gooders or the Amplified Deviants themselves when allotting responsibility for the escalation of the problem. The police are seen in a rather passive role, forced to bust more hippies as and when press and parliament demand it. In the course of the book he deals thoroughly with many of the drug myths; not only does he demolish old chestnuts of the 'Pot smokers escalate to heroin' order, but he also cuts the psychic perils of LSD down to size.

Drugs in, sex out

This is not a voyeur's book; if you want a contact high read Tom Wolfe. It's not for Woodstock Nation suckers either: '... it is not drugs per se, but hedonistic cultures which society reacts against ... the deviancy amplification of hippies is only historically tied to marihuana use. Reaction would still proceed even if the drug was legalised overnight.' One cannot tell from reading the book whether or not its author has had any drug experience, which speaks highly of either his objectivity or his insight.

It is only in the last chapter, when he discusses social policy and the drug-taker, that Mr Young confronts the reader squarely with the full dimensions of the problem. By purporting to sketch some ground rules for the development of a more humane and rational drugs policy, he succeeds in showing the utter impossibility of anything of the sort happening in our society without the precondition of radical political change. Dope may not be revolution, but in its small way it certainly indicates the need for it. For the time being, however, it would be no bad thing if politicians, doctors, lawyers, journalists, magistrates and police were forced by law to read this book. It's pretty readable.

7 Days, 26 January 1972

7 VERSE

OSTEOPATH

Quack!
Quack!
THUMP!!
(Crack!)

VERSE

Your Mum and Dad
(With apologies to Philip Larkin)

They treat you well, your mum and dad,
They don't know how to but they do;
They cuff you lightly when you're bad
And love you without planning to:
They teach you language, clean your mess,
Improve your spirits when you're ill –
Sugaring every needed pill –
They treat as theirs your helplessness,
Helplessly clothing you in the tissue
Of wise and stupid, glum and gay,
They too found irksome in their day . . .
Who fucked up whom is not the issue.

They do you proud, your dad and mum,
You don't deserve it but they do.
It's not their fault you're such a bum.
And they have feelings, just like you.

Femme Fatale

A sprinter and a model girl were dawdling over dinner;
The athlete nagged the odalisque for trying to get thinner.
He told her (as he shovelled down potatoes, beef and pasta)
She was living on amphetamines and smoking like a Rasta;
That pills and Scotch and cigarettes were kippering her guts,
And making her hysterical like All Those Other Sluts
And worst of all, the racehorse hissed (without a trace of pity),
She'd abused her constitution till she wasn't even pretty!
She ate an olive; sipped some gin; with dignity arose;
Swayed off into the ladies; stuck some powder up her nose;
Emerged, all eyes upon her smile so radiant and so smooth,
Saw the three private bailiffs round the athlete in his booth,
Sent by a former squeeze, whose mother's ring she'd nicked, to dun her:
So while they broke the runner's leg, the stunner done a runner.

BRICOLAGE

The Marquess of Bath
(With apologies to Linton Kwesi Johnson)

Mama
This the great legend of the Marquess of Bath
Who crash out of his house and skank away down the footpath
Not best please! In no mood to be tease!
Now the Marquess of Bath im don't like to be diss
And im in a hogly mood from a week on the piss
Night and day! Guinness and Wray!
Cause im car get mash up
Im wives give im grief
Im benefit cheque get cash by a tief
Im landlard get greedy
Im house fulla rat
And im otherwise hangry bout this and bout that
And all that booze
Kinda shorten im fuse
So im already seeing red when im get outa bed
Im fall on Cockney Pete and im kick im down the street
Im chase a man call Dick and im beat im with a stick
And what im do to Sid – you remember Yankee Sid? –
Backside man!
I cyaan't start to tell you what that evil marquess did!
Well: a police dem come to mash up the passersby
And kick in doors and windows and make people cry
And ax a lotta question of the deaf and the blind,
And them make a clean sweep man! Leave nothing but children
And dog and cat and budgie behind!
So: they drag up all the prisoners outa them cell
The fellers and the wife and them mother as well
But the Court have problem hearing anything them lawyer say
So them all get lengthy porridge for riot and affray:
Everybody bust! Not too just!
Everybody, that is, but the Marquess of Bath
Who come back outa the courthouse and skank back along the path
Having prove to the Court that im just passing by
And im never see nothing cause there something in im eye:
Im lawyer blow the judge a kiss. Case dismiss!

And that not all, Mama. The marquess name Thynne
And this judge think he a comic. Im say with a grin
Something about Bath belly. For this joking remark
The marquess smile, and ax the judge to visit im safari park ...
And when the judge get down there, that hevil Henglish sinner
Im seize the judge – I tell no lie –
And cook the judge and eat the judge
I swear it man, to bumboclaat!
With gungo peas and ackee for im dinner!

Mothertruckers

Crazed monarchs of the asphalt! Worthy avatars of Toad!
Your duty is to try to make a racetrack of the road.
Yes! Show your fellow humans that it's good to be alive:
Put a hundred in the hour on a packed M25.
You're quicker round the roundabout than through the underpass,
So just enjoy those generous excursions on the grass
As you undertake and overtake and squirt it down the shoulder
Using slip roads and embankments with decision ever bolder
Blasting your raucous klaxons as you exercise your toys
For it's just the joyous ticket
To really, really stick it
To those jiveass mothertruckers and those white van ladyboys.

The Ultimate Late Braker

There was a bloke who thought himself
The ultimate late braker:
One day he tried it in the wet
And shortly after briefly met
His disapproving Maker.

BRICOLAGE

The Marquess of Blandford

The Marquess of Blandford
Parked his secondhand Ford
In a slot behind the pits.
Then the little bastard
Got well and truly plastered
With a lot of other shits.
Flavio Briatore
Appeared in all his glory
And failed to see the joke;
Not knowing that sobriety –
Even in high society –
Is threatened by a mixture of dilaudid and malt whisky,
Amphetamine and oxygen (to keep the subject frisky),
Gin (to make him tearful), champagne (to keep him cheerful),
Heroin or Quaalude (to prevent him getting fearful)
And *bhang* (to take the edge off all the lines of uncut coke).

Currant Bun

Mean halftruths are our specialty
We grass folks up for fun
For we are Rupert's heroes
On the Sunday Currant Bun

We deal in false celebrity
We sting but don't get stung
(For we cosy up to coppers
On the Sunday Currant Bung) ...

We drink shampoo; we guzzle lox;
Our work is never done
On the Digger's dug-up baby
The Sunday Currant Bun

ARGY! GERTCHA! BARGEE! GOTCHA!
SUNDAY CURRANT BUN
OI!
SUNDAY CURRANT BUN!

All the Sixes

With stinking breath and curly horns and bloodshot, goatish eyes,
Scratching the vermin swarming on his hairy zigzag thighs
Smoke belching from his nostrils, farting to beat the band,
He reaches for his phone book with a twisted, furry hand,
Then trots across the halls of hell with cloven hooves a-clatter
And passes by the telephone: he knows it doesn't matter
But he hesitates to dial, even though he got the job
By knowing seven hundred names for Satan (or for Hob).
'Courage, young imp,' he tells himself. 'I'll ask the Boss at least.'

...

A long, black, trembling claw taps out the Number of the Beast.

Six Haiku on Sound

When you are speaking
I only hear sounds. Therefore
What is your silence?

My child is crying.
I go to him when ready:
His mother is there.

If what you are shouting
Is that you are not shouting
You can stop shouting.

Beautiful music
Is sounds in such an order
That we hear Nothing.

Silence, if golden,
Is of much less interest
Than confusing sounds.

I call for order:
Nobody can hear a word;
I call for order.

⑧ MISCELLANY

THE FIRST NORTH–SOUTH WAR

Without bloodshed, but with the threat of force, a British frigate in 1833 took formal possession of the Falkland Islands and returned some thirty or forty Spanish settlers to their country of origin: the newly independent Spanish colony of Argentina, then known as the United Provinces of the River Plate.

Since their discovery more than a century earlier, the islands – whose climate is uninviting but not excessively severe – had been claimed and briefly settled by various powers including France, Spain, Argentina and Britain. Now the islands, whose deeply indented coastline provides many sheltered anchorages, passed into the hands of the major maritime power, Britain. They were conveniently placed for shelter, rest and recuperation of ships plying the important but stormy sea-route around Cape Horn from the Atlantic to the Pacific.

Of course Argentina complained that the Malvinas – a Spanish version of the French name Malouines given to the islands by Atlantic fishermen from St Malo – had been stolen from them, but there was nothing the young colony could do against Britain's great and growing naval power. As the century progressed, Britons joined the flow of colonists into Argentina; British firms and financiers took a leading part in the development of Argentine cattle and meat industries and the country's railways. Most of Argentina's 30 million population is of Spanish and Italian descent. But among the minorities are 100,000 British-descended Argentines; 17,000 plus resident British nationals attest to long and close relations between the two countries.

These have persisted on all important levels – diplomatic, military, economic – despite occasional frictions on, as it were, political and ideological levels: Argentine sympathies for German Nazism; the struggle for independence by Argentine capital during the rise and subsequent decline of British imperial power; British arrogance and 'racism'.

Argentines are irritated by what they see as British superciliousness in regarding them as a Third World nation. With the stridency of all colonists, they point to the wealth and sophistication of their society and their European descent. There are British components in Argentine nationalism. The Argentine navy is largely modelled on the British Royal Navy which has helped train and equip it.

BRICOLAGE

Nationalist upsurge

The claim to the Malvinas, never renounced, was brought out and dusted off during the development of modern Argentine nationalism roughly since the 1920s. It was used by, among others, the populist leader Juan Peron and his wife Eva, the most notable figures in Argentina's recent political history. This nationalist upsurge coincided with changes in the role and status of Britain as a power.

By the 1960s, Britain had begun desultory negotiations over the future of the Falkland Islands apparently with a view to changing their status in Argentina's favour. But the Falkland Islanders effectively vetoed all the formulae discussed by the two governments. Less than 2,000 in number, the islanders apparently like living in an under-exploited backwater and do not wish to live in Argentina, even with the privileges offered.

Thus, negotiations dragged on without any useful outcome until Argentina lost patience. On 2 April 1982, with little bloodshed, but with overwhelming force, the Argentine armed forces took formal possession of the Malvinas and sent home the symbolic force of British marines stationed there. The next day, the British government ordered the dispatch of a powerful naval task force to retake the islands. The episode, which ended with the surrender of Argentine forces on the islands on 14 June, is rich in contradictions and shows both parties to have committed grave errors and miscalculations.

The worst miscalculation was that made by the Argentine government in imagining that Britain's apathy over the islands would survive an Argentine invasion. Certainly the British had no very special attachment to the islands. But General Galtieri's military adventure stung Britain, only recently a great military power, in its military pride: a pride upheld by the British taxpayer to the tune of £14,000 million a year. In the eyes of the taxpayer, this expenditure should ensure quietly efficient military forces, and the British public was content to wait for these forces to do what they are trained to do.

The British made several miscalculations. The first was to underestimate the depth of feeling about the islands in Argentina; the second was to misread the fairly clear indications that Argentina was planning invasion, despite earlier experiences which illustrated Argentine willingness to take the military option; and the third, and perhaps the worst, was to underrate Argentina's capacity to fight a modern war. All three can be linked with Britain's racist habit of underestimating the importance and the capacities of all foreigners. This is all the more astonishing in cases where Britain has helped over many years to train and equip another country's armed forces.

In the event, the Argentine navy and air force proved to be technically and militarily very capable, and the air force pilots in particular very brave indeed. This cost Britain substantial material and human losses. Argentina's troops were also often brave and fierce. But they could not cope with the Falklands weather and were let down by the strategic incompetence of their senior officers.

The moral positions of both countries, and of their various allies, were often laughable. Argentina, a colony in which no descendants of the indigenous population survive, has found it expedient to pose as a fighter against British colonialism, supported by Cuba and the Soviet Union which until three months ago were condemning it as a fascist country and pointing to the poor human rights record of recent Argentine governments (the present one is a slight improvement though far from perfect).

Deaf ear

Britain's government, which had long turned a deaf ear to left-wing complaints about Argentinian repression and continued to supply Argentina with advanced weapons, discovered with apparent surprise that the Argentine government was a 'fascist military junta'.

To avoid administrative problems, neither side declared war. To avoid an Argentine default rocking the world monetary system, the Bank of England continued to cooperate with other central banks in extending Argentina's overstretched international credit: thus in effect lending Argentina money for its war effort. The position of the United States was difficult. For some time it tried to remain neutral between its top NATO ally Britain and its anti-communist friend Argentina, whose troops it was using for military intervention against left-wing revolutionaries in Central America.

When Washington came down, inevitably, on Britain's side, giving some modest but useful help with intelligence, communications and arms supplies, Argentina felt betrayed; and went looking for its own weapon replacements in South Africa, Israel, Libya and various Latin American countries. Wars make strange bedfellows.

The British prime minister, Margaret Thatcher, claimed that Britain was upholding two principles: the right of peoples to determine their own political future, and the need to resist armed aggression. Few Africans will need to be reminded that Britain has not always upheld these principles with the same energy. In a speech after the Argentine surrender Shridath Ramphal, Commonwealth secretary general, congratulated Britain on performing a service to the world community. He felt obliged to remark that since Britain has sometimes 'acquiesced' in acts of aggression, its response 'in this instance is the more useful to the rest of the world'.

The Third World in general tended to adopt a pro-Argentina stance for two basic reasons: based on the proximity of the islands to Argentina (around 450 miles offshore, well outside internationally accepted territorial waters, but 'on the continental shelf'); and the existence of many past or present territorial disputes between developing countries and former imperial powers like Britain. The gut sympathies of most of the Third World were with 'developing' Argentina against distant, 'imperial' Britain. These sympathies are strongest in Latin America and in countries which have present or recent territorial disputes with Britain. Ireland is a striking example. In many cases, however, these sympathies have been tempered by awareness of Argentina's dubious legal position and perhaps by disapproval of what seemed to many – Brazil for example – a foolhardy venture doomed to failure.

In Africa reaction was very muted. Only Kenya, of all the Commonwealth African countries, openly condemned the Argentine aggression. However, several West African ports were used by the British task force ships for fuelling and resupply. In Black Africa, very little was said in support of Argentina. Here again, many leaderships will have felt the Argentine seizure of the islands to be ill-judged as well as illegal. The complication of Argentina's own 'racism' and its alliance with South Africa in a sort of South Atlantic hard men's axis may also have played a part. Something positive may come out of all the hard thinking occasioned in African capitals by the crisis.

Diego Garcia

It looks very much as if the new Mauritian government means to lead the way by espousing the cause of the Diego Garcians. These people, fewer in number than the Falklanders and of Afro-Asian origins, were evacuated by the British from Diego Garcia and the other islands of the Chagos chain in the late 1960s after Britain had formally separated the Chagos from

Mauritius. Diego Garcia remains a 'British possession' but is leased to the United States for use as a surveillance centre and military base in the Indian Ocean.

The point is that here, the British did not even pretend that the islanders were being consulted. Two disputes have arisen over the affair. One was over the question of compensation to the inhabitants, formerly fishermen and island cultivators who find it difficult to cope with life in the poor quarters of overcrowded Port-Louis, Mauritius, where they now live. They originally demanded $14 million, and the British have offered half this sum. The other dispute concerns the claim of Mauritius to the islands, which is being revived by the new government.

It would perhaps be useful, by underlining the difference between the way the Diego Garcians have been treated and the British official attitude to the Falklanders, to try to persuade the British to make some kind of backdated declaration of principle on the matter. It may be too late to try to persuade Britain and other powerful countries to uphold important principles whenever they are called in question and not simply when the interests of the powerful are threatened at the same time.

Africa magazine, 131, July 1982

MOVING TOWARDS CHANGE

Book review:
*Moving Towards Change: Some Thoughts
on the New International Economic Order*
(Paris: UNESCO, 1976)

We are now undergoing a period of profound and rapid, though uneven, and not infrequently crisis-ridden change. This change is largely connected with the ever-increasing power available to man, through the development of science and technology. The roots of the crisis phenomena lie, however, in the crucial sphere of social relations, which to a considerable degree are still not sufficiently adapted to cope with the rapidity of change caused by science and technology. Technology is ambivalent. On the one hand, it has brought enormous benefits to mankind. On the other, it has resulted in an incredible accumulation of destructive devices. Furthermore, the contradictions in the transfer of technology from the industrial centres to the developing areas of the world, with their characteristic socio-economic structures, have brought very serious maladjustments and disruptions. Inequalities have been accentuated and an extraordinary demographic growth is taking place. Millions of young people are being led to doubt and protest, and soon perhaps to despair with its accompaniment of violence.

A few remarks from the report of the Panel of Counsellors on Major World Problems and UNESCO's Contribution to Solving Them, printed as an appendix to this crucially important document. Well, it *should* be crucially important: nothing should be more essential reading than the 'thoughts' of the most intellectual and disinterested agency of that shadow world government, the UN, on the obsolete systems and psychologies now threatening to send the human race in an accelerating spiral of shortages, paranoia, starvation and violence, down the plughole of History to the final war... 'Existing stocks of nuclear weapons are already capable of liquidating several times over the population of the world', notes the Panel casually.

> Furthermore, several hydrogen bombs are manufactured each day, a hundred times more powerful than the Hiroshima bomb. Annual

> expenditure on the armaments race is very probably around 200 to 250 billions of dollars – a sum equal to the total national income of countries in which the majority of mankind is living. At the same time, twenty-five hundred million men and women largely live a precarious existence at levels of nutrition well below the acceptable minimum.

Food for serious thought, this kind of thing, if you take it seriously. The trouble seems to be, though, that not many people do. This book was published two years ago, but I do not remember seeing it mentioned anywhere.

Part of the reason for this is that there is nothing 'new' in *Moving towards Change*. The danger of nuclear war has been cited before – also starvation in the Third World, raw materials shortages, the growing gap between rich and poor, the unequal terms of exchange between rich and poor nations, etc., etc., etc. If the Algerians and other developing peoples want the world economic 'system' to be readjusted in their favour, there's nothing surprising about that, is there? Just doing what anyone would do in their place. Not everyone is in their place though, fortunately. 'The United States cannot and does not accept any implication that the world is now embarked on the establishment of something called "the new international economic order"', said the American representative to the Paris North–South Conference in December 1975 – five months after the Panel finalised the Report quoted at the beginning of this review. In other words: try to stop us by all means, but we'll screw you for as long as we can.

Not just the US, not just the West, but the big battalions everywhere, are *structurally* opposed to the changes to our outlook and comportment, to national and international political organisation, which are needed within twenty-five years if the survival of the human race is regarded as any sort of priority. *Moving towards Change* mentions these things clearly, but in the abstract; it cites the growing tendency of governments to seek 'authoritarian solutions', the need for a 'rational approach to socio-economic matters', the ambiguous role of 'capitalism' in Third World economies. It says nothing about what individual nations and groups must do to bring about the desired freedom and rationality: this is outside its scope. Each country's contribution to the new international economic order is the responsibility of its own people. And they must move fast, because what is needed – the new order – really amounts to nothing less than a world revolution, in some ways analogous to but in a different dimension from the trumpeted national 'Revolutions' embodying, alas, the state's religious faith more than anything else in a number of countries.

The reason why we need a psychological transformation first and foremost is that we don't really want to believe that all of this affects us. We are too eager to believe those who tell us that the abolition of waste, the juster division of resources between rich and poor (nationally and internationally) will affect our 'standard of living', deprive us of our cars, our steaks, our freedom. We cling desperately to our boring, nasty, insecure £80-a-week jobs because we are threatened with, not starvation, but the dole. We listen like hypnotised rabbits as the government, eager to be returned to power, lops a quid a week off our income tax. Beside this, the starvation of black millions, the threat of fascism and nuclear holocaust, and the UN's comments on them, pale into insignificance. Perhaps if there was a world government, we'd listen to its comments on our future with about as much attention as we give our own governments. As things are, most of us couldn't care less: we leave that sort of thing to the 'experts' we fondly imagine are paid to take care of them. We are making a mistake: our governments, our industries and experts – not the individuals so much as the organisms themselves – operate in the same way as you or me: keep a good thing going as long as possible. When it looks like collapsing, take the money and run.

The attitude, common to East and West, of any bourgeois, any organisation, or any psychopath.

c. 1976 (publication details unknown)

HOLY WATER

Father O'Flaherty's bowels turned to water as a traffic light changed to amber a hundred yards ahead and the car whose front-seat passenger he was swerved to the wrong side of the road and accelerated past the obediently slowing vehicle in front of it. The driver, a youth who, outside the presbytery two minutes before, had seemed the very image of fuddled bucolic panic and grief, now glanced rapidly from side to side, peering with total concentration in every direction, in the mirrors, switching the headlights on, hitting the horn button, standing on the brake pedal, changing gear with a tremendous scream of engine, a violent surge of acceleration in a shallow S-curve across the Shankill Road under the hooting noses of buses, cars and vans forced to stop, as it were, in mid-start. Clinging to the door, the sides of his seat which was set right back on its runners denying his feet purchase on the floor, bracing himself against the dashboard and transmission tunnel against unpredictable violent accelerations, Father O'Flaherty saw with unbelief the speed, flow and concentration of the driver's movements. Could this possibly be the same young man who, two hundred seconds before, slowly mumbled with downcast eyes a tale of a dying mother in need of the last rites two streets away? On climbing behind the wheel of this shiny blue new salesman's Ford, its engine already running, every panel on one side scraped and ripped in some recent collision, the incoherent country youth instantly transformed into a specialised urban animal of alarming efficiency.

The car slowed briefly, banged across a kerb, scattered children in a playground, passed through flapping clotheslines in a yard between old blocks of flats and raced, skidding in generous curves, through the muddy grass of a small mournful park. Father O'Flaherty slid lower in his seat as, engine howling, it bore down diagonally on a sweep of road busy with Saturday-afternoon traffic. 'Where did you say your mother was?' he managed to mutter. The driver, hideously busy with traffic, gave no sign of hearing him. Father O'Flaherty glanced forward through the windscreen at the tilting, heeling landscape, closed his eyes and sank back with a small moan. He began searching for a seat belt. 'Do you mind telling me where we are going?' he asked loudly.

'Just a short cut Father so it is,' said a voice quietly in his ear. 'Hold on now Father.'

Father O'Flaherty turned to the grief-stricken long-haired relative in the back seat, a young man older than the driver with a distant blue stare and wolfish satirical grin. The grin disappeared abruptly, the stare focused on Father O'Flaherty.

'D'you grudge Sean's mother the last rites?' the relative asked coldly in the snarling distinct speech of the city. He was wedged easily into the corner between the seat and the door, an anorak lying across his lap, the dull gleam of black metal between his knees. The car was passing along a narrow concrete road through a vast housing estate. Children, women with prams, two men working on a car, a laundry van, an armoured car, flashed past the window.

'You're a fucking funny-looking Irishman, Father,' the man in the back said.

Still fumbling for the seat belt, Father O'Flaherty turned to see the cold stare flicking back and forth among the dreadful blur of the passing landscape.

'Uncharitable persons,' he said irritably, 'might say the same thing of many of our people, my son.'

Banging and crashing, the car sped among and over piles of bricks and rubble in a large demolition site, launched itself briefly into space and landed diagonally on the high grass banking beside a new motorway out of the city. The driver switched on the lights, placed a hand on the horn button, swooped into the teeth of city-bound traffic in the nearer carriageway, rocketed across the grass of the central reservation and settled into a flat-out cruise away from the city.

'Will you step on it Sean for God's sake,' the man in the back said. Foot pressed to the floor, the driver made no reply. The sound of the engine was a strained blare. After their radical progress across the city, the smoothness of the road was blessed relief.

'For men with a dying mother,' Father O'Flaherty remarked, 'you certainly get a lot of enjoyment from your motoring.'

Both men laughed uproariously. 'You could say so, Padre,' the man in the back said. 'Couldn't he say so Sean?'

Father O'Flaherty's wrenching at the seat belt was rewarded. It yielded enough heavy nylon webbing to fit loosely across his shrinking, bewildered and nauseated form. He clicked the two halves of the buckle together, pinching his left forefinger.

'Is it here?' the driver asked suddenly.

'Yes.' The man in the back grasped the handle above the door and braced his left knee against Father O'Flaherty's seat.

'Teilhard de Chardin,' thought Father O'Flaherty. 'Lao Tze. St Augustine. Confucius. Leonardo da Vinci.'

Out of the corner of his eye, he saw the driver burst into a concentrated frenzy of manual and pedal activity. A dreadful scream of tyres, urgent engine noises and a series of bangs and thumps from under the car succeeded one another in no discernible order. Grass, bushes, a stone wall blurred at and past the car at unexpected angles. Father O'Flaherty was flung violently forward, then against the driver, then against the roof of the car.

'Jesus God,' he thought.

'Untidy, I'd say, Sean,' the man in the back said.

'Jesus will you hold on Father,' the driver muttered irritably. 'How can a man drive with the full weight of the church in his fucking lap? Polis,' he finished in a different tone, braking heavily.

'Stop,' the man in the back said. He threw the anorak aside, lifted a small machine gun from between his knees and laid it across his lap. The car stopped beside three policemen at a bend in the road, their grey Land Rover parked behind them. The man in the back wound down the window behind Father O'Flaherty and threw the grab handle from above the other door, which had come away in his hand, into the road at the feet of the three policemen. One of them approached the car and looked in. The man in the back cocked the machine gun with a loud multiple click, but left it on his knees.

The policeman paled, but looked searchingly at the three men in the car, one by one.

'Do you think, Father,' the man in the back asked in an urbane conversational tone, 'that Ireland should stay in the Common Market?'

The other two policemen had joined the first and were looking into the car. They, too, turned pale.

'Are you lads from Belfast?' one asked in a faintly aggrieved mutter.

'If you mean, as I imagine you do, should Ireland *join* the Common Market,' Father O'Flaherty at last managed to say in an unnatural voice, 'then I have no strong view of the matter.'

'Where are you heading?' one of the policemen asked.

Another walked slowly round the car twice.

'This vehicle's got two different registration numbers,' he muttered.

'Of course,' Father O'Flaherty resumed, 'Ireland's membership – that of the Republic as well as the North – is largely dependent under present circumstances on whether Britain joins.'

Two of the policemen had leaned their heads to the open back window to hear him. The other, excluded, stared at him gloomily through the front window. He began to wind it down. Cold air blew into the car and the three policemen stepped back to listen in greater comfort.

'Perhaps it is worth recalling at this point,' he went on, 'that – under the existing political regime – membership of the Six Counties would be included in British membership, while Eire's membership, in practical terms, is dependent on, but not dictated by, British membership.' Father O'Flaherty paused, unaccountably short of breath.

'Whose car is this?' asked one of the policemen. In the silence which followed, the driver turned on the heater fan whose noise suggested the presence of hyperactive metal rodents behind the dash. He revved the engine twice, like a racing car on the starting grid, and sighed heavily.

'Judging by the present signs,' Father O'Flaherty shouted above the clamour, 'the ruling class in Dublin favours membership even more than the British ruling class. Anything can happen of course, but it looks as if the announcement of British membership will come any day now, or at least fairly soon. And that, of course, will include Ulster. The Six Counties. Or Northern Ireland. The North-Eastern sector of Ireland which for historical reasons is considered part of Great Britain.'

Conscious of slight restiveness here and there in his audience, Father O'Flaherty paused again. The driver took a large steel watch from the left side pocket of his jacket and stared at it theatrically at arm's length, like a person with defective eyesight.

One of the policemen was pointing at Father O'Flaherty.

'Are you from Ulster?' he asked.

'Very interesting Father,' the man in the back said, 'very interesting to hear the views of a learned man like yourself on the issues of the day. Did you want something then Mac?' he asked the policeman in a different voice. 'Routine check, just a routine check was it?'

The policemen all looked away in different directions.

'Yes,' one said as he looked back. 'Just a routine check. Stolen cars, Taig terrorists, things like that. Sir,' he added bitterly.

The man in the back giggled. He took the magazine out of his machine gun and laid it on the seat, worked the bolt with his left hand and with his right caught in mid-air the live round that shot from the ejector slot.

'When you can do that I'll stand you a drink,' he said. 'We can depend on you for to keep order then?'

The driver was revving the engine again. The policemen appeared frozen. One moved a hand slowly towards the discreet holster at his belt, then dropped it to his side.

'Go,' the man in the back said.

The world tilted and shuddered, and so did Father O'Flaherty.

'They aren't coming, Sean,' the man in the back said after a moment.

'No matter if they was,' the driver said. 'We're a half hour late. Will you hold on now Father for the love of God.'

The car accelerated towards a stone wall and a clump of small trees. Green mountains, sad and lovely, were closing in. Feeling sick, Father O'Flaherty closed his eyes.

'Are you all right Father?'

'I feel sick.'

'Open the window for Christ's sake.'

'Out the window Father whatever you do.'

Father O'Flaherty was feeling too ill to derive much pleasure from the alarm he had caused. He wiped a hand across his slimy brow. As he opened his eyes, the car plunged off the road into dense undergrowth.

'Maria!' he shouted.

Both his companions laughed. Half a mile up the rutted, overgrown farm track the car slid to a halt facing a tubular steel gate into a field. Dust rose about them. The driver shouted something out of his window. A limping man carrying a shotgun and a small boy opened the gate and came up to the car. 'Who are you?' the driver asked. The limping man and the small boy looked at the ground.

'I am his cousin,' the man said at last. 'Market day. And who are you?'

'Father O'Flaherty,' the man in the back of the car shouted past the driver. 'Open the fucking gate.'

The limping man glanced at them quickly, then looked at the ground. The small boy pushed the gate open. The car rushed through it, across a field, into a thicket, uphill past stone walls.

Father O'Flaherty was feeling better.

'Who are you?' he asked. The driver turned off the engine. The car coasted into a farmyard and stopped. The driver got out, leaving the door open, and walked into a barn. The silence was astonishing. Father O'Flaherty discovered that all his limbs were braced against parts of the car: door, transmission tunnel, seat, arm rest. He began relaxing them one by one. They ached. He reached for the door handle. Something hard poked his shoulder. The man in the back was grinning.

'Sean is in training for to be an ambulance driver,' he said. 'Stay there a minute.'

The driver emerged from the barn carrying a heavy can and walked to the back of the car. Thumps and clanks resounded through its structure.

Three men stepped out of the door of the farmhouse. One resembled a clerk, thin, grey faced, sour, wearing a dusty grey suit and steel-rimmed spectacles. One was stout and florid with wavy silver hair, wearing a green tweed suit. The third was tall, with a dark moustache, wearing an expensive dark suit. The florid man, talking to the clerk, laughed loudly. He and the tall man walked to the corner of the yard.

The florid man turned towards the car and shouted: 'Are you right boys?'

Both men disappeared behind the barn. The clerk-like man walked quickly to the back door of the car and opened it.

'You're late,' he said. 'They want you for the bank in Newry. It closes in forty-five minutes. You'll have to hurry. No excuses.'

Father O'Flaherty's heart sank. He wanted very much not to visit any bank in Newry that day. 'Aquinas,' he thought. 'Assisi.'

'Who are they?' the man in the back asked, jerking his head towards the corner of the barn.

The clerk gazed at him through his spectacles, which glinted. A loud mechanical whine suddenly filled the farmyard and a small bright yellow helicopter rose from behind the barn, tilted in a curve overhead and vanished over the hill behind the house. The clerk opened Father O'Flaherty's door and said: 'Follow me please.'

He turned and walked into the house, leaving Father O'Flaherty fumbling wildly with his seat belt. The driver flung the can into the barn and opened the car's bonnet. The man in the back opened the last door and got out, dangling his machine gun from his left forefinger by its trigger guard. The driver slammed the bonnet, walked round to his door and slumped expertly behind the wheel. As he did so, Father O'Flaherty's belt parted and he sprang out. The car engine raced into life. The man with the machine gun, who now revealed himself as very tall, smiled down kindly at Father O'Flaherty.

'Nice to meet you, Padre,' he said with every appearance of sincerity. 'Till next time then. To talk about the EEC, eh?'

He fell into the front seat and raised his right hand in farewell.

'Newry,' he said.

Small stones ricocheted about the yard, striking walls and doors. All four doors of the car slammed instantly, but the boot lid flapped slowly up and down as the car drove straight through a deep bed of nettles between two buildings and vanished over what appeared to be a precipice. In a moment it reappeared running upwards across a steep ploughed field opposite. The boot lid was closed. Father O'Flaherty briefly saw its underside as it crossed a tumbledown stone wall on the skyline. His knees were trembling. A bird was singing and a cow lowed somewhere nearby. Distantly but clearly, he heard a scream of tyres and a familiar strained engine sound, rising in pitch as it decreased in volume.

The clerk-like man was frying bacon at a big modern range as Father O'Flaherty walked unsteadily into the warm cluttered farm kitchen.

'Sit down at the table,' he said without turning round.

Among the teacups and breadcrumbs at Father O'Flaherty's elbow sat two small radios of the type used by security forces. One of them emitted a continuous stream of short unintelligible messages alternating with bursts of static. The sizzling static blended with the sound of frying bacon whose aroma filled the room. Father O'Flaherty, whose lunch had been on the table when the presbytery doorbell rang forty minutes earlier, began to salivate.

'Cowboys,' an accentless voice said from behind him. 'It's dangerous. I don't like it.'

A stocky suntanned man was lying on a sofa under the small window with a tweed cap over the upper part of his face. His heavy brown shoes, grey flannel trousers and rough brown tweed jacket were nondescript but very new. His thick hands were joined across his belly and looked spotlessly clean.

'Agreed,' the clerk said, busy with the bacon. 'It's a mistake. We were rushed into it. We'll know better next time.'

'Unprincipled,' the man on the sofa said. 'And dangerous. The priest here. And the people at the other end. Criminals or worse.'

'Call it keeping ahead of the game,' the clerk said, taking a wrapped loaf of bread from the table. 'It's a lot of money.'

'There's always money to be found,' the man on the sofa said.

'We could drop the whole thing now. Pour it down the drain.'

'I'd like to go through with it now,' the clerk said. 'Not so much for the money. But to keep this young fellow on the hook. He's good.'

He handed Father O'Flaherty a plate with a bacon sandwich on it.

'Sorry to interrupt your lunch, Father,' he said.

'That's another thing,' said the man on the sofa. 'Freelances. There's no discipline. The whole thing's coming apart.'

'Got to stay ahead of the game,' the clerk repeated. 'Try to contain the explosion. Run with them a little and bring them under authority.'

He handed Father O'Flaherty a cup of stewed tea.

'It's your responsibility,' the man on the sofa said.

'OK. It won't come back to us. We won't do it this way again.'

'It's your responsibility,' the man on the sofa said again.

Father O'Flaherty, who liked chocolate and coffee but hated what he had been brought up to regard as 'English tea', found to his surprise that he had finished the cup and wanted another. As he reached for the pot, the clerk gently moved it out of his reach, and with his other hand laid an airline ticket on the table.

'Go back to your house and collect your overnight case,' he began without preamble. 'Take the bus to the airport. Catch the six o'clock flight to London. Do not miss it. Take the first airport bus into central London. Someone will contact you.'

'There must be some mistake,' Father O'Flaherty said. 'My name is O'Flaherty but I have only been in Belfast for three weeks. I do not know who you are. I have made no arrangements for travelling. It is possible that you have confused me with another priest of the same name.'

Fingertips together, the clerk looked mildly at him with grey-green cold eyes through spectacles reflecting the light from the window. From whose neighbourhood came a sound resembling a faint snore.

'Look,' Father O'Flaherty began again, 'the men who brought me must have made a mistake. I — '

'There's no mistake,' the clerk said, in an indifferent tone. He glanced at a watch on his left wrist, a delicately exaggerated gesture.

'Time is a little short,' he said. 'You have to be on your way and I have other things to do. Please remember, six o'clock plane to London. Bus to terminal, the first bus. OK so far? Someone will contact you there.'

The clerk held up his hand, turned the volume knob on the quacking short-wave radio at his elbow and listened for a full half-minute to its incomprehensible slogans. He turned the volume down again and pushed a heavy clear bottle across the table.

'Give this to the person who contacts you,' he said. He stood up.

Father O'Flaherty looked at the bottle. It was of the type used in laboratories and old-fashioned pharmacies, stoppered with a white plastic cork and sealed with green adhesive tape. On the side of the bottle, which contained about a litre and a half of clear liquid, was stuck a paper label bearing in large copperplate handwriting the message: 'Lourdes water'. He, too, stood up.

'This is ridiculous,' he said, 'as well as alarming and inconvenient. I am not going to London. I will not carry your bottle. Why should I not complain to the authorities? The police?'

'You won't do that,' the clerk said quietly. 'You can take my absolute assurance that any recourse to the police or other authorities, or failure to deliver this bottle to the designated person, will be punished. We are ... outside the British law. We do not play games here or make idle threats.'

He placed the bottle and the airline ticket in a plastic carrier bag and handed it to Father O'Flaherty.

'Believe me,' the clerk said. 'For your own good.'

'Or for your colleague's good in the presbytery,' said the accentless voice from the sofa. 'Or your housekeeper's good.'

Father O'Flaherty thought for a moment about these two people, whom he hardly knew: sour, depressed, gentle Father Gillick who never indulged his raging alcoholic's thirst until six in the evening; grim, silent, kindly old Mrs Finnegan, the worst cook he had met since leaving his native Mexico fifteen years earlier. Despite a sheltered upbringing, he also retained from Mexico an awareness of the coercive power of groups of armed men. He turned to the door with the bag in his hand.

'Don't feel bad about it. Don't worry,' the clerk said placatingly as they stepped into the cold, windy, sunlit yard. 'Just do as we ask and you'll be home again by tomorrow night. In time for lunch if you fly back.'

He pointed to the corner of the yard.

'Follow the track to the road and wait there. There's a bus in twenty-five minutes. It takes an hour to town. Get a taxi home and keep it waiting. Get your case. Take the taxi back to the airport bus stop.'

His head light and numb, the bacon sandwich sitting like lead in his churning stomach, Father O'Flaherty walked rapidly out of the yard. His knees still felt weak and he staggered slightly.

*

Mrs Finnegan opened the door as he mounted the presbytery steps. She was as silent as ever but less grim. She looked paler than usual. In the hall, she handed Father O'Flaherty his overnight case. Father Gillick, his face unpleasantly blotchy, emerged from his office with a handful of banknotes. 'Somebody telephoned,' he said. 'Better take some money to get back with. It's not enough for the plane I'm afraid. But train and boat is cheaper. I'm sorry this has happened.'

'Do you know these people?' Father O'Flaherty asked. 'I still don't know what is happening. Surely we should go to the police?'

'No,' said Mrs Finnegan.

'I don't know them personally,' Father Gillick said, 'but I know enough about them. It's best if you do as they say, believe me. We'll talk about it when you come back. Even that isn't a good idea. But we will. Mrs Finnegan's packed your bag, in case you miss the night train out of London. We were told you wouldn't be there long but it's best to be on the safe side.'

Distractedly, he patted Father O'Flaherty's shoulder. The whisky on his breath was today's, not last night's. Father O'Flaherty looked at him in surprise.

'Go along now. Don't miss the plane,' said Father Gillick. Avoiding Father O'Flaherty's eye, he pulled open the front door.

'Safe journey,' he said with a ghastly smile.

'Take care now Father,' Mrs Finnegan said.

*

Confused, irritable and afraid, Father O'Flaherty stepped out of the airport coach into a warm humid London dusk. Nobody approached him. He stood, undecided, on the pavement close to the taxi queue, which was long. Taxis drove up in turn, swallowed passengers and left. The fourth taxi passed the end of the queue and stopped beside Father O'Flaherty. The driver consulted a piece of paper.

'You O'Flaherty?' he asked. As Father O'Flaherty nodded and the driver crooked his right arm back to open the door, a sweating man arrived with a large suitcase and reached for the same door.

'I've been here half an hour,' he said, 'and you've just arrived. You wait in the queue like everyone else.'

'Taken, mate,' the driver said. 'Ordered this morning for the padre here.'

'I say,' the sweating man said. 'I mean half an hour.'

'Piss off,' the driver said shortly. 'Hop in, mate,' he added to Father O'Flaherty.

'Bleeding nerk,' shouted the driver over his shoulder through a gap in the glass division. 'Think they own the place some of them. Lot of it about, though, innair? Wankers. Sall the same to me though mate. Don't give a toss. Happy-go-lucky, that's me. Lot of them about though, like that, inney? Them coons! Think they own the place, some of them. Cheeky?

Don't make me laugh! Where you from then, don't mind me asking? Sall the same to me mate. I'm not a racialist. Don't give a toss.'

Shuddering and rattling, ringing its gears like a ship's bell, the taxi drove two hundred yards and stopped in a traffic jam. The driver gave a strangled scream, tossed something down his throat and swallowed rapidly from what appeared to be a small bottle of spirits.

'Garden party!' he bellowed over his shoulder. 'Late shopping Knightsbridge! Cunts! Cunts!'

Feeling that he might have misunderstood, Father O'Flaherty leaned forward politely to hear what the driver was saying. Although stationary, the taxi was trembling violently. The driver was sinking slowly lower and lower in his seat. A loud, furious muttering drifted over his shoulder.

'I think I have something for you,' ventured Father O'Flaherty through the gap in the glass partition.

The driver appeared to awaken and sat up again in his seat.

'Nah,' he shouted, glancing briefly at Father O'Flaherty from the corner of a narrow scarlet eye. 'Geezer in Great Titchfield Street. Rahna corner, geezer up the road, comprendy? Where you from, mate? Ang on! Not one of them wassernames are you? Don't mind my asking. Cor. Is it moving? Don't make me laugh. Wankers.'

The sound of a cracked Tibetan gong emerged from beneath the cab as he wrenched at the gear lever. Father O'Flaherty was flung back into his seat as the cab lurched forward amid mounting clamour. His overnight case fell over and slid across the floor.

After a moment of panic, his trauma-sharpened senses told him that the taxi was actually travelling quite slowly. He opened the overnight case and stared at the glass bottle, nested among his pyjamas and spare socks. It was undamaged. He felt a surge of anger, turning immediately to inexplicable grief. Lifting the bottle out of his case, he stripped the adhesive tape from around the stopper, which came out easily in his hand. He sniffed cautiously at the mouth of the bottle. He could discern no odour. He touched the bottom of the stopper with a forefinger, wetting a tiny area of skin, and cautiously touched the place with his tongue. An intensely salty flavour permeated his mouth. Saliva ran, and he swallowed it. He felt a slight, not unpleasant choking sensation and a powerful shudder rose from somewhere in his spine, just once. Still swallowing, he replaced the stopper in the bottle.

It occurred to him that he might have poisoned himself, but he did not feel ill. Like an ailing combine harvester, the taxi thrashed slowly up Park Lane towards Marble Arch. Night had fallen. Father O'Flaherty gazed out at the surrounding traffic. The salt taste had almost left his mouth, which felt dry. He had abandoned the attempt to communicate with the driver or decipher his profane monologue, touching at random on such issues as urban planning, sexual morality and racial integration, expressed in vivid images drawn from TV soap opera and popular spectator sports. The man's droning and cursing receded into the background clamour of his vehicle, which now hammered and shook its way into Oxford Street and lurched to a halt at a red traffic light with an agonising squealing of brakes. The nearside door opened and a man and woman climbed in. The woman sat beside Father O'Flaherty in a cloud of patchouli. She was tall and blonde, carried a string bag and was dressed in long pieces of chiffon and many necklaces and bangles. The man, in conservative dark clothing, was slight and saturnine. He took the bottle from Father O'Flaherty and frowned at it. At the same time, he handed a small sheaf of five pound notes to the driver and firmly closed the division. He stared seriously into Father O'Flaherty's eyes.

'When did you open it?' he asked in a metallic upper-class voice.

'Just now,' Father O'Flaherty said.

He pointed to the piece of green tape on the seat beside him. The man picked it up and carefully resealed the bottle.

'Shit,' the man said. 'I hope you didn't drink any. D'you know what it is?'

'I was wondering,' Father O'Flaherty said. 'What is it? Who are you?'

He felt suddenly talkative.

'Where are we going? Can I leave now? What is going on?'

He glanced down at the overnight case open between his feet. A moving bar of light from the street outside crossed the corner of his breviary, at which he had not glanced for more than a year. He felt a surge of affection and pity for Mrs Finnegan, who with simple faith had kindly packed the foreign father's prayer book, unable to comprehend the fact that it held no meaning for him.

'I licked a drop off my finger,' he said.

'Damn,' the man said. 'Damn. I hope it was a small one.'

He looked at his watch and scanned the Oxford Street traffic.

'Look, you weren't supposed to touch it,' he said. 'You may be in for a ... confusing time.'

He looked at his watch again, slid over to the right-hand jump seat opposite Father O'Flaherty, opened the division and spoke briefly to the driver. Slamming the division on a renewed monologue of overtly political content, the saturnine man turned back to Father O'Flaherty who was gazing at the play of light on the taxi floor.

'Listen carefully,' he said. 'We haven't much time. Don't be alarmed by what happens to you.'

Father O'Flaherty looked up and started at the sight of a green, moving face. As he watched, the left side of the still talking face disappeared and slowly reappeared, different in shape and outlined in red. The right side of the face now had golden highlights. Slowly the whole face, still talking, took on an appearance of kindly, vulpine depravity and faded into rippling shadow. It enunciated exhortations with exaggerated, earnest distinctness. Father O'Flaherty stared at its changing colours and realised that they were caused by the play of neon signs above the passing shops.

'Have you got it?' the face asked, fading rapidly through a vivid green-orange combination. The apparent changes of form, Father O'Flaherty thought, in Spanish, are an effect caused by changes in the angle of the dominant and secondary illuminations. How remarkable never to have noticed before the vividness of these effects, their beauty, so to speak. One had seen them often enough. With mounting interest, he recalled certain French Impressionist paintings at which he had looked without admiration some years before. He smiled.

'La lueur des magasins,' he said. 'La lueur des vitres.'

'Damn,' the face said.

The saturnine man looked at his watch, raising his wrist with a precise flourish to catch the light. The door opened and another man got in and sat beside him on the jump seat. Without a word, the woman took a parcel out of the string bag at her feet and gave it to the newcomer, who took a carrier bag out of his pocket and put the parcel in it. The woman took a cardigan out of the string bag, wrapped it round the bottle and put the bottle carefully in the string bag.

The saturnine man opened the division, said 'Holborn' and closed it again.

'He's tasted it,' he said to the man with the carrier bag, who stiffened.

'Did he take a lot?' he asked.

'No, no, it's OK from that point of view. But he wouldn't need much. I mean he's the one with the problem.'

'He'll have a problem all right if he's been tampering with it. He was told to leave it alone.'

'No need for anything like that. But he'll need somewhere calm and comfortable. A house where he knows someone.'

'He'll just have to need it then. He's got a train to catch.'

'Can't he come home with you?' the woman said. The man with the carrier bag stared at her. 'I have no home,' he said coldly.

These striking words, delivered in a brisk low tone, attracted the attention of Father O'Flaherty whose mind had been wandering. He did not know where he was or whom he was with. He began to feel alarm on realising this, but was distracted by a certain symmetry in the lineaments of his alarm which, in his mind's eye, had become a physical image although he couldn't put a shape to it. To his amazement, the image receded slowly to the strains of a powerful, intrusive, obviously very radical orchestral accompaniment. While one part of his mind continued to enjoy this music and the subtly integrated glowing and waning of the background light, another noted that the orchestra was in fact the myriad rattles, whines, creaks and rumbles of the taxi in which he sat as it thrashed very slowly down the bleak wastes of New Oxford Street. Part of the sound appeared to be coming from inside him. His stomach rumbled. He belched and was immediately enveloped in a sweet feminine scent as hair tickled his face. A scantily clothed youngish woman was whispering urgently in his ear. The waves of pleasure resulting from this unfamiliar experience prevented him from understanding much of what she was saying. The taxi stopped. The woman was shaking his left arm.

'... no need to panic, OK?' she said. 'Go and see a friend. If you don't know anyone, get a hotel room. Drink sweet tea, take sugar, eat if you want. Lie down. Take a couple of sleepers.' She shook his elbow again. 'OK?' the woman said, getting out of the taxi.

What were 'sleepers', Father O'Flaherty wondered. The woman's face looked in at him, frowning in concern. He liked her.

The door slammed. The taxi jolted slowly away with a horrible discordant hammering. Harsh, sickening light came into the vehicle from the bleak street lined with huge fascist concrete buildings, hideously stained with evil filth. Father O'Flaherty was alone with a short, burly man holding a carrier bag and staring at him threateningly. He said nothing but moving shadows chased a succession of grotesque grimaces across his features. The taxi turned left and stopped again. The burly man opened the door and took Father O'Flaherty, not gently, by the shoulder.

'Keep your mouth shut,' he said, 'or it'll go very hard with you.'

He spoke past Father O'Flaherty's head, hurriedly. He was uneasy, unwilling to look into Father O'Flaherty's eyes. I know his type, Father O'Flaherty thought, from the bars of Mexico City. He is a braggart, a bully. He has no power. He is afraid, a peon, a messenger. He disengaged his shoulder from the man's grasp.

'You have nothing to fear from me,' he said.

As he spoke he felt fear surging in his own gut. The man pushed a small wad of paper into O'Flaherty's breast pocket.

'Twenty quid,' he muttered. 'For expenses. Watch yourself now.'

The taxi door clanged, the man was gone leaving Father O'Flaherty paralysed and afraid. He felt faint and sick.

Diesel exhaust and unidentifiable stenches assailing his nostrils, Father O'Flaherty stood gazing at a lurid stain on the pavement outside King's Cross station. On the lower edge of his field of vision an unfamiliar suitcase hung down and away from a stranger's hand emerging from a slightly frayed black sleeve. Without recognising them, he was able from their arrangement to identify these objects as his own. Unanswerable questions flooded his mind. He felt extremely tired.

'Two shot in Newry bank raid,' a news vendor's placard said. A small elderly man in stained overalls carrying a small metal box and a newspaper approached at a fast shuffle, whistling through his teeth and gazing fixedly at the ground ten feet ahead of him. Father O'Flaherty gestured weakly towards the man and licked dry lips. With immense effort, he managed to say clearly enough to be heard: 'Where do I get the train for Belfast? Liverpool … Holyhead?'

The old man stopped and shrugged, then seemed to consider. Tired eyes looked out of a face speckled with grime, a gleam of humanity through layers of industrial damage.

'Dunno,' he said. 'Dan Air. Houston.' He pointed back down the street with an imperious but cracked and blackened finger.

Looking in the direction indicated, Father O'Flaherty froze at the splendour of the sight that met his gaze. Close on his right, a dark red castle rose, terrace upon terrace, to pinnacles outlined against the not quite dark sky. Here and there in the noble mass of brick, lighted windows softly glowed. Beyond it, and across the wide street, other structures in different styles, but all on a similar grand scale, marched two by two away into the distance. Discreet but adequate, artificial light sources illuminated the superb avenue for the convenience of travellers. Here and there in the distance, points and strips of coloured light – red, green, yellow – twinkled as if to beguile even the most jaundiced eye or philistine intellect, even the gaze of those fortunate enough to have become used to such splendour by living among it. Close at hand, friendly vehicles moved in orderly fashion with animal hisses and grunts. With a flood of emotion, Father O'Flaherty realised that he was standing amid an ancient civilisation, orderly, purposeful, humane and immense. He turned to thank the workman for bringing it to his notice, and found to his surprise that the man had vanished.

Palms sweating, knees trembling, he walked along Euston Road in what he hoped was the right direction, his eyes and mind wandering over the glittering grandeur before him. He moved slowly, pondering. What he saw was the embodiment of intellect in rearranged matter. God, if present at all, he thought happily, occupies a back seat here. He laughed aloud. His mind was free, although feverish.

Two men approached from the other direction and stopped in front of him, blocking his path. One was tall, heavy and elderly, the other young, slight and wiry. Both briefly displayed cards, and the younger man placed his hand in turn in several of Father O'Flaherty's pockets.

'Where is it?' the young man said.

His palpable criminality, among the noble mass of accumulated labour and intellectual endeavour over which Father O'Flaherty's awareness still joyfully hovered, struck the priest as comic. He began to laugh helplessly and experienced a painful desire to urinate. The taller man took his overnight case and held it indifferently in a large ugly hand.

'Special Branch,' he said, gazing past Father O'Flaherty's convulsed face. 'We want you, Paddy.'

Date unknown (not written for publication)

PAINTING THE LILY
Adapting Burroughs for stage and screen

People who had read *The Naked Lunch* all through, and liked it, were surprised to hear that David Cronenberg was working on a film of this title, and somewhat apprehensive about the result, although impressed by the film-maker's chutzpah. They doubted that it would be a film of William Burroughs's masterpiece whose lack of a central narrative and fragmented, episodic structure would not in themselves resist a scriptwriter's efforts, but whose breadth of reference and anecdotal richness could not easily be squeezed into the space of a feature film. The author's voice is most vividly present in footnotes and asides, anecdotes and descriptive passages. Was there going to be a lot of voice-over? And the book has a cast of millions: 'Power groups of the world frantically cut lines of connection ... The planet drifts to random insect doom....'

According to *Literary Outlaw*, Ted Morgan's brilliant Burroughs biography, there were two attempts to make *Lunch* films in the early 1970s. The first script was written by Burroughs's friend, collaborator and influence Brion Gysin, but the project foundered, Morgan says, over the mutual dislike between the film's would-be director Antony Balch and its financial backer, the lead singer of the Rolling Stones. Apparently Jagger thought Balch, a British film-maker and programmer, who had directed a couple of low-budget horror movies, distributed soft-porn movies and made the experimental monochrome *Towers Open Fire* starring Burroughs, had insufficient standing for the job. The second treatment was written by Terry Southern, but by the time he and Burroughs arrived in Hollywood to discuss details the money had again evaporated. It seemed that Burroughs fans were absent from the serious-money levels of the film industry, while people like Jagger who did like Burroughs, or the backer of the Southern film, a schlock-TV producer called Chuck Barris who may have thought the sensational aspects of Burroughs's work potentially exploitable, were subject to second thoughts or cold feet under the influence of their advisers. Given the commercial and physical impossibility of a nine-hour collaborative effort by (say) Roman Polanski, Ken Loach and Cecil B. de Mille, what was needed was a writer-director with industry clout who was also a Burroughs enthusiast willing to attempt the impossible.

Twenty years on, Cronenberg's product (despite two or three quotes

BRICOLAGE

from the book) is not a film of *The Naked Lunch*, and its undeniable production values are a mixed blessing. Instead of trying to edit the richly comic and lurid shapeless criminal blackness of the novel into a film equivalent (perhaps lacking detail but preserving tone and balance) Cronenberg cast his net wider and coarser, combining versions of a few themes from *The Naked Lunch*, the earlier books *Junky/Junkie* and *Queer* and the later *Exterminator!* with events from Burroughs's 'real life'. What we see is not an interpretation of Burroughs's oeuvre but a Cronenberg film in which William Lee – the first of a string of Burroughs aliases, author of *Junky* and author's representative in *The Naked Lunch* – is the central character.

Lee works as a pest exterminator. He lives with his drug-fiend wife Joan whose pyrethrum habit depletes his working supplies. Off duty he does pyrethrum himself and talks gloomily with his writer friends Hank and Martin. Taken in for questioning by city narcotics agents Hauser and O'Brien, he is left alone with a giant cockroach which tells him that it is his case officer and recruits him as an agent. It instructs him to kill Joan 'this week … and do it real tasty'. She is an agent of Interzone Incorporated. 'Why would a classy American woman like Joan want to work for a two-bit organization like Interzone Inc.?' Lee asks. 'Who says she's a woman at all? Who says she's even human?' the cockroach replies. Lee meets the sinister Dr Benway who gives him some powdered black meat. There follows a version of the notorious real-life shooting of Joan Vollmer by Burroughs in a drunken accident resulting from a very risky prank.

Lee goes to Interzone where his black meat habit increases and he meets Hans, a dealer, Tom and Joan Frost, writers, Cloquet, a rich foreign resident, and Kiki, a young local boy. Fadela, a local woman and friend of Joan Frost, takes over the black meat concession from Hans. Lee's typewriter turns into a giant cockroach – his new case officer – and kills the typewriter Tom has insisted on lending him. It orders him to seduce Joan, which he does with the aid of another of Tom's typewriters. Fadela arrives and throws the typewriter out of the window. Lee's case officer assures him that Joan's shooting was not an act of his own free will. 'Women are a different species', it says. 'Joan was an élite corps centipede.' Tom arrives and seizes Lee's case officer as a substitute for his own typewriter. Lee succumbs to black meat and despair after a visit from Martin and Hank, but is helped by Kiki who takes him to a repair shop where the typewriter is restored into a Mugwump. It orders Lee to 'seduce or otherwise compromise' Cloquet, an agent of Dr Benway who is inside Fadela's body. Lee tells a reluctant Kiki to submit to Cloquet, who turns into a giant insect and kills Kiki.

Lee and Joan drive off to Annexia. They are stopped at the border by two uniformed guards who are Hauser and O'Brien. Lee wakes Joan and shoots her. 'Welcome to Annexia,' the guards say.

Burroughs as an author is characterised by shocking juxtapositions: factual reporting woven into grotesque fantasy, learned footnotes under manic slapstick routines, a Midwestern bourgeois sensibility amplified by broad low-life experience, scientific knowledge informing a belief in gods, magic and telepathy, moments of great tenderness – easily missed by over-excited readers – in a discourse world-famous for its callous tone and black, desolate vision. What is magically sketched in *The Naked Lunch*, supported by the earlier works *Junky* and *Queer*, by numerous shorter pieces and by Burroughs's live discourse (with which he has been generous over the years), reflects a consciousness of great breadth and many registers, a genetic memory stretching far into the past and future, but humbled and humanised by acute observation and a range of overtly pathological obsessions. Vile quasi-sexual fantasies (during which Burroughs never lets the reader forget that he could if he wished do real erotic writing), grim prophecies, paranoid insights into the hidden agendas of power, are delivered in saltily economical lumpen tones with prim, academic, patrician asides, to irresistibly comic – and enlightening – effect.

These qualities, including the deadpan comedy, are noticeably absent from the film. So is another Burroughs hallmark, the sustained polemic on drugs which includes illustrative fantasy but is factually accurate and a good deal more informative than the average academic medical treatise. Cronenberg has chosen here to paint in very bold strokes. When we first see Joan she is injecting pyrethrum powder into her right breast. Later she and Lee become addicted to powdered black meat – the flesh of the giant centipede[1] – before Lee moves on to 'Mugwump jissom'. No less a person than Burroughs himself describes the substitution of imaginary drugs for 'the rather more mundane heroin and marijuana depicted in the novel' as 'a masterstroke'.[2] He goes on: 'One of the novel's central ideas is that addiction can be metaphorical, and what could underscore this better than the film's avoidance of

---

1 Although subject to the images of addiction that pervade the novel, Burroughs's black meat is not a drug but a prized gourmet food, unbearably disgusting and delicious, like an over-assertive European cheese. In his playful way the bourgeois St Louis puritan is attuned to all the perverse undergrowth of 'The Garden of Delights'. (Freud and his colleague Karl Abraham had a standing private joke about some cheese of this sort. The punchline is 'Coraggio, Casimiro!')

2 In a bland and somewhat disingenuous introduction to *Everything is Permitted. The Making of Naked Lunch*, ed. Ira Silvaberg, a promotional leaflet/£9.50 spin-off publication explaining and as it were providing an apologia for the film. Despite its partisan *raison d'être* this document contains writing of excellent quality, showing that the people involved in the film were intelligently sympathetic to their subject.

actual narcotics?' One is tempted to scribble in the margin like a mediaeval commentator: 'The Master here in error was'. One cannot help recalling the novel's documentary economy: 'Selling is more of a habit than using.' By addicting his characters to substances no sane person would want to ingest even in a reckless moment, Cronenberg underlines the dangerous and repulsive aspects of drugs but sidesteps their equally important seductiveness. The novel's pin-sharp, luridly substantive drama-documentary approach to this subject has become dangerously empty and uncontroversial fantasy of a type favoured by police spokesmen and government ministers.[3]

In the big game of commercially financed movies for general release, the film industry is subject to the same gigantist tendencies as other industries. It is obviously believed that without the sensory buzz of expensive production values, a film will be blighted in the marketplace if it ever gets there. Perhaps it is appropriate to suggest the industry is addicted to money and techniques.

Visual imagery and a close interest in the image itself, hallucinatory now-you-see-it-now-you-don't, on-off, signal-switching and image-mutation, infuse Burroughs's novel. He often refers to the manipulation of images for magical purposes, to alter reality:

> I knew they were out there powwowing and making their evil fuzz magic, putting dolls of me in Leavenworth. 'No use sticking needles in that one, Mike.'
>
> I hear they got Chapin with a doll. This old eunuch dick just sat in the precinct basement hanging a doll of him day and night, year in year out. And when Chapin hanged in Connecticut, they find this old creep with his neck broken.
>
> 'He fell downstairs', they say. You know the old cop bullshit.
>
> Junk is surrounded by magic and taboos, curses and amulets. I could find my Mexico City connection by radar. 'Not this street, the next, right ... now left. Now right again', and there he is, toothless old woman face and cancelled eyes.

---

3 This may be a response to certain kinds of political pressure. A film with a large budget has to try to get a certificate for general release. Moreover, the subject of drugs has probably become something of a dead albatross to Burroughs over the years, like the novel *The Naked Lunch* which stands between the readers and much of the work that followed. In OPEN LETTER TO MY CONSTITUENTS AND CO-WORKERS IF ANY REMAIN FOR THE END OF IT (*Evergreen Review*, No. 22, Jan.–Feb. 1962), Inspector J. Lee, Nova Police, says notably: ' ... Their Immortality Cosmic Consciousness and LOVE is second run grade B shit ... Stay out of The Garden Of Delights. It is a man-eating trap that ends in green goo. Flush their drug kicks down the drain ... Learn to make it without any chemical supports ... Use the sanity drug apomorphine ...' etc. (Apomorphine, a powerful emetic, had been used by a British doctor to cure Burroughs of opiate addiction. In this piece he was apparently trying to warn certain of his admirers against developing serious drug habits. He was only partially successful.)

But Burroughs is too intelligent, playful and benevolent to be a fundamentalist. Photographs and tape recordings, technologised instant image (now you see it now you don't) serve as well as wax dolls or nail parings, and have the added advantage of cheapness and hygiene. Although this helping hand extended to the film-maker, the suggestion of careful attention to sound and an imaginative use of camera and film-processing tricks,[4] is taken up in the film, on the whole it is ignored in favour of special effects models.

There has been much comment on these models. The problem with models in films – clear proof that the camera can only lie with a good deal of help – is that if we see too much of them it becomes difficult to sustain the illusion that they possess life. They are best used sparingly so that the viewer's imagination gets maximum exercise and the juices are kept flowing. When the camera lingers too long on some construction or knobbly bit of make-up its real nature becomes apparent, and the audience may start fooling about and making a noise. Cronenberg's earlier film *The Fly*, with its single main model and careful use of trick photography, has a lot of the quality advertising men call 'impact' (its flaw is that the shock-horror effect of 'man with fly's head' is mitigated by the faintly ridiculous, although still horrible, impression left by 'fly with man's head').

Of course the models in *Naked Lunch* are the best in the business, and the way they are deployed works in terms of Cronenberg's narrative. Indeed the most successful models (the 'bugwriter' and the hilariously frantic pink 'sex blob') are Cronenberg inventions which have nothing to do with Burroughs. The bugwriter telescopes several Burroughs themes: automatic writing, the typewriter as a prop, the phobic obsession with powerful giant insects, even the 'talking asshole routine' which Lee also recites late in the film in Cloquet's car. Various giant centipedes and slabs of black meat look authentic. The Mugwump has been expanded from a somewhat impenetrable Burroughsian sexual cypher into a character, mutating from a creature who is clearly basically human (thin purple lips concealing a razor-sharp beak of black bone, blank obsidian eyes, long black tongue, stylised hieroglyph hands, 'perfectly formed' genitalia, no liver) into a scaly alien.[5]

Burroughs's writing suggests the sinister intrusion of mythical elements into a real world sketched with deft touches of masterly, lurid

---

4 It seems that these are areas where bold effects need not be very costly by industry standards. In a very effective passage in Cronenberg's *Naked Lunch*, Tom Frost's voice tells Lee that he is slowly murdering his wife Joan, while his lip movements convey some completely different discourse. The voice explains that he is speaking 'telepathically'.

5 Of course only a purist would object to the replication and multiplication of the Mugwump's drug-secreting schlong.

precision, whereas the effect of these memorable models, combined with the non-factual attitude to drugs, the distortion of Burroughs's (admittedly unique) attitude to sex, and the straightforward if convoluted narrative, is to create a mythical world. In this setting the human characters seem to lack the models' passion and commitment, although Lee and both Joans, played by the same actress to support the device of repeating the shooting, give a convincing display of offhand junky irony. Four of them – Hank, Martin, Tom and Joan Frost – are clearly based on real, well-known writers who are or were friends of Burroughs in real life. It is strange in such company that the most faithful rendering of a Burroughs character should be the kind-hearted doomed catamite Kiki (also based on a real human being).

Two quotes decorate the screen at the beginning of the movie: 'Nothing is true. Everything is permitted', and 'Hustlers of the world, there is one Mark you can't beat: the Mark inside'. The second is pure Burroughs, but the first, attributed to 'Hassan I Sabbah', shows the hand of the late Brion Gysin who became friendly with Burroughs as he was finishing *The Naked Lunch*. Gysin's influence is also apparent in the misogynist material (women are a different species, etc.),[6] which is not a major theme in the novel but absolutely central to the film. Cronenberg's use of the shooting is certainly in questionable taste although Burroughs excuses it, writing that he was 'dismayed, naturally' to see the shooting scenes, but felt on reflection that they were 'so different from the tragic and painful episodes in my own life' on which they were based that 'no intelligent person can mistake the movie for a factual account'.[7] He comes closer to complaining about Cronenberg's treatment of Lee's homosexuality, and goes on: 'Whether this is because of David's own heterosexuality, or his assessment of the realities

---

[6] It was ungrateful of Gysin to encourage this quality, as he often lobbied rich women for money (he called this 'working the princess circuit'). Perhaps the ladies had not always honoured their promises.

[7] In the foreword written in 1985 to the first edition of *Queer*, Burroughs writes: '... I am forced to the appalling conclusion that I would never have become a writer but for Joan's death, and to a realization of the extent to which this event has motivated and formulated my writing. I live with the constant threat of possession, and a constant need to escape from possession, from Control. So the death of Joan brought me in contact with the invader, the Ugly Spirit, and manoeuvred me into a lifelong struggle, in which I have had no choice except to write my way out.' This is Burroughs's first reference for publication to Joan Vollmer's death, thirty-four years after the event. Everything written in the intervening period was produced under its unacknowledged shadow. While the importance of this horrible accident in Burroughs's life and work is undeniable, therefore, it seems reasonable to subject Cronenberg's use of it to a stern scrutiny which in my opinion it does not withstand. The film's character Lee is not Burroughs and the world represented is not the real world in which Burroughs lives, but the minutiae of the accident itself, or some of them, are faithfully reproduced. I do not blame the film-maker for exploiting a dramatic event, but I would criticise him for doing so disrespectfully. 'Faction', of which this film could be said to be a particularly fanciful example, is nearly always thought to trivialise and distort the events and persons represented. The usual industry excuse of ignorance does not apply in this case.

of making and releasing a multimillion dollar movie, or to other factors, I cannot say.'

Delicacy is not a quality often mentioned in connection with Burroughs, but the fabric of his literary vision warps and shrivels in contact with the vast, tottering baroque enterprise of a 'multimillion dollar movie'. Cronenberg's own intelligence seems to have become distracted from the effort to protect the original tissue, and to have seduced him into telescoping too much in too many ways. The result is a somewhat lumbering curiosity: a compulsively watchable pastiche, Burroughsesque rather than Burroughsian, repellent in ways that are not all attributable to Burroughs. Antony Balch's monochrome no-budget *Towers Open Fire*, made all those years ago, stays in the mind not so much for the voice and image of Burroughs (gas mask, fedora, ping-pong-ball gun) as for the shot of scattered papers blowing about an empty BFI boardroom, a wholly authentic Burroughs image of obsolescence, abandonment and desolation.

On stage

A more successful adaptation, because lighter-hearted and far less ambitious, was Graham Duff's stand-up performance *Burroughs!* (Film-Makers Co-op, 17 October 1992). The act, directed by Malcolm Boyle, was built around a selection of anecdotes and 'routines' from the first three books, somewhat expanded and modified. In a rapid-fire performance, Duff did about forty voices in a little over an hour. The Mexican lawyer needed more work and the 'Coleridge, Chemist and Minder' routine seemed designed to give the performer a rest among familiar English phonemes, but the authorial delivery – Duff had never met Burroughs but anyone interested could easily find out what he sounded like – was convincing. No attempt was made to imitate Burroughs's voice or appearance – no spectacles were worn, for example – but appropriate period dress and carefully tuned vocal cadences did the trick surprisingly well. That is what actors do, after all; and Burroughs himself, an increasingly above-ground underground celebrity for the last forty years or so of his life, could put on the style with the best of them.

PIX, 3, 2001

GOING TO THE CINEMA
Trincomalee in the late 1940s

The navy lived in the dockyard, a vast area overlooking Trincomalee harbour which Lord Nelson called 'the best natural harbour in the world'. In the late 1940s it was certainly a breathtaking spectacle, a mile or two across, dotted with green islands and a variable number of British and American warships. The rusting control tower of a huge floating dock, sunk by the Japanese in 1943, projected from the water, and a couple of medium-sized hulks destroyed in the same raid encumbered the main dockyard wharf. The army had its own enclave nearby. Both areas were enclosed by high, spiked steel fences and patrolled and guarded by armed police and servicemen.

Life in the dockyard was very luxurious and largely self-contained. Things available only to the rich in England – cars, telephones, refrigerators, boats, two bathrooms to a house, and of course servants – compensated service personnel and their families for the hot climate, exotic scenery and absence of rationing. Free buses drove around the dockyard and into 'town' and back. Apart from a political officer and a few businessmen and clergy, few Europeans lived outside the dockyard and army base, but I often accompanied my mother to 'town' when she went shopping in the afternoon.

In contrast to the space and somewhat rigid and inelegant military order inside the dockyard which, flora and fauna apart, might have been anywhere, 'town' was really Ceylon: crowded, hot, dusty, noisy with wailing discordant music and conversation, full of astonishing smells, fruit, meat and fish, fly-blown sweetmeats I was forbidden to sample, bespoke tailors and shoemakers, Chinese shops where excitingly dangerous firecrackers could be bought cheaply without any nonsense about how old you were. Sometimes on special occasions there were trips to 'town' after dark, to the cinema, for a rare Chinese dinner, or both.

Films were shown weekly in the Dockyard Club, a dreary building usually occupied by gin-swilling unmarried men in ill-cut shorts. But the cinemas in town were the real things: huge, leaky corrugated-iron sheds in which commercial films were projected for mixed, paying audiences. There were two of them and their names were the Nelson and the Wellington.

Both were laid out in the same way. The front two-thirds of the auditorium was filled with the cheap seats: rows of conventional wooden stalls in which the local population seethed, shouting and chattering in excited anticipation and then, during the film, cheering, laughing and yelling comments in Sinhalese and Tamil. These commentators would carve out partisan sub-audiences for themselves. From time to time scuffles broke out and occasionally the film would be stopped while order was being restored. The back of the cinema was divided into a maze of waist-high boxes containing ordinary chairs and tables. Here the rich sat. I believe that tea, beer and spirits could be served during the show to these members of the audience, who also enjoyed the downdraught from a scattering of noisy ceiling fans hanging from the cavernous recesses above them. All the adults in the building smoked incessantly.

The projection equipment was rickety and poorly maintained. Breakdowns and power cuts caused frequent interruptions, and the sound in particular was often distorted to the point of incomprehensibility. This would have mattered more if the clamour from the stalls had not anyway drowned out the quiet passages. When it rained – seldom for more than half an hour but usually with great violence – the roar from the almost flat roof drowned everything, and water would drip or cascade into the audience. Electrical short-circuits would often follow.

My father worked for the Admiralty and was responsible for immense quantities of naval weaponry that lay about in depots and dumps scattered through the Far East. A wild elephant had been flattening the fifteen-foot barbed-wire perimeter fence of one of these depots in the forest not far from Trincomalee: the beast would stroll through the fence, bringing it down for fifty yards, race about inside the depot leaving deep footprints everywhere, then bring down another fifty yards of fence on the way out. This sporting behaviour caused the elephant to be dubbed a 'rogue'. The police were terrified of it although they had firearms.

Eventually someone was found who was keen to shoot the animal, and he duly did so, bringing the fencing problems to an end. My father became friendly with the man whose hobby had proved so useful. He was a short, tough man, sophisticated and charming, in civilian life manager of the Wellington (or was it the Nelson? It cannot matter, as they have coalesced in my memory). When we went to his cinema after that he would greet us in his office and give my parents a drink before ushering us to our box. The wastepaper basket in his office was a hollowed-out elephant's foot, complete with toenails, painted a tasteless shade of bright red on the inside. I often wondered whether it had come from the famous rogue, but was too shy to ask. Later the manager killed a leopard and captured three of its cubs, which he took to our house for a visit. I was away at school at the time and had to make do with photographs of the occasion, but my sister was able to play with the baby leopards. She said they smelt pretty strange.

I have tried hard to remember what movies were shown in the Trincomalee cinemas, but the only one I remember is the Marx Brothers' *A Night in Casablanca*. I quickly forgot most of the film, but recommended it for years on the basis of the scene in which Chico and Harpo rush into the hotel manager's office and eat his lunch to prevent him from being poisoned, going on to crunch up the crockery with every appearance of relish. As I never read titles on screen and hardly listened to what was said to me, I believed that the film was called *Nineteen Casablanca*, a title that puzzled me whenever I thought about it. My parents adored the Marx Brothers, but at the age of eight or nine I found Groucho's discourse pretty impenetrable, although I liked Harpo's character for its combination of the childish and the superhuman. At the time I found the Three Stooges, who now seem to embody all that is flat, laboured and nasty about American humour, much more accessible. They too probably flickered and crackled on the screens of the Nelson and the Wellington, subtitled in Sinhalese, to vigorous comment from the audience and the roar of tropical rain on the iron roof.

PIX, 1, 1993–4

FRAGMENTS

Elephant House

That was the name of the big imported-goods emporium in Trincomalee which sold boring English stuff like cornflakes. It had a coffee bar where the mothers used to drink coffee and talk scandal, but for children it had another attraction: proper American ice cream sodas with cherry, two scoops of ice cream, shot of jam or toffee, lots of cream and a long spoon and two thick straws. The soda used in those is far better tasting than English lemonade. Nectar to an early post-war ten-year-old I can tell you. During the war you were damn lucky to get a bit of sugar on your porridge.

There was another big shop in Trincomalee that sold shoes. It was called The Royal Bootemporium, with the two last words apparently, to my young eye, run together into one word.

It had boring Clark's shoes and the like – one had to have them for school – but what I enjoyed was having crepe-soled sandals made to measure. The shoe shop man would draw a line round one's foot, and the sandals would be ready within a day or so. I don't think they cost much. The crepe rubber was glued onto the leather sole of the sandal, and often came off at least partially. It was cream in colour, but soon became dark as the rubber detached itself from the sandal sole and softened. Dark filthy flapping semi-detached soles were a feature of that part of my youth.

c. 2010 (not written for publication)

Blackout

For Mirabel, aged nine

Towns were supposed to hide their lights at night so that enemy bombers couldn't see anything to aim at. It was a terrible nuisance. If your house had proper window shutters you could close them, but if you had ordinary windows you had to cover them at night with black material. 'Air raid wardens', local men who had volunteered, used to go around knocking on doors and saying they could see chinks of light around the curtains.

Rationing

Meat, butter, eggs, milk, clothes and shoes were all rationed. Everyone had a ration book and you had to cut out the right number of 'points' – small rectangles from the right page of the ration book – to give the shopkeeper along with the money. Fruit and vegetables weren't rationed, but it was much easier to get boring things like potatoes and swedes, or horrible ones like cabbage and brussels sprouts, than nice things like apples and plums. As for imported fruit like bananas and oranges, there simply weren't any.

Every now and then shopkeepers would get something in that people actually wanted, and then they would keep them for their favourite customers, or for people willing to pay extra. Sweets, chocolate and so on were very strictly rationed. That was good for our teeth of course. You could only get ice cream sometimes, and most easily in remote country places, not towns.

I can still remember my first banana. I didn't like it much. Later at boarding school in Ceylon, where exotic fruit grew on trees, I had to eat two bananas for breakfast every day. That put me off them for years, although we even had them growing in the garden at home. I still eat them though.

People getting killed

The worst thing about wars is that they involve a lot of people killing each other in a systematic and determined way. My father wasn't in uniform because he had a quite important job supervising weapons and ammunition for the Navy. But my uncle Harry Skyrme – the first husband of my favourite aunt Georgie and father of my late cousin Jakki – was a bomber pilot who was shot down and reported 'missing, believed killed' fairly early in the war. I don't remember Harry although he was a good friend of my parents and I think Best Man when they married. His old parents lived in Ascot and I used to go and see them sometimes when I was at school. At the end of the war Georgie married again, this time with an Irishman who had volunteered for the RAF although Ireland wasn't part of Britain and he didn't have to.

A time when everyone was worried

I was born a week or so before the Second World War started, and the first five years of my life were spent during it. The adults sometimes used to laugh and drink and have parties, but really they were worried all the time, and you couldn't help feeling that, although they didn't talk to children about it much.

The adults worried all the time about aircraft noise. Were they 'ours' or were they the Nazis'? I was too young then to be able to discriminate, but the grownups were perpetually anxious, with their ears cocked, listening for Stukas and such.

Bath where we lived was bombed for a night or two, not very severely by the standards of big industrial targets like Swindon and Birmingham. Our windows were broken but we weren't hit. The Germans mistakenly bombed the town, instead of the Admiralty brick buildings above the town (those may have been invisible at night from the air, with camouflaged flat concrete roofs). But the houses across the road from us were gutted by incendiary bombs and stayed ruined till the end of the war. I used to explore the frightening, dripping ruins, although the parents had forbidden me to go there.

We used to retain edible waste for pig food. I sometimes had to cross the road to put the waste into the pig food bin. Of coure there were no cars in those days and nippers could be allowed out.

Very big rectangular 'static water tanks' (for firefighting, the Germans being expected to use incendiary bombs on us) were placed in Catherine Place, the elegant square where we lived. There were tadpoles and little fish in them, sticklebacks we called them, but the tanks were too high-sided for someone my then size to be able to catch them in my little net.

BRICOLAGE

All the iron railings in our square and in the park, indeed everywhere, had been cut off at the base allegedly to make weapons. They weren't replaced until a long time after the war. The new railings were flimsy by the solid Georgian/Victorian standards of the ones they replaced.

These days you wouldn't think anything untoward had ever happened, give or take a few changes to windows and so on. I think they have small panes now as they would have had originally in Georgian buildings, but until the Germans broke them they had in my day two big panes per window, one for each sash. Those would have been installed during the philistine modernism of the Edwardian era.

Funny the stuff one remembers. Something else: smoke from the coal fires, which everyone who could afford coal used in winter, had blackened all the buildings. Now that central heating is widespread the golden 'Bath stone' with which the buildings are faced has been cleaned and looks as it would have looked for a short time after Bath was expanded as a fashionable tonic spa in the eighteenth century. There are several crescents and 'the circus', a round open space with streets radiating from it in three directions, 120 degrees apart I think. A damn sight classier than Butlin's ... our egalitarian democracy has quite a downside in my arrogant opinion.

c. 2011 (not written for publication)

Carnival

Although I am not one of those who are paranoid about cameras, or not yet anyway, there is an anomaly in this area that is iniquitous and needs to be addressed.

While open police photography of peace demonstrators and the like (along with demonstrators of a more provocative and sinister sort) is said to be in everyone's interests, there is a new piece of legislation that appears to forbid photographing the police in the execution of their duty. Seems to me to be asking everyone to aim cameras and mobile phones at every copper they see, just to show what they think of this totalitarian rubbish.

The old bill have never been all that keen on amateur paparazzi. One carnival some years ago squads of riot-equipped rozzers were doing crowd control manoeuvres on my block after dark. Everyone could see that the manoeuvres were themselves provocative and had no other purpose (this used to happen all the time at carnival, and has now started to happen again). Being pretty well lubricated by that time I went out with a flash camera – film in those days – to record them. They shone powerful lights at me and eventually one detached himself from the line and chased me about as the neighbours cheered from their balconies and doorsteps (not sure why they were cheering though). My wife and daughter then came out of the house so I stopped evading plod who surrounded us, and then allowed my wife and daughter to 'take him inside, madam'. Most embarrassing. I gave them such a scolding for putting their lives at risk and making me look a wally ...

c. 2010 (not written for publication)

Hoppy

1937–2015

Hoppy was weightless in an elfin sort of way, but spiritually and intellectually substantial; he was sensitive and artistic but practical in a way we used to call 'fuck you'; he was radical and inherently democratic without the bureaucratic coldness, even brutality, so common on the political left; and he was hard-edged while remaining sweet-natured. You never knew exactly where you were with him, but he was a loyal and dependable friend.

2015 (not written for publication)